Thanks for Listening
Stories and Short Fictions by Ernest Buckler

Thanks for Listening

Stories and Short Fictions by Ernest Buckler

Selected and edited by Marta Dvořak

Wilfrid Laurier University Press

We acknowledge the support of the Canada Council for the Arts for our publishing program. We acknowledge the financial support of the Government of Canada through the Book Publishing Industry Development Program for our publishing activities. We acknowledge the Government of Ontario through the Ontario Media Development Corporation's Ontario Book Initiative.

Library and Archives Canada Cataloguing in Publication

Buckler, Ernest, 1908–1984.
    Thanks for listening : stories and short fictions by Ernest Buckler / selected and edited by Marta Dvořak.

ISBN 0-88920-438-1

    I. Dvořak, Marta. II. Title.

PS8503.U2T46 2004   C813'.54   C2004-903864-8

Printed in Canada

Pour Patrick

Contents

Introduction

Ernest Buckler is best known for his brilliant first novel *The Mountain and the Valley*, published the same year as Hemingway's *The Old Man and the Sea*, and to as much acclaim on both sides of the border. But just like Sinclair Ross and W.O. Mitchell, he also wrote dozens of short stories that began appearing in Canadian and American magazines in the 1940s. His first stories came out in *Esquire*, one of the central literary magazines that published leading American writers like F. Scott Fitzgerald, John Dos Passos, Sinclair Lewis, and Dorothy Parker. Other stories appeared in the better popular magazines like *Saturday Night*, *Collier's*, *Atlantic Advocate*, *Reader's Digest*, or *Chatelaine*. Still others appeared in *Maclean's*: the first one, "Penny in the Dust," became a favourite in countless anthologies, and the second, "The Quarrel," won the magazine's fiction contest. Along with his other productions targeting the new mass media—the radio and television scripts, essays, and newspaper columns—these family magazine pieces often blurred the borders between high art and popular culture. Certainly not the gentleman farmer that a rural writer like Faulkner claimed to be, Buckler grew up in a bookless society, but went on to earn a graduate degree in philosophy in Toronto before going back to the low-income region of Nova Scotia to farm by day and write by night. He set his stories in the farming communities of the Annapolis Valley, at a time when electric lights, a car, or a radio were miraculous things to have.

Like Ross (also born in 1908) and Mitchell, Buckler focused on the home and family when male writers rarely concerned themselves with the domestic sphere. Seeing saucepans and kitchens as objects worthy of artistic notice was more in line with the iconoclastic manifestos of fellow modernist—but female—writer Virginia Woolf. And while Ross's portrayals of misery and despair tend to be bleak, Buckler, more like

1

Mitchell, celebrated the land and the community in a sensual, romantic manner. The sentimental quality of the stories is highly revelatory of the idealistic mindset and tastes of the 1940s and 1950s in both the US and Canada. But today's readers will find more than the good storytelling they're looking for; they will also find that the questions he raises address their own concerns. They will find an authentic voice engaging them in fresh perceptions of age-old concerns: childhood, social bonding, and commitment, or the collision of cultures and values. Buckler's interest in time and memory as well as his interrogation of identity and ethics anticipate strong contemporary writing such as Carol Shields's or Jack Hodgins's, which is also rooted in the magic of the ordinary. Moreover, these stories satisfy the demand for books that evoke or recover our agrarian past—a demand even greater today than in the mid-twentieth century. Buckler's American publishers were right in believing that no one evoked that lost world better than he did. Readers will savour the authentic texture and highly coded rituals of a community in which party telephone lines were the cement of social cohesion, or in which romantic commitments were declared and measured in terms of pies or muffs—reminiscent of the turn-of-the-century courtships gauged according to the size of the young lady's ice cream dish in Sara Jeannette Duncan's *The Imperialist*.

These stories hold an important place in Canadian and American literary history, particularly now that demand for the short story form is exploding. While Buckler published forty or so stories over the decades, only one volume of selected stories ever appeared, initiated by Margaret Laurence. Arranged by Robert Chambers, fourteen stories appeared in 1975 under the title *The Rebellion of Young David*. That McClelland and Stewart publication was subsequently allowed to go out of print. Now this book contains those stories and more. With a view to providing new material from a writer remarkably adventurous with language, I have also selected previously uncollected stories, and even a certain number of previously unpublished pieces. One of these is the title story, "Thanks for Listening," an unusual, even troubling piece that engages the reader on multiple levels with astonishing lines such as, "Maybe you didn't recognize me sometimes because a face looks different with the blood on the outside." It can be seen in a way as a provocative story about storytelling.

≷●

The book is divided into two main parts. The first part contains stories that offer, on the whole, the traditional ingredients of narrative that implicate readers: event, character, and setting. The stories are organized into four sections revolving around social, artistic, or ethical concerns. These preoccupations are sites of questioning: they proffer but interrogate values that reveal themselves to be fraught with tension—values that are sources of the good when one is in a position to conform, but that deny fulfilment when one is not. Within a society of striking ethnolinguistic and religious homogeneity, otherness is generated through socioeconomic or urban/rural binaries—the store-bought/homemade dialectic in "Cleft Rock, with Spring," for instance, or the linguistic code-switching in "The Clumsy One." Readers cannot fail to note how Buckler's society furthermore constructs identity through conjugal status, how the community assigns the status of Other to those who are unmarried or who are childless. They cannot fail to wonder at a quasi-utopian stasis, undeniably reactionary in nature, which challenges the notion of historical progress but never challenges values that are seen as absolutes, such as parental or patriarchal authority. Yet readers can allow themselves to fall under the spell of a paradise glimpsed before the Fall, when time was young. They can be enchanted by this site of harmony, goodness, comfort, and joy, which is so astonishingly unaffected by notions of transgression, and unshaken by the forces of desire and loss that admittedly inhabit it.

Even in these stories designed for popular entertainment, however, the writing deviates from readerly expectations of traditional realism. The modernist privileging of subjectivity and consciousness over verbs and action, which was nourished by the growing fascination with psychoanalysis, is undeniably a guiding aesthetic principle for Buckler. It is visible in the focus on the small, or in the narrative strategy of indirection revolving around epiphanic moments, as well as in the hybrid combinations of free direct and free indirect discourse. One is struck by the transgressive techniques that distance the pieces from the conventional framework of realism: a self-conscious, shape-shifting narrator, a strong, complicitous relationship with a listener that generates timelessness and overshadows event, a labyrinthine structure that moves from one embedded story to another, and recurrent markers producing an effect of orality that privileges the telling over the story being told. Also striking is Buckler's trademark language-bending: his inventiveness with words and his gift for metaphor. When the narrator of "Thanks for Listening" equates death with "a breeze that dies in the air quicker than running," he is in effect designating the inexpressible.

The second part of the book contains short fictions that often break away from the constraints of narrative, and anticipate certain practices in contemporary North American writing that have been associated with poststructuralism. One can evoke, for instance, the hybrid genres and forms Margaret Atwood delights in. Her pieces in *Murder in the Dark* or *Good Bones*, which have been called sudden fiction, essay-fictions, or prose poems, are actually prolongations of the modernist penchant for fragmentation and blurring that we find in Buckler's short fictions. His pieces retain certain narrative elements such as characterization, scene, or temporality, but blend them with the lyricism or imagery of poetry, or the epistemological and metaphysical reflections of the memoir or essay. While some of the shorter pieces could be generically classified as short-short stories or sudden fictions, others as essays or sketches, and still others as prose poems privileging sound and signifier over referential meaning, such distinctions prove to be artificial more often than not. Buckler's early lyric essays or prose poems, often published years after they were written, belong to a romantic tradition that can be traced back to Baudelaire and beyond, to Thomas De Quincey's dream-painting. They are sites of haunting metaphors and startling conceits, such as the encounter in "The Snowman" of the future, of absence, and of impending death in the form of "a wall blanker than smoke, a nowhere louder than silence, a stare whiter than zeroes." Other texts like "Nettles into Orchids," structured entirely like a scene from a play, or "Education at Mimi's," call to mind Noel Coward, whose verbal acrobatics the young Buckler admired. Yet they are also a crossroads illustrating the evolutions and loops in North American production, involving recycling and radicalization. Buckler's reliance on verbal jousts, witticisms, (at times facetious) puns, linguistic scrambling, and rhetorical figures playing on the resemblances of sound or form also anticipates the postmodern predilection for flash fiction—essentially a double page that can be apprehended all at once—that we find notably in Atwood's *Good Bones*. Like hers, Buckler's texts work essentially with social stereotypes that pass for archetypal notions, and favour structures revolving around a flash of insight or twist. The "chance illumination" of "The Orchard," its metaphysical questioning and interest in nominalism, look back to James Joyce's *Dubliners* and *A Portrait of the Artist as a Young Man*, yet look ahead to, and even inspire, Carol Shields's *Unless* and Barbara Gowdy's *The Romantic*.

Since this book is a selection of stories and not a complete collection of Buckler's short prose, the selection process has necessarily involved compromise. Many interesting pieces could not be included, for reasons of space. Those in the previous volume now out of print deserve to be made available once again to the public. Beyond that, my selection criteria obeyed two almost contradictory wishes. First, I attempted to give a full representation of Buckler's trademark concerns, strategies, and modes so as to allow readers to perceive what is distinctive about his writing. (In a letter to Margaret Laurence, Buckler justified the apparently repetitive dimension of his writing as a legitimate part of artistic representation: how to vary the angle of light to make fifty similar subjects into fifty different stories.) Second, I attempted to represent the diversity—even eclecticism—of his production. The satirical material written over the years and finally collected through the instigation of Claude Bissell in the volume *Whirligig*, which won the Stephen Leacock Memorial Medal for Humour in 1978, springs to mind. Or a hybrid, meandering story like "No Matter Who's There," which offers a textured portrait of a society and period, along with shifts in voice and consciousness evocative of F. Scott Fitzgerald, all the while containing Buckler's distinctive use of neologisms and compounds. On top of these considerations, I have attempted to strike some sort of balance (in no way parity) between earlier and later works, published and unpublished ones, collected favourites and unknown pieces. A title has been modified only when it has lost its topicality and impedes readerly access.[1]

Among his very first pieces written in the 1920s or early 1930s (and never submitted anywhere to my knowledge) readers will find the lyric essays or prose poems "No Tongue for It" and "The Widow"—haunting, disturbing investigations of the inexpressible that lies beyond experience. In the early writing of "The Locket," readers may detect already a Faulkneresque predilection for hypnotic gerunds and conceits. Buckler's first published story (if we leave aside the stories that appeared in the non-commercial *Trinity University Review* in the early 1930s), "One Quiet Afternoon" (*Esquire*, 1940), deserved to be included for its vision and scope, as well as for the light it throws on the gestation involved in major works and on the creative process itself. A profusion of ideas, themes, characters, social and metaphysical concerns, and discursive techniques teeming and colliding in the lengthy, rambling story reveal themselves to be, twelve years later, the foundations of the writer's first novel, *The Mountain and the Valley*. But for reasons of space, I have given preference to the story "The First Born Son," which *Esquire* published the following year. Its radical streamlining of focus captivated both the public and critics, who selected it repeatedly for anthologies.

The question of readership is fundamental. The trends and tastes of the times, to which Buckler needed to conform in order to publish and make a living, accounted for certain choices in subject matter and narrative approach. Magazine editors determined to interest the largest possible audience notably rejected stories involving writers or artistic commitment. A story like "Glance in the Mirror" took ten years (and four different endings) to find a publisher, and the ironic ending of the original typescript disappeared completely in favour of a "happy ending." Seven years earlier, in a letter to W.O. Mitchell, then fiction editor of *Maclean's*, Buckler had indicated his own preference for the ironic ending, but offered to rewrite it with a less "grim" one.[2] The story that I have included here is the original version with the sharpest irony that Buckler tried to defend, against demand for a "formula" piece complete with what he elsewhere called a "built-in slushy ending."[3]

Buckler acknowledged a certain "molasses of sentimentality" in many of his magazine pieces, as well as his radio and television productions. In a letter to Claude Bissell, he explained that artistic integrity at times had to yield to the demands of the market: "I suppose it was whoring on my part, to keep the market in mind, but when one is starving, one does strange things."[4] Indicative of the state of the Canadian book industry even in the last half of the twentieth century, the income Buckler derived from his writing was meagre. With his longer fiction taking him years to produce, he depended on an occasional Canada Council grant and on his CBC dramas, magazine stories, and newspaper reviews and essays to supplement his farming income, which provided mere subsistence. But he remarked in the satirical essay "Muse in Overalls" (taken from *Whirligig* and included in this volume), that "the average writer's income is roughly that of a Burmese coolie." In an interview with William French, he also confided that "all the yachts you could build with your Canadian royalties you could sail in your bathtub."[5] Far from finding his writing overly sentimental, however, Buckler's American publisher, Alfred A. Knopf, and fellow writers such as Alden Nowlan, W.O. Mitchell, Harry Brown, Alistair MacLeod, and Margaret Laurence admired its sensitivity, poignant beauty, and spirituality. Along with the confrontation of the sacred and the brutish in stories like "The First Born Son," readers will find a profusion of Christmas stories that go beyond simple seasonal market appeal by presenting the holy/day as the materialization of a metaphysical quest or even unifying system, the manifestation, as it were, of the *noumenon*. Today, in what has been called a post-religious era, and in another aesthetic and epistemological loop in evolution, this is likely to strike a chord. A deep interest in spirituality is manifest in the contemporary fiction being published by authors ranging from Rudy Wiebe and Nino Ricci to Ann-Marie MacDonald, Sandra Birdsell, and Barbara Gowdy.

ò.

The 1975 volume of fourteen stories reprinted Buckler's texts as they had appeared in the magazines, often with the major cuts required by editorial decisions catering to market demand as well as allotted magazine space. I have chosen to include in this selection of thirty-six pieces some of the fuller, original versions. The lyrical prose poem "The Snowman" was rewritten and incorporated decades later under the title "Man and Snowman" in Buckler's collaborative work with the photographer Hans Weber, *Nova Scotia: Window on the Sea*. But the dramatic *memento mori* technique that animates the simple, moving story of an old man sliding into oblivion was subsequently transformed in the published version into a contrived, mawkish, and yet rather sanitized text. I have retained the early variant which does not spare the reader any of the ugliness of decrepitude and death. For other stories, I have kept the revised, definitive versions as they appeared in the magazines, notably when the tighter format corresponded to stylistic streamlining and aesthetic considerations. But I have often reinserted passages from Buckler's typescripts that worked well for depth or texture but had been sacrificed to suit magazine format. At times this involved working with and combining up to three variants. For example, "The Christmas Order," the earlier, original version of the story published in *Chatelaine* in 1953 under the title "Last Delivery Before Christmas," allowed itself the luxurious, roomy expansiveness of the long short story favoured by modernists like Katherine Mansfield and Thomas Mann. The piece exemplifies the manner in which Buckler's texts are drenched in time and filtered through memory. Yet among the contemplative passages that were excised in the published version, and restored here, was the opening paragraph foregrounding the fragility of our perception and remembrance of experience, and the retrospective stance of the self-conscious narrator. This is a trademark of Buckler's production, allowing a present consciousness to colour past event in a double exposure, as it were, superimposing anticipation onto retrospection. The technique, also used skilfully by Emily Carr, Gabrielle Roy, and Mavis Gallant, was to be widely adopted by postmodern writers: the younger narrated self, through whose gaze or eavesdropping an embedded story unfolds, notably anticipates Margaret Laurence's story cycle *A Bird in the House* as well as many of Alice Munro's earlier linked stories. Similarly, the piece "Goodbye, Prince" included here is not the truncated variant that appeared in *Canadian Home Journal* in 1954. It rests on the earlier, more contemplative, unpublished typescript entitled "The Christmas That Faced Both Ways," but incorporates stylistic revisions made in the penultimate draft—less lyrical and more event-oriented—all the while keeping certain judicious cuts made in the final version, such as the more open ending. Formerly deleted but restored here, for instance, is a child narrator fascinated by the transformation of wool to yarn on his mother's spinning wheel, or of heaviness to weightless movement when his unwieldy bicycle miraculously takes wing. A constant in Buckler's fiction is the exploration of process itself through the small, prosaic object—materialization of the abstract, site of a magical transfiguration.

At other times, privileging aspects of the original variant of a story restores the complicitous narrator/receiver relationship that is one of Buckler's strengths. "The Bars and the Bridge" generates more immediacy with its first-person narration than does the later third-person variant, "A Man," which appeared in *Ox Bells and Fireflies*, in spite of the latter's characteristic use of the imperative in the opening sentence to implicate the reader in the creation of a social archetype ("Call the man Joseph."). The early typescript "The Harness" was radically cut to become the story "The Rebellion of Young David" that appeared in *Maclean's* in 1951 (subsequently anthologized elsewhere). Many of the revisions were judicious: by tightening the narrative, they rendered it more effective. Yet restoring some of the excised passages allowed me to consolidate an important dimension that had been eroded, namely the modernist interest in psychoanalysis. Going beyond the dramatic functions of characterization, Buckler set out to investigate the construction of the self and of the other, and to explore our place in the world.

Still, earlier versions of stories were often much improved by later rewriting. "The Balance" is a much clumsier variant of the piece that was eventually published as the sketch "Another Man" in *Ox Bells and Fireflies*. Moreover, as Buckler often fed on one story to build another, the piece initially reproduced whole chunks of the typescript "Snows of Christmas, Snows of Spring," already included here under the title "Just Like Everyone Else." The story entitled "The Balance" that appears here is essentially the more concise published variant, with the addition of a few passages from the original, notably those that materialize the protagonist's obsessive characterization. These anticipate the practice of writers—interestingly enough, women writers—like Margaret Laurence, Alice Munro, Carol Shields, or Bonnie Burnard, in equating characters with the items to be found in their kitchen drawers.

A crossroads between the old and the new, between universal concerns and striking particularities, Buckler's stories and short fictions demonstrate the flow and overlapping of ideas across time and space, and show how representation mediates our access to reality. By rooting himself in his region, Buckler, the writer-farmer, inspired writers across Canada from Alistair MacLeod to Marian Engel. In the words of Engel, Buckler "provided generations of writers and readers with joy and self-knowledge." Margaret Laurence thanked Buckler for having shown Canadian writers how to be themselves, for telling them "where [they] really lived." Similarly admiring of the way Buckler's stories communicated a sense of place and structured a sense of self, Alice Munro confessed to the older writer that she was thinking of him as she was working on her story "Home," and that she felt "very close to [him] as a writer."[6] The vision she admitted to sharing with Buckler is beautifully expressed in her essay "Everything Here Is Touchable and Mysterious": "I name the plants, I name the fish, and every name seems to me triumphant, every leaf and quick fish remarkably valuable. This ordinary place is sufficient, everything here touchable and mysterious."[7] In stories like "The Dream and the Triumph," notably, written decades earlier, Buckler had already demonstrated that the ordinary place is sufficient and valuable, and that here is home.

Notes

1 "We Never Heard of Dorothy Dix," whose referentiality no longer functions as it was meant to, has for example become "Squares," a resonant locution taken from the piece itself.
2 Letter to W.O. Mitchell, 16 December 1950, Buckler Manuscript Collection, Thomas Fisher Rare Book Library, University of Toronto.
3 Letter to Michael Wardell, 9 June 1956, Buckler Manuscript Collection.
4 Letter to Bissell, 25 April 1975, qtd. in Claude Bissell, *Ernest Buckler Remembered* (Toronto: University of Toronto Press, 1989), p. 57.
5 William French, "Ernest Buckler: A Literary Giant Scorned?" *Globe and Mail*, 24 June 1972, p. 23.
6 Letters to Buckler, qtd. in Bissell, *Ernest Buckler Remembered*, p. 139.
7 Alice Munro," Everything Here Is Touchable and Mysterious," *Weekend Magazine/Toronto Star*, 11 May 1974, p. 33.

Stories

Just Like Everyone Else

The Balance

Call him Syd Wright. He was the odd one.

"Old Man Wright," the children called him. He wasn't old. No older than their fathers, but he lived alone.

He knew the name they had for him—he'd heard Lennie himself use it that very Friday night. But it had never bothered him in the least, and didn't then.

Friday night was Halloween. He was sitting close to the table lamp, reading the Almanac, when he heard the smothered giggles of the boys outside. He pretended not to notice. There was nothing to worry about. No turnips still in the field for them to root out and scatter, no odds and ends lying about in plain sight. Nothing to tempt their devilry as there might be around the other houses. The way Syd planned his work, all the straggle of summer was as neatly wound up and tucked away on October thirty-first as if that was the date of Judgment. He liked winter better than summer. It was so much tidier.

He never got mad at the children Halloween night. He'd wait until they put a tic-tac on the window. Then he'd go to the door and say, "Come in, come in, what's the hold-up?" As if he was a member of the fun too.

The children would sit inside for a few minutes, jostling together uneasily on the hard lounge, while he passed around the candy and cookies he'd bought to treat them with. None of them ever took more than one cookie, though, or more than one piece of candy; and soon they'd begin to nudge each other when his back was turned and shape an exaggerated *"Let's go"* with their lips. Then they'd leave—cramming through the doorway on each other's heels and, as soon as they

13

were outside again, letting loose a few wild yells as if they'd been unmuzzled.

This year it was a little different. Syd sat waiting for them. He heard their stealthy footsteps. And then, just as he moved to the door, he heard Lennie say, "Aw, let's not stop here!" Lennie didn't even bother to keep his voice down. "We don't wanta go into that old place! Ya can't even *tease* Old Man Wright."

"All right," Cale Wilson's boy said. "Let's go back to our place. Dad always gets rory-eyed!"

Syd stood at the door and listened, smiling to himself. They'd already forgotten him.

"Let's take Glenn's bain wagon apart," another boy suggested. "He never puts it under cover."

"No, he's got that big dog."

"Hey!"—another voice—"Let's tie Herb's pump handle straight up in the air and hang two turnips underneath, like it's ..."

"No," Lennie said, "I tell ya, fullas—listen, fullas, *listen*—after we go back to Cale's, let's come back this way to Wilf's and put his feed boxes up on the head scaffold. His barn door's wide open."

One of them threw a head of somebody's cabbage against the side of the house, but it was only a mechanical gesture. When Syd opened the door they'd already moved away.

He closed the door and sat down again with the Almanac. He picked out a few soft pieces from the bag of candy and ate them himself.

Then he brought his billfold out from the pantry shelf, with the saucer of change and the small black scribbler he kept his accounts in. Any day he earned anything or spent anything he made a record of it in the scribbler. There was an appropriate heading for every possible entry, even for Gifts (a doll each birthday to the child of a far-off cousin) and Liquor (a bottle of wine each December, to drink on Christmas Eve). On the last day of each month he added up the totals and checked their balance with the actual cash. The cash and the figures always tallied to the cent. He now checked the cash, before he inked in the current entries: the cream money on the Income side, and the price of a bag of middlings under Expenses. They balanced perfectly.

He was in bed, asleep, when the boys went back up the road on their way to Wilf's.

"Turn out!" they called automatically, but they didn't stop.

He awakened and again he smiled to himself. The long peaceful winter had begun.

❧

An hour later, the night cracked open and nightmare rushed out at the seams. There was not a breath of air; but the dark tossed like wind. Lights, never unsure of their path, lost their path in it. The window frames of light that came on one after another in houses that had been dark with sleep … the bobbing light of lanterns that the men with the news running inside them carried running … all had a core of trembling like horses in a fire. Eyes and mouth became unanchored in the face.

But Syd knew nothing of this. No one had come to rouse him. He'd slept straight through.

He heard the news next morning at the store. By then light was sure of itself again, the night had closed its seams, eyes and mouth were back at anchor: it was afterwards. Lennie, they said, had slipped from Wilf's scaffold in the dark and pitched headlong to the barn floor. He'd lain there without a sound. The other boys had thought he was clowning. But he wasn't clowning. He was dead. Chris and Ellen were taking it hard, they said.

Syd was struck still. A sadness real as anyone else's brushed him in stroke after stroke: he had never been a hard-hearted man. And if anyone, himself nearly crying, had been watching him to see if he might be nearly crying too, tears might have come.

But nobody looked at him like that, and he took his sadness home like a parcel, to be opened and examined in—"comfort" was nearly the word. The fact that Lennie was Ellen's child didn't affect him in any special way. The part with Ellen had been so long ago.

In the kitchen the sadness stayed with him, but it was almost like reading a sad book. The sadness itself made common cause with him; it didn't come at him from anything. The familiar household objects did not go strange. They were more like friends silenced by your own troubled silence, and so all the closer and more shielding.

He moved about methodically. His mind was full of what he'd heard, but filled as a sun stripe in a still room is filled with the whorls and tendrils of a puff of smoke blown against it, each shape dissolving so instantly into a different one that never for an instant is the pattern fixed.

That was Saturday. The funeral was on Monday, at three. As the hour came near, Syd felt grave. And quiet with himself. Nothing more.

Except that he dreaded the funeral. In a group, at a time like this, he always felt exposed—as if he'd lost all solid sight of himself and yet was the mark of every other eye. He knew there was no ground for this, and yet it crowded out every other feeling.

He kept a close watch on the clock. He didn't want to be conspicuously early or conspicuously late. Mechanically, he took from his pocket the change the storekeeper had given him and put it in the saucer on the pantry shelf. And then he thought: how much did them things I bought this mornin' come to? He couldn't quite remember. He knew he'd paid the storekeeper with a two-dollar bill, but exactly how much change had he got back? He hadn't counted it, either at the time or when he'd put it away, and now it was scattered among the rest of the silver in the saucer. What entry then would he make in the scribbler?

He felt a sudden stitch of uneasiness he couldn't help. He'd never been in this quandary before. And then the answer came to him. The monthly balance in the scribbler would tell him how much cash was in the house last night, and if he subtracted the amount of cash he had now from the amount he'd had then ...

He took the scribbler and the money to the kitchen table and worked it out. $1.08. But no, that wasn't it—now he remembered the right change exactly as it had lain in his hand. He was fifty cents short! Now where ...?

Had the feed man short changed him? He'd never made a mistake before. Maybe there was fifty cents in one of his pockets. He glanced at the clock. It said two twenty-five. He felt a flash of irritation almost at the funeral, calling him away perhaps before this could be straightened out.

He hurried upstairs and looked in all his pockets. They were empty. He came down, baffled and disturbed. It wasn't the money itself, he'd never been one to watch the penny that way. It was just the need of a lifetime to keep his reckonings absolutely straight.

He glanced at the clock again. Half past two.

He quickly looked back over the entries in other months, for suggestion there of how he might have spent the fifty cents. Household needs: kettle, door-knob ... nothing like that. Health? Bow for glasses, toothbrush ... no. Amusement? The newspaper! No, not today. Had he paid anyone at the door? Fred? Gus? Alf?

Aaaaaaah! It was like a sudden flash of light. He'd given Alf fifty cents towards the funeral wreath the community was getting for Lennie.

He ruled up the scribbler sheets for the new month and entered this figure on the debit side. He felt a little glow of release that in the same moment carried over to the sadness, releasing it too to its full nature so that he could join with it more wholeheartedly.

The clock said twenty minutes to three. That would give him ten minutes to dress, five minutes to walk down the road, and five minutes before the service began. The service would take an hour. Four o'clock. There'd be time enough for his raspberry canes. They'd been on his mind all last week. Other years, he'd covered their roots with sawdust long before this. But the best time to bank them was if you could catch a day when the ground was frozen and the first snow sure to follow right away—and this fall had been so open he'd had to hang off. There'd been a hard freeze last night, though. And it looked like snow this afternoon. He'd cover them after the funeral. He took great pride in his raspberry canes. They were the only cultivated ones in the place.

He took off his work clothes (except the grey shirt he'd put on clean that morning, anticipating this) and folded them carefully over the chair by the bed. His good blue serge suit wasn't large for him, but it gave the impression somehow that his flesh didn't quite meet it. His face too seemed to suggest that same subtle shrinkage from its own mould. The thick hair, once so light and curly, now lay almost flat. He combed it before the bureau glass, but the keyless eyes in the face made no search for the lockless eyes in the mirror.

He went downstairs, and looked all around to make certain everything was shipshape. Then he raked what coals were left in the kitchen stove carefully through the grate into the ash pan. The clock said seven minutes to three. He waited exactly two minutes more, and then he put on his hat and coat, to go down the road.

He got no farther than the door. From one corner of his eye he saw the hearse go past, and from the other the cabbage that had been thrown against the wall. By Lennie himself maybe.

The cabbage lay beside the woodbox. Its outside leaves were beginning to turn brown. And it was right then that he felt it. Without warning or preparation, as in so many moments of illumination, but shocking as a blow, and with total clarity. He saw Lennie's face then so suddenly and so clearly it might have been there in the room. He saw the other faces. He saw his own. He stood there without moving, staring stupidly at the cabbage.

No one even *bothers* me. Not even the children. Not even on Halloween. I am not like anyone else ... When anything happens no one ever comes to tell me first. I am never in on anything at the time. The afterwards is all I ever know.

The truth pierced him like a nail, going deeper second by second. He took himself back to the rocker in front of the stove as if he was leading a sick man, and sat down. He couldn't go to the funeral now. He couldn't.

The clock ticked on, past three o'clock. The stove turned strange. Every object in the room drew a line of blindness around its shape. But with every tick of the clock his vision became more mercilessly clear.

He saw the whole scene down the road. The kitchen tidied up by neighbours' wives to the last sink cloth, the last clutter on the windowsills. Things stiffening in the spots where they'd been misplaced. The way people moved, as if their very weight must be whispered. The heavy look on Chris's and Ellen's lips...

He had gone with Ellen before she ever met Chris. The school teases used to cross his name out with hers when they were in Grade Three, as far back as that. "Friendship, courtship, love, hatred, indifference, marriage..." He'd never mentioned marriage to her, he was waiting until he had a hundred dollars saved up. Then Chris had come here with a lumbering crew. Chris was always laughing or ready to laugh; and Friday nights at the dance in the schoolhouse he'd sometimes give the fiddler every cent he had in his pocket to play an extra hour. Children were crazy over him.

The first night Ellen told him Chris had coaxed her for her picture, he hadn't said a word. Had she been testing him? What if he had spoken up then? What good did that hundred dollars do him now?

They said that Chris and Ellen hadn't got along too well late years — but Syd saw how she would look at him now when someone nodded to the carriers it was time to come into the parlour. A woman will never look at me like that, he thought. Brad Ruggles was one of the carriers. He'd had a little trouble with Chris over some breachy cattle, but Syd saw how the two men would look at each other when Brad put his arm on Chris's shoulder — Brad had sons of his own. A man will never look at me like that... No one will notice that I'm not at the funeral — until afterwards. And then they won't wonder why not...

He wrenched his fists away from the funeral to the objects around him. The clock on the shelf, with the alarm that was set for five o'clock even on Sundays. The stove that was never filled to the top, even on the coldest nights, because that might warp the grates. The stack of Farmer's Magazines, piled neatly, issue after issue. The row of tin cans on the sink-room shelf with the used nails in them, each nail straightened with the hammer after he'd drawn it from the rotted board and all of them sorted out so that no can held two of a different length...

Fury seized him. These were the things that had cheated him. That was the way the minutes of his life had dried up and fallen down... while the other men were talking over their fences, or mending the hoe handles their children had broken, or looking in the catalogue with their women at the things they could never buy...

He opened and closed his fists. The fool... the fool...

The chill in the fireless kitchen grew. He put some bark and kindling in the stove and went to the pantry for a match.

He saw the scribbler lying next to the match box. He grabbed it up and crammed it into the stove. He thought about the raspberry canes and the sawdust.

"They can *go*," he shouted. "They can *go*..."

And then he sat down again in the rocker, and he cried. But he wasn't crying for Ellen. Or Lennie. Or for anyone else. His were the awful tears of a man who cries for himself—not because he has been hurt, but because he has never been hurt at all.

The clock ticked on past four o'clock, past the grave, and the snow began to come down.

ॐ

The men gathered as usual in the store that night. Each time someone new joined the group they went over the happenings of the day once more. Alf Fowler was sitting by the window.

"What's that lantern over in Syd's orchard?" he asked suddenly. "Surely to God he ain't prunin' this time o' night."

"No," Gus said, coming to the window, "he's got his fall prunin' all done. And that ain't the orchard. That's where his raspberry canes are. I bet a dollar he's coverin' them up."

Alf said, "He's a queer one. Wouldn't ya think he'd go nuts livin' up there all by himself!"

Fred chuckled. "I don't know, I think he likes it."

The men all greeted Syd cordially enough when he came into the store himself. But then there was a sudden silence. He knew they'd been talking about him. They didn't mention the funeral. Two men compared larrigans, two others spoke about the snow. And as he walked past them to the counter he knew that every ear was cocked to hear what his errand was. He almost never came to the store of an evening.

"Fred," he said to the storekeeper nervously, conscious of their listening, thinking ahead to going past them on the way out, knowing they'd be talking about him again as soon as the door closed behind him. "Fred," he said, "have you got any more o' them little black scribblers? Like... d'ya mind the one I got here last spring?"

A Present for Miss Merriam

There is nothing as still as a country schoolroom when only a stray laugh carries back to it from the children who have just left for the new kingdom of sleds and skates.

Miss Merriam had never felt the stillness so strongly before. It was the last morning of school before the Christmas holidays. The tree had seemed to have an evening glow while the children were there and the gifts were being distributed. Now they were gone, it had only a daylight blankness. The air of the room had the hollow smell of chalk and forgotten books.

She began to tidy up. The floor about her desk was littered with the wrappings of their gifts for her: the handkerchiefs, the cakes of toilet soap, the boxes of stationery. She gathered the wrappings and put them into the stove. She smiled to herself. Parents seemed to think a teacher had no other functions than to write a letter or wash her face or have a cold.

Well, *have* I? she thought.

It was one of those sudden self-questionings which seemed to stab her oftener lately. She would see a woman surreptitiously moisten a finger at her lips and perfect her child's curls before admitting a visitor, then make an elaborate pretence of believing that her child was no handsomer than anyone else's. Or maybe, from the road, she'd glimpse movement behind a lighted window, though no sound came to her. Or, try not to as she would, she might find herself ready too soon, and arriving earlier than anyone else, at anything that was going on. Sometimes then, she'd feel as if something had given way beneath her. She'd feel bleak and frightened, the way you do when you oversleep an afternoon nap into the dusk, and for a second when you awake you don't know where you are or how much time has gone irretrievably by.

❧

She was still young ... well, thirty-three certainly wasn't *old*. When she looked in the mirror *before* a party, her gentle face, though plain, would have such a careless "evening" expression that sometimes she'd feel like smiling back at herself. But why, looking in a mirror at the party itself,

would she have a foolish wish that some feature could be a little haphazard, out of balance? Why did she have the feeling lately that beneath
her own face, another stiffer one was accreting, to which her own would
gradually conform?

She dusted off the top of her desk, and aligned the small globe and
the dictionary and the bell neatly along the far edge. Then, as if in some
vague sort of desperation, she shoved the globe a little slantwise.

She took the register from her desk and inked in the daily atten-
dance. When she came to Robert Fairfield's name, she felt a momentary
pang. Bobby—her favourite—was the only child who hadn't brought
her anything.

But of course not. How could she expect a present from Bobby? Who
was there to remind him of it?

And, come to think, he'd seemed pretty bored with the whole affair
anyway. Though that might be only pose. When something was going
on that he couldn't join on the same footing as the others, he affected
a studied adult indifference which moved her more, somehow, than
any sort of wistfulness. You seldom knew what he was thinking. His face
didn't suggest an imaginative child. But when she'd asked them yesterday to make up some little "composition" about Christmas, the others' stubby sentences had all been about Santa Claus and toys: his had
been about a "lovely lady, with jewels on." His mother was dead.

She turned at a step in the porch. As if her thought had summoned
him, there he was, standing in the door. The look of indifference was
almost a frown. He took out a tiny box from his reefer pocket.

"I forgot your present this morning," he said abruptly.

She didn't know which struck her hardest: the clumsy wrapping,
with the seals only half stuck; or the transparency of a child who never
doubts that his little prevarication has been taken at face value. Obviously, whatever was in the box was something he'd been afraid the
other children might laugh at.

"Why, Bobby!" she exclaimed, peering as if with intolerable curiosity at the box. "What can it be?" She held the box up to her ear and
shook it. She made a mock grimace of utter puzzlement. "Tiddley-
winks?"

He had to giggle. "No," he said.

He couldn't keep the eagerness out of his face when she began to
undo the package. Then, just before she lifted off the cover, he said
suddenly, "Don't you want me to clean off the blackboard for you?"

"Why, yes," she said, "you can if you like." He picked up the eraser.

But he stood sidewise to the blackboard, keeping the desk in one corner of his eye.

It wasn't anything in the least like a cake of soap or a handkerchief. It was a pair of beaten copper earrings. They were of hopelessly extravagant design (for me, she thought)...but to a child, searching through the catalogue, they must have seemed like the very essence of elegance. For a second she couldn't speak. He began to rub the blackboard furiously with the eraser. "They had 'em with pearls too," he said, in a let-down voice. She knew he'd expected her to exclaim immediately. "But...."

"Oh no...these," she faltered. "They just took my breath, that's all. I never thought of such...."

He came over to the desk. He realized now that she was truly overwhelmed, even though he mistook the reason.

"Them was a little more than the pearl ones," he couldn't help adding.

"They're beautiful," she said. "They're the nicest thing I ever..."

"Maybe you *got* earrings," he said, protracting the thing now as long as he could.

"No, she said, "I haven't."

"You can change 'em if you don't like 'em," he said. "The slip's in the bottom there."

She knew what he was thinking. If she didn't like them! As if anyone wouldn't like anything as splendid as that! But it wouldn't hurt to mention the slip, so she could see they weren't just old ten-cent ones.

"*Change* them?" she cried. "Look!"

She slipped them onto her ears. His face broke into a great awed smile. "Gee," he said. "They just fit, don't they! They make you look..."

Then the elaborate indifference came back as suddenly as it had left. "I just noticed the jewellery page in the catalogue," he said casually, "and I thought..." He almost darted out the door.

Helen Merriam sat perfectly still for a second. Then, without knowing why, she found herself with her head in her arm, crying. She hadn't realized, until these first tears came, that she'd felt like crying all morning. But she was released enough in a few minutes to stop short and laugh at herself. She wondered if she should mention the earrings to Bobby's father when she stopped in this morning to have him sign her returns; he was the secretary. She really *should* thank him too, he must have paid for them. But, except with Bobby, he was such a withdrawn man, even for Grenville. And whenever he and she were alone together—when she dropped in to pick up her salary instalments; when he came to the schoolhouse, after hours, to fix a desk or a doorknob or the stovepipe; or when they stopped opposite each other in a Paul Jones at one of the rare dances he showed up at—there was a curious awkwardness between them, more than the ordinary awkwardness between two shy and quiet people.

You could tell a house with no woman in it the minute you stepped inside, she thought. There should be a plant in that alcove, there should be the smell of a cake just baked, or of something just washed or scrubbed. There should be something lying half-finished somewhere: mending, or knitting, or a garment.

Not that Chris Fairfield didn't manage far better than most men would have. The house was perfectly tidy, and Bobby never had the urchin look which most children do who are dressed by a man.

Chris was rather an unusual man for here. He'd gone through Grade Ten, and read everything he could get his hands on. (The neighbours all brought him their "papers" to fill out.) His large hands seemed incongruous in connection with anything subtler than a plough. But she'd seen a tiny statuette of Bobby he'd carved from a block of peartree wood. He hadn't made it an exact copy, but he'd known just which details to exaggerate a little, to catch Bobby's nature more accurately than a photograph.

He and Bobby were in the front room, trimming the tree. They too use up the last-minute things too early, she thought, because there is nothing to postpone them. They didn't hear her enter the kitchen.

"Walk right in," she called. She hated the prim facetiousness of her remark. But it was the sort of thing which always seemed to come out when most she wanted to sound natural.

"Oh…" Chris called back. "Is that you, Miss Merriam?"

"Is that you, Miss Merriam?" Bobby echoed. "Come see our tree."

Chris was in the kitchen doorway by that time. He had the almost Scandinavian kind of rugged blondness which makes a man look surprisingly young in dark clothes (and, in his case, so surprisingly at home in good ones).

"Oh, never mind your galoshes," he said.

She straightened up as abruptly as if his tone had been peremptory. She felt more awkward with him today than she ever had. She thought of the earrings. He too seemed more awkward than usual. Perhaps he was thinking about them also. She knew she couldn't mention them.

In the front room, though it was large, it seemed as if each must watch carefully before moving, lest they bump into each other.

The tree was a perfect fir. He and Bobby had hung oranges and tinsel cord on the boughs, and it seemed as if Christmas had really been
brought into the room from outdoors. The incarnate smell of the oranges
and the fir were like the true breath of the gentle mystery. But here, as
with the small tree in her boardinghouse room, she had the feeling that
the tree was abating some of its presence for being so privately, almost
defensively, possessed.

"Why, it's a beauty," she exclaimed.

"Oh, I don't know about that," Chris said diffidently. "We've no ornaments this year. I guess something got packed on top of them and broke
off that little stem thing."

"But that can be fixed," she said. "Just take a bit of match stick and
tie some red cord around the middle and...."

"Show us," Bobby interrupted eagerly, "will you?"

She showed them how you dropped the stick straight inside the
globe affair, then worked it into a crosswise position to form a support.

"Now that's an idea," Chris said.

Bobby raced to the kitchen for more matches.

"You do these ones, dad," he said, "and I'll do these, and Miss Merriam can do those. Or, no ... I tell you ... you two *do* 'em, and I'll hang
'em on, eh?"

They obeyed his enthusiasm without comment, as if it gave them a
curious docility.

Bobby'd test one against a bough and say, "There, Miss Merriam, do
you think?" "Well," she'd say, "there ... or over just a speck, maybe." Or
his father might say, "Think you should have two red ones so close
together there, Bobby?" With everyone's hands busy, the room seemed
to relax.

Then she and Chris reached for the same ornament at the same time.
Suddenly she had an acute consciousness of sitting there with her hat
and coat and galoshes on. "I brought my returns," she said abruptly.

"Oh yes," Chris said. He stood up.

"But we're not near done," Bobby said, dismayed.

"I guess we can finish all right now, son," Chris said. "Miss Merriam's
got other things to do."

"Oh, couldn't you just ... " Bobby began. But she had risen too.

She had nothing else to do. There was no way you could synthesize
that frantic rush the other women deplored, and which she envied so.
She always had her cards mailed, and everything ready a week ahead.
But how could she admit that?

Bobby began to hang the rest of the ornaments slowly, and any old place. She and Chris went back to the kitchen.

"I hope you have a good holiday in Halifax," he said, when she was ready to go.

"Thank you," she said.

(Now who'd have thought he'd remember my plans for Christmas, she thought. She'd forgotten mentioning them to him herself. But his remembering gave her a strange pleasure. She was so used to hearing the others say, "Oh, yes, I believe you did tell me that.")

"Will you be back for Christmas Eve?"

"No, " she said. "Not until Christmas Day." She couldn't tell him why.

If you had no family of your own, you'd think that to spend Christmas with an aunt, or at least at your boardinghouse where you knew the people, would be better than spending it among strangers. But it wasn't, for her. The last few years, she didn't know just why, those hours between first lamplight and twelve o'clock on this one day of the year were ones she couldn't bear to spend anywhere she was known. With friends, whose behaviour was so unfettered by the *predictable*. Who (no matter how kindly they included you in their circle) each had someone special they looked at, openly, in the way they'd felt about them only obscurely, throughout the year. Someone already there. Or someone they were waiting for, to come. Or someone they might make some spontaneous plan, at the last minute, to go surprise, themselves.

She went to the city a day or two ahead, and spent Christmas Eve in her hotel room. Not really unhappy ... just so long as she could shut out the carols. The others only half heard them, or were bored with them because they'd heard them so much. For her they carried an awful evocativeness of something, she couldn't say just what.

Christmas Day itself she didn't mind. At the stroke of twelve, everything was all right again.

"I hope you have a nice Christmas too," she said. The stilted sentence almost angered her. She didn't mean to sound like that. She wasn't *like* that.

"Oh, yes," he said. "It'll be quiet, but"—he hesitated—"I often think I should take Bobby to the city some Christmas time, to see the stores and everything."

She had a sudden impulse. "Why couldn't he come with me?" she said.

"Oh, no, no," he said. "I wasn't hinting. I just meant maybe sometime he and I ..."

"I know," she said. "But he could come."

"Where?" Bobby said suddenly from the doorway. He had heard his name.

Chris tried to turn it into a joke. "Oh, Miss Merriam spoke before she thought, I guess. What would she do in the city with you?"

Bobby almost lost his breath. "Oh, Dad," he pleaded. "Could I?"

"Now, now, son, you know ..." Chris said patiently. Maybe next year, you and I ..."

"Yeah," Bobby said, "I know ... but couldn't I?"

ঌ

Waiting for the train in town, Helen Merriam tried not to examine this new situation. She had done something on impulse, like the others. She didn't want to turn up anything that might be hasty or foolish in it.

It was different getting on the train with Bobby than it had been getting on the train alone. The Christmas look on the other faces no longer islanded her. She felt included and warm. Like the way she'd felt when Chris had brought him and his suitcase to her boardinghouse that morning, explaining to her about his clothes and entrusting his spending money to her.

The train was crowded. She searched for a double seat, but there was none vacant. Then a woman looked up at her and smiled.

"Sit beside me," the woman said. "And your little boy back there. I'm getting off next stop ... and then you can sit together. "

"Oh, thank you," Helen said. "Would you do that, Bobby?" "Sure," he said. To agree with even the simplest suggestion seemed to give him a brimming pleasure today.

A sudden ridiculous relief went over her that he hadn't added, "Miss Merriam." She'd had the strangest feeling when the woman said, "your little boy": then there wasn't anything about her looks to tell another woman such a thing would not be credible. She felt as if some vague disfigurement had all at once been sloughed off. She'd explain to the woman in a minute, but ....

The woman began immediately to talk about her own children. "I have a little boy about the size of yours," she said. "How old is *he*?"

"Nine," Helen said.

Now was the time to explain. The woman would slip away a little, instinctively. This only basis of immediate contact (she'd seen it in so many other women talking to each other about their children) would be severed at once. She hesitated.

"But he takes size eleven in everything," she said.

The woman laughed. "I know," she said. "Don't they grow? I suppose he's all excited about Christmas." She half-sighed. "Well, these are their best years, aren't they?"

Their best years. It gave her a sudden pang. Were what should be his best years slipping by, without his ever knowing what a child's best years, in a full family, should be like? Sitting alone, he had on that look of indifference. She felt like reaching back to touch him.

But sitting with her, later, he was exuberant as any child, with the spell of going somewhere strange and new.

And Helen Merriam herself practised a deceit she wouldn't have believed herself capable of. She deliberately fostered the impression now, of being an ordinary woman travelling at Christmas with her son. To be thought like the others, if only for a few hours, if only with people she would never see again .... She even pretended apathy at some of his eager questions about the country they passed through, to make the illusion more convincing.

"Miss Merriam?" he began at once.

"Who's she?" she said quickly, making a show of mock ignorance. "Let's not mention her name till school starts again, eh? We're on a holiday." She winked at him. He didn't understand, but he nodded and gave her back a willing conspiratorial grin.

About the time the lights came on in the train, she thought his face looked strained. He seemed restless. He kept asking, "How much longer before we get there?" She felt a flick of dismay. Was the trip wearing thin already?

Then it came to her. (And with it the thought of all the other times a lonely child might have suffered desperately rather than ask an embarrassing question.)

"Watch where that man goes," she whispered. "When he comes out, you better…"

His fearsome gamut over, Bobby's smile was almost triumphant as he came back down the aisle. "Gosh," he said, "this is a swell train, isn't it? I wish it could be Christmas like this all the time, don't you?"

In spite of himself he fell asleep soon after. And riding along in the lighted train, she was so safe in happiness that for the first time she was able to pronounce in her mind the shameful word "alone." She thought: even if it's only a child, and he asleep, it's not like riding in a lighted train alone.

ॐ

Showing Bobby the city was wonderful: she had something to communicate to someone else. He was fascinated with everything. And though it gave her an ache, it was a kind of precious one, to see him looking at the price tags in the stores and then surreptitiously examining the contents of his purse; to see the look of studied indifference when he was impressed by something, but not wanting to appear strange.

The second morning, the day of Christmas Eve, she was going out to buy herself a new dress.

"You didn't lose the earrings, did you?" Bobby said, coming into her room. "They were in such a little box."

She knew he was disappointed that she hadn't worn them. This was a hint to put them on. Well, they wouldn't look outrageous in the city...where half the people wore things that didn't suit them.

"Oh, no," she laughed, "they're safe enough. And I think now's a good time to try them out, eh?"

She took them from her suitcase and fastened them on. Then she went to the mirror, thinking she'd cover them as much as possible with her hair.

But it was funny. There is a certain type of plain appearance which a single bizarre touch—of lipstick, or ornament, or coiffure, or whatever—seems to lift right up into the remarkable. The earrings did that for Miss Merriam's face. She was astonished. She felt a sudden confidence, a strange buoyancy. It was funny too about the salesgirls. Before, they'd always shown her matronly dresses. Now they brought out simple but stylish ones. And it was funny that this was the kind of dress she bought. Before she'd always got one which, after it was no longer "good," she could take for school. Now she bought one she couldn't possibly wear in the schoolroom.

She bought a new coat as well; and when the girl asked if she'd take them with her or have them sent, she said, no, she'd wear them. Her old clothes, which the girl packed into a box, looked suddenly like someone else's.

She was really gay that afternoon, as she planned what they'd do Christmas Eve. Would he like to go to a big restaurant for supper, and then to a show? Or would he...?

But Bobby seemed distracted. "If you would," was all he'd say. He'd put on an eager face while she was looking at him; but as soon as her

glance shifted away, his face would fall into that unassailable preoccu-
pation a child has when he is secretly disturbed. She began to feel baffled.

"Miss Merriam, he said at last (forgetting their compact), "I don't
think I feel so good."

Oh, heavens!

"Where, dear?" she said. "How? Are you hot? Let me see."

She put her hand on his forehead. It was cool as ice.

"I think maybe it's in my stomach."

"Where?" she said. "Here? (Appendicitis!) Does it pain?"

"No," he said. "It don't pain. It's just kind of...."

She went quickly to the phone.

"You lie down on your bed," she said (and thought, as she spoke,
how that look of indifference had grown on his face last night when it
came time to undress—until she'd made an excuse out of his room),
"and I'll call a doctor."

"Oh no," he pleaded quickly. "I think maybe it's a little better now."
He hesitated a minute. "I think Dad would know what to do."

Her fingers relaxed on the phone. And suddenly she felt a little sick
herself.

"Would you like to go back on today's train?" she said. He had a
hard job to maintain the solemn visage of illness long enough that the
smile wouldn't take over too suspiciously soon.

"I'm having an awful good time, Miss Merriam," he said earnestly,
"but I guess we'd better. Besides, Dad might be kinda lonesome."

She couldn't believe that this was the same train of two days ago.

She felt the old exclusion. She couldn't forget how the excitement
of Bobby's trip had turned to ashes when he thought of being away
from his father on Christmas Eve. She might be an *ordinary* day's dis-
traction. She wasn't a Christmas Eve thing. He'd left her the way a child
you've been amusing leaves you so cruelly completely when another
child appears.

She hadn't had time to wrap the packages they'd bought. She had
planned that they'd carry some of them in their arms on the way home
tomorrow as a badge of belonging. Now, this almost professional talent
of hers to make a Christmas package look gay seemed like a fussy, mark-
ing, shameful one. She wished her fingers were clumsy and haphazard
like most other women's.

The lights came on in the train. They shone out onto the great-flaked Christmas Eve snow which had just begun its hushed expectant falling. She felt the old dread. If it were only twelve o'clock....

When they neared their station she noticed the curious light in the faces of other people who were gathering their luggage together, to get off: the special sight which comes to faces once a year; when you can almost see how they looked when they were children, and what kind of children they were. Her face didn't change.

There'd be no one waiting on the platform: glancing, glancing, and then, with recognition, the face-light flaring up suddenly as if the eyes had leapt a physical barrier. She made no pretence that she and Bobby were mother and son now. What she'd done before, now seemed like an indescribably foolish and shameful thing.

But they *were* met. Chris Fairfield was almost the first person she saw. Rather than the light of greeting, though, there was puzzlement on all their faces.

They moved toward each other through the jostling crowd. I suppose that woman would assume this was my husband, she thought. But wincing now, and wishing she could be somewhere alone, out of sight.

"Well!" Chris exclaimed. "What happened?"

"Hi, Dad," Bobby said.

"Bobby didn't feel very well," she said, letting her tone of voice tell the true story. "He thought you'd know what to do."

"Ohhhhh." He tilted his head backward and pursed his lips. "I see. But that broke up your trip too. That's a shame."

"You've got a new suit and coat," Bobby said quickly. Chris had. He looked almost boyish in them.

"Yeah," he said. "Y'know what? I took it into my head to go in on the evening train and surprise you tomorrow morning."

For a second he looked a little crestfallen. Like Bobby, she thought, when he was disappointed about something, never dreaming that the disappointment was showing on his face. And she thought too: he couldn't bear to have me share Bobby's Christmas entirely... not even once.

"Miss Merriam's got new clothes too," Bobby said, still trying to head off any discussion of his guilt.

"So I see," Chris said. He laughed. "Well, it looks like we're all dressed up and no place to go."

She'd never seen him in a jocular mood like this. It must be the new clothes, she thought. He looked like she'd felt when she first put on the earrings and looked into the mirror.

"I know," Bobby said eagerly. "Seeing you planned to go anyway, why don't we all go back on the evening train?"

Chris glanced at Miss Merriam.

"Oh no, Bobby," she said. "We couldn't do that. Now we're here."

The old awkwardness had come back to her more acutely than ever. His father's idea to surprise Bobby on Christmas morning would have been fine for Bobby, but she'd have felt like a stranger. She was thankful that Bobby had brought her home.

"Well," Chris said. "I guess ... if we're going home ... we better pick up a car before they're all spoken for." He moved off.

She didn't know why that should have anything to do with it, just watching him back-to, dressed up for town but not quite as glib and pushing as the others, his nature somehow crystallized and clarified by the presence of strangers, she realized something for the first time. I love him, she thought. She had the crazy, following, thought: if it hadn't been for my new clothes and his new suit and meeting here in this strange place, I'd never have known it. She knew too why she loved this child so particularly. It was primarily as an extension of his father. The whole picture came to her so quickly she felt faint. She felt like an old woman, glimpsing a vision of some other way it might have been if she'd only known...way back then.

Chris signalled for them. He collected the suitcases and they were ready to go. It was a car with no trunk.

"You two set in back with the suitcases and your son in front?" the driver said.

She winced again. Would people never stop making that mistake? It seemed now as if the whole world were in some conspiracy to mock her. She glanced at Chris. He was half-smiling, as if the man's implication were such a ridiculous idea he couldn't keep his face straight. He doesn't even take the trouble to correct it, she thought.

"I'll sit in front," she said.

"Aw no," Bobby said. "Let's all sit in behind, together. We can make room."

It was exactly the kind of Christmas Eve you saw on all the cards. Calm unhurried moonlight fell on the white road, polishing the sled-runner tracks like isinglass, except where the dark shadows of the spruces latticed them. The cold star-fire seemed softened, and flakes of snow drifted down dreamily against the headlights, like leaves from a twig. Even the car seemed to lose its machine-coldness. Its purr sounded cosy and animate. She saw the night with the awful clarity a night has for you, if your feelings are not attuned to it. We're part of the picture on the cards too, she thought ironically: a man and a woman riding home and the child between them falling asleep in spite of himself.

The car radio was playing "Holy Night."

"Maybe you're sick of the carols," the driver said.

"Well, I think they overdo them, don't you?" she said, as casually as she could manage. He turned the radio off.

When they'd almost reached her boardinghouse, she glanced at her watch. It was only half-past ten. She caught her breath. An hour and a half yet....

And now Chris would have to explain to the driver, when he let her out. They'd probably joke about it after she'd gone up the path, the mood he was in tonight. Opposite the driveway, when he still gave no sign to the driver, she sat up in the seat. But Chris shook his head.

"We might as well just make the one stop," he whispered. "It's only a jump. I'll walk back with you. And I got something I made at the house I want to show you."

She relaxed in the seat again, but she couldn't summon interest in even Bobby's Christmas things now. At the house the driver had no change for the ten-dollar bill Chris gave him. They both examined the contents of all their pockets in the light of the head lamps, but they still couldn't make it.

She looked in her purse. "I have some change," she said; and among them they worked the thing out. She had seen a man and woman doing *that* before too.

Bobby didn't awake when Chris took him out of the car. He carried him to the house in his arms.

"I guess you'll have to open the door," he said to her. "The key's in my outside pocket there."

She fished out the key, her fingers almost useless with self-consciousness, and opened the door.

"Perhaps I'd better take him right up and put him in bed, do you think?" he said. "You can light the lamp. I guess the big one's in the front room. The matches are there by the dish cupboard. I'll be just a minute. Then I'll walk back with you."

She lit the lamp. There was no fire in the room stove, but the tree sprang awake at the light, and its soft incarnate smell warmed the air.

Chris seemed to have lost most of his earlier sureness and jocularity when he came downstairs again; to be more his old awkward self. He was carrying something in his hand. Though the object wasn't wrapped, she couldn't imagine what it was until he passed it to her.

"It's for you," he said abruptly. She thought of Bobby with the ear-rings.

She gazed at it, speechless. It was the loveliest thing she had ever seen … but she couldn't very well say that. Because it was a little stat-uette of herself.

She could see that it was nothing he'd made in the last few days; he must have been working on it, carving and tinting, for weeks. Some-time or other he must have studied every detail of her face, to repeat them. And yet—the wonderful part—he hadn't repeated them exactly. It didn't repeat the tidy way she looked; somehow, its intricate perfec-tion caught the fluid, flexible, outgoing way she felt inside. And the dress wasn't like any he'd ever seen her wear. It was a dress more like the one she had just bought. And in the ears, in absolutely clear and per-fect detail, were replicas of the very earrings, the extravagant earrings she was wearing now.

She couldn't think what to say. He had turned aside. She thought of Bobby at the blackboard. "So *you* chose the earrings?" she said. "Well, it was his idea," he said. "I picked them out."

The breath he drew was so deep it was audible. "You should have a ring to go with them," he added.

She didn't pretend she didn't know what he meant.

But curiously, right then, she felt the exclusion more acutely even than in the train. It's for Bobby, she thought. He saw how well it went with the three of us at the tree the other afternoon. He knows that Bobby needs a woman in the house. I love him and he's asking me to marry him; but why, when it comes my way, does even this have to be a cold-blooded, reasoned thing … in connection with someone else?

When she didn't answer, he spoke again. Almost doggedly now; as if once he'd started it must all come out.

"I know it's asking a lot," he said. "There'd be Bobby to look after. And maybe Bobby… I don't know. But he likes you, you know that. And well, maybe even if he was jealous of you for a little while…well, if you would … a man has to think of his own life a little too, I guess."

He looked up.

Now what did I say *then*, he thought, to make her face change like that?

ॐ

He had no way of knowing that even before the full effect struck her of realizing that it was for herself alone … that so far from being in con-nection with Bobby entirely, even if Bobby should be *difficult* for awhile,

he'd still ... that someone, he, *had* been hinting to spend Christmas with
her — that even before that, she was thinking never again will I have
my cards mailed on time. That she was thinking: never again can the
others ask me somewhere without having to consider the possibility
of me having another plan. That she couldn't speak because she had just
glanced at her watch, and it was only half-past eleven, and she wasn't
afraid at all.

When she laughed, she looked like the statuette, physically.

"But can you afford a ring," she said, "after what the earrings cost
you?"

"What?" His face was comically irresolute between amusement and
embarrassment. "Did Bobby stick that slip in the box? Well, the little ...."

Then he chuckled, and she felt the earrings in her ears like Christmas stars. This was really like it was when she had seen a quiet man and
a quiet woman, who were nothing more than just quiet people in other's
eyes, chuckling together in the sharing of an understanding and humour
that was like no one else's ... at some action of a child. Or at anything
whatever.

"But listen to me, Helen," he said, "what about the ring? You haven't
said about the ring."

She nodded. "Yes," she said quietly. " But we'd better go now."

She was thinking that if they hurried there'd still be time for her to
turn on the radio in her room and catch one last carol anyway.

The Clumsy One

Did you ever strike your brother? I don't mean with a blow. Sometimes when we were children and a flash of child's anger would make a sudden blindness in my brain, I'd strike David any place my blind hands came to. I don't care about those times. He'd never strike me back; but afterward I would ask to borrow his jackknife or something. He'd know I didn't really want it to use. He'd know that when I said "thanks, Dave," the words were really for my contrition.

I didn't do it with a blow that day.

I was standing right where I'm standing now, the day I struck David. I still stand, with my hoe idle, and remember it, whenever I come to this spot in the row. It was just such a summer's day as this, with the bowing heat of the sun turning the petals of the daisies inward and wilting the leaves of the apple trees in immobile patience for the night dew. Little watermarks of heat rose from the asphalt road where the cars passed back and forth beyond the sidehill.

If David had been alongside me, it might not have happened. But they got out of the car and came across the field quietly, to surprise me. I didn't know they were there until their voices made me start. David was at the bottom of another row, and before he came opposite us again I had time to plan it.

That was my first summer home from college. David didn't go to college, though he was the older. There was only money enough to send one of us, and there had never been any question which of us it would be. Because even as children it was I who was clumsy with anything outside the shadow world of books, and it was David who had the magic sleight for anything that could be manoeuvred with his hands. I don't know why the quick, nervous way of my mind seemed to make me the special one of the family. I could see instantly the whole route of thought that led to the proof of a geometry theorem, without having to feel it out step by step. But surely that was a poorer talent than to have the sure touch of David's fingers on the plough handles, that could turn the long shaving of greensward from one end of the field to the other without a single break.

I remember the first day *I* tried to plough. The sod would ribbon back cleanly for a bit; and then just when it seemed easy, I'd move the handles too much one way or the other, because I was thinking about it, and suddenly the whole strip of sod would flop back into the row in one long undulation. As it happened again and again, a hairspring of anger kept tightening inside me. I stopped once and tried to catch the sod with my hands; but the earth split where my hands were trying to hold it and the tail of the sod went slipping back behind me.

"You're trying to plough too deep, Dan," David said.

The hairspring broke. "Oh, is that so!" I shouted. "Well, do it yourself then, if you're so smart."

I turned to leave the field. When I was in a temper, the blot of anger seemed to strike all light and breath out of the place I was standing, like a blow in the stomach.

"Danny! For God's *sake*..." David said. Not angrily, but patiently. Because, for all his own quiet mind, he understood me so well he knew there was no sting of meaning in the words I couldn't stop.

I don't care about that time. The anger was over as soon as David spoke. I put my hands back on the plough handles. When we got to the top of the row, I looked back and said, "Now that's a pretty job, what?" and we both laughed. And then I asked him, the way the asking of help from another can be such a warming thing when anger between you has just passed, "What do I *do*, Dave—do I hold them too much this way or *that* way?"

He said, "You're ploughing a little too deep, Danny, that's all."

I let him show me then. And the next time down the furrow I tried terribly hard to keep the sod from breaking, to show David how earnestly I was trying to learn from him—

ॐ

I went to college and David didn't, but I don't care about that. Maybe I always had the best of things, but it wasn't that I took them from the rest of the family, selfishly. It wasn't as if there was ever any dividing among us; our needs were met out of what we all had together, as each required. There was a sort of shy pride and a fierce shielding of me, because I was the one in the family who was weak in the flesh, but had the quick way with learning. One Christmas I got a set of books with real leather binding, while David got only a sled. But I knew that as they watched my face glow just to touch those books, the pride and wonder of knowing that one of their own family could feel a thing like that, was a better share in the books than my own possession.

It was I who got two suits the year I went to college, and David none; because I must look as good as the strangers I went among. But I don't care about that. If it had been David going away, I'd have given up my suit just as gladly. The thought that someone in the train might have the chance to laugh at his clothes, even though he bore their laughter quietly and without protest, would have made such a fierce hurt for him in me that I'd have given up anything I had to make his appearance equal to theirs.

I don't care about those things. But they were the things I thought about that day I struck him, just the same. I felt the shame of my action that day heavy in me, even before the others had gone; but I couldn't seem to help what I did. Sometimes there is a cruel persuasion you can't resist in the hurting of the one who understands you best, even as it hurts you more.

You see, the people who surprised me that day were some of the ones I had known at college.

I had just quarrelled with David about the distance between the potato hills. I told him he'd dropped the seed too close. He said there was no sense in wasting space. It was no more than a discussion, to him, until I shouted, "Yes, yes, yes, you're so stubborn—"

I wasn't really shouting at David. It was only the rankling at my own helplessness to hoe more than one row to his three, or to capture the knack he had of cutting the weeds and loosening the earth between the hills in a single stroke, just grazing the stalks of the plants themselves, that was speaking. The tremble of anger was still obliterating my attention when they sneaked up behind me. I never heard a sound of them until they spoke while my back was still turned.

"D'ya suppose he knows what he's doing?" Steve said.

I turned, startled. "Steve! Perry! Well…."

"We're taking the census," Perry said, in mock seriousness. "Is your name Daniel Redmond? What was your income last year? Can you read?"

"Come on," I laughed. "Come off it."

They had the smooth city way of talking, with a bit of laughter or a glib word always ready to bridge the small pauses; the way of not having to make the meaning that ran along in their minds match the sound track at all. David's straight talk, with the silences in it a way of speech too, would have seemed stupid to them.

I didn't call David to the side of the field by the fence. And when he heard us, hoeing over in the potato rows, I talked their way too—for him to hear. David had never heard me talk like that before. I let him think that was my real way of talking. The way I talked when I was with my own kind. A way he could never talk to me at all.

"How's Smokey?" I was saying. "And Chuck? What's Bill Walton doing this summer? It's funny, I was just wondering this minute if Bill had ever patched up his rift with Eleanor." (That was the year we were saying "rift.")

"I don't know," Steve said. "The last I heard, she was threatening to dump the whole complicated mess on the Security Council."

"Couldn't they work it out by algebra somehow?" I said.

"Yeah," Perry said, "or logarithms?"

"Yes," I said, darting a quick smile at him, as if we were really clicking, "or logarithms."

David hesitated alongside us, making patterns on the ground with his hoe, not knowing whether he should stop or go past. They looked at him without curiosity. I didn't introduce him.

"It's a scorcher, ain't it!" David said.

"Yes, it's really hot," they said.

"Has it been hot in the city?" I said, as if accommodating the tone of my remark to the stature of his.

"Not bad," they said. "Not so far."

"We always get a good breeze here at night," David said.

There was a pause, as if the real conversation had stopped.

I had been angry with David, and I did it that day the way the city ones did it after anger. That way, you waited until others joined you and then you talked with them. Not making a point of it, as if to show the one you'd quarrelled with that he wasn't the only friend you had; but just easily, as if the quarrel had become quite forgotten, now that these people you could really be yourself with were there. And if the quiet one doesn't leave at once, you draw him into the conversation, as if with kindness, from time to time; but you listen to what he says with patience, and sometimes after he has spoken you let his words hang in the silence a minute before you reply, and after awhile he begins to feel like someone trying desperately to cover his large inescapable hands.

They were asking me, why didn't the three of us get some rooms together next year, and cook our own meals?

"We could send you some sauerkraut," David said. We all laughed politely at his little joke. I saw Steve's eyes catch Perry's.

"Now, Dave ..." I said, tolerantly. There was quite a long silence.

"By the way," I said to Perry, "What brings you two to these hinter parts anyway?"

David stood there, with the self-consciousness that had made it so hard for him to stop and break into our talk at first making it just as hard, once he had stopped, for him to leave.

"Well, this ain't getting my work done," he said. We let his remark lie where it fell. We didn't help him out in the establishment of anything he said.

He bent over and began to cut the weeds again, but he still couldn't get clean away, because it was a slow business moving up the row with his hoe. The others scarcely glanced after him. I suppose they thought he was the hired man. I still talked their way, for him to hear. I let him believe that the glibness of my mind and theirs was a strangeness between him and people like us that he could never hope to overcome. That he wouldn't fit in with us at all. I put him outside, in the cruellest way it is possible to be put outside.

David, who once when I had cried because they wouldn't let me go to the back field for the cows with him, had felt so badly he'd gone out and broken the handle of my cart —so I'd hate him and wouldn't want to go .... That's the mean, rotten way I struck my brother that day.

It wasn't the same after the others had gone that day, as it had been times before when we had quarrelled. He didn't come over and ask me what time it was or something, to break the silence. It was I who had to speak first. I took my hoe over to him and said, "Will you touch her up a little for me with the file, Dave?" But it wasn't like the times I used to borrow his knife.

He said, "Sure"; but he said it too eagerly, and he didn't ask right away about the people who had been there. I hesitated to mention them too. And then after we had both hesitated, it wasn't possible to mention them at all. It wasn't true what I had let him believe that day— that they were my own kind and he was the stranger.

And walking back to the house that night, this thing between us that neither of us could mention lay on our tongues like a weight. He was quiet, without anger or protest, at the blow. And I had shame, which confession could only add to. The consciousness of even the movement of each other's limbs was so taut in us that if our feet had happened to slip and touch on the uneven ground, we'd have been struck with awkwardness beyond description.

Have you ever *really* lain awake the whole night? I did, that one. You know how, if you bruise your finger, it's when you go to bed that it really begins to throb. It was like that with my mind. How could I ever show David it wasn't the real me who had spoken that day—I had done my act so well. You can say, "I'm sorry I struck you, I guess I lost my temper"; but you can't say you're sorry for a thing like what I'd done, without stirring up the shame fresher still. How could my mind show me the answer now, the mind my brother was always so proud of, though he couldn't speak his pride—when it was that mind which I had used as the instrument to strike him!

I wondered if he remembered, that afternoon, the casual way I'd always answered him whenever he asked me things about college. I'd never thought he really cared about knowing. Maybe he had. That was a funny part about David. I had the quicker way with the mind, and still I couldn't feel how it was with him, the way he seemed to know, with a quiet sensing, exactly how it was with me. I wondered if he'd thought that I was putting him off when he asked me those questions. I thought, look Dave, I'd tell you about college now, if you could ask me again. We'd sit all afternoon on the doorstep, pulling the timothy heads from their stalks and talking the easy way.

I wondered if he believed now that if he were in a quarrel with some-one else, I might not take his side. (And I remembered—Oh Lord, I remembered—how David would always let me fight my own battles with kids my own size; but if any of the older ones so much as laid a finger on me he'd go into the only rages I'd ever seen him show.) I thought foolish things. I tried to console myself with the projection of foolish fictions: there was a war and David went first; because he was the strong one in the flesh and I was the one who had only the thin mus-cles of the mind.

But I lied to the examiners, and after awhile they took me too. I was small, but when I was angry I was as strong as the others. I was with David when he was in danger now, and so I was strong all the time. And the day David was killed I was right there, and in that last minute when all things are without falseness of any kind, he knew at last that I had been sick for what I had done to him. He knew that I wished we might change places. That the quickness of my mind would be nothing to part with, if it could save him. That I was never proud of it, myself, if it stood between us.

I started at the beginning again, making it happen a different way: I saw them when they got out of the car. Before they saw me. I ran down the row to where David was standing and grabbed his arm, with the anger all forgotten. "Dave," I said, "quick—there are some guys I knew at college over at the house and we don't want them stuck here all afternoon. Let's get out of sight in the orchard, quick...."

Oh they *did* laugh at David. They said, "Who's your friend?"

"Who's my friend?" I said. "That's my brother. His name is David. You wouldn't know anyone like him. They made him first, out of the muscles and heart and sense—and then they had some pieces of tongue and gut left over and they added a little water and made you. They added quite a bit of water. Would you like him to come over and turn you inside out, to dry? It'd only take a couple of minutes. One to do it, and one to wash his hands afterward. Don't worry, he wouldn't laugh at you. Dave's a gentleman. He wouldn't laugh at that smooth little city-face of yours, Perry, or those little cellar-sprouts on your mind, or that rugged little necktie you're wearing, Steve."

Oh I told them so surely just why their kind wouldn't even move the needle on the scales you'd weigh David in. With such a clean cutting that they wouldn't reply, for all their glibness. They believed it of themselves all right. They were glad to get away from our field quickly. The sharp sword of my mind shone and sang doing it, and I was really proud of its quickness. And then I leaped over the rows eagerly with my hoe, to where David was standing; the song sharp in me almost to tears. The song of one who takes up the cudgel for another with whom he has himself quarrelled, with the bright telling words the other could never in the world have found for himself—

But it was too late to do it that way now. It was foolish to take it out like that on Steve and Perry. They were good enough fellows. They weren't to blame. There was no one to blame but myself. And it would never be the same between David and me again.

ૐ

The next afternoon the wood saw came. I was so draggy I didn't know how I would ever work. Lift the heavy logs and carry them to the saw table, then lift and thrust, lift and thrust, lift and thrust—without a minute's respite. With the crescendo whine of the whirling saw rising so demandingly between cuts that it seemed it would shatter itself to bits if it were not immediately fed again.

I always dreaded the wood saw. But somehow David had always managed that I got a break in the work now and then, without drawing attention to my weakness. He'd call, "Danny, go get us a dipper of water?" or "Danny, go get the crosscut, will you? We may have to junk some of the big ones." (As if he hadn't left the crosscut saw in the shop purposely.) When he sensed that I was getting intolerably tired, he'd call, "Move her ahead, fuhllas, eh? We're getting too far from the pile." There'd be five minutes or so then, while the others were pushing the machine ahead, and having a smoke maybe before they started up the engine again, that I could get my wind. And somehow, without his planning it in any way that was obvious, when we all fell into our places for the first cut, David would be at the butt end of the logs, next the saw, and I'd be at the light end, on the far side of the pile.

Stan was sawing that day when we started, Rich was throwing away the blocks, David was next the saw, Joe and App were strung along the pile, and I was at the far end. We hadn't sawed more than three or four of the first small wire birches when David threw his head back in a motion for me to come up front.

"Take it, will you?" he shouted at me, above the roar of the engine, "I gotta get a stake for the wheel. Don't cut them too long." The one who was next the saw regulated the length of the block by thrusting the stick ahead just far enough between cuts.

David got the axe and drove a stake down tight against one wheel, to stop the vibration of the machine. I expected him to change jobs with me again as soon as that was done; but when he came back he went to my place at the end of the stick and left me in his.

It was all right while we sawed the birches. They were easy to lift onto the table, and there was a kind of exhilaration in the lightning rhythm of thrust, zing, thrust, zing, thrust, zing—and the transformation of the straggling lengths of trunk into even-lengthed blocks of firewood that flew from Rich's hands and grew into a neat mound before the shop door.

But when we came to the leaden pasture spruces, their weight became hostile, punishing; and the heightening scream of the saw between cuts more demanding. It seemed as if each time I lifted the butt end of one of them from the pile, it was not by strength, but by an effort of will. Then I had the butt of the stick off the pile, with my heart beating very slowly now after having beaten very fast, it was as if I were dragging it to the stable with the pit of my stomach, not my arms. My arms were trembling. Each time Stan tipped the table ahead so the saw could sever the block, I relaxed and let my weight ride with it. But the next instant it was necessary (would it be really impossible this time?) to lift, thrust, again. The others held up their part of the log with hardly any consciousness of its weight. Sometimes David and App would support it at the loop of one elbow and make a mock pretence of cuffing each others' ears with their free arms. David paid no attention to me at all.

We came to the big hemlock. I looked at it, and before I touched it even, I could feel its stupid sickening weight dragging at my stomach.

"Junk it?" I shouted to Dave.

"No," Dave shouted back, "I think we can handle that one all right, can't we, fuhllas?"

I bent over and put my arms around the butt end. I lifted and lifted, but it didn't budge. The saw was waiting, screaming higher and higher, threatening to shatter itself. I lifted again, until everything went black for an instant before my eyes. I couldn't move it an inch off the ground. I straightened up, for my sight to clear. And then I noticed that the others weren't lifting at all. David was motioning them back with his arm.

It was a kind of joke. They were standing there, sort of nudging each other with their grins.

"What's the matter, Dan?" Joe shouted. "Is she nailed down?"

I couldn't even laugh it off. It you weren't brought up in the country, you can't understand what a peculiar sort of shame there is in not being able to take as heavy a hoist as the next one. It was worse still because Joe had shouted. Everything that happened that day was worse still, because everything that was said had to be shouted above the sound of the saw.

They sprang to help me, and somehow I stumbled back and dropped my end of the stick on the saw table. I glanced at David. He was grinning too. I couldn't understand it.

We had to keep turning that one—the force of the saw would die about halfway through. The second or third block, Stan motioned us to wait until the saw had got up speed again. I let my end of the stick rest on the table and relaxed. I motioned to David to come up front.

"I've got sawdust in my eye," I shouted to him. I thought he'd send me into the house to wash my eyes in the eye-cup. He didn't.

"Let's see," he said. He drew my lower lid down. "There's nothing there. It must be just the sweat."

"Okay, fuhllas," Stan shouted. David bounded back to his place at the pile in an exaggerated comic rush. When he passed App, he pointed to his own eyes and sort of smiled. App caught on—the eye business was just an excuse. I couldn't understand it at all.

It got so I could only keep going by thinking about six o'clock. Six o'clock, when this would be over, must come somehow. Nothing could stop it. It got so I turned my face sidewise from the others, because it was twitching uncontrollably, like the tic of a smile that has to be held too long; and I knew it was pale as slush, despite the heat. My second strength came and went. I kept my eyes on the belt, willing it to go off the pulleys, as it had other times we'd sawed; but it didn't. It got so I could only keep going by thinking that when I absolutely *couldn't* stand it any longer, I could ask them, myself, to move the machine ahead; saving that, like a weapon.

"Move her ahead," I shouted at last.

"Move her ahead," David shouted to Stan, "Move her ahead ...."

Stan moved to shut off the engine. I took a great deep breath and relaxed.

"No," David shouted, "Don't shut her off ... unless anyone wants a puff. Anyone tired?" The others shook their heads.

"Will I shut her off?" Stan shouted again.

"No," David shouted. "This stuff's just kindling wood for us fuh-llas." He rushed front, worked the stake free in a flash, lifted the tongue of the wagon the machine was resting on, as if it were a match stick.

It wasn't a minute before the wagon was pushed ahead into place, with the saw still running. It wasn't two minutes before the wheels were chocked, the stake driven again, and we back in place for the next cut. My last weapon was gone.

It got so the pile was a looming, leaden, inimical mound of all the weight in the world. It got so the weight of the logs was there all the time in the pit of my stomach, whether I was lifting or not. My temples drew and beat.

Finally it got so I kept lifting at the log on the table, whether the saw was in cut or not, because I couldn't let go. It got so I was suspended somewhere by my arms, with the weight of my body intolerable, but unable to touch the ground with my feet. It got so my body was full of ashes. It got so my will began to tremble as uncontrollably as my arms. It got so I couldn't lift a straw. I motioned for David to come.

"I can't—" I said.

He did something that I wouldn't have believed. He turned and shouted to the others, "Dan's all in, fuhllas. We can finish that little bit all right alone, can't we? All right, Dan, you go in the house."

He needn't have shouted it out like that. He could have sent me to water the calves, or to put hay in to the cow that had been kept in the barn because this was her day.

I held my head down as I took off my leather gloves and walked to the house. But I could see the others out of the corner of my eye. Stan and Rich glanced after me, knowingly, though they hadn't caught what David said; but without much curiosity or concern. I saw David and Joe making a comic battle for each others' caps, even as they held the log.

I remembered the night David had taken me on his shoulders when I stumbled on the path from camp and carried me all the rest of the way home; pretending not only to the other kids but to me too that he thought I'd broken a bone in my ankle. So that even with him I needn't have the shame of tiring before the rest. I thought, I understood now. How he must hate me now—

We didn't make much talk with the others at supper. It was on the way down from the barn, with the milk pails in our hands, that he said to me, "Did you make up your mind to live with Perry and Steve next year Dan?"

"No!" I said, as automatically as if a trigger had been pressed—before I stopped to think that this was the first time David had mentioned them. "*Those*—?"

"You crazy old—" He called me a name as old and earthy as the land he hoed. That's what he always called me when it was a hundred per cent perfect between us.

I didn't speak, because tired as I was and so suddenly happy, I couldn't trust my voice. I understood then what had happened this afternoon: how else could he square it between him and me, between me and my conscience, than by doing something as mean to me as I had done to him? How else, since it couldn't be mentioned with words, could he show me that he'd known all the time the falseness of what I'd done, the burden of it afterward—how else, than by doing something as unmentionable to me today and letting me see, by his face now, the falseness and the burden of that?

Did I say it was David who was the clumsy one with anything that couldn't be held in his hands?

The Harness

There are times when you can only look at your son and say his name over and over in your mind.

I would say, "David, David ..." nights when he was asleep—the involuntary way you pass your hand across your eyes when your head aches, though there is no way for your hand to get inside. It seemed as if it must all have been my fault.

I suppose any seven-year-old has a look of vulnerability about him when he is asleep, accusing innocence. Above all, an assaulting grudgelessness. But it seemed to me that he had it especially. His head looked smaller and *rounder*, somehow, and there was a soft erasure over all his flesh.

It seemed incredible that when I'd told him to undress he'd said, "You make me!" his eyes dark and stormy. When I'd get him up to the toilet, his night-soft body absolutely pliant with sleep, it seemed incredible that those same legs and hands would ever be party to that isolating violence of his again.

His visible flesh was still; yet he was always moving in a dream. Maybe he'd murmur a scrap of the day's reading lesson, or cry, "No, right here." Or maybe he'd say, "Wait .... Wait up, Art."

I don't know why that was the most assaulting part of all. Where was I going in the dream, what was I doing, that even as I held him in my arms he was falling behind?

He didn't call me "Dad." He called me "Art." You see, the idea was, we were pals.

I had never whipped him. The thought of my wife—she died when David was born—had something to do with restraining me, I guess. And he had such an almost frightening perceptiveness, and a pathetic vulnerability about his wire-thin body contradicted so assaultingly its actual belligerence that the thought of laying a hand on him—well, I just couldn't do it. We were supposed to *reason* things out.

Sometimes that worked. Sometimes it didn't.

He *could* reason, with almost staggering clarity. ("How come your conscience can tell your mind to tell your tongue not to say 'Dammit'"?)

His body would seem to vibrate with obedience. Then, without warn-ing, reason would have no persuasion for him at all.

His friendship would be absolutely unwithholding, exquisitely can-did and intimate. "You stepped on my hand," he'd say, laughing, though his face was pinched with the pain of it, "but you didn't mean to ... that doesn't matter, does it, Art? Sometimes you can't see people's hands when they stick them in the way." Or if we were fishing, he'd say, "You tell me when to pull on the line, won't you, Art ... just right *when*."

Then all of a sudden he'd become possessed by such an automatic sort of mutiny that nothing—forbearance, open displeasure, ignoring him, nothing—would have any effect at all.

I'd get the awful feeling then that we were both lost. That whatever I'd done wrong had not only failed, but that he'd never know I'd been *trying* to do it right for him. That I'd *never* understand him. More assault-ing still, that his disturbed mind was rocked by some blind recalcitrance he'd never understand himself.

Maybe I'd be helping him with a reading lesson. I tried to make a game of it, totalling the words he named right against words he named wrong. He'd look at me, squinting up his face into a contortion of delib-erate amusement and ingratiation. He'd say, "Seventeen right and only one wrong ... wouldn't that make you *laugh*, Art?" Then maybe the very next word I'd ask him, he'd slump against the table in a pretended indolence, or flop the book shut while the smile was still on my face.

Or maybe we'd be playing with his new baseball bat and catcher's mitt.

His hands were too small to grasp the bat properly and his fingers were lost in the mitt. But he couldn't have seemed more obliteratingly happy when he did connect with the ball. ("Boy, that was a solid hit, wasn't it, Art? You throw them to me *just* right, Art, just *right*.") He'd improvise rules of his own for the game. ("If I'm on that bare patch there and I cross my fingers and say 'Keys,' I'm safe, eh, Art? I'm safe, Art, see?") His face would twist with the delight of communicating this particular variation in the rules to me.

Then, suddenly, when he'd throw the ball, he'd throw it so high I couldn't possibly reach it, or so hard that the physical smart of it on my bare fingers would sting me to exasperation.

"All right," I'd say coolly, "if you don't want to play, I'll go hoe the garden."

"No, no, no," he'd say, rapping a tattoo with his bat on the old licence plate he'd dug out for home base. "Nine hundred more times, Art ... nine *hundred* ..."

"No," I'd say coolly, "I've got to hoe the garden anyway."

"Please, Art," he'd beg, "three more pitches ... just *three* ..."

I'd go over to the garden, watching him out of the corner of my eye. He'd wander forlornly about the yard. Then I'd see him coming slowly toward the garden (where his tracks still showed along the top of a row of carrots he'd raced through yesterday). He'd come up behind me and say, "I have to walk right between the rows, don't I, Art? Gardens are hard *work*, aren't they, Art ... you don't want anyone stepping on the rows."

David, David ....

The curious part, it wasn't that my method of discipline had no effect because it made no impression.

One evening he said out of a blue sky, "*You're* so smart, Art ... I haven't got a brain in my head, not one. You've got so many *brains*, Art, *brains* ...." I was completely puzzled.

Then I remembered: that he'd called me "dumb" that morning. I'd countered with complete silence, as you might with an adult you loved. I'd forgotten the incident entirely. Now I could see that though he'd been less rather than more tractable since then, he'd been carrying the snub around with him all day.

Or take the afternoon I saw him looking in his small black purse. His funds were down to one nickel. I saw him take it out and put it back again several times before he came and asked me for another. He never asked me for money unless he wanted it terribly. I gave him another nickel. He went to the store and came back with a Coke for each of us. For some reason he had to treat me.

My face must have shown how curiously pleased I was. He said, with his devastating candour, "You look happier with me than you did this morning, don't you, Art? Parents know best, don't they?"

The assaulting part about that was that *he* had felt my displeasure, though on my part it must have been quite unconscious. I had no memory now of what his offence had been.

What had I done wrong? I didn't know.

Unless it was that, when he was small, I'd kept a harness on him in the yard. He rebelled, instinctively, at any kind of bond. But what else could I do? Our house was on a blind corner. What else could I do, when I had the picture of the strength of his slight headlong body failing against the impersonal strength of a truck, or the depths of a well?

(And then maybe one day when I'd forgotten to tie him, he'd come to me with the harness in his hand and stand perfectly still for me to attach it. David, David ....)

I said, "David, David ..." out loud, that particular afternoon he lay so still on the ground; because this is the way it had happened.

≽ઽ

I had taken him fencing with me that morning. It was one of those perfect spring mornings when even the ground-shadows in the awakening woods seem to breathe out a clean water-smell. He was very excited. He'd never been to the back of the pasture before, where it joined the dark-treed mountain.

I carried the axe and the mall. He carried the staple-box and the two hammers. Sometimes he walked beside me. Sometimes he walked ahead.

He always strode very straight, but there was something about him that always assaulted me when I watched him moving along *back to*. I'd made him wear his rubber boots because there was a swamp to cross. Now we were on the dry road again and the sun was getting hot, I wished I'd let him wear his shoes and carried him across the swamp. There was something that assaulted me about the heavy boots *not* slowing up his eager movement, and the thought that they must be tiring him without his knowing it.

I asked him if his legs weren't tired. "Noooooo," he scoffed. As if that were the kind of absurd question people kid each other with to clinch the absolute perfection of the day. Then he added, "If your legs do get a little tired when you're going some place, that doesn't hurt, does it, Art?"

He was good company, in an adult way. His unpredictable twist of comment kept catching you unawares, no matter how surely you'd learned to expect it. Yet there was no unnatural shadow of precocity about him. His face had a kind of feature-smalling brightness about it that gave him a peaked look when he was tired or disappointed, and when his face was washed and the water on his hair, for town, a kind of shining. But it was as childlike and unwithholding as the clasp of his hand. (Or maybe he didn't look much different from any other child. Maybe I couldn't see him straight because I loved him.)

This was one of his days of intense, jubilant, communicativeness. One of his "How come?" days. As if by his questions and my answers we (and we alone) could find out about everything.

We came to an ant hill.

"How come a little ant knows where to go, if no one can talk to him?" he said.

"Oh, they just know," I said.

"I guess they follow the big ones, eh, Art? Is that big one a father ant?"

"Probably."

"How come people can talk, Art?" he said, "*talk*?" I could see him trying to decipher the movements of his own tongue.

"I guess our minds tell us how," I said. I was afraid he was going to follow that one up. But his thought glanced away.

"We'd be pretty dumb if our minds didn't, wouldn't we, Art?" he said. "Do ants get cold in the winter with no clothes on?"

"No," I said. "They freeze right through, but they don't even feel it."

"Are they dead?"

"No, they thaw out in the spring."

"Yeah, but how come they don't feel it?"

"Oh, their blood and their nerves aren't like ours." That was as far as my entomology went.

"I tell you," he said eagerly. "I tell you what, it's because they don't have anything to *tell* them they're cold, you've gotta have something inside to tell you everything, haven't you, Art?"

"That's right."

"Humph," he said. "Maybe they *do* get cold. How would we know?"

We came to the place where a gale had torn up the huge pine that grew by itself in the birch chopping.

"How come trees can't move?" he said. "Does a tree get tired standing in the same place all the time?"

"I don't know, I never thought much about it."

"Maybe it got tired and tried to run away."

"Maybe it tried to run away and stubbed its toe in the dark," I said.

There wasn't anything very funny about my remark, but he worked himself up into quite a glee. "You always say something to make me *laugh*, Art," he said.

I knew his laughter was a little louder than he really felt like laughing. Each time I'd glance at him again, after glancing away, his face would twitch a little, renewing it, like the face of someone laughing when the joke is on himself. But that didn't mean that his amusement was false. I knew that his intense willingness to think anything funny I said was as funny as anything could possibly be, tickled him more than the joke itself. "You always say such funny things, Art!"

We came to the place where I had buried the horse. Dogs had dug away the earth. The brackets of its ribs and the chalky grimace of its jaws stared whitely in the bright sun.

He looked at it with a sudden quietness beyond mere attention; as if something invisible were threatening to come too close. I thought he was a little pale. He had never seen a skeleton before.

"Those bones can't move, *can* they, Art?" he said.

"No," I said.

"How can bones move?"

"Oh, they have to have flesh on them, and muscles, and ..."

"Well, could he move when he was just dead? I mean right then, when he was right just dead?"

"No."

"How come?"

I was searching for a reply when he moved very close to me. "Could you carry the hammers, Art, please?" he said.

I put the hammers in my back overalls pocket.

"Could *you* carry an axe and a mall both in one hand?" he said. I took the axe in my left hand, with the mall, so that now we each had a hand free. He took my hand and tugged me along the road again.

He was quiet for a few minutes, then he said, "Art? What goes away out of your muscles when you're dead?"

He was a good boy all morning. He was really a help. If you fence alone you can't carry all the tools through the brush at once. You have to replace a stretch of rotted posts with the axe and mall; then return to where you've left the staple-box and hammers and go over the same ground again, tightening the wire.

He carried the staple-box and hammers, and we could complete the operation as we went. He held the wire taut while I drove the staples. He'd get his voice down very low. "The way you do it, Art, see, you get the claw of your hammer right behind a barb so it won't slip ... so it won't *slip*, Art, see?" As if he'd discovered some trick that would now be a conspiratorial secret between just us two. The obbligato of manual labour was like a quiet stitching together of our presences.

We started at the far end of the pasture, next the mountain, and worked toward home. It was five minutes past eleven when we came within sight of the skeleton again. The spot where my section of the fence ended.

That was fine. We could finish the job before noon and not have to walk all the way back again after dinner. It was aggravating when I struck three rotten posts in a row, but we could still finish, if we hurried. I thought David looked a little pale again.

"You take off those heavy boots and rest, while I go down to the intervale and cut some posts," I said. There were no trees growing near the fence.

"All right, Art." He was very quiet. There was that assaulting look of suspension in his flesh he'd get sometimes when his mind was working on something it couldn't quite manoeuvre.

It took me no more than twenty minutes to cut the posts, but when I carried them back to the fence he wasn't there.

"Bring the staples, chum," I shouted. He didn't pop out from behind any bush.

"David! David!" I called, louder. There was only that hollow stillness of the wind rustling the leaves when you call to someone in the woods and there is no answer. He had completely disappeared.

I felt a sudden irritation. Of all the damn times to beat it home without telling me.

I started to stretch the wire alone. But an uneasiness began to insinuate itself. Anyone could follow that wide road home. But what if ... I didn't know just what ... but what if something ...? Oh dammit, I'd have to go *find* him.

I kept calling him all the way along the road. There was no answer. How could he get out of sound so quickly, unless he ran? He must have run all the way. But why? I began to run myself.

ॐ

My first reaction when I saw him standing by the house, looking toward the pasture, was intense relief. Then, suddenly my irritation was compounded. He seemed to sense my annoyance, even from a distance. He began to wave, as if in propitiation. He had a funny way of waving, holding his arm out still and moving his hand up and down very slowly. I didn't wave back. When I came close enough that he could see my face he stopped waving.

"I thought you'd come home without me, Art," he said.

"Why should you think that?" I said, very calmly.

He wasn't defiant as I'd expected him to be. He looked as if he were relieved to see me; but as if at the sight of me coming from that direction he knew he'd done something wrong. Now he was trying to pass the thing off as an amusing quirk in the way things had turned out. Though half-suspecting that this wouldn't go over. His tentative oversmiling brushed at my irritation, but didn't dislodge it.

"I called to you, Art," he said.

I just looked at him, as much as to say, do you think I'm deaf?

"Yes, I called. I thought you'd come home some other way."

"Now I've got to traipse all the way back there this afternoon to finish one rod of fence," I said.

"I thought you'd gone and left me," he said.

I ignored him, and walked past him into the house.

He didn't eat much dinner, but he wasn't defiant about that, either, as he was, sometimes, when he refused to eat. And after dinner he went out and sat down on the banking, by himself. He didn't know that his hair was sticking up through the heart-shaped holes in the skullcap with all the buttons pinned on it.

When it was time to go back to the woods again, he hung around me with his new bat and ball. Tossing the ball up himself and trying to hit it before it struck the ground.

"Boy, you picked out the very best bat there was, didn't you, Art?" he said. I knew he thought I'd toss him a few. I didn't pay any attention to what he was doing.

When I started across the yard, he said, "Do you want me to carry the axe this afternoon? That makes it *easier* for you, doesn't it, Art?"

"I'll be back in an hour or so," I said. "You play with Max."

He went as far as the gate with me. Then he stopped. I didn't turn around. It sounds foolish, but everything between us was on such an adult basis that it wasn't until I bent over to crawl through the barbed wire fence that I stole a glance at him, covertly. He was tossing the ball up again and trying to hit it. It always fell to the ground, because the bat was so unwieldy and because he had one eye on me. I noticed he still had on his hot rubber boots. I had intended to change them for his sneakers. He was the sort of child who seems unconsciously to invest his clothes with his own mood. The thought of his clothes, when he was forlorn, assaulted me as hard as the thought of his face.

I walked back the log road. Past the ant hill and the uprooted pine. Do you know the kind of thoughts you have when you go back alone to a job which you have been working at happily with another? When that work together has ended in a quarrel ... with your accusations unprotested, and, after that, your rejection of his overtures unprotested too?

I picked up my tools and began to work. But I couldn't seem to work quickly.

I'd catch myself, with the hammer slack in my hands, thinking about crazy things like the yellow sole-edges of his new shoes still unscratched, the Saturday I took him in town for the matinee ... Of his secret pride in the new tie (which he left outside his pullover until he saw that the other children had theirs inside) singling him so abatedly from the town children, the Saturday I took him to the matinee, that I felt an unreasonable rush of protectiveness toward him .... Of him laughing dutifully at the violence in the comedy, but crouching a little toward me, while the other children, who were not nearly so violent as he, shrieked together in a seizure of delight.

I thought of his scribblers, with the fixity there of the letters which his small hand had formed earnestly, but awry.

I thought of those times when the freak would come upon him to recount all his trangressions of the day, insisting on his guilt with phrases of my own I had never expected him to remember.

I thought of him playing ball with the other children.

At first they'd all play together in the normal way. Then they'd go along with the outlandish variations he'd introduce into the game, because it was his equipment. (Though he'd shown them his new bat and glove gleefully, with no reservations of ownership.) Then, somehow, *they'd* be playing with the bat and glove and he'd be out of it, watching. Soon, as if after an unspoken decision which didn't include him, they'd drift away.

I thought now of him standing there, saying, "Boy, I hope my friends come to play with me early tomorrow, *early*, Art"—though I knew that if they came at all their first question would be, "Can we use your bat and glove?"

I thought of the time I'd given him and another child each a quarter. He'd snatched the other child's quarter out of his hand. I let him see what a shameful action I thought that was—and then when they came back from the store I heard him say to the other child, "Here's your quarter. I didn't want you to use any of *your* money on the treat."

I thought of the night he'd said only, "Hi, Art," over-casually, when I surprised him crouching at the bedroom window listening to the voices of boys playing in a far field.

I thought of him asleep. I thought, if anything should ever happen to him that's the way he would look.

I laughed; deliberately. To kid myself for being such a soft and sentimental fool. But it was no use. The feeling came over me, immediate as the sound of a voice, that something *was* happening to him right now. I couldn't help it, I dropped my tools. For the second time that day I left the fencing unfinished.

It was coincidence, of course, but I don't believe that ... because I had started to run even before I came over the crest of the knoll by the barn. Before I saw the cluster of excited children by the horse stable.

I couldn't see David among them, but I saw the ladder against the roof. I saw Max running toward the stable, with my neighbour running behind him. I felt the chill you get when you see a country man running, as fast as he can. I knew, by the way the children looked at me, parting their circle and looking down with sudden silence at their own feet, what had happened.

"He fell off the roof," one of them said, with that strange, half-discomfited awe that was always in their voices whenever they spoke of any reckless escapade in which David was involved.

I held him, and I said, "David, David ...."

He stirred. "Wait," he said drowsily, "Wait up, Art ..."

This is foolish, but I had the feeling that if I hadn't been right there, right then, to call his name, he would never have come back. It is foolish, because he wasn't really hurt at all; he was only stunned. The doctor could scarcely find a bruise on him. (I don't know just why my eyes stung when the doctor patted his head in admiration of his patience, when the exhaustive examination was over. He always behaved with that assaulting perfection at the doctor's or the dentist's.)

I read to him the rest of the afternoon. He'd sit quiet all day, with the erasure on his face as smooth as the erasure of sleep, if you read to him.

It was the season of long days, so after supper, I decided there was still time to finish the fence.

"Do you want to help me finish the fence?" I said. I thought he'd be delighted.

"No," he said. "You go on. I'll wait right here. Right here, Art."

"Who's going to help me stretch the wire?" I said.

"All right," he said.

He scarcely spoke until we got almost back to the spot where the skeleton was. Then he stopped and said, "We better go back, Art. It's going to be dark."

"G'way with ya," I said. "It won't be dark for hours." It wouldn't be although the light *was* an eerie after-supper light and the night-mystery was beginning to isolate the woods.

"I'm going home," he said. His voice and his face were suddenly defiant.

"You're not going home," I said sharply. "Now come on, hurry up."

I was carrying an extra pound of staples I had picked up in town. He snatched the package from my hand. Before I could stop him he broke the string and strewed them far and wide on the ground.

I suppose I was keyed up after the day, for I did then what I had never done before. I took him and held him and I put it onto him, hard and thoroughly.

He didn't try to escape. For the first few seconds he didn't make a sound. The only retraction of his defiance was a kind of crouching in his eyes when he first realized what I was going to do. Then he began to cry. He cried and cried.

"You're *going* home," I said, "and you're going right to *bed.*

I could see the marks of my fingers on his bare legs, when I undressed him. He went to sleep almost immediately. But though it was perfectly quiet downstairs for reading, the words of my book might have been any others.

When I got him up to the toilet, he had something to say, as usual. But this time it wasn't the fragment of a dream. He was wide awake. The grudgelessness in his night-face was more assaulting than ever. I sat down on the side of his bed for a minute.

"Bones make you feel funny, don't they, Art?" was what he said.

I remembered then.

I remembered that the skeleton was opposite the place where he sat down to rest. I remembered how he had shrunk from it on the way back. I remembered then that the wind had been blowing *away* from me when I was cutting the posts. That's why I hadn't heard him call. I thought of him calling and calling, and then running along the road alone, in the heavy, hot, rubber boots. David, David, I thought, do I always fail you like that?... the awful misunderstanding a child has to endure! I couldn't answer him.

"I thought you'd gone home, Art," he said.

"I'm sorry," I said. I couldn't seem to find any words to go on with.

"I'm sorry too I threw the staples," he said eagerly.

"I'm sorry I spanked you."

"No, no," he said. "You spank me every time I do that, won't you, Dad?... *spank* me, Dad."

His night-face seemed happier than I had ever seen it—in, for him, a surprisingly quiet way. As if the trigger-spring of his driving restlessness had been finally cut. I won't say it came in a flash. It wasn't such a simple thing as that. But could that be what I had done wrong? It wasn't that a good trouncing was just what he needed, however hard it is to make it sound otherwise.

He had called me "Dad." Could it be that a child would rather have a father than a pal? ("Wait …. Wait up, Art.") By spanking him I had broken the adult partnership between us and set him free. He could cry. His guilt could be paid for all at once and absolved.

It wasn't the spanking that had been cruel. What had been cruel were all the times I had snubbed him as you might an adult—with implication of shame. There was no way he could get over that. The residue of blame piled up in him. Shutting him out, spreading (who can tell what curious symptoms a child's mind will translate it into?), blocking his access to me, to other children, even to himself. And to any kind of block an imaginative child's reaction is violence, deviation. Any guilt he can't be absolved of at once he blindly adds to, whenever he thinks of it, in a kind of desperation.

I had worried about failing *him*. That hadn't bothered him. What had bothered him was a shame—an adult shame I had taught him, I saw now—for failing *me*.

If he ever provokes me beyond my control again, I thought, I will spank him. That may be failure too, on my part, but I will do it. I will never treat him like an adult again. I will never, ever again, leave him with any unexpiable residue of blame.

I said, "Go to sleep now."

"All right," he said.

"Goodnight," I said.

"Goodnight."

"Dad," he said softly, when I was almost to the door, "how come you knew I jumped off the roof?"

I brought up short. "Jumped," he said, not "fell." Was it too late then? How much worse I must have done it than I imagined, if he was driven to jump off a roof to shock me back into contact with him.

Yet there was a curious hope to be had from this very question. Because it hadn't been a question, really. It had been a statement. "How come you *knew* …?" He hadn't the slightest doubt that no matter what he did, wherever I was I would know it, and that wherever I was I would come.

Anyhow, it is a fine day today, and we have just finished the fence. He is playing ball with the other children as I put this down. Their way.

Just Like Everyone Else

It was the hypnotic week before Christmas and the children were languid and adventurous by turns.

"I dare ya to ask Glenn right out about them logs," Puss Martin said to Danny Troop, adventurous. They were skirting up behind Glenn Chapman's barn with their sleds.

Danny had never been known to refuse a dare. But he didn't even bluff today. "Naw," he said. I wouldn't like to. Not Glenn Chapman."

The logs were a mystery.

Glenn had got them out ten years ago, on next to the last snow. He had yarded them on a knoll in the middle of his best field, so that (or so everyone supposed) it would be easier to load them for the saw mill when spring came. They had lain there ever since. They were dry-rotted now to the very core, but he hadn't even hauled them away. He plowed and mowed *around* them.

No one had ever found out why, Glenn was so close-minded. They gathered, of course, that it had something to do with that business of Flo Paige and the sleighing party. The very same snow had been involved. But even Maud Hennigar, who collected "Items" for the *Weekly Bulletin* in town, and could pick up a news scent no matter how obscure the trail, had never been able to fathom it out.

Glenn lived alone. A long sidehill stretched across all the farms from one end of the village to the other. His section of it was better coasting than anywhere else. But the children almost never coasted there. It wasn't that he was old and crotchety. He wasn't older than their fathers. Anywhere else he wouldn't have stood out from the average, except perhaps as his fresh-shaven color was a little higher and his thick black hair a little more positive and his body so unconcealably muscular even in his good clothes as to give any decorative pattern in his necktie an incongruous touch. But, here ... he wasn't married and he lived alone. It made him seem almost like an object of superstition to them.

Flo Paige lived alone, too. But that was different. That didn't give them the same kind of feeling. She was a woman, with a woman's pretty speaking-first face, and hair as soft brown as a schoolgirl's. She'd been

away to train for a nurse. Her house didn't seem like a cave, as Glenn's
did.

&

It was the week before Christmas, and almost every day snowflakes so
large they'd cling for a second like little white maps on the children's flesh
flocked so thick and spiraling in the Christmas-kindled air that to look
through them to the dark pagodas of spruces stretched far-off along
the ridge of the mountain affected the children like a delicious kind of
giddiness. It was the enchanted week exempt from time and space.
Ages leveled and faces were unlocked. And when you touched the fir
tree—the one it had taken you so agonizingly long to settle on, but now
you had it home seemed like the one tree in the world that was unmis-
takably the spell made shape—it was as if you put your bare hand on
the heartbeat of the mystery itself.

Glenn set the two brimming pails of milk down on the porch floor
and reached for the kitchen door knob. He glanced across the field to
where the children were coasting on Lev's sidehill. The children were
clustered around Danny, and Glenn wondered what recklessness he
was up to now. He watched to see, smiling.

The children broke ranks again and Danny started down the hill.
He was standing up on his sled.

You could see how quickly he picked up speed because his ear tabs
began almost immediately to stand out from his cap, and the strings
on them lashed the air behind him. By the time he struck the little hum-
mock halfway down he was going like the wind. The jolt took his cap
off altogether. The others shrieked with laughter. Danny righted the
sled with an expert twist of his small legs.

But there was nothing his legs could do when his runaway sled
struck the bare patch of frozen crust almost at the foot of the hill. It
jackknifed sideways quicker than thought and Danny's small body shot
out against the big rock like a diver's.

Glenn gave an involuntary grunt of alarm. He waited for Danny to
get up and cry. But he didn't. The children began to call his name and
run down the hill. Glenn half-expected Danny to get up and laugh
when they reached him. It would be just like that instant mischievous-
ness of his to be turning this into a joke. But he didn't move at all.

Glenn set the milk pails in on the kitchen floor with such haste that
one slopped over. A long finger of milk crept toward the stove. If it got
under the zinc ... he thought automatically. But he didn't wait to wipe
it up. He ran.

It was quite plain that Danny wasn't fooling. His body had the limpness that's one subtle degree beyond the limpness of any kind of sleep or pretence.

Glenn got down beside the child. "Danny," he said. "Danny ..." But it was the sort of deafness that no sound can be made loud enough to break through. He drew in one long deep breath himself, and put his hand inside Danny's shirt.

"Thank God," he said. He straightened up, suddenly brisk.

"Go get his cap," he said to Puss.

"Yes, Glenn," Puss said, chastened to intense obedience.

"And Hank..." Glenn hesitated a minute. "Hank, you go get Flo Paige."

"Yes, Glenn."

With a gentleness you couldn't believe his great hands knew, Glenn slipped the cap onto the boy's head. He looked at him. Danny was the kind of headlong child in whom stillness seems like a cruelty. With movement gone, it was as if he had been stripped of some pitiable shield.

∾

"What did Glenn and Flo say to each other?" Puss Martin's mother questioned him that evening.

"I don't remember what they said. I guess she told him his hands was freezin' cold. Why?"

"Oh, nothing. When did she say that? Did she touch his hands?"

"I guess. Yeah, I guess when she was showin' him how to carry Danny."

"Poor little Danny!" Mrs. Martin choked up. "Oh, I hope and *pray* he'll be all right." She paused. "What did Glenn say when she said that?"

"*I* don't remember what she said. I guess he didn't say much of anything, he never does."

"What made him call Flo?" Mrs. Martin persisted. "Why didn't he call Lev's or someone?"

"Lev's was all in town," Puss said. "And Flo's a nurse."

"I know, but ... How did they act?"

"Act?"

"Yes. Were they... friendly? Or did they seem to be ...?"

"I don't know. I guess they was too scared to ... And I think Flo was cryin' a little."

"Was it anything Glenn said? Or was she just...?"

"Oh, Mum, *I* can't remember," Puss said impatiently. "I guess she was cryin' about Danny but it was when she told Glenn about his hands she started. Why don't you ask Flo if you want to know?"

"Oh, no," she said, "no. And don't *you* say anything ..."

è♣

He sent for *me*, Flo thought. But, later, in the Troop kitchen, she saw (or thought she saw) that it was the nurse, not the woman, that Glenn had sent for. He didn't cold-shoulder her deliberately. But it seemed as if the way he'd shut her out ever since that fatal sleighing party was no longer dictated by feeling, but by mere habit.

Fletch and Mary Troop looked at each other beseechingly. Danny lay on the couch. They couldn't make him hear his name, either. Their faces looked like faces awakened by a knock in the middle of the night. And each time a different neighbor came through the doorway, it seemed a little harder for them to raise their weighted eyes to meet the glance that was almost guilty with helpless kindness but almost fascinated, too.

Mary wasn't a tidy housekeeper. When the woman from town who was visiting Clara Bensom came in, Mary cleared a chair and motioned for her to sit down. The mixture of desperation and compulsive courtesy in her face was somehow awful when she did that. And while Flo was phoning the doctor, she picked up the Christmas tree ornaments that were scattered over the sideboard and put them back into their sockets in the box, one by one, as if her hands were gently out of their mind.

The doctor told them to bring Danny in to the town hospital at once.

"I'll go along with him," Flo said.

Mary didn't protest the chilling word, hospital. "His pants ..." was all she said, in that lost crippled voice. "He's so hard on his clothes ..."

"His pants are all right, dear," Flo said softly. "We don't want to move him any more than we can help."

"But would it hurt if ... I washed his hands a little?"

Glenn turned to Fletch.

"I'll take you," he said. "All I got to do is separate the milk, and ..."

"Or I could take ya, Fletch," Aleck Carter said. "My double sled's all geared up and we could make some seats with bags o' hay ..."

"I got to go, too," Mary broke in.

"You can go," Fletch said.

"... and put some planks across the sled benches and set the couch right on."

"He wanted me to take him to town this afternoon and see the *stores*," Fletch said suddenly to Aleck. "I told him I didn't have no time to ... *I* didn't know anythin' was goin' to happen to him," he added savagely.

"Of course ya didn't," Aleck said gently, "of course ya didn't. "He put his arm round Fletch's shoulder. Fletch's face broke up for the first time in a harsh sob.

Aleck patted Fletch's arm. "Now I'll be right ready in fifteen, twenty minutes ..."

"And Jess Richards and I will look after things at the house here till you get back," Maud Hennigar said.

When they walked out to the sleds, Fletch took Mary's arm. He walked firm and steady, but bent forward a little as if he were breasting some invisible obstacle in his path. And Mary walked as if walking were some skill she was trying to remember.

Maud and Jess got themselves a bite to eat and tidied up the kitchen. They had their cry out, and then they settled to a thorough discussion of what had happened and of everyone involved.

"What a blessing Flo was here!" Maud said. "I don't know what there is about that woman, but ... did you notice how she got Mary quieted down right away, poor soul?"

"I did notice that," Jess said. She puckered up her forehead. "Isn't Flo the one that ...? Wasn't there something about her and Glenn Chapman one time ...?" Jess was new to the place.

"You mean the sleighing party," Maud said.

"Well, no, I never heard about *that*," Jess said, "but seems like a dream I heard someone say they ..."

Maud nodded. "About the sleighing party was this night ... they'd gone together all their lives, you know, everyone took them for as good as engaged ... and this night, all the young people had planned up a trip to the dance in Hamstead. Come along, *well*, nearly *dark*, and the rest of them had all gone, and didn't Glenn send word to Flo that it might be an hour or so yet before he could pick her up—he wanted to get his last load of logs out in case the snow should go! It was almost spring. They say Flo never unsealed her lips. She just walked to the phone and *hired* Wes Harvey to take her."

"She did?" Jess said. "That don't sound like her, somehow, Maud."

"I know it don't. But I tell you what I think. Glenn's good and kind and honor'ble and everything like that ... but he's so close-minded and set in his ways, and I think it must have just struck her that he was always puttin' his work ahead o' her. I think she just flew off the handle."

"Did he go, later?"

"Yes, he went. I don't know, of course, but I don't imagine Flo's mother ever told him Flo had *hired* Wes. She told him, I imagine, that Flo got a chance and knew he wouldn't mind."

"What happened at the dance?"

"Not a thing. But when the dance was over, Flo simply walked over to Wes's sleigh and come *back* with him."

"And she and Glenn never ...?"

"No. I imagine Flo was over it the very next day. But you know Glenn. And not long after that Flo went away to train. And them's the same logs you see right over in his field. Some says he left 'em there to grind her, but that don't sound like *him* altogether, does it. No one'll ever know the rights of it, of course, but I know there's more to them logs than ..."

"And yet Flo comes back here to live," Jess said.

"That's what I was goin' to say," Maud said. "When her parents both took that same terrible heart ailment—and both died the same week, one on a Monday and one on a Friday, wasn't that peculiar?—she come back to look after them, and everyone thought of course she'd sell the place. But she didn't. She's been here ever since. I think she still hopes ... well, I don't know just what she hopes, and I don't think she knows herself, if the truth was known ... but I think she still wants to be near him." Maud sat suddenly upright. "I shouldn't be talking about my neighbors at a time like this ... but I didn't say anything out of the way, now did I."

"Why, no. And Glenn never took up with anyone else all these years?"

"No," Maud said. "He still lives there all alone. Mustn't it be terrible! Especially like at Christmas ..."

Though Maud's guess about Flo was uncannily accurate, Flo herself wouldn't have recognized the truth of it. Flo told herself that she stayed on here simply because the clang and crush of the city had seemed, at the last, to be bruising not only her flesh but striking at her very bones.

But Maud was dead wrong about Glenn. He didn't find it terrible to live alone. Not any more. Habit had worked on him like a kind of anaesthetic.

❧

That was Monday. Tuesday night, late, Flo was putting the final decoration on her tree. She was the sort of woman whose touch seems to evoke in the simplest ornaments of any occasion that occasion's special radiance.

The phone rang suddenly. Sharp central strokes. One long and five shorts. That was Mary Troop's number. It might be further word from Danny. She felt no guilt at listening.

When she took off the receiver, a voice was saying, "... at your house yesterday. Mrs. Perry." It was the woman from town. "And I've been terribly anxious to know how your little boy is."

"Well," Mary said, "Fletch ... my husband ... just come from the hospital and they don't seem to think it's anything serious. He's conscious and everything, you know." Flo's eyes lit up. Oh, this was good news. "Of course, he's quite restless, there, and anyone can't help ..." Mary's voice broke.

"Now don't you worry, my dear," the woman said. "They must know. I'm just sure everything's going to be perfectly all right. And wasn't it wonderful you had Mrs. — Pace, is it? — right there when it happened!"

"Paige," Mary corrected her politely. "*Miss* Paige. She never married."

They went on talking, but Flo put up her receiver. There was the same curious strickenness in her hands that had been in Mary's when she took the garment off the kitchen chair. Her face looked equally lost. Mary hadn't said, "She isn't married." She'd said, "She never married." It was spoken in all innocence, but ...

So that's what I am, Flo thought. A woman who "never married." It's all settled. That's the way I've been written off. And other women *know*, she thought with a kind of fright, better than you know yourself. Yes, that's what I *am*. She stood staring at her hands as if there's where the blow had fallen.

A woman who never married. She knew what that meant here. There's no way you can escape the mold they assign you. They can predict everything you do. You take up little hobbies. You fall into little mannerisms which you hate, but can't help repeating. You get to be the one they come to for the dates of happenings and birthdays, though never with confidences. You get so you cast no shadow on anyone. And you parch ... And you never have a child ... A woman who never married. A woman who never lived.

"Glenn Chapman." She spoke his name aloud, almost violently. It wasn't what I did that night that separated us, she thought now. That was just an excuse. He didn't care. He never loved me. What ever made me think so? He never, ever, said a single word to ...

She looked at the room where the tree stood. It seemed as if everything in it bore a tag reading, "Made by Miss Florence Paige" — so typically clever with her "never married" hands.

She saw Mary's slipshod house, alive with disorder, and she saw Mary's face, intensely alive with pain for her son. She was intensely jealous of that pain. And she thought, absurdly, her ring is fifteen and mine is fourteen, only one short's difference, but...

And then her strickenness turned to a kind of defiance. I *won't* be like that ... I'll leave here. I'll ... she didn't know quite what. But they'll see if my chances are over to...

The next afternoon she made an excuse to Maud Hennigar's. She told Maud she was going away.

"But where?" Maud exclaimed. "Why?"

"Where?" Flo said. "Back to the city. To Norcross. For awhile, anyway. I have to get some ... clothes. And why...?" She smiled. "Well, there's going to be a big change in my life."

No one but Maud would have immediately read into that insinuation exactly what Flo meant her to read.

"Well, did you ever!" Maud gasped. "I never *dreamed*... Now aren't you the riddle, Flo Paige!"

"There have been so many obstacles of one kind or another up to now," Flo said. "But at last everything seems to be clear sailing."

"Is it someone you used to know there?" Maud said. "Or did you fall in with him on one of your trips?"

It was Flo's turn to exclaim. "Now, Maud! Whatever gave you *that* idea? You mustn't jump to conclusions!"

"No?" Maud said, with a playful arch of her eyebrows.

"No, really, Maud ..."

Maud smiled. "Do you see any green in my eye?"

Flo didn't realize what a real grass fire she had started. She hadn't the slightest idea it would take the form or the path that it did.

❧

It was Christmas Eve. The cloud of Danny's accident, which had kept drifting across everyone's mind at first like a kind of weather, had lifted. Fletch was bringing him home tonight. The snow lay gentle as forgiveness on the ground, and everywhere as a supper began to steam, or one voice called to another, or a light was lit, the magic and the mystery seemed to break into full blossom at last.

Glenn had milked half an hour early. Otherwise this might have been any other day.

It was almost dusk when he brought the papers in from the mailbox. He glanced at the local "Items" in the *Bulletin*. There was an account of Danny's accident ... a mention of Mrs. Perry's call on Clara Benson ...

And then: "Miss Florence Paige leaves shortly for an indefinite visit in Norcross. A little bird has it that she will soon be one of the principals in an interesting event!"

"Mr. Austin Reese," the item went on, "has purchased a new..."

But Glenn sat down as if his limbs had unhooked from their sockets. Flo! Married! The words about her stamped themselves on his mind as bright and challenging as pain. Exactly as with Flo, the events of this whole last week had been preparing the tinder. This was the flash.

It had never struck him until this very minute how totally Flo was the backdrop of his whole consciousness. Married to someone else! Marriage is the farthest country away there is. And as soon as there was a child ... Hers and someone else's ... Her face came before him so clearly and filled him with such longing that it was like one of those faces that assault you sometimes in the intolerably wistful light of a dream.

And then, as if the focus of some lens had shifted just the necessary millimeter, he saw the face of his whole life with merciless clarity.

The stillness of his kitchen and his fields struck him like a draft. A treachery in their neatness and their starkness—in these bare *things* he'd always had to have in order before he could turn to what was really important—seemed all at once exposed. Exactly as had seemed exposed to Flo a treachery in the *ornament* of her rooms.

I don't belong to anyone, he thought. I am not *like* anyone else in the place. They hardly separate me from the fields or the trees they look at. Not even the children. The children don't even sauce me when I catch them in the orchard. I am only a shape.

He saw Fletch's face when *he* had offered to take Danny to the hospital (and I had to say that about the milk even then!), and he saw it when Aleck Carter had offered. He saw the difference between those two looks. What did it matter then that Fletch and Aleck hadn't been any too friendly? Aleck had sons of his own. He knew what it must be like for Fletch. Fletch knew that. I don't know what anything is like. Fletch knew that, too.

He saw Mary's face as she held Fletch's arm walking out to the sleds. What did it matter then that she and Fletch didn't get along too well sometimes? A woman will never look at me like that. I will never know what a woman is like.

He saw Danny's gamin face. A child is a strange world to me ... I'll never know what it's like when the bad frights with them are *over* ...

When it came really dark he lit the light. But he couldn't read, as he always did. The silence of the kitchen was still a taunt. But there was nowhere else he could go tonight, Christmas Eve.

He picked up the paper and studied the words again, as if with concentration enough they might, by some miracle, be made to change before his eyes. But they remained the same.

And yet ... suddenly ... Or was this only another trap to torment him? Maud didn't come right out and say it was a sure thing. It could be only a rumor—he knew Maud. Hope sprang in him. And then he tried to beat it off like something treacherous. And then he was frantic in a different way. He was divided between a desperate urge and a terrible reluctance to find out the truth from Flo's own lips. Was it just talk, or wasn't it? He had to know. And there was only one way to find out for certain.

He looked toward her house. There was a light there. As if it strained every muscle in his body to lift it, he reached for his cap.

&

"Is it true?" Glenn said. "I'm not asking you anything more about it than that. Just, is it true?"

Words falling out. Flo had never known before how accurate an expression that could be.

"I'm going away, yes," she said. She spoke with a false calm, trying to get a grip on her tumbling thoughts. This intenseness she had never suspected was hidden in Glenn, this direct challenge, his coming into her house at all ...

"I didn't mean that," he said. "The other ..."

"But what difference would it make to you, Glenn?" she said in the same even voice. "You hardly ever see me. And when you *do* ..."

"I know," he said. "I know what I'm like. I know now. I can't talk things over, or ... like anyone else. I never could."

"And you were always so proud and stubborn as well, that you could never overlook anything, weren't you," she said. Much gentler, but still in the neutral voice.

He flinched. "Yes," he said. "I know. But ... I didn't *know*. I ..." The sentences seemed to be tangled up in his throat. And sooner or later each loose end he drew on would break.

Flo looked at him. It was no use. There was no savor in playing her advantage any longer.

"It's not true about any wedding," she said simply, "if that's what you mean. That was just something I said to Maud ... that she ..." She smiled ironically. Her bluff had lasted a long while, hadn't it.

His eyes lifted from his hands that were obsessively clicking each thumbnail under the nails of the other four fingers one by one. He looked her full in the face, and the pupils of his dark eyes seemed to dilate as if they had drops in them. They had that same look of soft velvety blinding. He took one deep breath, as if of deliverance.

"There's something I've got to tell you, Flo," he said then. "That night ... I mean the night ..."

"I know the night you mean," she said.

"That was the night I was going to tell you I ... I was going to ask you to marry me."

She didn't say a word. Don't you dare cry, she warned herself. She got up and put on the light in the room where the tree stood.

"But it was something that could wait until you got your logs all out, wasn't it," she said at last. She couldn't resist that.

"I don't blame you, Flo," he said. "I never seemed to realize that you can't expect people to read your mind." He hesitated. "They weren't just ... any old logs, though, Flo. I planned if you said ... if we ... I'd build a new house for us with them. I *had* to get them out while the snow lasted. Don't you see? And afterwards ... I couldn't bear to touch them. I hated them ... or myself ... or ..."

She stared at the tree. It seemed as if the cloak of its warm shining presence was folding softly over all the crevasses in her life where lately nothing else could quite block the chill winds from striking through.

"That snow did go the next morning," Glenn said savagely, "but there was another one after that. I needn't have ..."

Flo smiled. Really smiled. "It's funny *about* those last snows in the spring, isn't it," she said gently. "There's almost always another one."

Glenn looked at her, and his eyes seemed to catch light like a coal in the breeze. Could she mean ...?

"Flo," he said urgently. "If I asked you now? What would you ...?"

"Yes," she said quietly, without an instant of false hesitation. "There's never been anything I could do about it—I've always loved you and I always will."

એ

That's all there was then—not a thing more than just that. They slipped into that curious deep quiet almost like bottomless fatigue.

"I promised Mary I'd go over and see how Danny stood the trip home," Flo said later.

I'll go with you," Glenn said. He could go into *anyone's* house now, Christmas Eve or not.

"All right," she said.

At the door she turned and went back into the front room, which she had left lit, and took the small tree off the table.

"What's that for?" he said.

"It's for you," she said.

And when they came to his house they went inside and they put it on his table. And they lit every candle on it for a minute or so. They looked out the window at the other lights, and it seemed as if now the little chain of beacon fires was closed and complete. And they thought, when we have a child, the other children will tease and torment us sometimes just like they do everyone else. And they will not pass our house on Christmas Day as if no one lived there. We'll be just like everyone else.

They blew out the candles and she could not see his face in the darkness. But she knew there was a slow grin forming on it when he spoke. She had forgotten that grin of his, that grin you were always forgetting until it reduced his seriousness at the most outlandishly surprising moments.

"You know Maud may be right," he said. "This might be an interesting event after all."

Flo touched his hand. "And won't it tickle her to know she was a prophet?" she said. Glenn put his arm around her.

"I wish we had something to take Danny," he said. "Something real nice."

"You know," she said, "that's just what I was thinking. You took the words right out of my mouth."

But what Christmas present could they possibly take him that would match his gift to them?

Glenn thought a minute. "How would it be," he said, "if we named our first son after him?"

And they did.

Cleft Rock, With Spring

Madge Kendall took off her earrings and dropped them wearily into the tray on her dresser. It had promised to be a good party: the Pattersons were the kind of hosts who have a way of sparking you into a true party blitheness the moment they take your coat. But once more she'd brought home with her that odd sense of frustration. Jeff never used to act like that.

When Ken Patterson had said, "What makes you so quiet, Madge?" Jeff had said, "Oh, my wife is just bottling up her emotions. We use them for conserves in the winter. They have a flavour rather like quince." The tone, if not the words, had been almost derisive.

Not that Jeff was a smarty. His face corrected that. And if he were merely a smarty, the others would snub him. They wouldn't repeat him with the generosity they did.

Yet even when he was the hub of the party, he didn't seem to be satisfied. There was something hectic about his behaviour.

And lately there was a new edginess in the glibbest of his remarks. "You should see Madge whipping my Agatha Christie under a cushion when her artistic friends call. You see, she knows this character with a superb talent for writing unpublished mood pieces — and a radio actor that says 'straw'bris, black'bris....'"

Did the stubborn drive that had brought him, a village boy with a genius for figures, all the way from office clerk to chief actuary in eight short years and to more money than she'd ever been used to herself, explain it? Was that drive restless for new fields, now he knew he had his job — and his wife — in the hollow of his hand?

Or had it turned his head to have the strange women at parties like these almost invariably point out to him how much he looked like Laurence Olivier?

"And I'm only the poor man's Claudette Colbert," she'd said tonight. The rest had laughed, because it did describe her own rather plaintive looks so accurately. But Jeff hadn't even smiled. He seemed to resent her scoring anything that approached an applaudable remark.

He was taking out his cufflinks, with the same apathetic gestures as she. They didn't discuss the party. That's the worse sign of all, she thought: when you don't post mortem parties any more.

They never did now. That was the funny part: the moment they were alone, their own talk lapsed into a crippling matter-of-factness, like the talk of two people who have to keep skirting some sensitive topic.

She got into bed, but she couldn't sleep. She didn't understand him any more. You'd think it was he, not she, who was the city product. She felt shrunken, for being forever made conscious of her mediocrity.

He didn't use to be like that. He never used to have that relentless obsession to show her how totally he could eclipse her. It was her suggestion that they take this trip back home. To Dondale. The village where he'd been brought up, and where she had spent her childhood summers. With her mother's widowed sister, who had insisted that the company of simple village children would be the best formative experience possible for Madge. Those were the years when types like Aunt Emily fancied it terribly smart to refurbish an old mill like the one in Dondale and live in it through July and August.

Madge's desire for this visit now had something to do with the idea, persistent against all contradictions of experience, that reviving an original happiness is as simple as going back to the original scene of it.

They were staying at the small hotel in town, but Dondale was near enough that they could go back and forth every day.

Now, driving along the dusty road to the old picnic lake, this first noon, she was sorry they had come.

It was that hot, dry summer.

She had known that Jeff's family had moved away and scattered. That there were strangers living in his old house. That the old mill house had burned down — tramps, they suspected. And that any friends still here would be much older. She hadn't been naive enough not to know that you can never go home again, in that sense.

But it had never occurred to her that a place itself could age.

Dondale looked like a faded snapshot of itself. It seemed to her that the parched alders, their leaves crumbling away from the veining inside, were creeping in closer around the fields. And in the fields the grass reminded her of ribbon grass she'd seen one time, with a couple of peacock feathers, inside a vase in an unused parlour. They always planted ribbon grass on graves.

Around the bend beyond the long dusty hill below the church and the houses, and past the meadow where the rocks showed crusted with parched moss in the bed of the dry brook, they came upon a man and a span of horses. The man sprang upright on his load at the sound of the motor. He was so busy reining his horses to the exact edge of the narrow road that he didn't look their way at all.

But as they squeezed by, Madge caught a glimpse of his face in the rear-view mirror.

"Jeff," she exclaimed, "do you know who I think that was? That was Dave Woodworth!"

He braked the car. "That's what I thought," he said. "Do you want to stop?"

"Well, of course!" she said. And then she hesitated. "No," she said, "never mind. We're too far by now."

Everything had changed so, what would there be to say?

They ate lunch in the old pine grove by the lake. The pines had grown so tall they seemed now to belong more to the air than to the earth, and the warnings of fire hazard tacked to them seemed to annul their old intimacy. The lake was so low that huge rocks were exposed in the shallows where they used to swim. The water had a sweetish, withdrawn smell.

After lunch, it wasn't as it used to be. As soon as the dishes were packed, it seemed as if they were waiting to leave.

They sauntered up and down the road in either direction. The flying grasshoppers swivelled as if on a single axle in the dust, and the locusts spun the dry heat in their piercing monotone. It was like those walks you try to soak up the wait between trains with, in a strange city: when they got back hardly any time had gone.

They sat down, finally, on two rocks by the beach. Staring steadily at the hypnotic lap of the waves until they seemed to be floating too. They began to say, "Do you remember the time we...?"

Yet it seemed to her that they were doing even this doggedly. The images they dredged up wouldn't quite come clear. The dimension of spontaneity was missing.

"You know what we forgot?" she said. "Some drinking water. I'm thirsty. I never thought of bringing water here, did you?"

"No," he said. "Coals to Newcastle. But I'm thirsty too. Do you feel like walking as far as the old mill brook? There must be water there, surely."

But there wasn't. It too was dry. Jeff threw out his hands in a gesture of resignation.

"Well," he said, "I guess that's that. Do you want to start back to town?"

"Oh, no," Madge protested, "not just yet." She didn't know why, but it seemed important that they mustn't give this day up until they absolutely had to.

"Didn't there use to be a spring ...?" Jeff said suddenly.

"Yes!" she said. "The spring! *I* remember."

"Let's see," he said. "We used to go back that old log road and ...."

They didn't really think they'd find it. The log road was so grown up, and they couldn't remember how far back the spring had been, or on which side.

So that when they both heard it at once they stopped short. Jeff motioned excitedly for silence, as if they had been stalking a timid animal.

The spring was exactly the same as ever: starting somewhere in the root cavern of the same blown-up log, falling down the slight bank, and spending itself in the ferns. The ferns grew fresh and green all around it. The water ran clean and cool.

It seemed as unchanged as the huge cleft boulder it had always splashed against.

"Imagine!" she said. "After all this drought."

"Like love, eh?" Jeff said, with a flash of his hectic party levity that gave her a sudden chill. "*Ne*-ver parches, *ne*-ver parches ... I'll go get a cup."

Madge ignored the first part of his speech. "A cup?" she said. "In Dondale? Make a birch dipper, for heaven's sake."

"I don't know if I remember how."

But he located a birch tree and he made a conical bark dipper as expertly as ever.

He filled it with water and held it toward her, leaning across the boulder.

"Just a second," she said. She too was leaning against the boulder, extricating a sharp twig from one of her shoes.

Jeff set the tip of the dipper into the fissure that divided the rock, absently tilting it this way and that until its equilibrium was stable.

Suddenly he stood upright.

"It couldn't be!" he said.

"What couldn't be?"

"Come look."

Madge put her hands to the sides of her face and peered down into the deep cleft of the boulder.

Jeff pointed. "There."

"Of course," she said softly.

It was a crude ring. They used to make them by bending an ox-shoe nail into a circle. A child's imagination could easily transform the square head of the nail into a precious stone.

"Do you remember?" Jeff said.

Madge nodded. She remembered all right. It was the day's first distinct image.

"Do you know," she said, "I came back later that afternoon and tried and tried to fish it out with a long stick? But just when I'd get it almost to the top it'd slip back. I cried."

"You cried?" he exclaimed. "And who threw it there? You threw it there yourself, didn't you?"

"I know I threw it there," Madge said. "And you know why. You had to spoil everything."

I've been picturing it all wrong, she thought—he was never any different. A touch of anger sharpened her voice.

"Don't you remember? You were just fitting the ring onto my finger when some other kid came along—wasn't it Dave, actually? It was Dave—and you said, 'Maybe an ox-nail ring won't be fancy enough for Madge to wear, I guess we'd better take it home and put it in the pig's nose.' You had to turn the whole thing into one of your infernal wisecracks. For Dave's benefit. You're always doing something like that with me the minute you have an audience."

"For Dave's benefit?" Jeff said. "For Dave's benefit?"

He spoke almost involuntarily. The way you do in one of those moments when deliberate misrepresentations have reached the challenging point where, no matter what, they just can't be allowed to stand uncorrected.

"Now let's not twist things around. Since when have I ever done anything for anyone's benefit, as you put it, but yours? And it gets me exactly as far as it did that day."

"Jeff," Madge said, "now you know you...."

"This is what I know," he said. "Just let me finish. And listen carefully. Because, as they say, I can only give you the answer once." He paused. "I remember you had a 'boughten' dress on."

For some reason, that picture brought a flash of anger into his voice too and a kind of stumbling fluency.

"You were just *sitting* there, with your ... crisp ... boughten ... city ... dress on. You never had to make any effort whatsoever ... about anything ... to be ... well, automatically ahead of me. You knew you were city-grained and I was homemade ...."

He glanced at her, bristling against possible interruption, but she didn't interrupt.

"You know"—he seemed to slip into the present tense without noticing it—"that no matter how I go you one better in your own field—money ... cultchah ... or you name it, I'll try it—no matter how I knock myself out trying to impress you, I can never catch up on that head start of yours. All you have to do is let your ... entrenchment? *I* don't know what the word is ... sit back and smile."

He looked at her again, challenging her to interrupt, but she didn't say a word.

"I'm not one damn bit ashamed of being homemade, mind you. But you wouldn't understand. I remember one day I was trying to swing the scythe and my older brother came along and smiled at me. All you have to do is look at me, just look at me, and I get that ...."

He broke off all at once, suddenly self-conscious, and pointed to the dipper.

"All right," he said. "Were you thirsty, or weren't you?"

Madge put the dipper to her lips, and the touch of the cool water stopped their trembling. She felt a release as spilling as when some chance paragraph in a book you pick up defines exactly the way you are feeling right then.

But she took a long time drinking. Because she knew she must be very careful about choosing the next words she spoke. Because she felt as peculiarly shamed—though it was not for anything like exactly the same reasons—as if she'd been guilty of keeping her distance from a child who'd been trying to engage her with an approach he wasn't any too sure of himself. Or of surprising him, in the very presence of others to whom he was making some innocent boast, with the reminder that she'd actually been there when the thing happened.

Jeff looked about him nervously.

"Whenever you're through," he said, holding his hand toward the dipper. "I'd like to rinse off my own tongue." Trying to cover up. Trying to put his instantly regretted confession behind them, beyond reference.

And then he said quickly, "How would you like to stop and see old Dave on the way back?"

She knew then what she must say, for his desperate pride's sake. She knew all she must say, for now. Later they would get it all straight, but not now.

"I'd love to see old Dave," she said. "And thanks, darling, for trying to give your little city mouse such a terrific build-up. For a minute there you almost had me convinced."

"But you *are* ..." he began.

"Shush!" she said. "Or you will have me believing it. And fish me out my ring."

The Wild Goose

I've never stopped missing my brother Jeff.

I'm all right; and then I pick up the rake he mended so perfectly for me where the handle went into the bow; or I come across where he'd scratched the threshing count on the barn door, with one of those clumsy fives of his in it; or it's time for someone to make the first move for bed; or some winter dusk when the sun's drawing water down beyond the frozen marshes—do you know that time of day? It's as if your heart slips into low gear.

(I'm glad Jeff can't hear me. But I don't know, maybe he wouldn't think it sounded soft. Just because he never said anything like that himself—you can't go by that.)

I always feel like telling something about him then. I don't know, if I can tell something to show people what he was really like it seems to help.

The wild goose flew over this evening. The sky was full of grey clouds. It looked as if it was worried about something. I could tell about Jeff and the wild goose. I never have.

It really started the afternoon before. We went hunting about four o'clock. I was fourteen and he was sixteen.

You'd never know we were brothers. You could tell exactly how he was going to look as a man, and I looked like a child that couldn't make up his mind *what* shape his face would take on later. He could lift me and my load (though he'd never once glance my way if I tackled anything beyond my strength—trying to lead a steer that was tough in the neck, or putting a cordwood butt on top of the pile, or anything). But I always seemed the older, somehow. He always seemed to—well, look up to me or something, it didn't matter how often I was mean to him.

I could draw the sprawling back field on a piece of paper and figure out the quickest way to mow it, by algebra; but when I took the machine out on the field itself I wouldn't know where to begin. Jeff could take one look at the field and know exactly where to make the first swath. That was the difference between us.

And I had a quick temper, and Jeff never lost his temper except when someone was mad at *me*.

I never saw him mad at me himself but that one day. The day was so still and the sun was so bright the leaves seemed to be breathing out kind of a yellow light before they fell to the ground. I always think there's something sort of lonesome about that, don't you?

I'm no kind of a hunter. You wouldn't think I was a country boy at all.

But Jeff was. He was a wonderful shot; and the minute he stepped into the woods there was a sort of brightness and a hush in his face together, I can't describe it. It wasn't that he liked the killing part. He seemed to have a funny kind of love and respect for whatever he hunted that I didn't have at all. If I don't see any game the first quarter mile I get to feel like I'm just walking around on a fool's errand, dragging a heavy gun along. But Jeff's spell never slacked for a second.

You'd have to live in the country to know what hunting meant to anyone like Jeff. And to know how he rated with the grown-up men; here's just this kid, see, and he knows right where to find the game, no matter how scarce it is, and to bring it home.

Anyway, we'd hardly gone any distance at all—we were just rounding that bend in the log road where there's the bit of open swamp and then what's left of the old back orchard, before the woods start—when Jeff halted suddenly and grabbed my arm.

"What's the matter?" I said.

I guess I spoke louder than ordinary, because I was startled. I hadn't thought of having to be cautious so soon.

Jeff's gun went up, but he didn't have time for even a chance shot. There was a flash of the big buck's flag. He'd been standing under the farthest apple tree. Then in a single motion, like the ripple in a rope when you hold one end in your hand and whap the other against the ground, he disappeared into the thicket.

Deer will sometimes stand and watch you for minutes, still as stone. Stiller than thunder weather. Stiller than holding your breath. So still you can't believe it. They're cocked for running, but you get the feeling they weren't there before you saw them. Your eyes seem to have plucked them right out of the air. Their feet don't seem to quite rest on the ground.

But the second you speak, they're off. The human voice is like a trigger.

It would have been a sure shot for Jeff. There wasn't a twig between them. It would have been the biggest buck anyone had brought home that year. Even I felt that funny sag in the day that you get when game's been within your reach except for carelessness and now there's nothing. You just keep staring at the empty spot, as if you should have known that was the one place a deer would be.

Jeff turned to me. His eyes were so hot in his head I almost crouched.

"For God's sake," he said, "don't you know enough to keep your tongue still when you're huntin'?"

It was like a slap in the face.

The minute Jeff heard what he'd said the anger went out of him. But you'd have to live in the country to know what a funny feeling it left between us. For one hunter to tell another he'd spoiled a shot. It was as if you'd reminded someone to take off his cap inside the house.

I didn't say a word. Only in my mind. I seemed to hear my mind shouting, "You just wait. You'll see. I'll never ... never ..." Never what, I didn't know—but just that never, never again ....

Jeff rumbled with a laugh, trying to put the whole thing behind us, as a joke.

"Well," he said, offhand like, "that one certainly moved fast didn't he? But we'll circle around. Maybe we'll ketch him in the choppin', what?"

I didn't say a word. I just broke down my gun and took out the cartridge, then and there. I put the cartridge into my windbreaker pocket and turned toward home.

"Ain't you comin'?" Jeff said.

"What d'ya *think*?" I said.

I glanced behind me when he'd gone on. I don't know, it always strikes me there's something sort of lonesome about seeing anyone walk away back-so. I almost changed my mind and ran and caught up with him. But I didn't. I don't know why I could never smooth things over with Jeff right away when I knew he was sorry. I wanted to then, but I couldn't. I had to hang on to the hurt and keep it fresh. I hated what I was doing, but there it was.

It was pitch dark when Jeff got home that night, but he didn't have any deer.

I sort of kept him away from me all the next day. I hated myself for cutting off all his clumsy feelers to make up. ("What was the algebra question you showed the teacher how to do when you was only ten?") It always kind of gets me, seeing through what anyone is trying to do like that, when they don't know you can. But I couldn't help it.

(Once Jeff picked up about fifty bags of cider apples nights after school. The day he took them into town and sold them he bought every single one of us a present. I followed him to the barn that evening when he went to tend the horse. He didn't hear me coming. He was searching under the wagon seat and shaking out all the straw around the horse. He didn't want to tell me what he was looking for, but I made him. He'd lost a five dollar bill out of the money the man at the cider mill had given him. But he'd kept the loss to himself, not to spoil our presents. That's what he was like.)

It was just about dusk when Jeff rushed into the shop the day after I'd spoiled his shot at the deer. He almost never got so excited he forgot himself, like I did. But he was that way then.

"Git your gun, Kenny, quick," he said. "There's a flock o' *geese* lit on the marsh."

It would be hard to explain why that gave even me such a peculiar thrill. Wild geese had something—well, sort of mystic—about them.

When the geese flew south in the fall, high in the sky, people would run outdoors and watch them out of sight. And when they turned back to the house again they'd have kind of a funny feeling. The geese seemed to be about the most—distant, sort of—thing in the world. In every way. You couldn't picture them on the ground, like a normal bird. Years and years ago Steve Hammond had brought one down, and it was still the first thing anyone told about him to a stranger. People said, "He shot a wild goose once," in the same tone they'd say of some famous person they'd seen, "I was close enough to touch him."

I was almost as excited as Jeff. But I kept rounding up my armful, pretending the geese didn't matter much to me one way or the other.

"Never mind the *wood*," Jeff said. He raced into the house for his gun.

I piled up a full load before I went into the house and dropped it into the box. It must have almost killed him to wait for me. But he did.

"Come on. Come on," he urged, as we started down across the field. "And put in a ball cartridge. We'll never git near enough fer shot to carry."

I could see myself hitting that small a target with a ball cartridge! But I did as he said.

When we got to the railroad cut, we crawled on our bellies, so we could use the embankment the rails ran along as a blind. We peeked over it, and there they were.

They were almost the length of the marsh away, way down in that mucky spot where the men cut sods for the dike, but their great white breasts looked big as pennants. They had their long black necks stretched up absolutely straight and still, like charmed cobras. They must have seen us coming down across the field.

Jeff rested the barrel of his gun on a rail. I did the same with mine. But mine was shaking so it made a clatter and I raised it higher.

"I'll count five," Jeff whispered. "Then both fire at once."

I nodded and he began to count.

"One. Two. Three...."

I fired.

Jeff's shot came a split second afterward. He gave me a quick inquisitive glance, but he didn't say a word about me firing before the count was up.

He threw out his empty shell and loaded again. But the geese had already lifted, as if all at once some spring in the ground had shot them into the air. They veered out over the river. All but one, that is. Its white breast was against the ground and we didn't see it in the blur of wings until its own wings gave one last flutter.

"We got one!" Jeff shouted. "Well, I'll be *damned*. We got one!"

He bounded down across the marsh. I came behind, walking.

When I got there he was stroking the goose's soft down almost tenderly. It was only a dead bird to me now, but to him it seemed like some sort of mystery made flesh and shape. There was hardly a mark on it. The bullet had gone through his neck, fair as a die.

Then Jeff made a funny face. He handed the goose to me. He was sort of grinning.

"Here," he said. "Carry her. She's yours. That was some shot, mister."

"Mine?" I said.

"Sure." He looked half sheepish. "I'm a hell of a hunter, I am. I had two ball cartridges in this here pocket, see, and two shot in this one." He put his hand into the first pocket and held out two ball cartridges in his palm. "I guess I got rattled and put the shot in my gun instidd o' the ball. You know how far shot'd carry. It was you that got him, no doubt about *that*."

I carried the goose home.

It didn't mean much to me, but he didn't know that. He could only go by what it would have meant to him, if he'd been the one to carry it home. I knew what he was thinking. This would wipe out what I'd done yesterday. And the men wouldn't look at me now the way they looked at a bookworm but the way they looked at a hunter.

I'm glad that for once I had the decency to pretend I was as excited and proud as he'd thought I'd be. I'm glad I didn't say a word—not then—to let him know I saw through the trick.

For I knew it was a trick. I knew I hadn't shot the goose. While he was counting I'd felt that awful passion to wreck things which always got into me when I was still smarting over something. I had fired before he did, on purpose. Way over their heads, to scare them.

The day Jeff went away we sort of stuck around close to each other, but we couldn't seem to find anything to say.

I went out to the road to wait for the bus with him. Jeff had on his good clothes. They never looked right on him. When I dressed up I looked different, but Jeff never did. I don't know why, but every time I saw Jeff in his good clothes I felt sort of—well, like *defending* him or something.

The bus seemed to take a long time coming. He was going away in the army. He'd be with the guys who were twice as much like him as I was, but just the same I knew he'd rather be with me than with them. I don't know, buses are such darned lonesome things, somehow.

When the bus was due, and I knew we only had left what few minutes it might be late, I tried to think of something light to say, the way you're supposed to.

The only thing that came into my mind was that day with the goose. It was a funny thing to bring up all of a sudden. But now we were a couple of years older I thought I could make something out of it to amuse him. Besides, when someone's going away you have the feeling that you ought to get everything straight between you. You hardly ever can, but you get the feeling.

"You shot the goose that day," I said, "didn't you?"

He nodded.

I'd never have opened my fool mouth if I'd known what was going to happen then. I'd felt sort of still and bad, but I hadn't felt like crying. How was I to know that the minute I mentioned that day the whole thing would come back so darn plain? I'd have died rather than have Jeff see my face break up like that.

But on the other hand, I don't care how soft it sounds, I'm sort of glad I did, now. He didn't look embarrassed, to see me cry. He looked so darned surprised—and then all at once he looked happier than I believe I ever saw him.

That was Jeff. He'll never come back. I don't even know which Korean hill it was—the telegram didn't say. But when I tell anything about him like this I seem to feel that somewhere he's sort of, I don't know, half-smiling—like he used to when we had some secret between us we'd never even discussed. I feel that if I could just make him absolutely clear to everyone he wouldn't really be dead at all. Tonight when the geese flew over I wished I knew how to write a book about him.

The geese didn't light this time. They never have since that day. I don't know, I always think there's something lonesome about wild geese.

But I feel better now. Do you know how it is?

Desire

The Quarrel

Do you know what quarreling is like between a man and a woman to whom the language of quarreling is an alien tongue?

When you go outside from the kitchen afterward, if you are the man, the leaves wave absently in the movement of the August air that is more heat than breeze; and everything you work with, the fork or the scythe or the handle of the plow, sags, heavy to the touch. Your thoughts stumble inside your head, and time comes inside and hurts there. You think it must be noon a dozen times, but scarcely an hour has passed.

If you are the woman, you reach into the corners of the zinc beneath the stove legs as carefully as ever with the broom, and stoop as carefully as ever to pick up the twist of white thread embedded in the raised roses of the hooked rug, but the rug doesn't seem like anything your own hands ever made. You were going to have a change for dinner, but it's too late now; there is a cast of irrevocable lateness about everything. You catch a glimpse of your face in the mirror over the sink, and it seems as if the mirror must be lying, to show it enclosed and with shape. You press the tip of the flatiron into the fancy points of rickrack braid on the apron, but you don't feel the inner smile that was always there at a thing that was extra trouble to be made pretty.

The kitchen and the fields go dead, with a kind of singing remoteness. And when the hum of the anger has died completely away, there is nothing left—nothing but that curious drawing between you, as if you were tied together with an invisible cord on which all the minutes were strung to intolerable heaviness, but never to actual breaking.

I didn't know that all this was happening between mother and father that Saturday morning, of course, because I was only ten. But I knew the day was spoiled. And the next day. I knew what Sunday would be like.

It wouldn't be the perfect August Sunday, the first Sunday after the hay was cut, with the nice hiatus about it as if even the fields knew it was a day of rest, and the tail ends of all the jobs that weren't quite finished lacking the insistence they seemed to have on a weekday. My father would not drowse on the kitchen lounge in the long restoring forenoon, while mother wandered with that special Sunday leisure through her flower garden, pulling a weed here and there, stooping to hold a bright poppy in her hand like a jewel, bringing a dipper of water from the well and holding apart the spicy leaves of the geranium so the roots got all of it, and tiptoeing in past him with a bouquet of the splashy nasturtiums for each of the lamp rests on the organ.

And after dinner, father would not change into the striped drill pants with the size tag still on the waistband and his fine shirt and his fine shoes. Mother would not go upstairs and come down adjusting the wonderfully intricate coral brooch at the neck of her dress. And I wouldn't wait with the thrill of a minor conspiracy, though it were a simple thing, to walk together with them to the garden.

The hay was cut, but we wouldn't walk to the garden with that funny feel of freedom, because, though we could still see the darker-green line of the crooked path we had used through the stringy grass, now our feet could go anywhere they liked. Nor through the garden, where it lay exposed at last to the full kiss of the sun; looking for any cast of ripening in the tomatoes, parting the secrecy of the cucumber vines to see if any fruit lay on the ground beneath, gauging the number of days before the corn would be really yellow, or calling a greeting, smiling though our faces couldn't be clearly seen that far, to a neighbor strolling through his garden the same way.

Father would not change his clothes at all tomorrow. As soon as he had milked and fed the pigs, he would fill his tobacco pouch and get a handful of matches from the canister behind the pantry door and go outside, without asking mother what time she planned to have dinner. She might be doing the chamber work or putting clean newspapers under the rows of preserves down cellar, but she seemed to feel the instant he left the house and I would see her come to the dining room window and watch, in that curious secret way, to see whether he went to the wood lot or the back meadows.

The whole kitchen would seem to catch its breath when his step sounded on the porch again, exactly at noon. As we ate silently, mother would seem to know, without watching, the minute he was ready for his tea; but she'd set it down where he could reach it, she wouldn't pass it to him. And if they both put a hand out for the sugar bowl at the same time, something so tight and awful would strain across the table that I'd feel like screeching.

Right after dinner, father would leave again. Mother would dress up a *little*—I don't think, if she were dying, she could have sat through Sunday afternoon in a housedress—but she wouldn't go outside. She'd be quiet with the catalogue for a bit, but just when I'd think her mind was taken up, she'd drop the catalogue and begin that awful wandering from room to room. As if each familiar thing promised her absorption and then failed her.

When I'd hear her swivelling up the organ stool, her intake of breath, caught before it became a real sigh, and then the first pitifully inaccurate chords of "Abide With Me," I'd rush outside, myself.

And no matter how late I played, or with whom, or at what fascinating game, or no matter how angry I got with myself that I couldn't be insensitive to my parents' quarrels as other kids were, I'd get that awful feeling in the pit of my stomach when I came near the house again that evening. Then we would sit silently, but each moving when another moved, with the Sunday hiatus stifling as a thunder pocket now.

I'd go to bed early, to escape it. But it was no use. I'd listen for the movement of mother taking the clock from the mantelpiece, and start when I heard it. I could see father then, sitting there in the loud-silent kitchen with even the tick of the clock gone, staring at the floor a minute after he had taken off his boots, before he followed her. I would hear the softer than usual pad of his woollen socks on the stairs and then there would be nothing. The very boards of the old house would seem to sing with that listening stillness.

è▲

That's exactly how it turned out to be. I have no trouble to *remember* the particular torture of that day.

You see, that was the August Sunday which was to have been twice as wonderful as ever before because it had in it the looking ahead to a tomorrow more wonderful than any day I had ever known. Monday was the day that we, and we alone from all the village, were going to the Exhibition in Annapolis.

I had never been to the Exhibition before. There was to be a travelling show. (I had studied the poster so long I knew the face of Madame Zelda as well as my own, she who would tell my fortune though she didn't even know I existed.) There was to be a merry-go-round. ("Mother, do they really go as fast as an automobile?") There was to be the excitement of so many strange faces. There was to be ice cream. And those were the days when ice cream was something that made a high priest of the man who scooped it with such incredible nonchalance out of the deep freezer, and it didn't seem as if the ten cents you laid on the counter could possibly pay for it.

I should have had warning of the quarrel. The moment before it had been so perfect.

We had been wrapping the tablecloth of tiny, tiny, intricately mortised blocks, that mother was to enter in the fancywork class. She kept folding it, this way and that, trying to find a way it would not muss; even father hung about the table, wanting to be in on the thing; and I stood there, tingling with willingness to hold my finger on exactly the right place while mother tied the second knots.

She had made a great show of pretending that she'd never have dreamed of sending it in if the others hadn't kept at her, and we never mentioned the possibility of its winning a prize. But in our hearts, none of us had any doubt whatever that it would be the most beautiful thing there and would get first place.

When I took it out to the mailbox, the laborious lettering on the wrapper completed at last, there was that wonderfully *light* feeling in all of us. The moment was so perfect that even the consciousness of its perfection sprang into my mind.

Always before, when this had happened, I had thought of something sad at once, as a sort of protection. If only, I castigated myself afterward, I had not neglected to do that this time ....

It doesn't matter how this quarrel started. The thing is, their quarrels always ended the same way. Actually, what happened, my father began poking about in the bottom of the dish closet where mother kept the wrapping paper.

"Did you see that sheet of paper with the lumber tally on it?" he said.

"What did it look like?" mother said.

"It was just a sheet of paper with some figures on it," he said.

"Where did you put it?" she said.

"I put it in here," he said. "It ain't here now."

"Let me look," she said. She went through exactly the same papers he had, but she didn't find it.

"It ain't there," father said, with the first hint of annoyance. "I ought to know it when I see it."

Mother looked through all the papers again.

"You didn't burn it with them scraps from the package, did you?" father said.

"No," mother said, "of course not. I never burn anything that's any good." But she went and looked in the stove just the same. There was nothing but ashes there now.

"Well, what did you stick it *in* there for?" she said suddenly.

"I'd like to know where I'd put anything that—" father said. "You're always burnin' somethin'!"

"*Ohhhhhh*—" mother said. She sighed. "I wish I'd never bothered with that tablecloth."

"*Ohhhhhh*—" father said. He started to pace about the kitchen, the way he always did when he was angry. The cat brushed against his legs and he stepped on her tail. Her screech startled him so he gave her a kick with his foot. "*Git* out from under my feet," he said. Mother put the cat outdoors, without saying a word, as if he were a man who was cruel to animals and she couldn't bear to watch it.

"Now I'll have to count that lumber all over again," father said.

"Oh," mother said, "you'd think that was going to kill you—"

I ran out of the house then, because I knew what the rest of it would be like. Now they were both angry beyond embarrassment or caution at their quarreling; whenever they could think of nothing else to say, they'd say something false and cruel. "Oh, no, no one ever gets tired but *you*—" "Well, what do you think it's like for *me*?" "I got feelings, too—"

I ran around in circles outdoors, the whole day burst and tumbling about me. They had broken it, like glass, and no matter how perfectly you fitted the pieces together again, you'd know that the mending was there. I was such a foolish child that when a thing which was to have been perfect was spoiled the least bit, it was spoiled entirely. If I as much as scratched the paint on my new wagon I wanted to take the axe and smash the whole thing to bits.

I hated them both then, equally. I'd never speak to them again as long as I lived—I'd run away to town—I'd die…

❧

We were all up Monday morning before dawn. But it wasn't like other mornings when we'd eaten in the magic minutes of lamplight, preparing to go somewhere special. That awful speechless synchronization of movement between mother and father still went on. She was taking the strainer off the clothesline exactly when he set the milk pails beside the scalded creamer. His blue serge suit was laid out on the bed just before he went up to dress; and just as he was walking back through the hallway to the kitchen again, she was on *her* way, through the dining room, to dress, herself. I hated them separately, then. First one and then the other. When father took every cent of his money from the tureen in the dish closet and then came back and asked me (because mother hadn't offered) to brush off the back of his coat, I hated mother. "Father, why don't you get someone to *help* you mow that old back meadow next week?" I said, loud, so she could hear. When mother came downstairs and took the precious little bottle of perfume from behind the pendulum of the dining room clock, her face with the same tight look on it that his had, I hated father. "Let me take that creamer down cellar," I said. "It's too heavy for you."

There is something about changing one's clothes and the prospect of movement that stales the validity of an old quarrel. I think either of them might have spoken then. But I suppose that whenever father was tempted to speak the watchful drop of acid would touch a spot where his pride was still raw: "The time I set the boiling kettle on the new oil-cloth, I said I was sorry, but she made out I did it on purpose just the same—She says *she* has a hard life." And when mother was tempted to speak, the same whisper would stir up the whole wind of forgotten hurts: "The time I scrubbed till I thought my back would break and then he tracked right through the house with his muddy boots on, just because he couldn't keep Tom *Hannon* waiting a minute for that pair of traces in the attic—He says *he* has a hard life." And when they'd let the minute pass, the silence itself had a kind of unshakable fascination.

ॐ

We had a sixteen-mile drive before us. It was one of those glorious mornings you get sometimes in late August, with a cleanness about it more of spring than of early fall. Little hair nets of dew clung here and there on the glistening grass. The waking call of the birds sounded sharp and new. It would be hot later, very hot, but now it was cool. Dark shadows of the alders fell across the dusty road, cool as shadows inside a well.

We didn't keep saying what a perfect day it was for the Exhibition, though. No one spoke at all. I didn't ask questions about any of the things that had happened in any of the places we passed, waiting with more, rather than less, excitement, because I already knew the answers from so many stories before. It was all right when the horse was jogging. But when he slowed down to a walk, with the spinning of the wheels a sound of scraping only, as if we were bound to the road, the stretches from turn to turn looked endlessly long. The only way I could sit still at all was to pretend that, with hard enough thinking of the town, some elastic tension would draw us suddenly from here to there.

This was the day that was to have been the most wonderful in my whole life …

I suppose the moment when we turned the corner by the old blockhouse and first came in sight of the Exhibition itself was most like the moment when the forces of the ingoing and the outgoing tide balance exactly. I think it was then that the quarrel lost all its *colour*, like the flame of a lamp that has burned on into the daylight. There suddenly was the high board fence that encircled the actual wonder and all the throng. We became different people.

We seemed to shrink a little, somehow. Each of us could see, helplessly, as if noticing it was a kind of betrayal, that our clothes were Sunday clothes that had stiffened in the midst of the townspeople who had no idea that they were dressed up.

I think mother must have longed to straighten father's tie, and I couldn't help wishing he would put his coat on again, to cover up the sweat marks that edged the straps of his braces. I wished that mother would take off the sprig of fern she had pinned on her coat lapel, so wilted now that the safety pin showed through. I wiped the dust off the shiny round toes of my brown shoes and for the first time I wished they weren't so patently new. I took off the red-banded straw hat I had spent so long tilting at the right angle, and thrust it beneath the tasselled sewing-machine throw that mother had brought along to protect our good clothes.

≈

Mother and I waited at the gate while father put out the horse. I forgot almost everything else then but the excitement to come. I watched the throng of people going in and the trickle of people coming out. It seemed incredible that there was no change of any kind in their faces the instant they stepped from the inside to the outside. How *could* they not look back, in soberness, or in satiety, or in longing? How could they *bear* to leave while it was still going on?

When father joined us again, silent still, and with that subtle little flicker of adjustment in mother when she saw his approach, we moved toward the ticket window. Just before we got there, he said to her, "Do you want any money?"

I don't know what there was about that question. It was a curiously hurting thing, to have to ask, and to hear. No matter what had happened, the thought of her maybe having not enough *money*, on a day of pleasure —

"I got money," she said.

At last we were inside. I wish I could say that I stayed close with them all that day. But I deserted them almost at once. They moved through the clotted crowd so slowly. The stream of townspeople kept dividing us and father would step aside to let them pass. I wished he would walk straight ahead and let them move aside for *him*. I was suddenly angry with them because they didn't talk and laugh together as the others did. I left them, though father had given me a bright fifty-cent piece, so much more wonderful than if it had been in small coins, and mother had given me a quarter though I could see there were no bills in her purse at all. I left them because I thought the only way I could savour the wonder utterly was to know it alone.

ॐ

It's an odd truth that when a child who has played too much alone pictures himself in the scene of a carnival occasion, he is invariably at the hub of its spirit; but when the time actually comes, he finds himself at the farthest point of its periphery. It was like that then.

Not that some of it could have been more wonderful. The ice cream. The ecstasy of the merry-go-round, heightened by the very dread of the horses beginning to slow down. The songs of the cowboys. It was not they, it was *I* who was singing. But in between the moments when the movement or the magic swung me irresistibly out of my own body, the sea of strange faces was like a kind of banishment. I stood there among them with such a feeling of nakedness that I wondered why they didn't seem to notice it.

When I came to the howdahlike booth of Madame Zelda, the sense of my fortune being a thing between just the two of us was gone altogether. The others crowded so close and surely everything she said could be heard. I stood there with my quarter tight and ready in my palm, but no matter how often I struck myself cold inside with the certain resolution to speak to her after she was through with that very next person, when my chance came my heart would beat so hotly that I simply couldn't get a word out. An agony of heat and cold alternated inside me until she put her jewelled hands flat on the counter, leaned out, and called, "Have your future propheciiiiiied-a." It seemed she was staring directly into my face. I made a frantic pretence of looking for something I had lost on the ground and moved quickly away.

I joined mother and father again.

We came to the machine that registers your strength by the height a ball shoots upward at the blow of a hammer.

"Try it," I whispered to father. The man before him, a tall man with thin white town arms, had sent it up two thirds of the way. I wanted father to show them he could send it right to the top. Father swung the hammer and the ball shot up almost as far as it had gone before, but not quite, and then fell back. "I guess I need more beans for that," he said, half-addressing the men about us. They glanced at him, without smiling, as if they didn't understand what he meant, or as if his futile little joke was out of place. He stepped back, his own tentative smile twitching and drying up on his face. And it was just after that that a man and a woman went by on mother's side, and we couldn't help hearing the woman whisper to her husband, "Did you get the perfume? I wonder if she took a bath in it. What is it, Cauliflower Blossom?"

&

The day was very hot now, and our legs were tired. We walked on past the lunch counter where scraps of bitten food lay on the ground with the dust adhering to them, and past the booth where the sweating men waited for a dead-eyed attendant to set up the Kewpie dolls.

"Are you goin' to take the tablecloth home with you?" father said. "I might as well," mother said.

Father walked ahead, inside the building, to the central bench where the prize-winning objects were displayed, hut it wasn't there. Our hearts skipped in dismay. Had it arrived too late? Had it been lost in the mail?

The tablecloth was there all right, but not on that bench. It was back in one corner, half-concealed by a hooked rug. It hadn't won any prize at all. And now all of us could see why. It was *not* as beautiful as the other things. We couldn't help seeing now that the pattern we had thought so involved was really plain alongside the peacocks in the prize-winning centrepiece, and that the texture of its material lacked altogether the light spiderweb delicacy of the other's crochet.

I couldn't stand the silence then. I clipped away, hardly able to keep from running before I got outside.

I ran so fast down the steps when I did get outside that I collided head on with a boy from town. We both tumbled. I picked myself up and half smiled at him.

"Do you want to fight?" he said, coming close and puffing out his body.

"N-no," I said.

"Well, then, watch where you're going," he said.

When mother and father came out of the building, mother with the tablecloth wrapped up under her arm, I said, "Let's go home." Mother looked at father. "I'm ready whenever you're ready," she said.

He said, "I'm ready to go whenever you are."

We must have been halfway to the gate before I remembered Madame Zelda. I *couldn't* leave without that. "You go on—" I said.

?♠

I ran back toward Madame Zelda's booth without any explanation. The customers had thinned out now. She was sitting sidewise, with her chin cupped in one hand, talking to the man who ran the merry-go-round. I was so close I could hear what she was saying. She said, "If I have to set here and dish out much more o' this tripe in this bloody heat, I'm gonna murder the next one that comes along." I was so close I could see the green mark that the bright ring she was twirling on one finger had left on her hand beneath.

I turned. I couldn't see father and mother anywhere. And then I started to run again. I think if I hadn't caught up with them before they reached the gate, if they had left me in there alone, I'd have burst out crying.

Now here is where I wish for the subtlety to show you, by the light of some single penetrating phrase, how it was driving home. But I can only hope that you will know how it was, from some experience of your own that was sometime a little like it.

Do you know how my father felt, remembering the woman laughing at the perfume mother had thought such a touch of splendour, and thinking of the time he'd known she wanted to go to the magic lantern show in the schoolhouse because she changed her dress right after supper, in case he should offer to take her, but he'd been angry from chasing cows and said nothing, and she'd taken off her good dress again, saying nothing either, because she knew he was tired? Do you know how he felt, remembering the clothes of the town women that he could never afford to buy her the likes of, and thinking how he'd told her she should have *some* men, they'd show her?

Do you know how my mother felt, remembering his face when the town men had made him appear weak and silly about the strength machine, and thinking of the time she'd gone to the cabbage supper alone, giving him to think he was only pretending to be tired, and coming home to see the single plate and the cup without a saucer where he'd got his own supper on the pantry shelf? Do you know how she felt, remembering him spending all his money on us today as if it were not the price of a bag of flour, and thinking how she'd told him that if he had *some* women they'd put him in his boots?

Do you know how I felt, remembering I had wished father would put his coat on, and thinking of the Christmas when there was hardly money for bread, but when there had been a sled and crayons for me just the same?

Do you?

Perhaps then you will understand why a different kind of silence had mounted all day, sorer still, after the shifting of the tide. Perhaps you will understand what it was like driving along that night, thinking about the tablecloth, but being able to say nothing more to mother than "Let me take that basket over here, out of your way," or "Are you *sure* you got lots of room?"

And perhaps you will see how a point of fusion might be found after all. In the moment after the cat had brushed our legs in an ecstasy of welcome home, and the faithful fields had been found waiting for us, unaltered ... after we had changed our clothes, father flipping the straps of his overalls so easily over each shoulder, mother tying behind her, without looking, the string of the apron that seemed to be the very personification of suppertime; and me feeling the touch of the ground on my feet as immediate as the touch of it on hands, when I took off my stiff shoes and went, in my sneakers, for the kindling. Then it was that mother unwrapped the tablecloth and put it on the dining-room table again.

"It's the prettiest thing I ever seen," father said. "I don't care —"

ॐ

That was the moment of release. Everything of the quarrel vanished then, magically, instantly, like the stiffness of a sponge dipped suddenly in water.

Because he spoke no less truly than with penitence. The tablecloth *was* more beautiful than anything else now — *here*, where it belonged.

I think I saw then how it was with all of us. Not by understanding, of course, but, as a child does sometimes, with the lustrous information of feeling. My father could lift a bale of hay no man at the Exhibition could budge, but there was a knack in a thing like the strength machine he was helpless against. It hadn't been humbleness that made him step aside for the town men to pass, any more than it had been fear that made me retreat from the town boy who wanted to fight. My mother's hat was as lovely as ever, now it was back in the bag in our closet. This sureness when we were home couldn't be transplanted; but that's why, when we had it all about us and in us, like an invisible armour, it was such a crying thing to hurt each *other*.

Bright pictures of the things I had seen that day still echoed like heat lightning in my mind. But they were two-dimensional. Mother coming to the corner of the shop as if she knew just when our feet were beginning to stumble, and telling father to make that the last furrow, she was having dinner a little early — Father edging the borders of the flower garden so perfectly by just his eye, while mother and I stood by with such strange closeness, because this wasn't *his* work at all — Watching the cows race to the tub after a day on the sun-baked marsh, to fill their long throats ecstatically with the cool well water — These things only were real.

I listened to father and mother talking in the kitchen that night, after I had gone to bed. I listened to them coming up the stairs together. I heard father take the change from his pocket and lay it on the bureau. I heard the murmur of their voices, low in the room, like the soft delicious drum of sleep in my ears. I thought of the quarter that had been so miraculously saved from squandering on my fortune — I could buy father a staple puller and mother a mixing spoon with it, for Christmas. I had never been so consciously happy in my whole life.

But I didn't take any chances this time. I repeated the words from my prayer, quickly, intensely, "If I should die before I wake ... If I should die before I wake ..."

ૐ

I awoke and I heard mother and father talking in the kitchen. I thought, the hay is cut, the hay is cut ... and this morning we will all walk together through the garden. I could feel already the exaltation when I chose the largest stalk and, as they watched, pulled the first new potatoes from the sweet crumbling earth.

Goodbye, Prince

The moment Gus Sanford spoke to Father that day a stone dropped into my heart. Everything had been so perfect just then.

It was the week of Christmas. The once-a-year cakes with all the colored peel in them were cooling on the pantry shelf before being wrapped in a cloth and put into the earthenware crock. All sorts of Christmas smells and secrecies seemed to make the house deliciously boundaried, to give it a face, as benign as firelight. In another way, nothing was boundaried at all. Everyone seemed fluid with everyone else. We helped Mother crimp green tissue paper for the flower pots with a table fork, though to have touched this green paper any other time would have been such a sissy thing as to make us wince, and she came outside to watch us rig up a crude press for some Russet cider, which at any other time would have been almost an intrusion. The ground was bare, and frozen hard as bone. But the air felt like snow. Soft, mysterious, Christmas snow. And though the twitch log they were sawing up was only half-finished, Father and my brother Chet had left their saw, abandoned it right in the middle of a cut, and were going with me to get the tree.

Prince was "my" colt. As the brockle-faced steer was "Chet's" steer. It wasn't that they were ours to really own or dispose of. But somehow every animal that was born on the farm got to be known sooner or later as "mine" or "Chet's." Prince wasn't a very glossy black, no matter how much you curried him, and his head was way big for the rest of his body, but I don't know—just to *think* of him sometimes on the way home from school was like secretly touching in my pocket a glistening new-minted coin that I could never bear to spend. "What would ya take for that colt o'yours, Bart?" Gus said.

If we'd got out onto the road five minutes earlier, I thought—if I hadn't urged Father and Chet to wait till I made sure Mother embedded the once-a-year walnut kernels in a perfect pattern on top of the fudge she'd just turned out into the pans, so that they'd come out in the exact centre of each square when it was cut—we wouldn't have run into Gus at all. But it was too late now.

Father looked at Gus and sort of half-grinned. "Oh I dunno," he said. "I don't know as I'd want to part with him right now, Gus."

It was the way Father spoke that gave me the shock. Despite his words, his tone had negotiation in it.

I glanced at his face, hoping it would contradict his tone. I couldn't make out the look on his face at all. He was looking hard at me. With a funny, sort of studying look.

"But you must have *some* kind of a price on him, Bart," Gus said to Father. "He'd just about match that little mare o' mine. They oughta turn into a good team."

"He's twice as big as that old ... rack o' bones ... o' yours!" I cried.

But Gus just smiled. I guess Dick don't like to see anything leave the farm," he said. "I was like that when *I* was a kid."

I hated him for seeing through me, for calling me a "kid."

Father gave me that odd, studying glance again. Then he turned to Gus. "Well, *I* don't know, Gus," he said. "How would fifty dollars strike ya?"

"Hmmmm," Gus said. "Fifty, eh? Tell ya the truth, Bart, that's a little higher than I planned to go. I thought, maybe around forty, forty-five ...?"

My heart took hope.

"Yeh?" Father said. "Well ... I don't know. Maybe we could do business."

"We could go back and have a look at him anyways," Gus said.

"Sure," Father said. "No harm to do that." He turned to Chet and me. "I guess you fuhllas can get the tree all right alone, can't you?"

"Sure," Chet said.

Gus looked so pleased with himself I could have struck him. He winked at Father. "Y'know, Bart," he said, "I see Dick shinin' around my Molly there quite a bit lately. It wouldn't surprise me if them two made a match some day."

Molly Sanford. That ... girl! What good was any girl? You couldn't even net pollywog nests with a girl and have any real fun; she was always thinking about her old dress, afraid she'd get a spot on it or something. But Gus could tease me any way he liked now, I felt too sick to care.

Chet and I turned away. Sure we could get the tree. It didn't matter whether Father was in on it or not. What difference did it make who got the tree now? The day was bleeding to death minute by minute. I knew Father always had to sell something off the farm to get a little extra money for Christmas, but … my breath snagged in my throat. Gathering up a handful of oats automatically when I opened the linter door, and then letting them dribble back through my slack fingers into the barrel when I suddenly remembered …

It took all my concentration not to cry as Chet and I walked across the pasture. I guess Chet sensed why I didn't speak.

"Never mind, Dick," he said. "We had to sell him *some* time. You know he'd never be no good for a saddle horse. And if we didn't sell him soon, no one'd buy him, 'cause he'd be too old to break. It wouldn't pay us to break him—Dad really ain't quick enough now, anyway, and we ain't got work enough for *Queen* hardly."

If Chet had been like he was a year ago I could have let my tears come right out when he said that. Then we could have talked it over and I'd have felt better. But I couldn't talk things over with Chet anymore.

Two things had changed him. He'd earned money of his own, working *outside* the farm, this past year. And he had bought his first pie— Freda Marven's—at a social in the schoolhouse.

I couldn't understand the subtle change that having a girl had made in him. It was as if he'd moved into some different kind of daylight that made the things he and I used to do together go suddenly transparent and boneless. He just sort of smiled this year when I made such a touse about moving the tree stand to the *other* corner of the parlor so we could see the tree all the time we were eating supper Christmas Eve. It was the way, the first time I swam right out over the deep part of the pool, that I looked back at the younger kids making tiny canals between the little puddles on the bank and sailing timothy heads down them so intently. Lord, I hated girls as we walked across the pasture! Freda Marven especially, for what she had done to Chet.

The firs stood singly at the edge of the pasture, then groved, thicker and thicker, until finally they became dense woods. We had scarcely stepped into the first fringe of them when we came upon this tree. Lying on the ground. Last month a Christmas tree company had gone through our woodlet, paying Father so much a bundle for the ones they cut. This must be one they'd missed when they tied up the bundles. Chet spotted it first.

"Say," he said, "there's a humdinger! Already cut! What's wrong with that one, eh, Dick?"

I couldn't tell him what was wrong with it: how awful it would be to get a tree that someone else had picked out. That was lying on the ground. That had been cut a month ago. But I didn't protest. The day had now bled so white that somehow I took a sullen pleasure in *every-thing* about it that fell short of the way I'd pictured it. Chet wouldn't have touched a second-hand tree either, last year. How I hated girls!

Father always went to town the day before Christmas. And I had always gone with him. It was the best day of the year. The bright glittery side of Christmas, with all the rush and the strange faces, was all the more exciting for thought of the Christmas Eve supper waiting for us at home where nothing was strange. And the Christmas Eve supper was all the more deliciously snug for my body being a little luxuriously tired from the buzz of the gaudy stores we had just left. But I didn't go with him that year.

"You ain't comin'?" he said to me after breakfast, when I started to oil my larrigans instead of making any move to get into my good reefer and my Sunday boots and rubbers.

"No," I said.

I thought his face would fall. I thought he'd protest. But he didn't. He looked almost relieved. He didn't coax me at all. I had never felt so baffled and alone. I couldn't have gone with him, even if he had coaxed me. But just the same ...

I couldn't go. Because this was the afternoon Gus was coming to take Prince. I had to have this last morning absolutely alone with Prince, to say goodbye to him. Somehow I couldn't do that, I couldn't even touch him now, if anyone else was around.

The moment Father left I started for the barn. When I got as far as the shop I glanced back at the house to see if Mother was watching. She wasn't.

But I saw someone else. I saw Gus. The road past our house went down one long hill and up another before it reached his place. He was just coming over the crest of the near hill. He had a length of rope coiled over his arm. He was coming for Prince. Now!

I felt myself turn white. My mind went all sort of crazy. I thought of running to the barn ahead of Gus. But there'd be no way of escaping him afterward. I couldn't bear the thought of him being in the barn with Prince and me, maybe teasing me while he fixed the rope ... maybe asking me to go along behind them and keep Prince moving with a switch. I couldn't stand the thought of seeing Prince's hind legs go out over the barn door sill and knowing it would be for the last time.

I dived into the shop and squeezed behind a row of empty apple barrels.

I heard Mother come to the door as Gus passed the porch.

"Bart's gone to town, Gus," she said. "I suppose you're after the colt. But Dick can help you. He was here somewheres a minute ago. I'll call him. Dick!! Dick!"

I didn't answer.

"Oh, I guess I kin manage," I heard Gus say. "I paid Bart, yistiddy, y'know."

"Oh, that's all right," Mother said. "But I'm sure Dick's just around here somewheres."

"Maybe he skinned out when he saw me comin'." I heard Gus chuckle. Lord, how I hated him then.

"Well, now, *maybe*!" Mother exclaimed. "I never thought of that."

They said something then in a lower voice, something I couldn't catch. Then I heard Gus chuckle again.

When I heard him close the barn door I stopped my ears so I wouldn't hear Prince's feet going past the shop. And when I thought Gus must be completely out of sight I went outdoors again. But I hadn't waited quite long enough. I glanced toward Gus's place, try as I would not to. Gus and Prince were just turning in his gate at the crest of the far hill. I shut my eyes and shook my head as if I could loosen the image from my retina. But I couldn't. It was still there when I went to bed that night.

This was Christmas Eve, but I went to bed as soon as it was dark. Mother couldn't believe that I was *that* tired. "Why, we haven't even had supper! She exclaimed. "I suppose we could eat now, but I don't like to eat without your father ... Christmas Eve. He should be here in a little while."

"That's all right," I said. "I'm not hungry." I wasn't, but she fixed me a place at the corner of the kitchen table and made me eat a piece of sparerib from the steaming platter of it in the warming closet, and a couple of doughnuts.

I didn't even glance toward the parlor to see if I could see the tree. I was so terrified that I'd hear Father's bells before I'd finished eating. I didn't want to have to hold the lantern for him while he unloosed the tugs on the horse's harness. Not even to help him carry the exciting last-minute packages of eats to the house. Not even to sample, with a delight so intense it seemed almost to call for a sense of guilt, just one sprig from the magical clusters of once-a-year grapes which he always brought home for Christmas Day. I couldn't go near the barn tonight.

The Christmas order had arrived in the afternoon mail. I walked past the dining-room table where Mother had taken off the big wrapper. For a moment I forgot Prince when I saw the exciting pile of packages. I couldn't help glancing at the little sheaf of "bills" that always came with the order. The one right on top said: "Jackknife … $1.00." In big red letters on the bottom was: SOLD OUT.

Now, in bed, I couldn't help calculating. I knew exactly what the suede windbreaker for Chet (he'd kept looking down at the elbow patch on his homemade one, this last year, every time he got ready to go to a dance or anything) had cost; and the pipe for Father; and the serving tray with the landscape scene under glass that we'd put down for Mother (it would be the handsomest thing in the house). I totaled the three amounts. I knew also what the complete order had come to. Mother always managed to get hold of a twenty-dollar bill somehow throughout the year and saved it for the Christmas order. The postmistress couldn't break it the morning Mother sent the order off, but the next day she sent the change back by me, with a little accounting slip attached showing the amount of the order, the charge for the postal notes, and the balance. I subtracted the first total from the second and the difference was exactly $1.50. That's all there had been then for me. The jackknife. And it was sold out. I didn't complain, even in thought. But I had that little snubbed feeling you still have, though you say: "Why, of *course* not, I didn't expect you to … I never *thought* about it." And again the bitter, self-biting little pleasure.

I heard Father's bells. Then I heard them stop. At Gus's place, I supposed. Gus was always coming out to the gate for a chin with someone passing by. It was quite awhile before the bells started up again. I felt betrayed somehow, thinking of Father taking his time chatting and laughing with Gus. He must have had some idea how I'd miss Prince.

I heard Father stop at the door and *Chet* take the lantern out to him. "Where's Dick?" I heard Father say. I didn't hear what Chet answered.

Then, later, I heard the clink of their dishes at the supper table. I felt, for a moment, so unbearably exiled from something wonderful that was wasting away even as I thought of it that I almost got up and went downstairs. But I didn't.

After supper, I heard Chet go out. I knew where he was going. Over to Marven's. Likely he had a present for that foolish Freda! How could he do it—tonight? I could keep by myself upstairs. But I couldn't bear to spend this evening anywhere outside the *house*. Then I heard Father go out. To take the grain box from Queen's manger, I supposed. It was so quiet then that I fell asleep.

It seemed hours later that I awoke. I heard all three of their voices again now. Conspiratorial Christmas Eve voices. But this time I wasn't even tempted to go down. *Let* them have a good time without me, I thought. Once more I felt the sullen little pleasure: that I wasn't down there with them; that even if I had come upstairs of my own accord they hadn't awakened me and *made* me come down.

I went downstairs the next morning still sluggish and sullen. When they heard my first step on the upstairs hall I heard all theirs head toward the parlor — not hurrying, so as to appear casual, but as if after an exchange of signals. I took my time.

"Merry Christmas!" they said. Casually, too, but they couldn't keep their eyes from flicking toward the tree.

"Merry ..." — and then I saw it standing there. Something my wildest yearnings had never considered in the realm of the possible.

A bicycle! A *bicycle*! That's why...

I can't describe what it was like — in those times, and in our circumstances — to know that it was mine. I had studied the pictures of bicycles on the colored pages in the catalogue minutes on end, but it was like a sightseer staring at some precious object under glass. The price was so beyond our means that even longing had shrunk back. I got one of those queer sensations you have when you touch something out of its element, like holding a live wild bird in your hand. Or like having a famous man single *you* out of a welcoming crowd for a nod and a smile. I don't know which of my feelings was strongest. This glory of possession. Or the hurting shame of having taken for unconcern what had really been a plot to surprise me with something splendid. Or the sudden sense of betrayal toward Prince — as if I myself had exchanged him for this. I was so mixed up I couldn't move or speak.

And then I looked at the others. They were standing around watching my face. It would be too awful to think that they should be made to feel there was any reserve in my jubilance.

"Well, gosh all hemlock!" I cried. "Ain't ... that ... a ... beaut!"

It was. When I first mounted it, it felt heavy, stubbornly awkward. It seemed full of jerky miscoordination, put together wrong, with no *knowledge* of movement built into it at all. And then, later, once in awhile there would be a sudden beautiful smoothness in its motion, as if it had awakened for a second or so to a fleeting memory of speed. By the third day there'd be those long delicious swoops of movement when it seemed as if suddenly the bicycle and I had lost all weight and grooved into the very track of speed itself.

Yet it was right then, sometimes, in the very same trajectory, that the thought of Prince would also swoop down on me—like some great black bird planing down, to land.

                                    ❧

That third afternoon I saw Gus and his wife drive out his gate and up the road. Molly was in the wagon with them. She turned and waved at me, but I bent over and tinkered with the pedal chain as if I hadn't noticed her. And when I glanced up again and across at Gus's barn, there were Prince and Gus's filly standing in the cattle yard, where he had turned them out for a little exercise.

Here was my chance, I thought. I could go say goodbye to Prince now. I could see him alone—one final but somehow healing goodbye— and get shed of this terrible feeling all in one lump.

Mother had been carding wool into rolls. She called now and asked me if I wanted to help her spin the rolls, more as offering a treat than dictating a job. It had always fascinated me to watch the long gossamer rolls turn into yarn, without ever being able to catch just how it happened. I fed them to the spindle while Mother turned the big wheel, for perhaps half an hour. But I wasn't restless. I'd seen the bag of hay in the back of Gus's wagon, so I knew he was going to town. That he'd be away all afternoon.

I was thankful for the bike. Somehow I would have felt unbearably foolish to have my family—nodding and smiling— see me walk up the road, knowing I was sneaking off to see Prince. This way, I could let on I was just trying out the bike. Then I could slip into Gus's yard when I got over the crest of the far hill.

The moment I got in by Gus's house I yelled, "Hi, Prince!" He whinnied and ran over to the bars. The sadness that had been distributed all through me since the first day we'd met Gus in the road seemed to come to a head all at once, right in my throat. The tears started to sting behind my eyes.

But just as I took the first step toward the enclosure, I heard the kitchen door, and Molly stepped out into the yard. I could almost have struck her.

"I thought I saw you goin' to town," I said.

"Oh, no," she said. "I only went up as far as Freda's, to see her tree. I come right back across the field. I have to keep the fires while Dad and Mother are away."

The snow still hadn't come; the air was still hard and cold. But she was standing there with no coat on. I knew why. She had on a brand new dress. She must have got it for Christmas. It was kind of a sky-blue flouncy thing, with little bows of black velvet tacked all over the shirring at the waist. She wanted me to say something about how pretty it was. I didn't even let on I saw it.

She aligned the bows at her waist very pointedly. I turned my bike toward home.

"That's some bike!" she said. She giggled. "But I saw it before you did. Your father left it here Christmas Eve till he made sure you were in bed. Ain't it a dandy?"

So that's why Father..."It's all right," I said.

"Did you come over to see Prince?" she said.

"No," I said almost savagely. "I was just tryin' out my bike."

I turned toward the gate. I glanced over my shoulder toward the barnyard. Prince wasn't looking my way at all. He was over by the filly, muzzling her mane. They looked as if they were carrying on some sort of whispered conversation.

"You ain't goin' to ride *down* the hill, are you?" Molly said.

"Sure," I said. I'd no idea of riding down the hill—Lord, I wasn't expert enough for stunts like that! But what else could I say?

"You better not," she said. "*Please* don't." She came right close to the bike. She was shivering a little with the cold. She gave me a look I'd never had a girl give me before. Half-pleading. Concerned for me.

"Look out," I said. "There's dirt on that wheel. You'll get it on your new dress." I tried to speak grumpily, but I couldn't help thinking, a girl *is* kind of a pretty thing, with a clean new dress on.

She seemed to make no account of her dress anymore. "You better not ride down the hill, Dick," she said again, her tone pleading openly now. "It's dangerous."

"Aw," I said, "there's nothin' to do."

She walked with me to the gate, to watch. As if she dreaded to, but couldn't help it.

I didn't say a word when I got on the bike, to start down the hill. I couldn't. I was too scared. I had never felt so small and childish in my life. The bike seemed like an alien, threatening thing. This old hill, which I'd never given a thought to one way or the other, seemed suddenly to break out with a menacing inexorable face. From top to bottom. It was like a nightmare when the present minute is suddenly split by a terrifying impassable chasm from the safe one next. But I couldn't appear to hesitate.

And then I was starting down the hill.

And then I was moving fast.

And then I was moving faster still, and the bike and I and movement became a single unit again.

And then I had no fear. My movement was as sure as flight. My pants legs were flapping a frantic tattoo against the spokes as I'd seen the older boys' do sometimes on Mike Parry's bike —the only other one in the place. I seemed to have stirred up a glorious wild freedom in the air that sang past my ears.

And then I thought of Molly watching me. Standing there in the pretty soft girl's dress and watching me do this wild hard male-thing. It was as if I were rushing into a brighter and brighter daylight that made the old things suddenly transparent and boneless. I didn't think about any of them then. But if I had thought of things like checking the way Mother put the walnuts into the fudge or watching the rolls somehow transfigured into yarn —these snug, cloistered pleasures— I'd have thought of them with the same kind of tolerant embarrassment Chet had for them now. The intoxicating wind my speed set up seemed to be sieving right through me and blowing all those things behind and away.

When my speed leveled off at the foot of the hill, like one long delicious exhalation, I turned and waved to Molly. She waved back. It seemed now as if, if any time after this I looked up that long steep hill and she was not standing there, the hill would not look alive. It would look like a face without one of its features.

And then I noticed that the snow had begun to fall. The soft, dreamy, Christmas snow. It would come down and fill up all the ruts, and cover all the bare brown places in the fields, and tomorrow this would be like a different world. A shining immaculate one. The snow would change it as if by a long passage of time.

When Molly had gone back into the house, I looked again toward the barn. Prince was still in sight. I silently coaxed him to look at me, but he didn't. He was still nuzzling the filly.

I said, "Goodbye, Prince," to myself. I *willed* myself to cry. But in the same instant I caught myself thinking, "I hope Molly didn't get any dirt on her new dress off the bike." And then I realized that the tears were never going to come.

It Was Always Like That

It was no use, I couldn't work at all that afternoon, I had the feeling every writer has constantly, that his last story was the end. There were no ideas. Then there were too many ideas. It was all there, if I could get at it, how it is with everybody and everything, but the sentences for it were broken up, and stuck inside my head, and when I read over the words that did come, that was not it, or any part of it, at all.

Time itself tantalized me, distracting me with its new sensations before I could get the old ones down, and mocking my helplessness to strike a chord inside me so it would be easy then. I felt nothing but the panic of too much awareness, like the empty beat of a heart shrunken and bled white with defeat.

But the need to get it all down, somehow, was there just the same ... and I would keep putting the blank paper away and then taking it out again. God only knows how relieved I was when my brother came in and I saw that he was dressed for hunting and had brought both guns.

When I saw Peter's lively, quick-smiling face, the band between the inside and outside seemed to thin away.

ﾞﾞ

.... But there were plenty of things to write. There are always plenty of things to write. I *need* not have gone hunting that day. It need not have happened at all.

There was the night I first hated Peter, I could have written that. A cold winter dusk was thickening and mother kept walking to the frosted-over window pane oftener and oftener now, straining her eyes towards the fast-fusing woods. She made a little grimace of relief and annoyance when the tiny blur of movement showed at last against the snow.

Then when father crept up the cellar-way, and winked at the blood-stains on his mittens, we knew he had killed a moose in closed season.

That night was the most wonderful night of my whole life.

The neighbours dad told thought I was too small to help carry out the meat, but at last Peter said, "Oh, hell, dad, let him go, if he wants to ... " And I could have cried, Peter seemed all of a sudden so wonderful.

Then the exciting stealth, carrying the lanterns beneath our coats until we reached the edge of the woods, the friendly-warm conspiracy with older men, wonderful now too, no sound but the steady frost-squeak of our larrigans as we crept along in the cosy, safe, woods-dark ... and at last father's whisper, "Well, boys, here she is."

I remember how strange the faces of the men looked sometimes, half in and half out of the little yellow hole of light in the dark, and the coarse jokes they made when they skinned about her hind legs, and how proud I was when it was all over, to stand up and piss with them, holding my hand flat-open, like a shield, as they did.

I remember, too, how absurdly light my load seemed when I first started home, and then, later, how the muscles began to come alive in my back, and ache ... and sometimes there would be a sudden little sky of stars before my eyes. The men's voices sounded heavy now, and the sore places in my back would come so much sooner, each time we started on again from resting our backs against a tree.

Peter was not tired at all. I staggered once, and he whispered, "Let me take your load too, Al ..."

God, how I hated him then ....

ॐ

Peter walked ahead, today. The breath of the ground was cool, places where the trees overhung; and as soon as he caught the spicy smell of the sweet fern and the faint urine-odor of the leaves that rotted in the still puddles of late October sunlight, I knew my company was half-forgotten. I knew he was thinking how the first partridge twitters, before her heavy headlong flight ... or the perfect target a rabbit makes, sitting there back-to, like one of those rabbits children draw ... or the deer that has seen you first, every line of it taut with watching, waiting one second, motionless as stone, for you to pick out its heart or its brain along the lovely steel-cold gun-barrel. Those are the best excitements there are, if you were ever a child in the country. Maybe if the deer goes off in long smooth loops of running the minute you pull, you stand there and swear and give up hunting for good. But you forget that disappointment before next time.

Peter could aim and shoot in one hard-calm second. Somehow I always waited too long, for a better shot, and then the deer would bolt, and I'd curse myself afterwards for the things I hadn't done.

Once in a while I would think about the pain the deer must feel... although that part of it didn't really affect me. It didn't spoil my hunting any. If Peter had thought of it as I did, I don't believe he could have hunted at all.

We stopped at the edge of the burntland, to smoke. Peter held the match for my cigarette.

"I didn't see Anna this afternoon," he said, "where was she?"

For God's sake, Peter, why must you mention Anna's name today? The afternoon was spoilt now.

"I don't know," I said, "I'm afraid I don't watch her movements as closely as you do."

"Oh don't be a damn fool, Al..." Peter laughed.

He looked at me suddenly, as if he might be seeing for the first time something that made clear so many things he had puzzled about. Peter used to whisper with me, nights in bed, about how it was to grow up. He could hardly wait to try it... but it didn't keep him awake. I would wish I was like him as I lay awake myself. He looked so safe and sure, even then, one arm always thrown carelessly outside the quilt, and his heavy hair moist on his sleep-pale face.

But it was not that Peter I heard talking now. It was the stranger whose step made my wife start, although she had been listening for it all the time, even when her thoughts were somewhere else. It would make her start as if she had been caught at something she should be ashamed of. But Anna was not ashamed. I knew she had never let herself be that. And if she was kinder to me then, it was not to deceive, but because, I suppose, it is so easy to be kind when there's one shape of flesh whose mere nearness makes your heart sing, what if it is desperately. How kind I could have been to Anna, too... if hers had been another woman's face, and another woman's face had been hers.

I knew Anna was in love with Peter because I spied on her eyes. They would give her away because that thing she tried so desperately to put in them now when she looked at me, was only a shadow of the same thing she could not hide in them, except with the lids, when he would first come into the room. And I knew that. It had been my business as a writer, to watch for those things... and it was my curse to see them now as often almost as I cared to look.

But it did not help any, to understand it. And when I would hold Anna in my arms and sense her wanting desperately to warm my body with something, pray as she would, she could not make herself feel, there would be a taste in my heart, sicker than the taste of death.

I was never quite sure if Peter knew about Anna or not. And I don't think I ever blamed either of them, or hated them. It was the circumstance itself I hated, that it had to happen at all ... and I could not stop a sick loathing that would swell up in me for everything that touched it.

I felt it rising then, when Peter mentioned Anna's name ... and there was only the driving wish to hurt myself and to hurt them and make the whole thing as desperate and irrevocable and without remedy as possible. I wanted no quarter whatever from this hateful thing none of us could help.

ঌ

........Or that other night, that cold March night there had been something between father and mother, why didn't I stay at home and write that. I had come home from coasting alone, into the dusk-shadowed kitchen. I heard loud voices before I went through the door, and I thought someone must be sick or hurt. But only father and mother were there.

They seemed like strangers. I had never seen father's face broken up and beaten like that, and mother's face looked as if it had been lashed. I heard mother say, "Ada ... and after all the years I've ..." and I heard father say, "a damn lie ... if you had lots of men, Martha." It was never quite the same in our kitchen again.

They stopped talking when they saw me, and mother told me to go out and play. I took my sled out again on the ice in the flooded field. And I remember how blue and cold the ice looked when I had my face near it, belly-down on the sled ... and how sad the bare trees seemed against the pink-cold spring sky, like people who couldn't ever get close and warm to each other again ... and the feelinglessness of the frozen, hubble-rutted road. It was the first time the bleak wind of loneliness penetrated inside me.

When I went in again, the lamp was lit, and mother was bringing in the basketful of frozen clothes from the line. Her hands were blue, and there was a cold look about her lips that the fire did not take away. She did not speak to father all evening as she ironed the sweet-smelling clothes and hung them bright-smooth on the bars, and when she spoke to one of us or answered us, her voice seemed to come from far-off where we could not reach her. Father sat there reading ... but he just seemed to be staring at the same line over and over because he hardly ever turned a page. All the little sounds like the wood dying in the stove or the steady rattle of the flat-iron handle seemed as loud as a scream.

I felt it only as a sort of fear, like a child feels when he is lost. But I have come to understand these silences well enough now, since Anna has known Peter ... the knot-tight, soundless cry of them ... the dull-burning quiet of the other drawing against your own quiet ... the silence-heavy load of the minutes inside you. I know now just how sick a thing it really is when two people fight to suck up all the sound in a room and hold it tight inside them.

When it came time for bed, mother lit the lamp and went upstairs. She didn't ask father if he was ready to go. Father did not take the paper from his face, but I had the feeling they were both watching each other with every part of their bodies. After they were both in bed, I waited to hear mother cry, it would have made me feel better somehow ... but there was no sound at all but the creaking of the walls, as if everything in the whole house was full of that horrible listening.

I whispered to Peter, "What's wrong with mother and dad?"

He said, "Oh, it's mother's fault ... she's so damn jealous." Peter always stuck up for dad.

But it was thinking of mother's face that kept me awake. Dad looked as if he might get better, if mother would only smile ... but mother looked as if she would never be happy again, even when she was busy.

๖

Peter was not angry yet. And he was smiling at my anger, which did not warm it away but made it more sullen. It was always like that ...

He was half-serious but still good-natured, when he spoke.

"Want to know what I think, Al?" he said. "I think Anna puts up with a darn sight more from you than any other woman as fine as she is would. You're the kind of guy that doesn't give his wife a *chance* to use him decent ... you're such a damn *jealous* fool."

(That's true, Peter, but God knows it's not as simple as that ...)

"Thanks very much," I said, "but if you don't mind, I'll ask for an opinion on my wife and myself when I want it ... and I'll ask someone disinterested."

The gibe went home. I saw a flash of the quick rage Peter always had for deliberate unreason. Then suddenly he was baffled, trying his best to be persuasive, to make me see. He could never seem to learn that that was hopeless.

"For crissake, Alan," he said, "don't be so childish."

"*Is* it so childish?" I said. "Maybe *I'm* childish, but I'm sure you and Anna are adult about it all. Adulterous even."

"Well, whose fault is it but your own?" Peter said. "You know damn well you've no one else to blame but yourself ... you *drove* Anna to it."

There. The hated truth was out in the open at last. Peter looked as if he had been surprised into saying something he wanted to recall the minute he heard it uttered. Maybe he was just mad and saying anything that came into his head, like he used to do as a child. But I didn't want to believe that.

"Just how?" I said.

"You know how."

"Still," I said, "you didn't decline *your* part, with any particular emphasis, I must say."

"I had nothing to do with it."

"Isn't that nice?" I said. "Nor Anna either, I suppose ... it was so beautifully spontaneous. Anna had *no* will of her own, *no* pride, not the *slightest* power of choice left her at all ... Oh no."

"Maybe Anna couldn't help it," Peter said. "For God's sake, Al, what if she couldn't help it ... there are lots of things that people can't help, if it kills them."

I know she can't help it. Why can't you see that's it, Peter? If Anna could help this thing, it would be just for me to hate her then ... if she had my own cursed clarity, I could blame her for what she does. But I *know* she can't help it. That's what makes me so sick. I envy too much to forgive it that confusion and helplessness I have hungered for but never known, not even in my anger. I can't even surrender to the blind heat of my anger now, things are forever so cruelly clear and plain.

"Well," I said, "can you think of any way to settle it, once and for all, without shattering any of the moonbeams?"

Peter's face had a hot look, but he was still steady and persuasive. He would never understand how I could want so desperately to discredit my own hope.

He made a comic grimace of exasperation with his hands.

"But, Alan, you damn fool," he said, "I tell you there's *nothing* between Anna and me. Maybe I did let you think so but ... hell, you asked for it. The whole damn thing's your bloody imagination, and you know it. Do you think Anna and I could be *that* rotten to you?"

"Thanks again," I said ... I twisted his meaning around in a nasty way I hated even as I did it ... "but if that's what's holding you back, you can keep your bloody kindness, the pair of you."

Peter threw down his gun. "Goddam you ... you can't bait *me* ..." he shouted. The sudden anger in his eyes was so strong it seemed to choke out the vision in them altogether. "You goddam ... I'll knock you sense-less."

"Come ... right ... ahead," I said. I made each word cold and sepa-rate, as if I despised him, as if he was a stranger.

My own anger was like the beautiful, learned anger of an actor, now. Now I was on safe ground, fighting where I knew I would lose, no pity for me to spoil the sureness of it. The shame of striking my own brother was sweet.

ह

... Like another time when we were children, I could have written that. It was that hot-still afternoon at the baptizing pool ... one of those sum-mer child-days when time seemed so long to have fun in. I lay on the bank, with my eyes closed, listening to the dream-sound of the laugh-ing that seemed so much further off when you couldn't see the faces that went with it, and planning man-feats that would be so easy, so very easy, when the time came. There was a drowsy, melting feeling in my whole free body as I lay there.

It must have been much better even than I can remember it, now.

The town-boy kept asking me did I want to fight, but I didn't bother with him. I wasn't scared ... but it was no fun fighting with someone you didn't like.

Then Peter said. "Go on, go on, Al ... don't be such a calf."

I never hated Peter like I did then. I knew he didn't mean it, I know your brother *had* to say things like that, but I hated him just the same. I hated them all ... they could all go to hell, every damned one of them. I didn't want *anybody* on my side. I leapt into Peter with my fists.

Peter could always beat me, but I didn't care. I didn't want to be the one to win, anyway, because then I'd hate the other boys for seeing me beat him, and that night after he was asleep I'd cry because I couldn't tell him I was sorry. But when Peter beat *me*, he could win, but the sweet part of it was he couldn't make me forgive him. And, later, if he asked me what was wrong, I could laugh and act surprised, and he'd think I wasn't sulking, that unconcerned was just the way I felt about him any-way ... Maybe when he'd try to do things for me after that, and then watch me, hoping I'd laugh like old times, I'd feel like crying then too ... but it would be sweet, just the same.

He struck me another hard blow on the mouth. I fell. "Attaboy, Peter ... paste him ... give it to him ... give it to him ..." the town-boy yelled. The fight went out of Peter all at once. He turned to me, shame all over his face.

"Come on, Al," he said, "let's go home."

"What for?" was all I said.

So he put on his clothes and walked up the long dusty hill alone.

He would look back, making out he stopped to tie up his sneaker laces, but I tried never to let him see me glancing his way, and to make my laughing loud enough to reach him.

That night at the supper table, he said to dad, "Al's getting to be *some* swimmer. He can swim farther than *I* can now, dad."

Dad said, "Is that so, Alan?"

"I don't know," I said, "I've never noticed."

After we went to bed, Peter whispered, "Let's sneak the axe tomorrow, Al, and build a camp. We won't tell anybody…not a damn soul…just the two of us, what?"

And I lied, "I guess I got to go fishing with Herb, tomorrow, Pete."

"Oh," he said, "alright. But we will sometime, won't we?"

"Yeh, maybe I can, "I said, "sometime."

It wasn't until the next afternoon when he lost his knife that I started to ask him questions and it was the same again.

Well, we had come a long way since then, and learned a good many words, but we hadn't really changed any…

The hard-breathing second we stood there seemed very long. I think I was steady but Peter's whole face was working with anger. His eyes had a heavy look, as if he had been running, and I knew what a swirl of broken thoughts his mind was.

I only wish he had struck the first sharp knuckle-blow then, without waiting. Then with the cases of our anger burst, and at last the beautiful, free, pulse of muscle choking muscle, the other thing might have drained away. I might have beaten him that time … and, later, we could have laughed as we picked up our cups and wiped the blood from each other's face, and it would have been settled between us forever. I could have forgiven him, then. Perhaps I could have forgiven Anna too … or listened to her, no need for hate or pride between us, giving pity and taking it, and she and I could have come closer with the new understanding, warmer after hate, than she and Peter ever could with only love. Or if I had lost, that too would have been as sweet as it was to lose when we were children. Much sweeter than what happened.

But the deer had to come out, that very minute, on the far side of the clearing ... everything was against us that day.

When Peter's eye caught the deer, his fists fell, and every spark of fury went out of his face, so all at once it was almost comical. "Holy old asshole, Al!" he whispered.

He nodded and winked at me, in his excitement, and pointed, like a quick-forgiving child. "It's a buck, too ... We'll creep around the edge of the clearing ... and go easy, for *God's* sake."

It would have been incredible to Peter that I could feel the same, and the deer there ... that I hated him then, worse, than if he had struck me.

He crept along on tiptoe, testing each twig we stepped on, for sound. If one did snap, Peter would turn his head and frown at me. I don't suppose he looked at my face, to see if it had changed.

Once when the deer threw its head up, he halted suddenly, and put one hand back on my shoulder, to stop me too. He seemed to forget its pressure there altogether, as we waited for the deer to start feeding again ... but I wanted desperately to shake it off, to draw away from it. The deer put its head down again, and we went on.

We must be getting near now.

... For God's sake, Peter, bend an inch, just one more inch more for that branch ... we still have a chance ...

The deer spots us and runs a little. Peter doesn't see it. I do, and I open fire, suddenly. This one day, I don't wait.

...but there is still a chance, Peter .... trip and fall ... anything ...

The deer springs, and stops dead-still, watching.

Still Peter doesn't see it. And I don't tell him where to look. He springs up on a knoll, in front of my gun, just so I know what I'm doing, but can't save it. My hard-nosed bullet finds his soft flesh, sure as a die ... O God, Peter ... the afternoon has stopped. But you're only stunned, Peter, that's all ... it *can't* be a *bad* wound ... the blood will stop ... see, it's stopping ... a little ... isn't it ... isn't it, Peter ... you're alright. I'll feel it there ... there ... a little lower ... there ... I'm clumsy, that's all ... there ... higher ... there ... there ... Peter ... Peter ... PETER ... O Jesus, Peter ....

I carried him home, a loose, easy load on my shoulder, but the warmth of his body did not keep me from shivering ... It was Peter made excuses to go with me the first time I had to water the new horse, because he knew I was crying-scared, but he never let on ... he came along that night it was getting dark and I had to go in soon and tell them I'd broken the new axe handle. He said he'd cracked it the day before, but he was lying … I tried to keep my glance away from that sprawling, lightless look in his eyes.

I forgot even to watch for the same look in Anna's eyes, when she saw what I was bringing her … that wasn't important at all, now.

The First Born Son

The pale cast of fatigue smudged Martin's skin and little grooves of it emptied into the corners of his mouth. But this land was his own, and a son of his own flesh was holding the plough that broke it. His thoughts were tired half-thoughts but they did not ache.

He felt the wine of the fall day and for a minute his feet wandered, inattentive, from the furrow. The dogged, slow-eyed oxen followed him, straining nose-down at his heels. The plough ran out wide in the sod. David tried to flip over the furrow with a sudden wrench of the handles, but the chocolate-curling lip of earth broke and the share came clear.

"Whoa!" David yelled.

"Whoa!" Martin roared at the oxen.

"For God's sake, Dad, can't you watch where you're going? It's hard enough to hold this damn thing when you keep 'em straight."

"Now don't get high," Martin said. But there was no echo of David's temper in his voice. He knew David was tired. And David could not learn to handle his weariness. He fought it. It was no use to do that. If you let it come and go, quietly, after supper it made a lazy song in your muscles and was good to think about. Martin remembered the night David was born. They had thought Ellen would die. It was Christmas Eve. There was not a breath of wind in the moonlit, Christmas-kindled air. Snow lay in kind folds on the ground, shadowed in the dead-still moonlight like the wrinkles of a white cloak. On the brook Martin could watch the gay, meaningless movements of the children skating. And sometimes a fragment of their heartless laughter would break away and fall inside the room. Ellen's pain-tight face stared at her pale hands outside the quilt. The kind-smelling Christmas tree was a cruel mockery. Now and then Martin would go outside and listen, bareheaded, for the doctor's sleighbells, trying to separate their faint, far-off tinkle from the frost-crackle of the spruces. He would think he heard them. Then there would be nothing. Runner tracks shone like isinglass in the moonlight. He heard nothing but the heartless laughter of the children.

It seemed hours later, when he was not listening at all, that he looked out and all at once the dark body of the horse turned in the gate, by the corner of the house. His heart gave a great leap. The helplessness left him. This man could hold Ellen back from death. The moonlight seemed to turn warm. After the doctor went in with Ellen the laughing of the children did not seem so far-off and strange.

The quick white grip of fear came again when he heard the doctor's hand on the door again ... but Martin looked up and the doctor was *smiling*. Suddenly the whole night was a great, neighbourly, tear-starting friend. He had a son now. He knew it would be a son.

Martin felt shy to kiss Ellen in front of the doctor, but there was a new peace and a strange swagger in his soul. When he got the doctor's horse for him, it seemed like the best horse in all the world; and half-ashamed and half-afraid not to, but somehow wanting desperately to thank *someone*, he knelt down for a minute on the hay and prayed. Outside the barn, the voices of the children laughing were a glad song in his ears, now. In the bedroom, Ellen murmured "My own little Jesus" ... and the thick spruce-cosy smell of the Christmas tree and the shining moonlight outside and the soft peace after danger past clothed the minutes in a sweet armour.... A son.... A son.... And Ellen well.... Martin couldn't believe how good it was. He would never die now. He had a son, now...when he was too old to break up the land he loved, any more, this son would come in at night and they would plan together, just the same. This son's sons...

"Well, maybe you think it's *easy* to hold this damn thing," David said. It *must* be that he's tired, Martin thought. He can't mean that...this same David...my own son cannot find it hard to plough this land of our own. I never found it so, when I was young. Ploughed land was always the prettiest sight in the world to me. It was always good at the end of the day, to stand and look over the brown waves of earth and know that I had opened my land to the sun and the air and the rain. I don't like to hear this son of mine talk that way. He says too many things like that. I don't like to hear my son talk that way. The ploughed land was here before us and it will last after us and our hands should be proud to work in it.

"Haw," Martin called, and the lip of the earth curled back and buried the grass again.

In the city, David thought, their bodies are not dead-tired now. They have not walked all day in their own tracks ... back and forth, back and forth, in their own damn tracks. There is movement and lights and

laughing. Every day there is something *new* … something to keep alive
for. The same people here … the same talk … the same eternal drudg-
ery … your nose in the ground all day long, from morning till night,
like a damned ox … cooped up in that damned circle of trees.

The last brown beech leaves on the hardwood hill drifted down to
the ground, dreamily, a little sad to die. A flock of partridges made their
heavy headlong flight into an apple tree and began to bud. In the fields,
the potato stalks lay in blackened heaps. The earth was grey and brown.
All the colour was in the sky or hung in the thin air. Only the stray
pumpkins, left to ripen on the withered vines, gave back any of it. They
were like bubbles of the sad October sunshine. Martin loved these quick
chill dusks, and then later the kind eye of lamplight in the window,
and the friendly, wood-warmed, table-set kitchen.

They came to the end of the furrow. Martin split the rest of the acre
with his eye.

"Will we finish her before supper, son?" he asked.

"Do you want to work all night too!"

Martin stopped the oxen.

"What's wrong with you today, Dave?" he said. "If you planned to
go after the partridges …."

"Partridges, hell!"

"Well then, what's …."

David hesitated.

"I'm so damn sick of this place I …."

"Is *that* so!" Martin said slowly. "What's wrong with this place?" He
kicked over a sod with the toe of his shabby boot. An old man looked
out of his face for the first time. It was true, then …. It had never been
because David was tired or lonely or weak or young …. It was because
David had always *hated* this land … the land that would be his own
some day. A sick little cloud settled on his heart. He *had* no son, then.

"What's *wrong* with it?" David said. "The same damn thing over and
over from morning till night … every day and every day … what future
is there for anyone here?" David kept his back bent to the plough handles. He felt a little mean and ashamed when he heard the sound of his
own words.

"What future is there here?" The question sounded meaningless to
Martin. He had the truth, to contradict it. There is the first day in April
when the fields stir again and it is good all day just to feel your breathing …. There is the sky-blue August day when the whole green wind is
full of leaves and growing, and Sunday morning you walk in the wav-

ing growth-full garden rows and wish you could keep this day forever, hold it back from going …. It is good, too, when the snow whistles cold and mournful because it can never get inside the pane to warm itself …. It is *all* good, all of it …. Men live here as long as their sons live, to see the clearings their axes have made and the living grass that sprang from their tracks in the first furrow and the green things their hands gave life to …. "The same thing over and over…. " Martin did not speak. Only his sick thoughts pleaded, patiently, silently, incredulously. We did not plough yesterday, David. We took the day off and last night this time we sat at the edge of the woods and waited for the shy-eyed deer to come out into the old back field.

I thought it was good to sit there and smoke with my son after we boiled the supper kettle, not talking much but not feeling the silence either, and watch the dead leaves drifting down past the rocks in the cool-talking brook. The fire itself felt good, in spite of the sun, and it was good to hear the nervous twitter of the partridges in the apple trees just before it got too dark to pick out their heads along the sights of the gun…. Or is this like the day last spring we nodded at each other across the pool with the foam on it each time we held a broken-neck trout throbbing in the tight of our palms? Or the day we cursed the heat in the alder-circled meadow and our shirts stuck to our backs like broken blisters? The hay smelt good that night, just the same, and it was good to hear the wagon wheels groan on the sill just before the dark thunder-frown of the sky burst and the barn roof beat back the rain. I remember the night we ate our first supper in the house I had built with my own hands. That night the neighbours came in, and we danced half the night to the fiddles. It was easy with everyone, like with brothers, and we loved them all … and it was good that night to lie in bed and let sleep's drowsy wind blow out the candles of thought. The day they brought your brother Peter home loose in their arms before it was dinner time, his dead body so broken your mother could not hold it, that day was different …. And the next day…. And the next day….

"Well what kind of a place suits *you*?" Martin said at last. David straightened.

"The city, of course! Who'd want to live in this God-forsaken hole when you can get a job in the city?"

"Did you say the *city*?"

"Yeah. The city," he said laconically.

Martin listened with sick wonder to this stranger who had been his son. The city…. It's *there* the days are the same. I thought it was very lonely in the city, the time I was there. The stone things move, but they do not change. My feet were always on stone. I could not walk on the ground and look over it and know it was my own. They never looked at the sky there, or listened for the rain.

When I looked at the sky there, the sun I saw was a strange one ... it did not make friends with the stone. The stone houses were alike, and the days were alike, and never till they died could the people lie in bed at night and listen to rain on the corn after a long heat. They had nothing to breathe but their own tired breaths. I remember their faces. There was stone in them, too. They were all alike. They looked as if they never awoke from their tired dreams of the night. Their minds kept turning in their own tracks, like the weary wheels that could find no rest on the pavements. The soft-fingered women-faced men lived in houses, and the house-smell clung to everything they said or did when they went outside. When they talked, it was empty, because their eyes saw nothing but the stone things that their hands had not built ... and none of them had anything to say that could not be said with words. It was very lonely there. They laughed too much. But not even love or death could melt their aloneness. Even when they laughed, their eyes did not change. And when they died, no one remembered, and there was nothing left of them.

I liked it in the city, now, this time, David thought. The street lights began to come on, a little before it was dark, and excitement seemed to stir in the busy pavements. The wind was not strong enough to lift itself above the street, but the women's skirts clung to their bodies as they passed. So many different women's bodies! What if they *didn't* speak? The bright, metallic faces of always-rich women seemed to shine in the shop-window light, and you knew you would feel clumsy and ashamed with them, but it was good to think of having their soft flesh alone somewhere in the dark. There was so much light there, then ... and life. Like when you took off your work-clothes and shaved and felt smoother and brighter and ready for things. There was life, not death, at the end of the day. Here, my God ... the same old bare maples weaving back and forth against a sky that made your lips blue just to look at it, and never the sound of a strange voice, and later the snow sifting lonely through the spokes of the wagon wheels .... What a God-forsaken place to be *young* in. Maybe his father didn't mind, they didn't seem to mind *missing* things when they got old. Old people didn't seem to dread being quiet and letting things slip like this. They thought it was because they were wise ... it was because they were half-dead already. If he thought he'd ever get like that about things when he got old.... He'd never get old. He swore a desperate promise to himself that he'd never, never, never get that awful patience like his father... standing there now, with that stupid look on his face, like one of the oxen....

ও

"But Dave, Martin said slowly, "this place will be *yours* some day, you know that."

"What do *I* want of this old *place*?"

A whiteness came into Martin's face that was different from the whiteness of the cold or the weariness. He remembered the day his father had said the same thing to him. They had both felt shy and awkward, and he could say nothing, but as soon as he was alone, he had looked over this land, the tight tears of pride came warm into his eyes. He had kept this place, the best thing he had, till he could give it to his own son, and now when he offered it to David he saw it meant nothing. That he despised it. He had known through and through how his own father felt.

"It was always good enough here for *me*," Martin said.

"All right, but what did you ever *amount* to?"

Martin was stung into a sudden anger. "As much as *you* ever will, you ...."

Then he looked over the fields, slowly, and a break came into his anger. Why today, only a few hours ago, starting to plough, it had been, without a thought, so sweet, so safe, so sure... he and his son ploughing and him trying to show David how to turn the furrow better and David trying his best. Things just didn't come handy for David, it must be that. He had half felt Ellen working quiet and happy in the house and the smoke went straight from the chimney into the clear, sun-filled air and there had been no hurry or fret in the fields or the slow oxen or his thoughts. Now... it could never be the same again between him and David, now. Every time they said a sharp word to each other now, these sick things would all come back.... What if David was right? What *had* he ever amounted to? Well, he had been young here, and youth was very fresh and full here in the fields and the sun and very long, some of it never died, it grew green again with each April sun. He had had a wife of his own kind, and everything they had, they had got with their own hands, his hands and hers. There had been a lot of tiredness but there was always the quiet night afterwards and the slow kindly talk. There had never been an end of work, but you could always stop to talk across the fields to your neighbour, and you got along just the same. There had not been much money, but there had always been the sweet smell of bread in the kitchen and the soft song of wood in the kitchen stove. There had been no strangers among them, and when you died these men you had lived your whole life with would not work that day, even if there was clover to be hauled in and rain in the wind ... and you would lie in the land that your hands and your feet knew best, and the same breezes you had breathed would always blow over you. Surely that was enough for a man. If your son .... If David .... It was hard to believe that your own son was not like you wanted him to be. But, Martin thought sadly, you couldn't make him see, if he didn't feel that way. You wished ... but if he felt that way, there was no way to make him see.

"Well Dave," Martin said slowly, "if you're *bound* to go away, I suppose ...."

"Oh," David said impatiently, "let it go, let it go ... I'll stay," he added sullenly.

He is almost afraid of me, Martin thought. He won't even talk it over with me. He has no use for my talk. He wants to keep me away from him. He don't think I can understand him at all. I try.

He walked around to the oxen's heads and picked up the whip.

"Haw," he said quietly. "Just cut her light here, son."

David put his hands back on the handles but he didn't speak. He threw the plough around when they turned the furrows, so the chain jerked taut in the yoke. "Easy now, boys," Martin cajoled the oxen.

A bare little wind started in the bare maples. The sun burned cold and lonesome in the blind windows of the church across the road and the long withered grass bent over the cold grey sand in the middle of the built-up graves. Peter's grave .... Peter would coax to hold the whip. He could hardly make his small voice loud enough to stir the oxen, but they obeyed him. Martin could see the crazy nostrils of the running horses and then Peter's small crumpled body on the rock heap where the wheel had struck ....

The cows came up from the pasture, calling hollowly to be let in. The sky looked away from its own darkening face in the mud-bottomed puddles of the road. The blood in Martin's face came blue to the skin, and his blue eyes, a little faded with weariness, looked like frozen spots holding up the weight of his face. He walked back-to, guiding the oxen by the horns to help David keep the furrow straight, but David did not straighten his back, even when Martin stopped for a rock. Martin would come around and kick out the rock himself.

Martin blew on his hands and tried to start a smile in the corners of his tired, cold-thin, lips.

"Time for mittens, I guess. *Your* hands cold?"

"No," David said.

A shaft of the sun broke for a minute through the blue, wind-cold clouds. Long bands of it searchlit the grey rocks, without warming them.

"Snow comin'," Martin said.

The sun went down, and the sky made a few cold-pink patterns at the horizon. It would not be as sad again until April.

Martin turned the oxen for one more furrow. He could not stop, until he was *sure* how David .... Maybe if he kept on, David would say something himself about stopping, and he could show him then how ready he was to listen to him and take the oxen off the tongue.

"*I'll* never ask him to stop if he ploughs all night ...." David was so tired the muscles of his legs felt like a frayed rope and a tight cord drew his temples together. The blood seemed to drain from his face and throb heavy in his neck. The ashes of weariness sifted through the bright surface of his thoughts. The oxen lifted their heavy feet and deposited them carefully on the ground. The plough dug its slow way through the earth.

"I guess we're just gettin' her done in time," Martin said.

David said nothing.

"I guess this clears things up, about, for winter. You'll have a little more time to hunt, now, Dave."

Ellen came to the corner of the house, holding down her apron with one hand against the tug of the wind, and called supper.

"All right," Martin called back.

"Hungry, Dave?" he said.

"No."

Dave glanced at his father's face. For the first time he noticed how tired it looked. He felt sorry for his father, for a minute, and a little ashamed. He'd *have* to stay as long as his father was alive, he supposed.

They came to the end of the furrow. Martin hesitated.

"Well, I guess we'll let her go at that for tonight," he said. "We can wind her up in the morning, easy." He hesitated again.

"David," he said, "if you really *want* to go away ...."

David's impatience flared again. He forgot his father's face.

"Oh, for God's sake," he said, "can't you let that *drop*? I said I'd stay, didn't I? What more do you want? I'll stay here as long as *you're* here, anyway. So you need not worry."

So it is that way. A small coal touched suddenly against Martin's heart. He will wait, but he will be glad ... so he can go away. If he was waiting for it, so the place would be all his own then, it would be ... but he will be waiting, so he can go away. There will be a stranger here, and nothing will be done the same. There will be a strange name in my house, and maybe they will let the alders creep back over the acre field because they did not clear it for the first time and plough it with their own hands ... and the grass will grow tall and strange over the graves.

He pulled the bolt from the tongue. It was true. It was true, then. He *had* no son. David took his hands from the plough. Martin waited for a minute to see if he would line the plough up for the next furrow in the morning. David did not move. Martin walked around to the plough. David went to the oxen's head, took up the whip and started with them to the barn. Martin pulled the plough around and lay the chain straight out along the next furrow. Ellen came to the corner of the house and called supper again, but Martin did not answer. He watched David take the oxen past the house. He saw Ellen say something to him, but David did not reply.

He bent down and dug the mud from the ploughshare. It shone underneath, where the earth had polished it, like a sword. The earth smelled cold and silent. He moved a few stones, absently, with his foot and stood for a minute with his eyes on the ground. Like the night they buried Peter. He felt lost in the long, dead day.

In the porch, he listened to see if David might be talking to the oxen. There was no sound but the bells, as David jerked the yoke-straps. Martin caught his breath quickly. He had no son. Peter was dead. He *had* no son, now. He scraped the dirt from his heels with a stick from the chipyard and went inside the house.

"Well, what in the *world* have you two been doing?" Ellen said, moving across the scrubbed soft-wood floor from the stove to the table. The warm breath of food rose sweet in the oil-lamplight. She held the dipper of water for Martin's hands over the basin in the sink. "Are you goin' to do a coupla more acres after supper?" she joked.

"Yeah, I was kinda thinkin' we might," Martin laughed.

But his laughter was heavy and grey, like a hawk rising.

Return Trip to Christmas

It must have been Friday, because that's the day Mother always cleaned the lamps. I was sitting at the corner of the kitchen table, cracking walnuts for the Christmas fudge. I was ten, then. I can see her now — after she'd washed and dried the chimneys, misting her breath inside them and polishing them until they shone. I had the foolish notion that the shine came from some delicate vitality in her breath that she could ill afford to spend. She wasn't a fragile woman, but she looked like Helen Hayes looks sometimes in a play.

I knew Mother wasn't sick; she never complained, she never put a hand to any part of her body involuntarily. But sometimes she would stare at the most familiar object for the longest time. It wasn't much, merely the sort of thing you avoid doing except in the presence of children — forgetting that children are the first to sense it. Father wouldn't have noticed at all.

She got up off her chair when Father came in for a dry pair of mittens. He was hauling wood. She often sat down at her work lately and she always sprang up when Father came through the door. It wasn't in the least that Father was intolerant or unfeeling about anyone else's weakness. But he was so rock-strong and solid himself — his was an almost Scandinavian appearance — that just to look at him made you feel that any listlessness of your own must be fancied or a defect of will. I had something of the same reaction about being inside the house.

"You can finish these now, can't you?" I said to Mother, as if it were only to oblige her that I was cracking walnuts.

I got my mittens off the oven door and went out to the porch for my cap. I couldn't be comfortable in the kitchen while he was in the dooryard unloading. There was nothing I could lift, but I could make a show of loosening the bunks on the chains and, when the sleds were clear again, hook the chains over the back bench and wind their loose ends around the peavey stock.

Father glanced at what Mother was doing. "How would it be if I got you one o' them hangin' lamps for the front room ... for Christmas?" he said self-consciously.

Mother was a moment replying. And then she said, "Well, they're real nice, Arth, but now I don't want you to go ..."

I knew what made Mother hesitate. Father "thought he was doing something" and it would be too shameful to think about to show disappointment. But a hanging lamp would be the worst gift possible. I knew that her heart was wistfully set on electric lights—however much her head contradicted it and though her tongue never mentioned them. That particular gift would be like the time I had let my imagination play with the picture of those trim hunting boots with red scalloped tops in the catalogue, and he had brought me home the stub rubbers as a surprise. As the hanging lamp would be, they were the best of their kind. So uncompromisingly sturdy and reinforced at all points of greatest wear that it seemed as if I could never escape them.

My mind sputtered to itself. "What do we want of an old hangin' lamp? Why can't we have the lights, like everyone else?" I banged a stick of wood against the side of the woodbox.

Electric lights were a small miracle to us then. No other country place had them. It just happened that the new power line went through our village on its route to the big central dam. Almost everyone else in the neighbourhood got them in by paying so much a month on the installation cost.

That we didn't have them was just an instance of what was typical in Father. I never knew a more generous man, but he'd have nothing whatever that he couldn't pay cash down for. I remember one spring grain was sky-high he let a whole five-acre ploughed field go unseeded because the storekeeper couldn't even persuade him to accept a month's credit.

"You'd never guess what's goin' on over to Stan Wheeler's this mornin'," he said to Mother.

"No," Mother said. "What?"

"They're puttin' in a radio!" Radios were still a novelty, even in town. "Stan told me himself he only paid twenty-five dollars down on his lights ... and ... now a radio! He must be runnin' his face for every *cent* o' that. Where is that man's ...?"

Mother shook her head and gave a little laugh of bewilderment. "Don't ask me," she said. "Debt don't seem to mean any more to them than ..."

Mother always sided in with him. He wasn't in the least overbearing. But because he was the sort of man to whom the truth about things seems to be so plainly legible—and because we loved him so much for being the kind of person who'd be utterly helpless to know how to win anyone's love if it weren't given to him naturally, and because his love for us was of such bedrock certainty—it never occurred to us that he might be mistaken in any of his attitudes. Whenever we were tempted to think differently about anything it seemed like a failing we should know better than to indulge.

That's why I felt guilty even as I continued my silent sputtering. "Yes, yes. *We* never get anything until we can afford it. After it's an old story to everyone else. It's no fun that way." I banged another stick of wood against the side of the box.

"Peter!" Mother called. "What in the world are you doing out there in the porch?"

"Nothing," I grunted.

I stood in front of the oxen while Father unloaded the sleds, to give myself the appearance of having a function. Once in awhile I'd shout "Whoah!" though they'd given no sign whatever of starting ahead.

Father never smiled at these transparent little actions of mine. He never treated me like a child when I wanted to be treated like a grown-up. On the other hand, he could almost always sense when I wanted to be treated like the child I was, and never, then, treated me like a man.

I watched him toss the leaden beeches onto the pile as if they were fence posts, and I forgot about things like the lights. He seemed like everything anchored and sustaining. I had never heard him mention anything selfish *he* wanted in my whole life. And one of those sudden little vertigos of exaltation which had spun inside me at odd moments all week possessed me then.

Because this was the enchanted week before Christmas. Snow had fallen steadily until finally the branches of the spruces on the mountain were lipped with pure white, and the frozen wheel-ruts in the road were evened over, and everything rough and harsh and plaintive from the fall seemed to be soothed into a dreamless sleep. It was the week when everything had a face. The days ... the nights ... the kitchen, alive with the intoxicating smell of oranges and spices ... the closets, delicious with secret packages. The room where the tree already stood, even though the tree had no trimming yet, really breathed, you could almost see it. And a child, used to being fenced off in the company of his own years, might look into the face of an adult and see, miraculously for a moment, the face of another child.

I looked at Father's face.

He was watching the operation over at Stan Wheeler's. They were putting up the radio aerial. "Well now, if that ain't ..." he said to himself. His face was completely encased in incredulity at anything so outlandish.

Then he turned to me. "Do you want to go back with me this trip?" he said.

"No," I said, my voice suddenly short. "I guess I'll stay home and help Mother. I don't think she feels any too good."

"Don't feel good?" Father said. "Who said? Did she say?"

"No," I said. "She'd never let on till she dropped." It was the old-fashioned speech of an only child. "I don't think she's what you'd call sick," I added. "I think ... she's just old before she's young."

It was ridiculous talk for anyone my age, and of course I was just mouthing phrases I'd heard my elders use on occasion. And yet I half-knew what I was talking about just the same. Mother was forever picturing little refinements that would take the bareness off mere sufficiency, and tracing out her dream of them down to the last detail, even though common sense told her there wasn't the slightest chance of their ever becoming fact. And Father was so ... No, "practical" isn't the word, it wasn't anything like as cold as that. He never disputed or ridiculed our fancies, they were simply harmless. But for anyone to be always coming up against being made to see that your habit of mind was a vacant one ... Until you got so you stared that way at things you held in your hand.

"She just sets and stares at things sometimes," I said.

Father made no comment whatever. "All right," he said. "You stay and help her."

"It ain't her *work*," I started to say, contradicting what I'd said before. But it was quite beyond me to explain what I'd mean by that, so I didn't answer him.

I glanced at Father when the ponderous oxen, with the gait like movement stunned, turned into the bend of the log road beyond the barn. He was hunched forward a little on the sled bench, striking the thumb-and-forefinger angle of one mittened hand inside the same angle of the other. He had that look of the big forthright man who doesn't quite know what it *is* that's on his mind, let alone how to work it out. Then, I wished there was something I could side with him against.

る

At the dinner table that noon he said to Mother all of a sudden, "Annie, why don't you take a little trip down to see Ella before Christmas?" It came out startlingly loud from having been over-rehearsed to sound casual.

Mother was so embarrassed she didn't know where to look.

Ella was her sister in the city. She was married to quite a well-off man quite a bit older than herself and she "had everything." They'd been down to visit us a couple of times. Uncle Clyde's automobile was sleek as a racehorse, with so much room in it that everyone could sit sideways and talk to each other just as if you were in the house. And when he drove us in to town, with him and Aunt Ella looking so much more sophisticated dressed *down* than we did dressed up, and when his urbane desk hands (ours were like naïve faces) did their transactions in store after store I directed him to in his search for some special city food that half the storekeepers had never heard tell of, I kept praying all the time that everyone I knew would see us.

Father didn't have a jealous bone in his body, and you couldn't say exactly that he and Uncle Clyde didn't get along. But when Uncle Clyde would tag along with him at his work and ask him questions about it, as if his interest in this extraordinary way of making a living were some kind of flattery—or when, in all innocence, Aunt Ella would say to Mother, "Oh dear, Annie, I'm so *used* to throwing all our scraps in the garbage, I forget you save them for the pig," or when she'd take the pitcher of hot water in the morning for Uncle Clyde to wash in the spare room basin—Father's face would go kind of set.

I remember one day Uncle Clyde said to him, "Could you make use of these old pants if I left them here when I go back, Arth? In fact, I must have all kinds of castoffs you could get a turn out of, for everyday. Ella could bundle them up and mail them to you."

"They'd be too small for me," Father replied, but the way he looked Uncle Clyde up and down said more than that.

Except for the usual standing invitation, only once before had the question of Mother's going to visit them come up. Aunt Ella had written, asking her to come on a specific date. She'd added a P.S.: Clyde says to tell you not to worry about expense. It won't cost you a cent. He'll send you a round ticket."

"By God," Father exclaimed, when Mother read that part out to him, "when I can't pay my own wife's way anywhere ..."

Mother folded the letter as if his voice had been a blow on her hands, and when she wrote back to Aunt Ella that night she stared and stared at her pen before she could get the (what possible?) words on the paper. She and Father had never mentioned it again.

That's why she was so taken back now. She didn't know anything about our conversation that morning.

"You know I couldn't go now, Arth," she said. "I'd need clothes, and ..."

"Well, *get* clothes," he said.

"And it's such a busy time. No, I couldn't," she added, as if she were stamping firmly on a little flame of yearning that had sprung up in spite of her, "I couldn't."

"You got your cooking all done ain't you?" he said, "and your presents all wrapped?"

"Yes, but ..."

"Well, then ..."

"Would you go too?" she said.

It was his turn to look confounded. "Me?" he said. "No. What would I want to go for? I got my wood to get out in this snow, and ... But that needn't make no odds to you goin'. It'd give you a change." He hesitated a moment. "You never have any pleasure." Mother looked as if she wanted to cry.

I felt like she did, I don't know why. I was all confused. I knew that again Father "thought he was doing something," and I knew how hard it must have been for him to come out with this particular suggestion. I knew how totally a gift it was, because he could never understand why anyone should *need* a change.

But again his gesture was subtly wrong. If he'd pitched in with us and said he'd go too, the heck with the wood ... But how could Mother go off in a holiday spirit alone, even though it wasn't begrudged to her one iota, even though he urged it on her? Why couldn't people like Father see that no outward "change" whatever which they might arrange for you could take the place of an inward change in *themselves*? And wasn't this week in any way special for him as it was for everyone else, that he wouldn't specially mind being separated from us during it?

Yet I felt the same little flicker of longing as Mother. At Aunt Ella's — where everything that was luxury to us here would be like an everyday thing, without any need for conscience about it. And I had never been to the city. The city, this particular week, with its special excitement ...

"Now you just make up your mind to get ready and go," Father said. "I'll drive you to the train tomorrow and come meet you on the train back Christmas Eve. I got to go in to town that day anyway."

"What about the tree?" Mother said.

"Trim it that night," Father said. "Or if there ain't time, trim it Christmas Day."

Christmas *Day*? I thought, in a kind of incredulous horror.

"I couldn't," Mother said again. But now I could see that something fresh was complicating her indecision: a conscience about going against Father's wish, and a weakening before his will. "I couldn't content myself, with you worrying along here all alone."

"Me and Pete can run the ranch here all right, can't we, Pete?" Father said.

"Sure," I said.

It was my automatic agreement with anything Father asked of me. But I'm afraid it came out pretty limp. It had never occurred to me that Father would assume I'd stay here with him. My dream of the city crumpled down over my breath like a kite sailing high in the sky when the wind suddenly fails.

And yet, when I gave it second thought … To be a full partner with Father, just the two of us, in the management of everything on the place. Planning adult things together, and joking together when either of us, as men, were clumsy with some woman's task in the house. *We* could trim the tree, and Mother would be amazed at what a good job we'd do.

I looked at him looking at me as an equal and I felt tall. My heart gave a great surge. Why, this would be *better* than going!

"Now, we both want you to go, why don't you go?" I said to Mother.

The next morning, Father didn't take the oxen to the woods. He said he'd chop a load ahead and come out early to drive Mother to the train.

Mother had decided she'd get Aunt Ella to help her pick out a new dress in the city, and make the rest of her clothes do. "I don't see anything wrong with that hat, do you, Arth?" she said.

"No," he said, "I always thought that was a pretty hat."

I felt curiously hurt for them both, as if for a moment *they* were the children, to know that it wasn't any kind of hat whatever for the city, but I didn't say anything.

Mother kept posting me: "Now don't forget, the buttermilk pies are in the cellar-way, under the cheesecloth. You better eat them up first, they won't keep like the apple," and, "Remember to keep the cover on the breadbox," and, "You can cook yourselves some eggs, they're hearty and they're easy to get." And I kept saying, "Yes, yes." But I was scarcely listening. I could handle things all right! Again, it was with Father that I felt the team spirit. Men didn't ding at you the way women did.

Around ten o'clock, I thought: I'll go water the oxen, and he won't have to have *that* to do when he gets home from the train. I'd never watered them before, but heightened with my new responsibility I felt equal to anything now.

Father always led them out to the tub one at a time, by the horn. Bright had his head down in the manger, using his long tongue like a hook to lash strands of hay through the chinks in the cow stall next him. I took hold of one horn to try out the feel of it before I undid his chain. He swung his head up and sideways (I was on the wrong side, to lead him), and I felt the iron strength of his neck go like a charge through my arm. I let go and reached down the whip from the yoke rack behind them. I'd just undo their chains and team them out and back.

Brown made a kind of calf caper and took a playful hook at one of the cows he passed, but it wasn't until they were both out in the yard that I saw what a mistake I'd made to turn them out together. I remembered too late how they acted the first day Father turned them out to pasture in the spring. How he always screwed the blunt brass knobs onto the points of their horns beforehand.

You wouldn't have believed that these were the same stupefied beasts that had stood side by side in the barn and lumbered along in the yoke sluggish as stones, taking no more notice of each other, though their bellies touched, than if they were blind. I watched from the barn doorstep, dismayed.

They acted as if the touch of the ground drove them mad. They raced up and down and criss-cross the yard like runaway horses. They braked their front feet suddenly and arched their backs and threw their rumps up in the air and from side to side like someone snapping a whip. They got down onto their front knees and battled the snowbank with their horns, tossing their heads back and forth like a dog worrying a bone, and when they stood up again their big eyes rolling in their snow-whitened faces gave them a frenzied look.

"Bright!" I shouted. "Brown! Git over there and drink!" I cracked the whip.

If oxen can sneer, they sneered. Brown did pause for a minute at the tub and push the icecakes back with his nose to clear a drinking space, and I let out my breath. But he merely tasted the icy water with his teeth and then, disdaining it, tossed his head in the air and started that violent charging again.

And then suddenly they headed for each *other*. I felt the way you do when a grass fire gets out of control like some demon you've unleashed.

Only they weren't running now. They approached each other obliquely, with a deliberation I found more terrifying than anything before. They held their heads down, stalking like cats and seeming to look in another direction, until they were almost touching, and then, *crack!* — I screamed — their horns locked in a flash.

And then there was nothing but that deadly intent buckling against each other with every ounce of their strength. Gaining a foot, losing a foot, breaking free for a few seconds to try to gouge (I saw a little white pencil mark streak up Bright's side where the hair was laid open and he gave that hollow unearthly chilling bark which is the ox's only exclamation), and then, *crack!*, their horns locking again...

I came out of my paralysis and fear. I ran up to them with the whip, striking first one and then the other and screaming, "Bright! Brown! Stop! Stop!" I beseeched them, "Please...Please..." I might have been the wind.

I thought: the feed boxes. I raced into the barn and dumped meal into both boxes, banging the boxes against the side of the mangers and shouting, "Come, boy...Come, boy..."

I heard Bright bark again. I ran toward the door with a dipper of meal and just before I got there Bright bounded in, with Brown right behind him. Brown had him on the run. If they keep fighting in the barn, I thought...If they tackle the cows tied up...What'll I *do*?

But each went into his own place as docilely, and buried his nose in the mealbox as rapturously, as if nothing had ever happened.

In my crying relief I crowded between them without the slightest fear, to fasten their chains. I fastened Brown's first. It was shadowy in the mangers and slightly blinding after the sharp sunlight on the snow, and it wasn't until just as I had both arms in position around Bright's bent neck, to drop the bar pin on one end of his chain into the big round link on the end of the other, that I noticed anything wrong. I let the pin fall through as if I were loosing my grip on an intolerably heavy stone. Your heart *can* sink. I felt mine do it, then.

For where Bright's big hard left horn should be there was only the "peth" of it now, glistening and streaked with blood like the inside of a rabbit's pelt. That last bark — Brown had knocked its shell right off.

Bright was ruined. You could never strap a yoke on him now. I knew the peth would harden in time, but I knew that Father would never have a stunted, unsightly thing like that in his barn. That's why he'd *bought* this team, because their horn spreads had matched so perfectly.

Father. What would he ever say? But that was the worst part of it. He wouldn't rage at me (if only he would!) or whip me. He'd just ... I could see his uncomprehending face.

I stood there, hating myself. The very first thing I'd tried to do ...

I stood there and everything was in ruins. Our partnership, Mother's trip, Christmas, Everything ... You can truly wish that the earth would swallow you up. I stood there and wished desperately that I could turn into nothing.

Such wishes are always denied, of course. And sooner or later you have to make a move of some kind. I went out into the yard. Sure enough, there was the horn. I picked it up. It was still warm.

And then I had this crazy idea. I had knocked down Mother's best platter one time and broken it in two, fishing for the cookie jar. I had stood it up again and fitted the edges together so well that Mother had never known the difference until the next time she came to use it. It wasn't an act of slyness, really; it was just until I could get over that terrible "gone" feeling at the time.

If I could slip the horn back on. I took it back into the barn and I gave Bright another dipper of meal to keep him quiet and my hands were trembling, but I must have got just the right twist on it for it slipped into place like a glove. Bright paid no more attention to what I was doing than he would to a flybite.

The horn felt absolutely solid unless you tugged on it. Would there be such a thing that it'd grow back on as good as ever? I should tell Father about it, ask him that. Maybe there was something he should do—tar around the base, to seal it off from the air, I now seemed to remember having heard someone say.

But I just couldn't tell him. I knew it was cowardice, but I knew what I was going to do. I was going away with Mother, before he found out. Let him think Bright had loosened his horn somehow in the manger.

I wasn't afraid he'd yoke them up without noticing it. The bleeding had matted a little circle of hair right where the horn joined the head. He'd see that first thing when he went to water them after coming back from the train, and do anything that needed to be done.

The next hour or so I don't even like to remember. White and shaky inside, and sick with the traitorous feeling of secrecy. My heart lurching like a leaf at the clout of a raindrop when I saw Father coming out the log road. Holding my breath while he harnessed the horse—though the horse stable was on this side of the barn, with a separate door—lest something would put it into his head to have a look at the cattle.

I like least of all to remember Father's face when Mother told him I'd "put up a touse" to go with her at the last minute. "Well, if he'd rather," was all he said. I sat speechless on his lap in the sleigh, thinking every minute of the way to town that if he tumbled to my deception before I could make up my mind to confess he'd never have any faith in me again.

Trips that begin disastrously often rally and become all the more splendid. This one didn't.

Uncle Clyde wasn't there to meet us when we got off the train, though Mother had spent a whole dollar to phone Aunt Ella when we would arrive. We waited almost an hour, hungry, and islanded with strangeness in the gaunt dusk-dreary station before they appeared. (I told Mother I wasn't hungry at all, because I couldn't bear to think of elbowing our way to those high stools before the counter with the mirror behind it that would keep giving us back our unease, and where the hectic waitresses seemed to slap the food around as if it were something contaminous.) And when they did show up, they exchanged a few peevish words before they greeted us properly.

"I *told* you to call the station and check on the time," Uncle Clyde said. "You might know you wouldn't remember it right."

"Now, just because Tom Carlton gets a raise at Christmas and you don't, don't take it out on me," Aunt Ella said.

Both of them were as nice as could be to *us*, but by turns. It wasn't until we reached the apartment that they joined forces in welcome. The drive there wasn't anything like I'd pictured it to be.

I knew it wasn't because they were in any way ashamed of us, but almost the first thing Aunt Ella said to Mother in the car was, "Annie, you ought to wear a hat that's off your face more. Here, try on this one of mine, just for fun. You can have it if it fits you." And I couldn't help noticing Uncle Clyde's eyes smile at my clumsy mail-order cap a whole size too large.

Strangely enough, I didn't much care, though. Uncle Clyde didn't seem like anyone so special *here*. Not the way Father seemed special amongst the men home. Nor did his car, either. There were so many just like it or a little better.

I felt funny going up in an elevator for the first time. But I felt funnier still that Uncle Clyde and Aunt Ella merely nodded to the neighbours who got off on the same floor, and made no move whatever to "make us known" to them. What would people think if you acted like that with company home?

The apartment was so much finer furnished than any house I'd ever seen as to seem altogether elegant to me. It was like a rich plush pocket you stepped into out of the teeming day. But it was like a pocket in other ways too. Once you'd become familiar with what was strange about it you couldn't seem to take a dozen steps without meeting yourself coming back. The radio I'd looked ahead to so eagerly was broken. Uncle Clyde explained that he was getting Aunt Ella a new, much bigger, one for Christmas, but she didn't seem to be in the least excited about it. Their Christmas tree was already decorated, and as elegantly as everything else, but it looked like a homesick child you are trying to distract with blandishments.

The whole city struck me like that. Aunt Ella took us to see all the Christmas displays in the big stores, but there seemed to be something iron-grey striking through the glitter of everyone's and everything's face, like when the stove polish burned off. And all the snow looked soiled.

One night Uncle Clyde said to Mother jokingly, "I suppose kids are easier to satisfy once they know there isn't any Santa Claus. Or is it the other way around?" I had believed in Santa Claus until that moment. And there was nowhere in an apartment where you could go, to be alone for awhile with such a discovery.

That was the night I had the nightmare. On the bed they had to assemble and take apart for me each day. Santa Claus was coming toward me and just when he got touching close two ox horns came out of the side of his head and one of them was bleeding.

It was the longest and the shortest week I ever spent. Long and wasteful by the hour, for having had my dream of the city turn out to be such a subtle fraud; and short and chilling by the day for having each one bring me nearer to the showdown with my crippling secret when we got home again.

It wouldn't be anything like the truth to say that Aunt Ella and Uncle Clyde were glad to see us leave. There was an extra spurt of sincere feeling when we said goodbye. But if we'd missed the train or anything, and had to re-open our visit, no one would have been able to conceal the awkwardness of it.

I had little spells of shivering in the train. But it wasn't the usual delicious shivering on the day before Christmas. This whole lost "week before Christmas," I thought … that could have been so different if I'd never set foot inside the barn that morning.

Mother was very quiet too. She wasn't returning to something she dreaded, like I was, but I knew that her "change" hadn't done her any good either. It wasn't one of those changes that make you fancy that the things you are coming back to must have been rejuvenated by it as well, that you'll find them altered in all the ways you've always hoped for. That little rigidity of Father's in certain things would be just the same.

I thought of saying I was sick when the train blew inexorably for our station. For I knew now that Father would be in possession of the whole truth. Think of any plausible deception long enough and some shark's fin is sure to break through its surface. It had come to me not ten minutes ago about the tell-tale hoofmarks in the snow.

ह

I got the surprise of my life.

Father was there to meet us—no fear of *him* getting the time wrong— but however I had expected him to act, this wasn't it. For one thing he was all shaved and dressed up. And though I couldn't put my finger on exactly what the change in him was, he almost behaved as if *he* were the one that some penitence had taken the starch out of and made awkwardly thoughtful. He had hot bricks for our feet, and ... Mother laughed: "Arth, what in the world made you think we'd need the buffalo robe on a mild day like this?" He kept asking us question after question about our trip. He even enquired about Uncle Clyde.

Mother scarcely heeded his questions for plying him with her own about how he had managed by himself.

"It's a shame you had to break up your whole afternoon coming in here to pick us up," she said as we drove out of town. "Just when the hauling was at its best."

"Oh, the wood'll keep," Father said. "There'll be wood after we're dead and gone."

I had never heard Father make a remark like that in my whole life. It, too, came out awkwardly, but I could tell it wasn't any attitude he was putting on. What had come over him? It was already dark and I didn't see Mother stare at his face, but I fancied I could feel her doing it. I imagined that a tension went out of the way she was holding herself in the sleigh, as in a limb released from the cramp of one steady position.

But I couldn't exult. I was too consumed with the exasperation you feel when someone, however innocently, goes straight to the very topic you've been dreading.

"And I suppose you could only make two turns a day, with everything else to look after," Mother said. I seemed to shrink up, and my exasperation turned to anger. Oh, *why* couldn't women let anything drop! I held my breath for Father's answer. This was the moment.

"Matter o' fact," he said, "I've knocked off haulin' for awhile." He leaned forward and flicked the horse's flank with the tip of the whip. "I got rid o' the oxen."

"Got rid of the oxen?" Mother echoed him. She might have been saying, "Got rid of the place!"

"I'm sleepy," I put in suddenly. It was a dead giveaway, but I couldn't help it. "Can I get down in the front of the sleigh?"

"All right," Father said gently. "Get right down on the bottom and rest your back against my legs."

"Yeh," he said to Mother. "They was gettin' along. And I got a good trade on 'em. Beef's sky high, y'know. The meat man give me a pair o' yearlin' steers and two hundred dollars boot. I had use for the boot."

My whole body breathed out. It was like waking from a nightmare. He was going to let it slide. He wasn't going to mention a thing. Oh, Father ...

"I suppose you needed the boot, that's why you sold them," Mother said. "And us wasting your money on this trip!"

"Now, now," Father said. "I guess we ain't gone starve jist yet awhile." I had never heard him make a remark like that before, either.

"But they wasn't old cattle, Arth?" Mother kept at it. "They couldn'ta been more'n seven or eight, were they?"

"Well, no, they wasn't *dead* old," Father said. But Bright was always either crowdin' or haulin' off. Pete and I kin break these new steers in ourselves, so they'll work right." He added, as if it were the most trivial afterthought, "And Bright'd knocked a horn loose somehow."

"Knocked a horn loose?" Mother exclaimed. "How did he do that? Did you see him when he did it?"

Oh, *Mother*! It was the way she'd kept quizzing me about the platter even after I'd confessed. There hadn't been a suggestion of punishment about it, but why did women have to keep dinging at a thing? When Father ... When men ...

"Are you comfortable there, Pete?" Father said to me. I didn't answer.

"I guess he's asleep already," Mother said.

"It looks like," Father said. But somehow I was sure he knew better.

"Arth?" Mother harked back. "Didn't you see the ox when he did it? He couldn't do it in the barn, could he?"

"I don't know, I suppose he could," Father said.

"Well, I don't see how," Mother said. "Arth," she continued after a minute, in an entirely different voice, "Peter was up to the barn a long while that morning. You don't suppose that little monkey turned them out or anything...?"

"He might have," Father said. He moved his legs—to rouse me, I think, if I should really be asleep. He must have known by the way I readjusted my body against them that I did it consciously. "But why would he be scared to own up to me about it?" he said slowly. "Surely he don't think I'm that kind of a ..."

I turned my cheek flat against his knee and I clasped his leg with my hand for just a moment. He put one hand on my cheek for just a moment. I knew that that was all the exchange that would ever be necessary between us.

I fell asleep that way.

è⬤

I slept until we were almost home. When I awoke, mother was still asking him questions. There was a curious—well, kind of freedom—in her voice. I don't know why, but it reminded me of the way a calf that's always been tied up acts, when you first let him loose. First he only goes as far as his rope used to let him. Then he ventures a little farther, and stops short, surprised. Then a little farther still, but still doubting. Then a little farther still. Until finally, in one great bound, he *believes* that all limits are gone.

"What did you do with yourself evenings?" she was saying.

"Oh, I don't know," he said. "Stan made me go over and listen to the radio one night, and ..."

"That was nice," she said. "How does the radio work?"

"Fine," he said. "Perfect."

"What was on?" she said.

"That night, they was actin' out kind of a play," he said. "'Ile', they called it."

"I'll?" Mother said. "I'll what?"

"No," he said. "Like kerosene. Oil." I thought about the hanging lamp. "This old whaler captain in the story called it 'Ile'. He ..." But he stopped short. "I don't know how they kin make them things sound so real," he said.

"Was it really just like real people?" I exclaimed.

"Well!" Father said. "Did you have a good sleep? Yessir, it was just as plain as if you was right there."

è⬤

It was pitch dark when we drove in the yard, but still early evening. We'd have lots of time to trim the tree. I leapt out of the sleigh. I felt suddenly sorry for Uncle Clyde and Aunt Ella—for everyone in the world who wasn't us. Mother seemed wonderful all over again. *She* didn't know... and what a blessing she *had* kept at the thing until it was all cleared up!

"I'll fetch the lantrun," I said eagerly.

"Just a minute," Father said. "You get the things out of the back, till I find the key. Now which pocket..." It was odd that he'd locked the house. We never thought of locking our doors. He was knotting the reins around a big twitch on the woodpile and throwing the rug over the horse. "Wait a minute, now," he said, "till I go ahead and show you where the path is I shovelled out." It was a path to the front door.

We followed him up the path and through the front door. "Are ya in?" he said. "Now don't stumble there, till I get a light."

He went over to the side of the room where the lamp stand was. But he didn't strike a match. He bent down on one knee to the floor board. And then...

"Merry Christmas," he said. There was an almost sheepish smile on his face.

The sudden light made us blink after the pitch darkness outside. But it wasn't harsh or blinding. It was the soft magic light of I couldn't count how many little coloured bulbs strung over the Christmas tree.

"Arth!" Mother gasped. "Oh, Arth!"

"You never noticed the wires or a thing," he said, "did you? I was afraid you'd notice the pole by the gate."

"Not a single solitary thing!" Mother said, like someone dazed. And then she began to cry.

I couldn't open my mouth. I just ran across the room and hugged him around the waist. I didn't care if it was childish or not.

Mother fought for control of her voice. "Arth," she said, "they're... it's... I can't tell you. But..."

"But what?" he said.

"But it must have taken every cent you got out of the oxen. I hate to think of you..."

"What's the odds?" Father said. "We're only goin' this way once."

I could hardly believe my ears. And I knew it wasn't the lights then that gave Mother's face that shining look.

"Maybe you won't like the fixtcher I picked out for the kitchen, I don't know," Father said quickly. We followed him into the kitchen with a kind of rapt and speechless obedience. The radio was in the kitchen.

"Turn that knob on the left there," he said to me.

I turned the knob without a word, though I could tell by his eyes that my own must have been glistening. The most exquisite choir I had ever heard came right into the room. "Sing in exultation…"

"I thought first I'd get you one o' them washin' machines," Father said to Mother, "to save you work … and then, I didn't know, I thought maybe you'd just as leave have the radio …"

And that was the finest thing of all. It meant he understood. He really understood at last. We stood there, listening, and three people were never more like one. I knew there wasn't any Santa Claus — but I knew now that there'd always be Christmas.

It wasn't until years later that I found out about "Ile." That it was the famous play about a hard inflexible man so proud and set on his own goals that his wife lost her reason from having her womanly fancies so stonily disregarded. That his wife's name was Annie. It gave me the sharpest pang. To think that Father could have imagined for one minute — and maybe because of what I'd said that morning at the wood-pile — that there was any likeness whatever of that man in himself.

But I was sure he must have known — certainly from that Christmas on — that *we'd* never thought so.

The Locket

I was running away from home that night. I waited until the house was still.

The still moonlight was outside. The heavy June moonlight that lay like a waiting over the growth-full fields. The leaves of all the growing moved a little all the time, but there was no breeze you could feel, and they moved as if they were drowsy and burdened, not shivering bright the way the sun had made shot silk of the swimming grass in the still-hot afternoon. The only sound outside was the patient sound of the cowbells, muffled because the clapper barely touched the sides of the bell, but it carried close and near into the room.

I lay there, loving all that now that I must leave it and a little frightened now that the time had come to go, but having to go just the same.

My father and my brother Michael were sound asleep. They didn't lie awake and remember the way the sun had moved over the grass, because they belonged here. I noticed those things because I was a stranger.

I lay with my clothes on, and waited, and now, I thought, it is safe. My heart was beating fast when I tiptoed by the door of the room where my father and mother slept. And suddenly I thought, I can't do it after all. It was like stealing, somehow, because they were asleep. They are sleeping because they are tired, I thought, and I can't go away without a word, when they are tired. I thought, I'll wait till morning and tell them then and maybe they will see.

But how could I do that? In the morning the sun would be bright again and everything solid and real, and how could you speak suddenly to your father and Michael, standing to listen with the milk pails in their hands, or to your mother, stopping her work at the stove to listen, and tell them you did not belong in this place, when for them the thought of any other place in the world as home would be almost as strange and shameful as a lie? How could you look at their faces then? You couldn't. You would put it off till noon, but at the dinner table your breath would come too fast with just the thought of beginning to speak and you would put if off till evening, but then when evening was come, the thing would be dulled with the silting of the day's work through your mind and your muscles so you could find no tongue for it at all.

Not until you lay down on the bed at night would the shimmer of the sea and the places beyond it stir in you again like a madness.

I could never explain a thing like that to my father, I thought. It was not that there was no love between us, but when we were silent our minds were not moving alongside each other; and if I spoke this secret thing of mine to him in words, so it would always be there then, spoken, between us, every time we were angry or alone together it would come back.

I whispered softly, "Goodbye, mother and dad," and passed by their door to Michael's. I whispered to myself, "Goodbye, Michael, we had good times."

I could have told Michael and it would not be like trying to tell my father. Michael and I had felt that first strange lightness inside us to see a girl's dress cling to her in the wind, the same first secret summer, and talked about it together, and after that we could talk about anything at all. But he wouldn't understand this. He wouldn't understand a thing that was stronger even than girls. He wouldn't understand that your home was not where you were born, that it was some place you had to find.

I couldn't bear to think of telling my mother at all, the way her face would be.

I tiptoed downstairs and the guilt went a way a little, until I came to my grandmother's door. I thought, the others ... but I will never see her again. And she is old and blind. She has never seen me.

And suddenly I thought, if she were young I could tell her. I know she of them all would understand. I thought, when she was young I know she was restless too sometimes, and sometimes she must have been struck still in the midst of her work and scared, for a minute, because the circle of trees everywhere she looked seemed small and closing about her and she was young and there were so many things her eyes would never see and her heart would never find out.

And now she was old and blind, and she had never been on a train. A thing like that could happen. The thought frightened me, so I wanted to hurry.

But she stirred. "David," she said softly, "what is it?"

I stepped into the room quickly and stood by her bed. "Nothing," I whispered. And then I couldn't lie. I said, "I'm going away."

"Away?" she said. "Where?"

She spoke softly too, as if it were already a secret thing between us. "I don't know," I said.

I didn't. I didn't know which place would be home. I had money for the train. And then there would be ships. A ship was like a dream, then. The land was still and rooted like the noon of the day, but the sea was running and free like wide thoughts that came in the night.

"Why?" she said.

"I don't know," I said.

I didn't. I didn't know what it was I was looking for. If it weren't in one place it would be in another. There were all kinds of places and it must be in one of them.

"Will you tell them," I said, "the others ...?"

I knew she could tell them all right. Far better than I. There are some people who can tell things, and some who can't. She could tell things and you couldn't see where her words were much different from the words another would use, but you would forget you were listening to a story, you were there.

I think that's why she had never seemed old to me. She had told me stories since I was a child. I think it was the way she told the stories that made me believe when she was young she had felt as I felt. Because sometimes she seemed to forget I was listening, it was as if she were telling these things to herself. A story of hers had started my thoughts of leaving, although I did not think of that now. It was a secret story between us, a story she had told to no one else. I can only give the facts. I cannot tell it the way she told it.

One day she'd been helping my grandfather in the fields and when she came in to kindle the fire for supper, before she reached the house she had a funny feeling that someone was inside. There was. A man was standing in the kitchen, by the wall near the window, where he could watch to know that she came alone. He was very young, no older than she, but the sailor's middy he wore was clothing so strange that he was like someone from another world.

She didn't scream. She said she stepped back to the bake oven where the great poker for turning the firewood lay, but although the house was alone by itself and the woods ran up behind it, somehow she was not afraid.

He spoke to her and told her she must hide him. Until his ship sailed. The port where his ship lay was only fifty miles from home, but that was as five hundred then, and he told her they would not come searching for him there.

He told her why he must hide. It was a strange reason, but she said she knew it was true. And she listened, because she was so startled she couldn't find her voice to deny him yet.

He had gone with his captain on some errand to a great house in the city. It was funny how she could make you see what a great house in the city was like as plainly as if she'd lived in one all her life. In the garden there had been a peacock. And she could make you see what a strange and wonderful thing a peacock was in the cool garden of a house in the city. The peacock had fascinated him. He had thought, if I could just have one feather from its tail. To carry to Bermuda in my blouse, to show them there.

He had managed to sneak into the garden while the captain was inside the house, and stealing close to the great bird he'd given its tail a sharp wrench. The bird screamed. He had never heard a peacock scream. He had no idea a bird could scream so loudly. The captain had rushed out and there he stood, with the feathers in his hand.

He knew as soon as they were back on ship he would be whipped. She told me what it was like to be whipped on a ship and my own body could almost feel it. Her eyes were angry and hurt. "The heavy thongs would have split his soft flesh like the blow of an axe lays open a maple's flesh when the sap is running ..."

He had run away while the captain was in a shop, on the way back to ship, and travelled through the woods by night and now he was here and he said she must hide him.

When she found her voice she said no, go away at once, she couldn't do it. I know she was thinking of my grandfather. He was a good man, and in his heart a kind one, he was like my father; but he would never be party to hiding a man, although giving him up might be a harder thing to do than to feel the lashes on his own flesh. If you were guilty you must be punished according to the rules that stood, and there could be no tampering with justice as it was written, even if you might not understand it.

She was thinking that there was no way of making my grandfather see about a thing like that. It would have been like trying to make my father see why I must go away. He would listen patiently, but words that went against the things that were strict and plain would mean nothing to him at all.

She told the young sailor no, but he kept saying yes, you must, you will, and at last she said, for one night.

I have looked at the picture of my grandfather that hung over the organ in the parlour and I know what that decision must have been like for her, who had never kept anything from him before in her life.

I think she must have said yes because the sailor was so young. My grandfather's age was almost twice hers then. I know she never loved anyone else and had been happy. But I think that afternoon, after all the years when there'd been so little youth about her that she'd ceased almost to feel the brightness of her own, now suddenly she felt her own again sharply, like clean linen in a breeze, and suddenly burstingly and sadly too, like something that had been yours and neglected and that sometime would die without notice that it was gone. And then she could not refuse safety for the youth in another.

The sailor stayed that night, in the loft. And the next day. And the next night. And then he made her promise that he might stay until his ship was surely gone.

" It was wrong," she'd say. "I should have told your grandfather... but he had stayed one night, it was already a deception ... and what could I do?"

She brought food to him, secretly. At first she had refused to talk to him. And then I think someday he must have begun a story of some far place he had seen and her hand had lingered, in spite of herself, on the door-knob.

It was a strange thing to think of, my grandmother listening to those stories, maybe when she should have been at work in the fields, guiltily, in fear that my grandfather might find her out, not wanting to listen but the sun slipping down towards the trees while she sat there with her hands still on her apron and the words about those far places sounding in this little building of our own.

Her eyes would have a strange look when she'd repeat those stories to me, and I knew she forgot that I was there.

" The ship goes slower now, going into a place called Marseilles, only they don't spell it the way it sounds, because it is far-off and the words there are not the same as ours are, and the water there is blue and deep like the colour of a flower..."

"... They call it China and the people there eat with little sticks, and the feet of the women are bound with wood, and in the market-places the fowls are hung with the feathers on until the head drops off..."

"... and there all the people have flaxen hair and everyone knows how to play a tune and they dance in the streets and they seem to be always laughing ..."

"...and there their skins are all dark and everywhere there is the smell of spice and fruit, fruit everywhere in the streets, oranges, and limes, and grapes, and melons, and dark sweet fruits I have never seen, and the dark women have combs in their hair and lace, even in the smallest houses..."

"...The wind is sharp on deck when you leave and sharp on your skin as knives and when it is night the waves break their dark tongues against the sides of the ship steadily, as if they were blind, but when you come there it is summer all the time..."

And then I would scarcely be listening either, because I *was* that man, in all those places, listening to the story but moving along with it, in it now, like the way you watch the current of the brook so steadily that after awhile you are floating along too...and when I helped Michael to water the cows that night or carry in the wood my body would be slow and the place where my body was did not seem to be a real place at all. I had to go everywhere and do everything that man had ever done.

One night the sailor told her something I didn't believe he could have meant. He told her the sea was a lonely thing. He told her if she'd bring him some old clothes, he'd find work somewhere on the land, that's where he wanted to stay. She said she had thought he spoke the truth, because he spoke so earnestly.

The next morning he was gone. She took the clothes for him, but he was gone.

$\approx$

"What do you want me to tell them," she said, "the others...? "

I don't remember the words I used then, they were probably not the same at all for any of it as these, but I remember what I was trying to say. I may not have talked that way then, but it was the way I thought.

"Tell them..." I said. "Do you remember when you were young? Were there sometimes...when you heard the whistle of a train... did you stand still and it was like your own life was going by in the train and everything in the place where you stood was struck with a quiet, it was a quiet you couldn't call to, like the way the flowers lie on a grave after everyone has gone home...?"

"I am an old woman,"she said.

"But think," I said, "sometimes, when you were young... in the fall when the hay was cut and the moonlight was on the fields and you stepped outside, was it lovely, but like a mocking, was there something like you couldn't wait, like it was all somewhere else... or in the winter when the sun went down and the wind was sort of blue over the frozen fields … or even in the summer, like now, even in the hot growing afternoons would there sometimes be a minute when you'd think of somewhere else or something or someone else somewhere and a fright and a shiver would go through you like the shiver of the grass in the sun … or when you thought of the sea …?"

"What do you say?" she said sharply.

"Or the sea. Did you ever see a picture of a ship sailing … just a picture … and all at once you were there in the picture, and life moved in you then, sharp and clean and not waiting, and the sea went everywhere, moving a little always, bright and blue and deep, going everywhere, touching everywhere…?"

"David," she said, and her voice was funny, soft but sort of frightened, "come here by the window. Let me look at you."

I went to the head of her bed and she reached up and took my face between her hands.

"You have blue eyes," she said, "haven't you?" I suppose she must have heard someone speak of my eyes, because she'd never seen them with her own.

"And your hair is dark, isn't it … very dark … and thick at the temples?" I supposed she knew that because she was passing her hands over it.

"And somehow your face seems to move all the time even when it is still, like there was a breeze behind it, lightening and shadowing … and your eyes go away, they keep going away…"

She had certainly never heard anyone say anything like that. She said that as if suddenly her eyesight had come back and she was really seeing me for the first time. I thought, she is an old woman, wandering.

It gave me such a funny feeling that I moved away a little. I began to feel restless. It wasn't quite midnight, and there was a shortcut across the fields and over the marsh and down the cut to the station. But I wanted to be there in lots of time for the train. I kept one hand in my pocket to make sure my ticket was still there.

"I must go," I said.

"Will you kiss me," she said, "before you go?" Suddenly I felt foolish. I didn't want to do it at all. But I knelt over and kissed her cheek.

It was strange then. Her face didn't feel like the faces of other old women who had kissed me when I was a child. It seemed almost like a young woman's cheek. I don't know why, but it made me think of Helen.

I don't know why, but I thought of Helen then stronger than I had thought of her all that night. I had kissed Helen that afternoon, down by the river where the sweet smell of the clover and the clean moist river-smell had seemed to get into the kiss too. I didn't tell her I was going away, because it was light and I thought I will come back someday and nothing between us will be changed, the way nothing here changes, it did not seem like good-bye. But now in the darkness, suddenly I knew it was good-bye, that I would never kiss her again.

The thought of Helen was so strong then, the way the first girl you've kissed when you are young can seem to have in her all the places there are to go to too, that it was stronger almost than the voice of the places that were beyond the sea. I thought, I can't leave her.

And then, ever so faintly and from far-off, the whistle of the train crept like a cry across the still fields and into the room and I knew that if I did not run across the fields soon, soon the train would go by and then it would blow again, leaving the station, and the sound would come back to me and there would be a stillness after that more terrible than the still-ness of the moonlight. I felt in my pocket for the ticket. It was still there.

"You *will* tell them?" I said quickly.

"Yes," she said. "I will try."

I must go now. I must. I said, "Good-bye." And yet I hesitated because it seemed as if there should be something more than that.

"It's all right," she said softly. "You have said good-bye."

I was almost at the door when suddenly she called me back.

"Look," she said. She pointed to a tiny drawer in the bureau. "Inside a book. Is there something there?"

I thought, she is wandering, but I opened the drawer quickly and took out the book. A tiny locket dropped from between the pages onto the floor.

"It's a locket," I said.

"Yes," she said," take that. It's for you. "

I looked at it. I had never seen her wear the locket herself. She was never a woman for things about her neck or her arms. I thought, she is wandering again. Did she think *I* could wear a locket?

Or maybe she thought it was valuable, that I might need money, that I could sell it. I could see it was not a valuable thing, the workman-ship was poor and the metal was tarnished, but I didn't tell her that. I felt a lump in my throat.

"It's lovely, grandma," I said. "I will keep it."

"I am an old woman," she said so softly that I could scarcely hear her voice as I turned to go.

I ran across the fields, dark now because the moon had gone, and across the marsh where fog lifting from the river made a dew almost as cold as the first fall frost, and through the long dark cut where the train ran, not thinking at all now because the time was so short and the great body of the train was already humming in the rails where my feet touched them. I didn't have time to think at all until I was on the train, until I was really there, and I could feel in my pocket and know there was nowhere I could lose it now.

I had time to think then. But somehow there was something funny about the whistle of the train. It sounded the same as ever, leaving the station. It sounded as if I were not close to it even yet. It was still ahead of me and the lonesome sound was still there, as if it did not know I had heard, really heard this time, as if no one would ever really hear, as if I were not following behind at all.

The faces of the people were all strange, and the easy way they talked and laughed about things that had no body in them was all strange, but I was still alone. These faces were strange, but somehow they were not real, because they were here and now, like the faces were real in the places you could think of, the places where the faces would be strange but you would be with them. The places that were not yet.

My ticket was gone and I was moving, moving now through the dark against the pane, and then I thought of home. I thought of them sleeping at home.

I thought of them at home, and I had never before seen as sharply as I did then the way the shadows of the maples latticed the ground where they met over the mountain road that was cool even in the summer, or how the field sloped up behind the barn so you could lie in the grass and narrow your eyelids and make the dark mountains come as small and close as you liked, or the faces of my mother and father tired and quiet when the lamp was first lit at the supper table in the fall ... or felt so plainly the curling of my bare toes on the hay stubble when the hay was first cut ... or heard so clearly Michael's good voice that night I was lost in the swamp ...

I thought of my grandmother and I wondered if she was sleeping too. I wondered if she would be able really to tell them.

I thought of the locket, and I went out between the cars where there would be no one to see me. I took it from my pocket and turned it over in my hand. The wheels were racing beneath me and the darkness was running by and I opened it and looked inside.

I held it up closer in the dim light then, because there was an old-fashioned picture beneath the oval glass. The face was the face of a sailor in a middy, a face about the age of mine. It was one of those pictures where the eyes always follow you.

I knew then who it was and where it had come from. He must have given the locket to her, as a keepsake, or left it for her, that morning he went away. I closed the locket and put it back into my pocket.

But the eyes still seemed to follow me. Something about the face made me look again. The face was familiar, that was it. It was like someone. It was like someone I knew very well. I thought. It wasn't like my father, or my brother, or any of the neighbours, but I had seen that face before.

And then suddenly I knew where I had seen a face like that, beyond any mistaking. I had seen it in the mirror. It was my own.

I knew then how my grandmother had seen my face. "But what could I do …? I shouldn't have listened, but what could I do?" I knew too what she had meant when she said that. There was no guilt anywhere. I knew she had loved her husband all the time, deeper than anything else, but I understood now what it was like to love a thing the way I myself loved home, and yet when the sun is still on the fields and something like the whistle of a train calls, what can you do?

I knew too why the train whistle would always be ahead for me and have the lonesome sound, but I having to follow. I knew whose blood my own was echoing, although my father's had not heard it.

And Helen, or Annette, or Maria, or any of you, if you should see this, will you understand? Will you understand that it was not ever you that was lacking, that your part of it was enough, that I meant to stay but …? Will you understand that I can believe it now, that the sea is a lonely thing … that I have been to all the places now and I know now that every place you come to, as soon as it is here and now the faces are not quite real, like the ones ahead? The places are all alike when you get there. I know there is no one place where I will be really among them.

That you may understand. This you will not. But will you *try* to understand about the whistle of a boat? How you forget all you *know* then. Maybe this time. Maybe this place. Will you try to understand what it is like to hear the lonesome sound in the whistle of a boat and know it's lonesome always for you alone?

Will you try to understand what it's like when no matter where you hear the whistle of a boat, what can you do?

❦

The Choice

I don't pretend to be any authority on it, but everyone has his own theory about love. For what it's worth, mine is: the idea of a single perfect mate for every man is silly. Otherwise, look at all the guys and all the dames who'd be fretting their hearts out because one lived in Vancouver, say, and the other in Tibet. I just don't think there's that much difference in women. I don't think it's a case of one thing being love, and all the rest non-love. I think there are degrees of love. I think it's possible to love two women so equally you almost have to flip a coin.

Anyway, that's what happened with me. There were Sally and Anna and I... and it was a triangle about as near isosceles as you could get.

That's not to say the hairline between true-love and not-*quite*-so-true-love isn't important. I just mean, it's luck if you stumble onto it at the time. It's only afterwards that it pops up and makes all the difference. If you make the right choice, you know it then, every day after awhile, consciously or unconsciously. If not, well, I don't think you're apt to be really miserable. You're just like a guy whose hemoglobin count has always been a little below par, without him knowing it.

I was lucky. I got the right one. Everyone has his own idea about love, and in my case I guess I'd say that I love my wife because she's the person I'd hate most to overhear someone poke fun at in clothes she didn't know looked queer, herself. And I guess that makes very little sense.

But as I say, *at the time*, there were Sally Hindle and Anna Benson and I...

Let's say of me only that I am a thoroughly ordinary guy, who doesn't pretend to be even the poor woman's Gable, and I could never figure out what either of them saw in me. I'll have to introduce Sally and Anna more thoroughly, though, or there's no point in the thing at all.

They didn't look alike. Sally was what you might call the ripe-wheat type. Her complexion always looked as if this was the day it was at its peak, as if it had the clean smell of fruit. Her hair grew in crisp curls, and she wore it cropped short all over her head, like Maria in *For Whom the Bell Tolls*. She could get away with it.

Anna I guess you could call the October-brown type. The type that
is either mousey or wonderful. Her hair fell long and light to her shoulders, no matter what the current style happened to be, like the hair of
a girl much younger. She could get away with that, too.

I guess Sally had her on complexion, but maybe Anna had her on
eyes. Maybe. I don't know. Maybe, for another guy, they wouldn't be
lookers at all, that's the way it goes. The point is, as far as self-readings
could discover, my own systolic hit exactly the same high for each of
them.

As for getting *along* any better with one or the other, it was also touch
and go. I could be quiet with either of them, when I felt like being quiet.
I wouldn't feel their attention picking at me, either in an effort at dis-
traction or what can be worse still, the nibbling at your peace of a deliberate patience with mood.

They both thought I was funny (so help me), and what more can a
guy ask for than that? We had a sort of private, binding humor between
us that wasn't repeatable with any effect to anyone else. Maybe it was
wacky, but it wasn't formula-wacky; it wasn't anything like a man putting on a woman's hat for a laugh, or it wasn't anything like the jokes
in the left-hand corner of a newspaper.

Neither of them was jealous of me; but if I talked too long about
someone else, unconsciously, I'd begin to notice that funny little-girl
look about them they never had any other time. I don't mean I like a
jealous woman, but a little of that stuff makes a guy feel alright, just
the same.

If I walked into a street-car and one or the other of them happened
to be there, or if one or the other of them turned up unexpectedly at a
party, I'd have the same feeling, do you know what I mean, as if the space
between us became instantly contractual and exclusive. I could let either
of them straighten my tie just after we'd rung someone's bell, without
minding a bit.

I don't mean to idealize them. They both had faults.

Sally looked like she'd be a wonderful dancer, but she was heavy as
lead; and I love to dance. Anna had no absorption whatever in the the-
atre, beyond the transient absorption while she was there. A good stage
performance ebbs out of me like a drug wearing off; and sometimes
when I'd be holding forth on something we'd seen at the Alex in the
restaurant afterwards, I'd catch her in that curious maneuver of submerg-
ing the beginnings of a yawn into her throat muscles and widening the
mouth part into a deliberate smile.

Both of them were quite capable of venting a fretful womanly spite against some irrelevant trifle, to let you know that the irritation was really you—maybe if you were feeling good and they weren't, and you'd been too bright about something. Sally had a bad habit of saying "Yowsah!"at the time when everyone was saying it like the late Ben Bernie said it; and Anna used to do something with a nail file against her teeth that could, at the right moment, darn near drive me nuts.

The point is, they were equally fallible and human. As far as I could see, *at the time*, exactly equally.

They were equally intelligent, too. I don't mean that there was anything like flat-heeled knowingness about them. I just mean that you could talk to them about almost anything and they wouldn't start distracting themselves with scrutiny of their nail polish.

And they both knew how to act. I don't mean they had that deathly sureness of being naturally at ease anywhere. They could wonder, like anyone else, what the hell you'd say if you were introduced to Edith Sitwell; but when they weren't quite at home with anything, they knew the proper frank way of making light of their confusion. Best of all, you didn't have to worry that when they were with your friends who had none of their poise, there'd be any of that curiously insulting trimming of sails, as it were, in gracious accommodation.

Do you see why I was beginning to wish that the three of us lived in Salt Lake City?

The funny part was that *I* clicked with either of them. Neither of them had ever been mink-coat-over-ostentatiously-cheap-denims rich, but security had always been in them, integrally, like a feature. Their houses had the contained atmosphere when you stepped inside them. It was like the difference between poise and pose. It wasn't like the atmosphere of the big houses in your own home town—where you felt they weren't quite sure that anything was just right unless it had been copied rigidly from a page in a magazine.

And yet I was never quite happy with their parents. Everything was fine when I was alone with either of the girls, but there'd be a little constriction of ease whenever their parents were around—when Sally would ask me to wheel in the tea-wagon for her mother, and when Mrs. Hindle would give me that quick, inclusive smile as she passed me my cup, or when Anna's father would turn to me after dinner with the proper father-of-daughter talk about how was medical school coming on and did I have the same job lined up for next summer.

You see, I was brought up on a farm. I'd learned most of the answers now. I could talk fairly well about serious things, with observations that had meaning for myself, and I could do a fair job of dovetailing the light remark. I'd learned that intricate little protocol of men about women, introductions, entering a room, restaurants—that stuff—without any rigidity about it. I didn't have any moments of staring at anything strange that was said or done, anymore. But I had learned it, and I still had to watch a little. That's not quite the same.

And if you have been born in the country and have always been poor, there remains always that peculiar—what shall I call it, snug alertness?—in the core of you. No matter how intimate you become with city people who have never been poor, no matter how much you fall into their ways, there are always moments, something they say, some little way they look, when—and the feeling is not subservience or anything the least bit like it—you are struck with a total blindness for everything about them, as if they were creatures from another planet.

The funny part is, I never felt that with Sally or Anna at all.

The funny part is that they never cared about that awkward part, even when I was learning. I don't mean they overlooked it, or ever tried to cover up for me. That's a different thing. I mean they just didn't care. There wasn't a smidgen of the attitude in either of them which you get sometimes among the papier-mache upstarts in a small town.

For instance, I was having dinner at Sally's one night when I was just learning. You didn't begin the meal at the Hindles with the food you were to eat lined up on your plate so there was only the silver to worry about. You started with an empty plate, and built up from a series of covered dishes. Whenever one of those came at me, I sat as tight as if a cobra might strike when the lid was lifted. Except for a flat "yes" or "no" when the rest of them tried to catch me up in the swim of the talk, I was literally dumb with concentration.

There was a brief respite between the main course and the dessert—which would probably turn out to be one of those pastry-and-pudding affairs which they manipulated with a fork and spoon, simultaneously. Sally's sister had broken a small bone in her arch, in a skiing accident, weeks ago. I looked across the table at her and said, right out of a blue sky, "How's your foot?" The remark sort of went "plunk," like a rock dropped into a well.

When Sally and I were alone later that evening, she looked at me with that smile I can't describe—mischievously incredulous, enveloping, and somehow, if I do say so myself, strangely idolatrous. She said, "You said, 'How's your foot?'"

There's no way you can tell it so it doesn't sound as if she were laughing at me. If anyone else had said it, I'd have been angry at one. But I laughed instantly; and the way we laughed together then about me saying to Muriel, "How's your foot?" was about the best way you can laugh together with anyone.

Or take the time at Anna's when I was trying my darndest not to kill the demi-tasse with one gulp. I had begun to take Anna out a good deal, and there was some discussion just now of an overnight trip, with some married friends of hers, to a football game in Montreal.

"But we don't know anything *about* you, Steve," Mrs. Benson said. Jokingly, but with a certain gentle prying, just the same.

"I come of poor but honest parents ..." Anna interrupted, in a stilted Frank Merriwell voice.

That sounds kind of foolish, to tell it, too, and with anyone else it could have been insulting. But when Anna said it, we all laughed, and everything was easy at once. Even the demi-tasse cup seemed to swell into the comfortable proportions of the Clover Leaf china I'd always been used to.

And now do you want to know how the choice between them came about?

They were always asking for stories of my school years. Their interest wasn't curiosity about something "cute." These stories seemed to have an *importance* for them, in a way they had no importance for me, myself; as if these things centred me in a curious kind of light they stood at the edges of and absorbed a funny kind of warmth from.

One night I told Sally about the famous Christmas concert. I told her about Fred's white crepe paper stockings unwinding in the angels' drill and involving us in a tangle worse than the Laocoon; how the carded wool whiskers of the Wise Men twitched so when they sang "Star of the East" that they couldn't finish the last verse for giggling; how in the sketch about the "Titanic," my sister and her cousin sang "Nearer My God to Thee" in the porch outside, with their heads in a pork barrel to make it sound like music over water ...

She laughed that quick, infectious, somehow-commending laugh of hers. "Steve," she said, "I don't believe it!" Of course she *did* believe it. It was just her way of saying that it was incredible, but wonderful, that I had been there.

I told her about the boy who had had no present for the teacher that morning.

Our Christmas present to the teacher was always a handkerchief or a cake of "Baby's Own" toilet soap. But when the other kids called for him that morning, with their presents under their arms—some of them in tissue paper even—he had nothing whatever. He said he wouldn't go.

"How could he?" Sally said.

You would have to understand about his mother too, I told her. His mother would give you the last thing she had. I remember "Moose" Ramsay laughing, long after he grew up, about one day he was there to dinner. He asked for a boiled egg. When she boiled the egg, he wanted a fried egg. When she fried an egg for him, he decided he wanted an egg mixed up in milk. She'd have stood there and broken the last egg in the house. But this morning she had absolutely nothing. She had tears in her eyes.

"Didn't he go?" Sally said.

"Yes," I said, "he went. His mother made one last desperate search of the house and spotted the picture. It was tacked up over one of those victrolas with the morning-glory horn, did you ever see one?" She nodded." I remember it was a colored picture of King Edward, cut off an old calendar. It had a date scribbled on the back, I remember—the date she'd set a hen or something. She took it down and scrubbed the date off clean as anything with a bit of bread crust and wrapped it up in a piece of newspaper and gave him that."

"Aw, bless him," Sally said, "starting off to the teacher with his little cut-off calendar! Steve, how do you ever *remember* all those things? You ought to write stories about them."

I told Anna about the concert too. You told one of them almost exactly the same things you told the other.

I told her about the "Faith, Hope, and Charity" tableau that was made up of the three girls with the longest hair and the yards and yards of white cheese-cloth, doled out afterwards to cover spoon-holders and stuff when the table was left set ... about the recitation of "Poor Little Mike and Bill" which I couldn't bear to rehearse even before my own family, but which seemed to come out smooth as anything when the magic of the kerosene footlights really sent me.

I told her about the boy and the calendar.

"What did the teacher say?" she said.

"She picked it up the very first thing," I said. "Even before the stuff in the tissue paper. She made out she didn't know what it was. Someone snickered, 'It's a calendar' ... but she never let on she heard."

"What did she say?" Anna said. "Steve, can't you remember exactly what she said to him?"

"I remember exactly," I said. "She said, 'Well now, I just bet that's the only picture I got. But it's much too nice to hang up here, isn't it. I'm going to take it home for my own room.'"

"Oh, bless her," Anna said, almost inaudibly, "bless her heart!"

Bless *her*, she said, not him. And she didn't say anything about why didn't I write it up. There was the funniest look on her face.

Anna and I have a son, eight years old. She looks at him sometimes when his gamin face is lit up and the water glistens on his subdued hair at the school closing, but his name will never be called up for any prize because he gets the wildest answers when he multiplies thirteen by three. Or when we come across the wilted thistle—not a bunch of daisies or a sheaf of goldenrod, but a thistle—that he has toted around through the whole day's trip, in a broken preserve jar. It's a little like the look Miss Temple gave me the day I believed, shiningly, that my cut-off calendar *was* the nicest thing she got.

How could I know, beforehand, that if Anna and I were married we'd have a son like that, and that it would be more wonderful than with any other three people in the world (though David, of course, hasn't any idea why), just because he isn't good in arithmetic? I catch her looking at me like that sometimes, if I say something not quite funny enough to make them laugh, when I'm tired. She looks like that when *anyone* acts as if she might have been expecting to be brought something. How could I know, way back then, that a little thing like that could make all the difference?

As I say, it's silly to think there's a single perfect woman for every man. Just because in this one case ... And maybe Sally's. Sally is married too. What the tiny little differential that makes all the difference is, in her man, I don't know. But they seem to be as happy as we are.

A Million Things to Tell

Thanks for Listening

They're all telling about the war now, but no one will mention me. No one ever guessed that any of those faces was mine.

I'm small for twenty, and quiet; and always there I had the way they had when they walked along the streets in their uniforms together, with the danger they didn't think about running into their faces like an extra sort of health. So perhaps that's why they never recognized me.

Do you remember the picture of the kid giving his cigarettes to the men off the raft? That was me, and that was one of the really good times. And the one running up the beach at Iwo? You could only see the back of my head in that one and my mouth was misshapen and dry with fear, but it was me all right. And the one where the actress talked to me in the hospital where they had taken off my leg and I smiled and forgot because she was kind and soft like any other woman, this one was really kind, and there had been no woman's face for a long time...? I was in the ones they took at Tripoli and Falaise and in the North Sea too, but perhaps they didn't recognize me in some of them, because the flesh looks different when the blood is on the outside. And sometimes they didn't recognize me maybe, because there was that look on my face that comes from seeing too much broken flesh, you know. The actors can't quite get that look.

But they don't believe I know what any of that was like. And now it's over, I can't say it clearly enough so that someone will really believe I was there ... do you know what I mean?

If I could tell you exactly how it was going away that first day, would you believe me ... the eyes and the flesh and the thinking trying so des-

161

perately hard in the loud minutes to drain it all, the now and the was
and the will-be of her and me, but knowing that a last little thirst would
always leaven in the heart?

Or do you remember the quiet picture on deck that morning we had
the bread and the wine before the battle? The very-white of the padre's
garments floating a little in the breeze we did not feel and the cross
behind him, bare but firm against the sun on the sea, looked sort of
beautiful, didn't they? Well, that was a true picture, that's the way it was.
We had been cussing before and we would be cussing after, but I think
we were glad it was a thing we had to do together. It was as if we were
all on a little island in the swift current of death and laughter which
was strange to our rough feet but where we knew enough to tread
softly. Are you listening? Will you listen if I try to tell you a few more
things so maybe you will believe?

I don't think you could find any better way to be with the other guys
than the way it is with the face of the sea possessing you like a funny
song you'd never think of singing out loud. And the land always a fine
place, like the far-off places people think about when they're home,
but when you're there always a little strange for one of you alone.

But please don't think I'm a dreamy guy when I say this. The other
guys didn't think I was. They'd kid me about this stuff all right, but I
could make them laugh too. I wasn't that kind of dope, honest. I remember one night we were talking about what we wanted most when we
came back and I said what I wanted most was the chance to take a quick
pass at that damn chocolate sundae we were all over here fighting for,
and after that I knew I was all right.

There were the girls too. Sometimes there would be two or three of
us sailors and two or three girls, and they were none of your lassies
with the delicate air, we were young and no one was going to keep
anything away from us we felt like; but it was loud like that because it
was the thing we were all alike in and doing together in a land where
one of us would have been alone by himself, and sweethearts, you
shouldn't mind, because it didn't mean the same thing as ours at all. Did
it, Joe?

I know you didn't recognize me the time our ship was struck and I
was the doctor, because I was much older then than I am now. I don't
mean to sound cruel, or phoney in any way ... I'm just trying to tell it
truly ... but that was a sort of splendid night for me. Because I had been
an old man among them, but now their young flesh was broken, and
touching the flesh my hands might heal and feeling it grateful, my own

flesh hurt for the quiet eyes that watched the movements of my hands until my own old flesh too was young again with the pride of its craft, and the guilt in it for being old and whole while the soft whisper of death lay on the faces of the young went away altogether. You won't think I was glad it happened, will you, if I tell you that my humbleness and my pride and the fierce breath of youth again in my flesh that night were like a wild and splendid kind of song.

Maybe I shouldn't tell you about the time I won a battle, because you might think I'm trying to sound brave. And I'm not trying to sound any way at all. I'm just trying to say it truly, so you will believe. I *was* brave that day, though. I was alone but I didn't go back. And afterwards when they gave me the medal I'd make a joke of it with the other guys like it was nothing, but sometimes when I took my tunic off in the dark I'd touch the ribbon, secretly, like the first prize I'd won at school.

You believe I know how it was, don't you, Joe?

There was no picture the morning Joe died. I don't think there was anything a picture would have shown. We were there alone, and it had to come right in that little place ... the same little place his heart took up from the day ... and I saw all the hearing and the seeing and the touching go out of him like a breeze that dies in the air quicker than running, and I saw the strange soft whisper on his face even before his body became only a weight against the deck. And my own breath was like a guilt in me then.

I said, "Joe!", but I knew. And then after I knew quite well I put my arm beneath his shoulder and lifted him up a minute before I called the others, and I said "Joe" again.

And I suppose when I said "Joe" the second time I meant all the bright times we had had together because we were young together in a place where death was jealous of our breaths and the times were stolen, and the first moments of the never-again dark on the day ... I suppose I meant that he was dead, but that somehow I would save his part of the pain and the laughing in the world for him always, fiercely somewhere, where it could not be lost ...

When the others write the history of the war they'll say we were fighting for this thing or that, but none of the words for them will be a guy's name. But I think I was fighting for Joe. I think we were all fighting for the guy next us. I think the way it could be when I spoke his name the second time that day was the nerve of my fighting, and the way it could be, remembering, after they let him over the side that bright morning into the sea the muscle of it. But perhaps I mean those words after all. Maybe the way it is when you are in the laughing and the fearing and the suffering and the sharing of a thing like that with the guy next you, fighting for the way he feels fighting the same way for you, maybe that *is* for Freedom and Justice, maybe that *is* for America ...

I remember the morning it came to me. I had more time than Joe, and there had been pain and there was no pain at all now, but I knew. You can tell when you're young and you've never heard the sound the minutes make before, louder than the guns. But Joe was such a good guy to have with you then there was hardly any thinking at all.

For Joe had done all the things, even the ones you'd missed, he had been in all the places where the going was tough and the going was tired and the going was gay like the sound of the dance music and the laughing when the door to the room opened for a minute before you were quite there, and he had been in this one too so that it could not be a strange place for the young. And so there was no evening part to it and you didn't think of the springs that would come again, for someone else. Because it was the first time you'd ever seen him quiet like that and you knew it was the same way with him then that it was with you that other day. And in a minute like that when the meaning of brother is first clear and the way one can keep for him the things that would have been another's, the meaning of all the other things is clear too, so that time denied does not make an ache in you even if you're young, or any crying at all.

And somehow the springs were safe again, and surely there'd be another time for you both when breath would not be grudging in the air and you would still be young, with the drink light in you and the sharp-soft thought of the girls and the door of the room would open and let the dance music come out to meet you.

You won't be jealous, wife and sweetheart, will you, that it's these guys I wanted to be with again those other springs. Because I thought of you too, and I knew it was you who must keep the soft summer part for me. I knew that Joe would keep all the bright way it could be with the guys, and that you would keep all the sharp-soft way it could be with a girl, and that's why the day did not seem dark or too soon. That's why I didn't cry.

The only time I cried was the day it came to me and there had never been a girl at all. I cried a little that day, even after I was dead.

And now I should tell you about the way it is to come back. But I can't. Although it isn't because I died that I can't tell you that.

I can't tell you about coming back, you see, because I was twenty and they were twenty and they went marching by my window, all the Joes, and I have never walked in my life. That's why I was in all the pictures, in every one of them. That's why I wanted you to listen, that's why I wanted you to believe. Do you understand that?

Do you understand what it's like when you've been there and it's over but they won't believe you, so you can forget like the others, so you can come back?

Glance in the Mirror

He was right on the verge of capturing it exactly, just before she came into the study. And that was wonderful.

They thought that writing was always wonderful, but most of the time it was the loneliest job in the world. That crippling stillness when you sat down to try the first few lines. As if everything you looked at was tensed for you to make a sound and you were tongue-tied, like someone in a nightmare. If that lasted long enough you would sit there then and hear the sound of your own life going by. A lifetime is not forever, and yours was already half gone. You would think of all the other times you'd sat here alone, while the rest were building something tangible. Together. Really together with the real thing, not this shadow of it. The laughing and the touching and the joining with the same thoughts .... It wasn't wonderful then.

Then maybe it would begin to come. In a gathering rush. Like the coursing of blood through a vein again after thumb pressure has been relaxed. You could seem to hear the voices of everything, all at once. You would have words for the touch of flesh, and words for the way of two people who were really together, and words for the wordlessness in the mouths of people who had never had anyone, and words for all the incommunicable shadows on the heart that the face hid—the morning ones of love and hope and being young, and the still afternoon ones of failure and of someone gone away and of growing old .... And time itself could be caught and said.

And *then* you'd sit there and feel what it's like when a man first knows that he's done only bits of the thing that it was meant for him to do wholly. And again just one word would pulse in your brain: alone ... alone ... alone ....

But it could be wonderful. Like now. The day when there would be a single thing to fasten on. A thing that had been cloudy and coreless inside you, like an ache; but you hadn't given up, and now you read the words, there it was, almost exactly in the shape you could see it must have, and *outside* you.

Then it would seem that you could possess anything whatever, by telling it. That nothing would be intolerable if you could find words for it. Time was not a fear any more and loneliness was beaten. Then you were free like no one else. You wouldn't exchange places with anyone.

He was reading over what he had written, when she opened the door.

Her name was Anna. And they were really together. That is possible. It doesn't happen with everyone, and to those who have never known it, time makes a steady sound like a far-off bell. But it happened with them. And they knew it. And it was wonderful. It was an over-all thing like the quiet song of health or the subtle mending of sleep ... to have your voice come back to you, not in its own thin echo, but with the edges gone as if with the smoothing and softening of fire-light, because another had heard it exactly.

Her name was Anna, and it meant a face ... and the inimitable safety. The great sweet wonderful safety from the cry of things not understood, and things said and things not said, and things done and things not done, and the sound of time and the sound of time gone by ....

She came in, and he saw her glance at the mirror, instinctively, before she spoke. She took off her hat and ran her fingers through her curly, close-cropped, wheat-coloured hair. He caught the clean fragrance coming from it, like a breath.

Then she came over and sat down in the chair next his desk and lit a cigarette, frowning a little at the first inhalation of smoke. Then she smiled at him, a long settled smile, as if she were all ready to talk.

Her name was not Anna. Her name was Sheila, and she was his wife.

He felt everything leave him, the instant she came into the room. He turned the sheet back on the roller, faking a correction.

"How's it going, darling?" she said.

"Terrible."

"Oh, you always say that." She laughed. "You're so serious about it, Jeff. You know it really isn't a matter of life and death, darling ...."

I don't suppose it is, he thought ... to anyone else. I don't suppose I should expect her to understand that.

"Let me see it," she said. "I'll bet it's wonderful."

"It's terrible," he said.

He took the paper out of the typewriter and tore it lengthwise and crosswise very thoroughly and dropped it into the waste basket.

"Jeff," she said, "I think you're mean. You never let me see anything you write lately. Why do you have to be so darn secret about it? Honestly, you'd think it was something I'd *caught* you at."

It's funny, he thought, the way she can hit it right on the head like that sometimes.

He didn't speak, and she said, "Jeff, could the reason be that you don't love me?"

Oh no, he thought, it's nothing as simple as that. Just the hint of a wry smile twitched his lips: and I suppose some people believe that I married her for her money ... that it's as simple as *that*. He shook his head.

"I love you all right," he said.

"And I love you too, darling, believe me," she said eagerly. "That's why I wish you'd let me help you."

"Okay," he said. "Go ahead. Help me."

"Well," she said, "not so much with the writing, maybe .... But to tell the truth, darling, I don't think you ought to be writing at all. You should be doing something else. You sweat and fuss and get all steamed up and it's got to be *just* so." She laughed tolerantly, but incredulously. "And what *difference* does it make? You're wasting your whole life puttering around with a few old words, and what difference do they make?"

That's nice, he thought, that's very nice, to hear someone else say that.

"What else could I do?" he said. "I'm not a kid any more."

"Oh, there are lots of things to do. For instance, if you'd just be sensible about this money business, Jeff—I don't understand you ... if you'd just let me give you a *start* in something, some business or something ...."

He didn't say anything.

"First," she said, as if it were already settled, "we'll take a nice long trip and get this old stuff right out of your head. We'll go to Gaspé and Banff and the Cabot Trail and oh I don't know where, and get all those stuffy old words right out of your head. Like the sound of that? Eh?"

"I don't think so," he said. "I'm sorry."

"It's because I said it would be my treat, isn't it? Jeff, you're so darn silly ...."

"But you just said you bet what I was writing was wonderful. You say everything I write is wonderful."

"Of course it's wonderful, silly." She said it quite sincerely, with no consciousness of self-contradiction whatever. "I just meant ...."

"Maybe you meant it didn't bring in much cash."

"I didn't mean that at all. You're so darn silly about money. I mean, it doesn't bring in much money, really, does it ... but I certainly don't worry about that. It isn't as if I had to depend on .... I'm sorry, darling," she interrupted herself, "I didn't really mean it like that."

"That's all right," he said.

What is it, he thought, this business of loving someone that particular way? They say it isn't love at all. But it is. It's not the flesh, wholly. The little shock whenever our hands touch even now, some of it is that perhaps, but not all of it.

What is this business of the flesh, anyway? She's not really beautiful. I can understand why another man might not find her so, and yet with what part of me would I find such blindness on his part incredible? What is this business of the single face? There are women who resemble her almost exactly. You'd think the feeling for them would be almost exactly the same as the feeling for her. But it isn't. It's so different it's a different *kind* of thing.

Why *is* it that I can forget her when I'm alone, but that the instant she comes into the room she brings the love and the destruction both?

And then suddenly he felt the warmth creeping back. If I could just get that outside me, he thought ....

She glanced at her watch. "Heavens!" she exclaimed, "I didn't know it was so late ... the time goes so quickly when I'm with you, darling, aren't you flattered?... I told Helen I'd pick her up at five and we'd look in on that art show at the Museum, although Lord knows I might as well try to read a page of Gaelic ....Would you like to come?"

"No, thanks," he said.

He put a fresh sheet of paper into the typewriter and wrote the title, THE SUMMER'S GONE.

"Have you got something?" she said.

"I think so."

"Good," she said. "Good luck with it." She picked up her hat and went over to the mirror. "And darling," she added lightly, as if it might have been the weather they'd been discussing before, "you don't mind anything I said, *do* you. I didn't mean to discourage you, or anything, you know that. If you want to go on trying I think that's wonderful. It's just wonderful."

He was writing quickly.

She had close-cropped hair, soft as a kitten's, and her skin was soft and smelled nice because she had always been rich and had never had any of the thoughts so sharp they gouge the skin a little too. The always having of money was in her, integrally, like a feature. Her face was fine, and it gave him that wonderful feeling which nothing but another face can, if it's the right one, and he loved her, but they were never really together.

She didn't know the way of any kind of silence. Silences were something she ran away from. The long safe silence of being together with someone was something she didn't know at all.

He realized that, but it didn't help anything. He didn't blame her. It was no one's fault. But she was destroying him. A writer is alone. A watcher is always alone. Yet if he has someone to be alone with, then his voice is sure and strong with the speaking which only the voices of the lonely can ever know.

But they were not together at all. She could destroy his voice, without knowing it, because she couldn't enter into any of the things that were his. He would feel a sort of shame he couldn't help for any part of his own way which was different from hers, and a deeper shame for the shame itself. If you build bridges, and a thing like that happens, you can go on building good bridges in spite of it. But if you are a writer ….

She was still in front of the mirror.

"Why, darling," she said, "listen to you. You're going like a house on fire. May I read it before I go? Please … just this once?"

Okay, he thought defiantly, go ahead, look in this mirror for a change. Just this minute he felt that wonderful free feeling again.

She took the sheet from him and began to read.

"Darling,"—she laughed suddenly—"her hair's like mine." She glanced in the mirror. "I'll bet you were thinking of *my* hair. I think you're sweet."

She put the paper down after a few more sentences, and lit a cigarette. Then she picked the paper up again and read it through quickly. She passed it back to him.

He looked at her, penitent already. Hoping there would be anger, and not hurt, on her face. But there was neither. Just a puzzled look and a mild amusement.

"It's wonderful, darling," she said. "I think it's wonderful. But why do you always have to make them so *grim*?" She laughed again. "Why don't you ever write one about you and me?"

Another Christmas

Christmas comes to the city too, in a way .... The air is clean and cold that day and in the streets the faces come alive and sometimes childlike, and people smile at strangers. This one day there is the strange warmth and excitement and kindness abroad, and when the dusk of Christmas Eve falls on the busy streets, for the first time the great green trees with all their artificial lights look happy. When the dark falls, the trees lighted behind the windows seem almost as kind as lamplights, and even the shopping crowds feel the strange stir in their hearts as if something incredibly thrilling were about to happen....

ᶻ👄

Inside the apartment, Eve in her cool sure way had everything bright and in order. The other lights were carefully subordinated to the glimmer of the tree which stood in one corner with a few exotically wrapped packages of assorted sizes piled beneath it. The table glowed properly with simple crystal and silver and a single English holly centrepiece. The wine bottles each had a great bow of red ribbon. Eve herself with her easy silver way and luminous skin moved among the guests, listening, talking, and laughing with her pale bright laugh, like beads falling. They often wondered why Steve never wrote about women like his wife. He always wrote about the simple girls he had known as a child in the country.

This party Eve had arranged specially for him because it was an occasion. His first book was just out, and even the most chronically churlish reviewers had used no adjective smaller than "great." It ought to be the best Christmas Steve had ever had.

ᶻ👄

"Merry Christmas!" "Merry Christmas!" they were all shouting ... the women with their quick eyes and nervous bodies and the men who could hold a glass in that casual way Steve had never quite mastered; and laughing with them, with the wine lifting vaguely inside him, it felt like Christmas all right, the real thing, he thought. The bright things they said seemed very funny, with the wine, and he liked these people.

"My dear, you should *see* the strange package I found tucked away in Toby's closet. It must be for me and I'm simply frantic about it. It all goes up to a peak, but he *swears* it isn't a metronome ...."

"No thanks, Eve, I'm sticking to scotch tonight. The other seems to upset my metabolism or something ...."

"Good King Wenceslas ... how about a chorus of Good King Wenceslas?... I like the part where it goes Stee-*eee*-ven. What do you know, it *is* the feast of Steven, isn't it! Eh, Steve?"

"We ran into Anne's on the way over and she had the most adorable little aspic ... all reindeers and things, even to the antlers ..."

"That's damn good stuff, Steve ...."

"We should have Jackie here ... he knows the most *salacious* little parody on 'The Night Before Christmas'. Have you heard Jackie ...."

"Why don't we call him? He'd be at Ginny's."

"But Ginny is *especially* dull on Christmas Eve, don't you think ...."

And of course in one corner, very seriously, over cigarettes:

"I suppose what Shaw really meant, if he meant anything at all ...."

"But really his *nudes* are appalling ... they're all so sort of utilitarian, if you see what I mean ...."

"Why don't *we* attack for once, down through ...."

And then they were talking about Steve's book.

"It's uncanny, Steve, the way you seem to see right through people. It makes me definitely uneasy ...."

"Nice going, old man, *damn* nice going."

"That part about the little country girl ... what's her name, Ellen or something?... that's *really* cute, Stevie ...."

Cute!

"But how do you keep from turning handsprings, Steve? To be able to write like that ... good Lord, it must be so damned *wonderful* ...."

"Lucky beggar, you! Only having to work when you *feel* like it ...."

So it's wonderful to write, he thought. So it's such an easy job. Well, you don't know how white paper can be. You don't know what it is like in the ghost-world of words.

8.

At first it had been a great new space to walk into and wonder, it was exciting to be another-time-and-space builder yourself, and you had a pity for the others with only one narrow life to live, their own, as it was. But then the real thing got less and less, because you were always watching it, it was only something to tell. And the first day you tried to tell a thing that had happened, truly, and the right-feeling words would not come, the ones that had a move and a speaking in them, the ones that brought the thing outside you, clearer and shapelier than you had ever thought you knew it ... the first day those would not come at all but only the springless bones-of-words, and you sat there feeling the white-tight silence of the very doors and everyone else, seemed to be busy with something alive, the real thing, and you thought surely in a little while, but you had to get up finally and leave it, you couldn't get your hands on it at all ... they could not even *guess* what that sort of emptiness was like. And the other times when you did get something truly, then your mind was feverish and swarming with everything there was, to tell. If you walked in the woods then, there was the untold story in the way every single fir-tree was, to tantalize you, the small ones and the large ones and the straight ones and the one that leaned lonesome against the horizon all through the dark secret night ... there were not only the big things then, the never-to-be-fathomed stuff of space and time, the human heart, the way the face is, the great gossamer-drifting mists of thought, but all the little things too ... the pebble and the snail's eye and the sleepy cat-thoughts and the worm's track you never saw and the billionth blade of grass. There was more in any *one* of these little things than you could ever tell in your whole lifetime ... there was more in the way the wagon-wheels stood there, lonely in the snow, that grey-blustery winter afternoon than you could even suggest. When you came out at dusk with your gun and stood there on the cold hill at the edge of the woods and there were the lonely wagon-wheels with the snow sifting through the spokes, and the dead apple-tree limbs, and you felt that nice lonely feeling about the whole world when it is dusk in the wintertime, and it was quiet, then, like death, when the dying is over and only the stillness is left ... you couldn't tell that because there were a million things in it to tell, and a million ways to tell every one of them, and only one way for each of them was right. And you tried desperately to find a single light that would come suddenly so that everything would fall into place as if you were looking at a picture that was only broken lines at first but as you looked at it, steadily, suddenly all the broken lines flowed into a single image, and the separate lines were gone and everything was part of the same thing.

But you never found that single light ... that single plan. No one ever did. So how could the little separate part you had told matter at all?

And then they were all gone and he and Eve were alone.

"Shall we open them tonight?" Eve said.

"Why, yes, I think we might as well." He laughed. "I remembered one time when we were children we opened them on Christmas Eve, and then cried afterwards because we hadn't saved them for morning."

Eve's present for him was a brand new typewriter. She waited for him to exclaim.

"Don't you *like* it, darling?" she said.

"Of course!" he said. "It's a beauty. But really, Eve, the old one .... "

"But that one's *so* old, Stevie. You must have had it ever since you started."

It would be a little hard to explain to Eve, he thought, how he felt about the old typewriter.

The clock struck twelve.

"Merry Christmas!" Eve smiled at him.

"Merry Christmas, darling," he said softly, kissing her.

They were silent.

"What are you thinking about?" Eve said. "That's the trouble with you, Stevie, I never know what you're *thinking* about."

❧

He was thinking about the Christmas he got the new skates.

He had gone with his father the afternoon before for the Christmas tree, and he had wondered how his father could be so calm. He knew *he* could never get calm about Christmas, no matter how old he got to be. The snow he prayed for had come and it lay smooth over everything except where the rabbits had made their odd snowshoe tracks across it, and it sparkled in the sun. Strange lips of it hung over the middle of the brook where he could still see the water running under holes in the shell ice. He made rabbit tracks of his own with the end of his mitten, the long-foot ones and the small dot with the thumb where both hind feet came down together. How good his father seemed. How good everyone he thought of seemed that afternoon. That night, when the lamp was lit and the fascinating smell of oranges was through the house and his mother busy with all sorts of mysterious things, he would sneak off now and then into the room where the tree was, and put his nose as close as he could to the little blisters of balsam and the places where the bark was skinned away to the glistening trunk beneath. The smell of the fir and the oranges was like a wine in his senses. Later, in bed, he could hear his mother and father laughing and making strange rustling noises behind the closed kitchen door, and he swam further and further and further off to sleep in an almost intolerably delicious excitement.

And there they were, next morning, the first thing he saw. Gleaming and clean like speed itself. And screwed right into the boots! That was the wonderful part. He was afraid they might be spring skates but these ones were screwed right onto the boots like the big boys' skates were.

He took them down to the meadow that afternoon all by himself. And that was the day ... he could remember the very time it was in the afternoon, with the dark spruces just beginning to creep closer around the blue meadow-ice ... that it came to him how to cross your skate over when you turned a corner. So you got the long clean sweep the bigger boys had when they were so sure of it they could do it faster, or slower, or clown it, or do it any way at all it was so sure with them. Once before on the old spring skates he'd almost got it, but the next time he tried, it was jerky, and after that if anyone was looking he wouldn't try to cross over at all, he'd just coast around and bend down to make out he was tightening his bootlace. But that afternoon ... Lord, it was lovely that afternoon, he thought, with the new skates and half remembering all the time that the Christmas tree and the oranges would still be there when he got home ... that time he had done it and he didn't know, in his head, just how, but he knew it was right, that now his legs knew it, to repeat it, whenever they liked. Now he was sure of it. And that first time you crossed over on the new skates and felt the cool wing-sure dip of it and knew that now you had it, really had it ....

"What *are* you thinking about, Steve?" Eve said.

"I was just thinking about one Christmas I got new skates."

"And," Eve laughed, "I suppose you're going to tell me that pair of skates made Christmas more fun than a best-seller! Stevie darling, you're getting sentimental in your old age."

"It's just possible," he said.

No Matter Who's There

He went to the mirror and looked at his face. It was like a drawing of a face, without the one right line that would put life into it. That's the way you felt, he thought. It was as if the current had been cut. You pressed the button the same as the rest, but the light did not come on.

He was trying to think when it had started to be like that. The little white core of emptiness in everything he turned to had never been there when he was a child in the hills. That seemed a long time ago, a different time ago.

Just the day was enough, then, he thought ... just the day filled you up. You didn't notice the sun or the sky or look at your own face or feel that time was fast, or slow, but everything in the day was *enough*, everything was as much as possible. And when night came, there was the sweet river of sleep to dissolve into, immediately, deliciously, completely. If he could just go to sleep once again like that. Just once again not to hang onto the tired things even in his dreaming. But everything was enough, then, because you had not broken off from the day that ran through you, into your private bit and the awareness of it.

It was still enough, he thought, that early-cool May morning when you were ten to wake up all at once, after no dreaming, with the blood running happy in your body beneath the sleep-warm sheets, and remember with a quick bounding that the day was here, this was the day, right now the day that your father was going to take you back fishing and stay all night in the woods for the first time. There would be little patches of snow, still, under the big trees, and you would feel the cool breath of it as you walked along, but when you sat on the big rock and looked at your line so steadily in the rock-slapping current of the brook that you seemed after a while to be floating along with it, the sun would come out on the back of your shirt and you would be warm and quiet and pulse-happy all through. Then when the trout would take the hook and the sudden shock of it would come along the tighter than current-tight line now and right up through the pole into your arms, and then the great, taut-swerving surge and you held him at last in your hand with his neck broken and a little shiver running through his smooth body and his gills opening suddenly but closing very faintly, now ... that was enough.

And it was enough, later, when the whole night was cool like it had been, on the way back, only under the big trees where the cool-breathing snow was, to come to the camp and find the dry wood his father could always find and build the brisk-talking fire and feel the food and the tea and the heat warming and filling up all the empty and tired spots inside you until the fishing seemed a little far off now, as if it had been another part of you that had done that. You were glad it was over now, this now was the best. You would have felt afraid when the woods first got strange with the dark, and like crying, if you had been alone. But with your father there and it dark and quiet and warm in the camp and this the first night you had ever slept in the woods, there had never been anything like it. And you knew it would *always* be as good as this first time ... because you were sure you could always make it the very same.

Well, it wasn't as good the next time, not quite as good. Things never were as good the next time, that was just something you came to learn. But there was always something *else* to do then ... still the first time for so many other things.

ख

There was that cold day when the ice showed blue and heartless and the mourning wind scooped out the tight drifts in a long scythe-shaped curve. The men broke out the roads, bending to the wind with their mittens held over their ears, but before the frost-whiskered oxen had passed from sight their tracks were covered again with the vicious snow. The bite of the cold went clear down to your lungs, and when the cows went to drink they shied their heads down into the biting wind and tested the water carefully with their teeth before they gathered up a mouthful of it and swallowed it down their long throats in a great ball. Coming back from the barn you had to walk back-to, to hold your breath at all ... and sometimes when you looked out again you couldn't see the barn for a sudden bluster of snow. Little corners of snow piled up outside on the sashes of the window, and you could make circles on the inside of the frost-needled pane with your breath. But when the quick dark fell and the water was in and the box was full of wood and everyone was settled for the night and eating supper in the oil lamp-light with the table drawn a little closer to the fire, you felt all over you the snug little warm-swollen feel of your blood, swimming with the heat again after being out in the biting cold. And when the dishes were cleared away, the wind was still howling out there in the dark and fans of the blown snow would slap suddenly against the frosted pane like a broom, and when you held up your hands to your face and looked through the breath-holes in the pane, it looked cold and hard and mournful outside. But around the fire again where you all sat close and you knew none of you would have to go outdoors anymore that night, you felt the snug-swollen feel in your blood again, and there seemed to be something very exciting holding you all there together, with the roads blocked and the storm at the pane, but the lamplight and the wood-warmth and the slow-cosy talk melting you all together. You all sat up late to keep the fires. And it was enough, then, just to be staying up late that cold night with the storm outside but the chairs and the table drawn up close to the fire and mother making a lunch and this the latest you had ever stayed up in your whole life.

ֶ֊

When I was fourteen, he thought, trying to follow along to the place where he had got off the course, it was different altogether. When you were a child, the best things were really inside. You had your own secret fun in a private way no one ever suspected, and that's what made it so special and important. But it would have been lonesome now, if you had kept on the childish way, no matter how good the things were you had to yourself. What made it exciting now, was to have a secret with somebody else ... those warm, swelling, day-lasting, thrilling-to-be-suddenly-remembered secrets with somebody else. When you did a little thing when you were fourteen, he thought, so it would be good to have it with your friends, it was better than to do the big things now. Because now when you got the thing done, all the friends you had done it for, that it would be the best part of it to tell it to, had died, or gone away, or changed, they had almost all changed when you came to tell them; and to yourself, now it was done, it was done, and meant nothing. If he could just have it again now like it was then ... those few body-fresh, warm-wise, never-to-be-doubted planning, wonder-chocking years. For then you knew for sure that you could be the best of anything you wanted to be. He remembered the first good violin music he ever heard ... how good it was to know all of a sudden in bed that night, that that's what he'd be, the best violin-player in the whole world. He remembered the day the teacher herself couldn't get that tricky problem about the sphere. It was three grades ahead of him, but he had worked at it secretly and quietly and quickly, praying that he could just get it before someone else, and when he was ready to divide his final quotient he saw that the number he'd have to divide with was the same queer number, 23 or something, that was on the bottom of the answer in the book, and then he knew it was coming out right, and the sharp clean thrill went all over him that always came in mathematics when it was hard but you could see it was coming out right. You knew then, with a strong clean thrill, that you'd be the best mathematician in the whole world.

Well, he couldn't be the best of anything now, it was too late … and the first times for things were all over. But, then, there was still the first feel of boy and girl … and when it was new that was the best there was.

You noticed a softness in their hair and the flesh of their legs and the way they walked and in their voices. Something secret and very strange and burstingly soft. When you were with boys and girls together you just clowned, you just had to act silly … but when there were only two of you, you and a girl, you felt awkward with this new secret softness in them, and the softness in girls was like something that had *belonged* to you sometime, that someday you would get back again through touch. When your leg was against one of theirs, touch had a new dimension altogether. And after that, walking home, you felt stronger and bigger and the awkwardness all gone, and all the kids you met seemed so much younger, never to have had this feeling you'd had, that they didn't seem like the same kind of thing you were at all. And sometimes in bed you'd damn near sweat all over just to think about this new, secret, scaring way there was to feel about something … this hot-secret, warm-teasing, moist-swelling way of feeling about something, with just a little seed of emptiness in it, just a little thirst always left … and you'd be damn near scared to death to think what it would be really like to touch a girl anywhere you liked.

ॐ

That was the summer Toby came down from the city. And perhaps, he thought, that's when the emptiness started at first, a little …

The easy-laughing, right-word way of talking Toby had seemed to make the other boys feel awkward and strange, and they had a slow-minded way of being very quiet and watchful with him all the time. But right away, he had felt more at home, older, with Toby, than he did with these boys he had lived his whole life with. The others seemed to feel that Toby was born in the city and that made him a different kind, and they never got over the slow-minded watchfulness. But it was always easy between Toby and him, the way Toby talked seemed to be more his way than the other, and he and Toby could talk without a bit of watchfulness between them. It was very exciting for him to know he had the way that Toby was, himself ... and the others all seemed a little stupid. If I had never had his way, he thought, or some of the way the other boys were, too, I could have been one or the other now ...

Things had seemed empty after Toby went back and you felt a little sheepish when you were alone with the other boys now, as if you had betrayed them ... and it was never quite the same with them again. Not ever. But soon the fullness with Anna came, and from then on the things that were not with Anna did not matter at all.

He had never dreamed of doing it with Anna that first afternoon, that close August afternoon. It was after swimming, and the sun was still lazy and clean in his legs and the soft after-swimming sensuousness was all through him. And in his mind there was a nice not-thinking, like the close-hot way the waiting afternoon had. Then, later, they were sitting at the edge of the pasture, out of sight of the houses, where they had gone when it had got too hot to pick any more berries in the sun. They were sitting there and he started clowning. You had to clown with the girls, and make out you knew all about it ... but he never really thought of doing anything more than talk. It was so hot, he kept wondering how many clothes Anna had on. What if she didn't have anything on under that dress? It almost scared him. If a girl had *two* things on, she seemed so far away from you didn't start wondering at all. But if you thought there was only one, it was more tantalizing than if she was naked.

"It felt good, swimming today," he said, "boy, it felt good to get your clothes off."

He liked to have Anna think of him being undressed. It gave him a nice feeling all over. As if he could be showing himself to her, undressed, without any of the shyness he'd feel if it was the real thing. He wondered if Anna had ever seen a boy undressed. It was funny, the boys wondered about the girls, and the girls wondered about the boys, half the time, and all that covered his body was this shirt and these thin pants, and maybe Anna just had that dress on ... and still they had to keep guessing about each other.

"How far can you swim?" Anna said. She was lying almost flat now, turning her head a little from the sun, and the way the dress moved with her breathing, it didn't look as if she had anything underneath it.

"Half a mile," he lied. He could feel again his bare body in the water, and then later the lazy sun-sensuousness creeping into his naked legs on the bank.

And maybe Anna just had that dress on ... The sun must be warm, through it, he thought. It made him feel a little light-headed and queer to think of Anna's body being warm and moist, like his, beneath that one thing she had on. But he never really thought of doing anything. You'd have to wait till everything was perfectly ready and you'd thought about it for a long time, to do that. You talked about it, though, as if you just hadn't got around to it.

"I wish *I* could swim," Anna said.

"You should have come down today," he said, clowning, "I'd have showed you how."

"Oh now, don't get smart," Anna said, but he knew she wasn't really mad. The girls always made out you better shut right up, but he knew they liked to have you say things like that. They always made out you'd said something terrible, but he knew they told each other all these things you said, afterwards, and giggled, and that it tickled them right through. He wondered how much girls really knew. When you said anything like that they'd come at you to cuff your ears, but he knew it wasn't because they were really mad, it was because they knew you would hold their hands and make them promise they wouldn't do it again, and all the time they'd wriggle up against you, making out they were trying to get away. And they wouldn't give in for a long while, just so they could feel you holding them and wrestling with them and touching them in different places, as long as possible. It was pretty good for you, too ... Maybe Anna just had that dress on. He felt the slight-swelling sun-sensuousness all over him now.

"I didn't say anything!" he said, mock-serious.

"You did *so*," Anna said, snippy. She sat up and threw the hair back from her face, trying to look mad. He just felt nice, warm and horny and nice, making Anna thinking about him undressed, and making her think he'd do anything. He knew he was only talking, but it gave him a nice feeling.

"I just said if you'd come down I'd show you ... a few things. About swimming..." he teased.

"Oh, you shut up!" Anna said.

She got up and broke off a bush and struck at him. He got up too, and pressed the hand with the bush in it behind her back. He had to hold her close, and they stood there straining against each other, first struggling and then quiet and then struggling again, Anna still trying to look mad, and his own eyes brighter for the feel of her body with just the dress on, he was sure that's all there was, now. Every minute or so Anna would move a little, suddenly, to surprise him, but he always had her tight, and then they would be quiet again, but always tight against each other so that she could not get the stick free.

Then he started to wish that Anna would stop fighting altogether so he could let her go, because every time he touched her now the little moist-swelling itch was growing greater ... he wished she would stop fighting, because if she didn't he couldn't stand it any longer. He wanted to get back to just talking, before this feeling got so much stronger than you were that you couldn't put it away and forget it. He was tense and quiet now, and scared, because the minute would pass without bursting but then it would come again and you couldn't help going along with it.

Anna made another sudden movement and as they wrestled, they fell. Anna dropped the switch and he let her hand go ... but she didn't make any move to get up ... and suddenly, without any planning ahead that this would be the time for it, at all, he had to do it ... because the strange compulsion of touch swam through him so swelling and tickling and reaching and strong, so much stronger and faster than thinking, now, that he just had to do it, without thinking at all ... and the still-hot afternoon stopped dead.

Surely it was more than enough then, the first time with Anna. It was so much more than you had known anything could be ... this sweet-creeping, hollow-tickling, flesh-flooding, exquisite and more-exquisite and more-exquisite and more-inundating-exquisite dismemberment. And then the soft, faint, softer-fainter-echoing ... until you saw that the trees were still there but that nothing would ever be the same as it used to be, and this girl was a new thing altogether in the world for you.

Carrying Anna's kettle on the way home, he had felt the first kind, owning feel of man for woman ... and that was enough. There was the new tear-soft feeling for every movement she made, every sound of her voice ... the new, fierce-defensive love for every part of her. All the empty child patterns of fun that had been enough before that afternoon were completely gone. And the funny part of it, he never once thought of bragging about it to the other boys as he had always planned to do when it came. He was proud of it, but it wasn't that kind of proud, now, at all.

It was always that good with Anna. It was only with Anna, he thought, that the next time of anything had ever been as good. In between, maybe the seed of emptiness would grow, but it never got really bad, because the minute he touched Anna again the current would come on.

ě●

It had never been that way with Claire ... not once.

There was a little fear of Claire, he thought, even before he married her, a little kernel of country-fear ... but she had had the deep black eyes in the cool health-pale face with just the faintest brush-stroke of pink-luminous blood beneath the full skin, and she had had the same easy way as her perfect-fitting skin in her words and her laughing and her clothes and everything she did — the easy city-way that Toby had. But Claire had always been a stranger. He had learned all the things she stood for, so well he could write about them ... but he had learned them, and no matter how much he came to despise them now that he could do them himself and find out their emptiness, he would always feel that unsureness before them, that little fear before their strangeness, because he had not had them always. He would feel with Claire like a simple man who hates it where the talking is smooth but covers up his large hands, a little ashamed of them in spite of himself.

So with Claire the current had never come on at all like it had with Anna. Although the things she had brought him had seemed so good at first, like the way it had first been with Toby was. The well-coolness of her, her round silver kiss, or the new way she had taught him to know lateness at night ... their way of breaking up the darkness everywhere with a light and gathering in these bright hard places of light to talk and laugh very fast and easy and close into someone else's face. It was good sometimes when you were working and they would come in on you, suddenly, to include you in something ... a drink or a joke or something. It was good to hear them coming before they opened the door, their chatter with always the one not-really-laughing woman's laugh like glass breaking, and then bringing in with them the small fever of their being together and darting through each other and saying nimble things, and the women with their eager snake-bright eyes and shining teeth wearing the expensive wraps thrown back lightly from their nervous bodies as if they were nothing and talking a lot of jangling half-sentences out of their night-creamed, faint-smelling faces, and one of them kissing you lightly and beginning, restively, like her quick eyes, "My God, listen, Dave darling ..." and you knew you were one of them.

With Claire he had come to know that delicious colding of the blood when the footlights begin to die and all the pleasant sound patterns people have made with catgut or brass or their own breath and all the pretty little shapes you could make out of just talking and laughing ... things like that. But these things were not like the first time he had gone fishing with his father when the breath of the snow was cool under the big trees and the big trees whispered together their lonesome not-man-talk outside the camp in the dark. And now there was this emptiness.

Now, he thought, there is this emptiness in me even while the people are laughing, even behind the warm wine-screen, ticking empty like the stillness of a clock ticking ... because there is a pale spot that the blood never runs through rich and warm. And the rest of you goes on doing the same things and no one notices anything but a tired look, but it is like the walking of a man after his legs lift themselves with no further direction from the mind, like the eating of a man after he has come home to supper and they tell him his wife is dead, the laughing of a man who finds he is waving long after the one on the ship that will be sunk can see him any longer. Once you stop to watch that spot inside you the rest of you goes on, but the pale beat of it is in your heart and the dead-white of it holds your eyes always. And the things of every day drain through you like a sieve and leave nothing. And that is the whitest emptiness there is.

So now, he thought, is there nothing left to drown the white ache of this sick spot inside me? To make it like it was when I was a child, that different time ago. Like it was with Anna. With Anna, he thought, there had been the emptiness, the always-reaching in between, but as soon as he touched her again the current would come on and the separateness would go. There is Anna, he thought, suddenly. That might be possible. My God, that would be possible. Still. There could be Anna again, to drown it. It was so simple and relief-full he felt the sudden smart of tears that come when all at once everything seems clear and generous and warm about a choice you've always wanted to make without knowing it. He had always belonged with Anna and that part of him. He had been wrong about Toby and Claire and the things that were with them now. It would be so simple, really, he thought, because Claire was so civilized. She was just the sort of woman who would make a thing like this least awkward. He felt a sudden rush of kindness towards Claire.

"Claire," he said immediately she came in, "you remember me telling you about Anna, the first girl I ever loved?" He wanted to get it over as soon as possible, not because he found telling Claire unpleasant, but because he had wasted half a lifetime already, and a lifetime seemed so short now and so precious, now that he had found a sure way in it.

"Yes, darling," Claire said, not very seriously. She scrutinized her blood-red nails as she crushed out an almost fresh cigarette. The cigarette looked like a bleeding worm, he thought, with the bright lipstick on it. "I was very jealous for a couple of days. You know, I always felt a little lost with that part of you. I didn't have anything to *compete* with Anna for that part of you. I did get a print dress, though ... do you remember that little print, Dave darling ... Toby said I looked like a milking sequence with Carole Lombard ..."

Claire laughed her quick immaculate laugh, and David felt a little of his mood go. He felt tempted to say some bright easy thing to make Claire laugh again and see in her eyes the flash of constant surprise and satisfaction that this boy from the country could be so much more accurately amusing, in the glib way she liked, than the rest of her friends.

"Claire," he said, "I've been thinking it over ... and over ... and over, today. I want to go back to Anna."

"Anna?" Claire said, laughing. "But you're not serious, Dave."

"Yes, I am serious," he said.

She looked at him. "I believe you *are* serious, Dave," she said. "Yes, I can *see* you are serious, now."

"You don't mind, do you?" he said. "You wouldn't mind?"

"But of course I wouldn't mind, Dave, if you mean it."

"But why shouldn't I mean it? It's quite fantastic, I know ... but it's quite natural to be fantastic, really. When we're sensible it's only because we're afraid."

Claire lit another cigarette. "Don't you love me?" she said. "Love" was an important word for Claire but a practical one, and she never spoke it with any special accent.

"I suppose so," he said. "Part of me, anyway, loves ... part of you."

"I never thought it was all of you I had, Dave," she said. "But I always thought my part of you was at least half. I always thought it was something more than half. But maybe you're right."

I've *got* to be right, he thought. But how white her skin is and it might be hard to forget. It might be very hard to forget your wife, he thought uncertainly. A little of the sureness was gone.

"Well," Claire said, "it sounds awfully quaint to me, darling, but if you want to try it ... why of course I'd be most understanding, as they put it."

Try it? That wasn't the idea at all. If you weren't so *sure* of it, it would just be wild. If you weren't sure, it wouldn't be … well, it would be impossible.

"I don't belong here, Claire," he said. "You know that."

"Are you quite sure you belong *there*?" Claire said. She reached over and turned on the radio, regulating the volume softly. "It's four o'clock, dear… the Philharmonic … Sibelius, this afternoon, and that new man…"

Claire was following the music intently. It was his favourite music too, and listening there with Claire, Anna did not seem very real.

"Are you quite sure you belong there, Dave?" Claire said again after the part they both liked best was over.

"Yes, I am sure," he said. Damn you, Claire. Damn your white flesh, I'm not sure at all now.

"Well, I just wanted to be certain of that … for *you*. You'd have to be *very* sure of a thing like that, wouldn't you."

"Yes, you'd have to be sure." If you weren't sure, absolutely sure, it would just be wild. Nothing could be worse.

"Well," Claire said, "do as you really wish, darling. But half of you will always be mine, I know that."

Oh damn you, Claire, you're right … you and your white skin and your eager eyes and your clean metallic loving. I don't belong with you, but I don't belong with Anna either. I don't belong anywhere. That's the way of it, really, I don't belong anywhere … because I am not all of a piece. And the white-tight emptiness he knew now for the lonely loneliness of being alone no matter who was there because it was always a loneliness for whichever part of him he was away from. It was cureless like the loneliness of old people in the country watching all their friends die and their own children growing strange.

"Anna would be older and different now, you know," Claire went on. "People you don't see stay the same in your mind, but they are all different when you actually go back. Sometimes they're much stranger than strangers."

Damn you, Claire, do you think I'm not sure now … not sure I was wrong. I could never go back now. It was just wild. It would be like the other boys were with Toby, now.

"Perhaps we'll just forget it, Claire," he said. "I think we'll just forget all about it. Anna *would* be much older now. She'd have that hollow look about her cheek bones they get in the country, that little colour of ashes the thin women get," he said, wanting to hurt himself with hate for the things he was making himself say, "and her hair might not be very nice. She'd probably run and put on a clean apron when she saw me coming. She'd be very polite with me in that funny sort of way, wouldn't she."

"Darling," Claire said, "I do think you're right. I really *don't* think you could love Anna again now. If you live with country women and love them right along, I suppose you don't notice ... but to come on them suddenly after a long time of ... well, me, if I may say so ..." She put her blood-red nails lightly through his hair.

"And Anna'd be sure to have bad teeth," he said, stabbing meanly, willfully, at his last dream. "Women seldom brush their teeth in the country. They get all spotted and eaten away."

And Claire has such nice teeth, he thought, such nice, cool, shining teeth, he thought, hating himself and the way he had happened to be and Claire.

Sentiment/Sentimentality

The Christmas Order

Most memory is like a blurred negative. When you hold it up to the light of conscious recollection, searching however carefully for the precision of its several features which you are sure intentness enough cannot fail to decipher, you are finally faced with only a baffling irreducible off-focus. But when I glance back at my life, the years from eight to ten stand out with absolute line-clarity, like buildings in the foreground of their shadowy penumbra. The Christmas of my tenth year I can see as plainly as if its features (of sharpest pain and of brightest joy) had somehow been sealed immobile under glass. In memory there is always the question of how much is original fact and how much is the conscious coloring of later knowledge. But whenever I think of that particular Christmas this distinction disappears almost entirely. It comes back to me with such immediacy that my thoughts of it keep slipping into the present tense. I even *feel* again something of its peculiar anguish and delight.

ࢌ

My father had been dead two years, and that August my mother married again. She married Syd Weston. It was that circumstance which.... But you would have to understand quite thoroughly about Mother and Syd and me to have any of that following Christmas make sense.

For Mother's sake I tried not to let resentment of my stepfather show. But a child of ten doesn't have the technique for that kind of acting. *I* didn't, anyway. I remember how angry I used to get with my face sometimes. Other people's faces could keep a secret for them. But whenever

I'd glimpse mine in any reflecting surface it seemed to be tattling everything that went on behind it.

I suppose I got that from my father. Though with a crucial difference. His face used to be right out with everything, too, but in an expansive entirely unselfconscious way. I believe, if you'd asked him to describe his face, he'd have had to *think* a minute to know what it really looked like. (Where had that outward look gone, I wondered, the day they took me in to look at him, with the flower smell like a silence gone sickly in the parlour, and the yellower sections of the drawn-down blinds like the first hint of a mortality even in the green fields outside?)

He never turned things over in his mind as I did. I suppose I got that from Mother. I have that curse of sensing immediately the degree of discordance among any group I enter—with a sort of responsibility, as if the guilt for it were my own. Mother had that too.

That's why most of the time I tried to hide from her how Syd and I jarred. Syd's face hardly told on him at all. It just seemed to listen.

Syd was no stranger. His small tidy farm was right next to ours. There wasn't even a fence along the line between us. I remember that when Father would mow there first the swath would go across the line and back, crooked as a ram's horn; but when Syd made the first cut his swath would be straight as a die, just inside the line on his part.

The only time I had ever seen Syd's face give him away was the day of my father's funeral. Heartbroken though I was that day I studied everyone's face, as any child will, to see how they were feeling and to see what kind of look each of them was giving me. A simulated grief sat on the other faces like a kind of demureness, but Syd's face had such a look it startled me right out of myself. It had a sort of desperate waking-in-a-strange-place look, especially when he glanced at Mother.

                                    ❧

He would never come into our house after that. But how many times, it seemed by accident, he would be working alongside the road when I went by and ask me how we were making out. And it got so I went over to his place quite a bit. He would let me take the reins of the team until we came to a ditch or had to cross the main road, and let me pick out small rocks to chink the well with, in a way that made me feel as if I were grown-up and doing a man's work. I remember how I'd spit sideways when both my hands were busy, the way men do.

I never felt any constraint with him then—unless some of the other kids came by; then I'd make some excuse to leave immediately. Because, among ourselves, we called him "old man Weston." Not because he was old or cranky, but because he lived alone. And no one is as cruelly ostracized by kids as someone a little "different." no one so embarrassing to be caught being friendly with. Not that Syd was a bit like "Old Man Talbot." whose orchard we raided chiefly for the fun of having him chase us out, shouting and throwing apples. But *anyone* who lived alone...who must have to wash out his own frying-pan and—if you thought about it—never said "good-night" to anyone when he went to bed or "good morning" to anyone when he got up....

I remember one day I said to him, "Syd, why didn't you ever get married?" It used to be a gig of mine to try to startle people with odd questions like that. But Syd's face didn't alter a bit.

"Well now, I don't know." he said.

"Y'know, Syd." I said, "you look real *good* when you're dressed up and Mum said you used to be the best dancer she ever danced with!"

"Did she now!" he said. His face didn't change then either, but he brushed away the shavings from the auger hole he was boring, with a sudden little movement that reminded me somehow of the way a dust devil will catch at a neat windrow of hay and disarrange it.

He never talked about Mother directly. But occasionally when I would do or say something that I couldn't see was any way different from the way anyone else would do or say it, he would murmur: "Ain't that Laura for you!" Laura was my mother.

I knew, of course, that Syd had gone with Mother when they were both young, from hearing the women joke her about it sometimes. "Do you mind how we used to cross out Syd Weston's name with yours in school and they'd both come out 'marriage'?" or "Is it true that Syd was hangin' off till he had a hundred dollars in the bank?"

And I knew how Jess Matthews (that was my father) had come here to Westfield with a lumbering crew and married her within a month. It was a sort of local legend how that night at the pie social when he did the tricks (he could do tricks that *no one* could see through) he got Mother to come up and hold out her left hand and, after exhibiting his own empty palms and rolling up his sleeves, made a quick magician's gesture in the air and before she knew it there was an engagement ring on her finger, and she standing there looking as if she didn't know whether she wanted to laugh or cry.

Father was always laughing, or ready to laugh. He'd pay the fiddler as much as five dollars to play an extra hour at the Friday-night dances in the schoolhouse; and there was always a bunch of kids hanging around him. He could turn out to have completely forgotten something he'd promised you, something you'd counted on for days; and then with just some conspiratorial little nudge or wink become as infallible as ever, and make you feel as big and wonderful as he was.

I mentioned that pie social affair to Mother one time. "Was Syd there that night?" I asked.

"No." she said. "He had to haul in grain. He said, 'It looks like rain, and if that load of oats gets wet again tonight it won't be good for anything.'"

That'd be Syd all right. And then I thought: wasn't it funny that anyone would recall the words — the exact words — someone else had said about a little thing like that so long ago?

Syd never came inside our house again until that August evening. He'd give us a load of wood now and then, but he'd haul it into the dooryard some afternoon Mother was away. And she'd send *me* to thank him and try to make him take pay for it. When he made the arrangement to put our hay in on the halves he'd sent *me* to ask her about it. And whenever Mother would bring out a plate of cake and a jug of lemonade to the men in the afternoon, Syd always seemed to be off in a corner some place, clipping around a rock (every haying season Father planned to blast the big rocks in the field that fall, but somehow he never got it done) with the hand scythe.

I can still remember that August evening. I remember how peculiarly still it was. I had gone to bed before dark, so I could run off all by myself, like a reel in my head, the excitement of going away. Mother had finally made up her mind.

From my bed by the window I could see Syd sitting on the front doorstep of his small house. To a child the idea of oneself going away makes sober rooted people seem almost incredible, unbelievably stupid. You feel that somehow someone should make them *understand*.

The stillness didn't bother me but I know now the kind of stillness it was for the older ones. It was one of those nights of drought when the slamming of a screen door or the tapping of a neighbour's hammer sounds astonishingly near. And yet everything else seems untouchably far away. There is only the fitful pulse of the blind against the screen where you sit, hearing only your mind not-think.

I saw Mother go outside. She walked along the edge of the flower bed, picking off a wilted nasturtium leaf here and there, or straightening a little corral of sticks that kept the peony plant's huge burdening blossoms from weighting it to the ground. But she did these things inertly,

as you do things on a day you are trying to whittle away with movement—a day when it seems as if each time you look at the clock more
time must have passed than the clock has counted.

I knew Mother wasn't happy, like me, about going away. But what
could she do? A farm can go on for a few years without a man's steady
care, but what can a woman do when the ditches in the low parts grass
over and fill in, and the shingles blow up on the very top of the barn
roof, and the time comes when all the fence wire is rusted too brittle even
to splice? Even if she could hire these things adjusted, what about the
night when the gale blows the big shed doors open, or the day the cow
is choking on an apple and no one within sound of your call?

It was coming dusk when I saw Alf Steele walking up the road. He
stopped for a minute opposite Syd's. Their voices came to me clear as
voices over water.

"Ain't ya comin' to school meetin', Syd?" Alf called.

"I guess not." Syd answered. "Not tonight."

"No? Well…. " And then, just before resuming his pace, Alf added,
"Did ya know Laura's goin' away? Anyhow, that's the talk."

"Goin' away?" Syd said. "No. Where?"

"They say her brother Frank's got her a job in the city. Montreal, ain't
it, Frank is?"

Syd came to his feet so quickly I thought he was going out to the
road to question Alf further. But he didn't. He turned abruptly and
went inside the house.

I think I know, now, what happened then. I think the stillness of his
empty kitchen sink struck him like a draft; that an awful treachery in
the *things* around him, to maintain the neatness of which had been his
one passion, was exposed as suddenly as if some lens which had tricked
his vision all his life had shifted just the necessary millimetre for absolute
clarity. For older ones, "going away" is in the same class of words as
"dead." His would be the shock you have when the only life tied to
yours with memories the others have long ago found replaceable is
seen now to have been as liable to—yes, inescapable from—change as
anyone else's. Gone away! Even the slight comfort of a few exactly
shared memories is snatched away when *a different set of objects*—no
longer these same houses, this same sky, these same fields—is to become
daily before the other's eyes.

I think he was divided between a desperate urge and an awful
reluctance to go find out if this rumor were really true. I think he reached

for his cap. Then put it back on the peg. I can see him pacing up and down the room, picking up this thing and that and then setting it down again, as if each thing he touched, for reassuring contact with solidity, itself touched the quick of his indecision.

Or maybe I do imagine here. Maybe it was just one of those moments that come only to solitary people: when a sudden bold spontaneous hope—and the resolution to match it—breaks the bonds of caution that have fettered hope of any kind before, in one great soaring bound.

Because it couldn't have been more than fifteen minutes later that I heard our screen door open and close.

"Why, Syd!" Mother exclaimed. The heat hole over the kitchen stove was right beside my bed, and I could catch everything that was said below.

"I can't set down," Syd blurted out. "I just came over to...."

I knew he did sit down though. In my mind I could picture him snapping the crown of his cap to the peak and unsnapping it. And I could see Mother taking off her apron and smoothing out the wrinkles in her skirt. I could see her place a smile on her face, consciously. It wouldn't be a false smile, but it wouldn't hide her feelings half as thoroughly as she believed.

"Laura." Syd said—and the words came out propulsively, as if they were a stoppage in his throat—"you ain't goin' away, are you?"

I could see the precarious smile drop off Mother's face.

"I don't know, Syd." she said. Her voice sounded freer, now that her thought and her speech need not keep to separate channels. "I guess so. I don't know what to do. I can't seem to think. Frank wants me to go out there with him. I wouldn't like the city, I know, but things here have got to the point where...." She would be sitting there ironing one arm with the palm of her other hand.

There was quite a long silence. And then I heard Syd say, "Don't, Laura...don't.... " I knew what had happened. I always hated to see Mother cry. She'd draw in a deep breath and hold it hard, as if against the muscles of her face. But then the muscles would begin to give way, one group after another. And her mouth would look as if it hurt her, physically.

"I guess I'm making a fool of myself." Mother said, all at once contrite. "Do you remember what you used to say: 'I never saw how crying over anything ever helped'?"

I heard a chair scrape out then. Syd would be standing there, clumsy with the thought of his hand lying on her shoulder and equally clumsy with the thought of taking it away, because it seemed to help her, touched for a moment by that curious glow you feel when someone puts a particular memory of you into words, when you had feared that nothing more than a general memory of you might exist in anyone anywhere.

"Laura." he said suddenly, "*don't* go 'way. Why couldn't you and me…?"

I think she looked up, surprised and not surprised. And then he spoke almost with savagery. "I ain't the old —" (the word seemed to escape him) "—people think I am. I got feelin's too."

I had a moment of consternation. It sounded as if Syd hated the way he was. All people in any way strange —it had never *occurred* to me that they might have to go on being that way because other people kept expecting it of them.

And then I covered my head with the bedclothes, not to hear any more. I knew we would not be going away now.

But even that was crowded out of my mind. I had only one bitter, burning thought. You needn't be openly rebellious against a usurper, but if you observed forever one little obstinacy known only to yourself, your original loyalty would still be intact. For Mother's sake I wouldn't make any fuss. But I would go right on calling him "Syd." I would never, *never* call him "Dad."

ঽ৶

I think that at the beginning Mother didn't really worry at all about me keeping Syd at arm's length. It was to be expected. But in a few weeks, when the situation hadn't changed, a constraint fell over all of us. This constraint was not continuous, of course —three people cannot live together in the country without being unreservedly fused most of the time by little excitements, little catastrophes, and the news brought in by one or the other from outside. But I had the child's talent for that most punishing rebuke: of withdrawing a little, as if behind an invisible boundary, just when the other has begun to think your estrangement must have been something he imagined.

Syd would show me how to mow, placing my hands just so on the scythe and I trying to hold them right there; and then, following my swath, he'd say, "That's right, that's right, you got the hang of it." and I'd say, "I guess you can finish it." and go hang up the scythe in the crotch of a tree. Or we might be preparing to go raspberrying in the back burntland, searching about for the water jug, gathering the tins, checking in the lunch basket to see if the salt and pepper for the eggs hadn't been forgotten, and I'd turn to Mother and say, "Is *he* going to stay all day with us?"

It was then that Mother's face would get that awful look: resignation, but resignation worse for never being safe from a hope perpetually renewed and as perpetually struck down. She would sometimes pass her hand over her forehead vaguely as if there were some possible kind of motion that would wipe this film over things away. And for a while after that it would seem as if everything Syd and I said (or didn't say) to each other would sound sort of loud.

The situation was never openly admitted, and at first Mother tried to overcome it. If I let slip something spontaneous like, "I'd like to see Syd on that mowin' machine o' Reg's. I bet he could mow that field in two hours!" she'd seize upon my remark and repeat it to him ever so casually. Or if Syd were to say, "Why, that kid can sow grass seed as good as a man—better'n *some* men!" she'd repeat that to me. But her casualness was so transparent (each of us *knew* what the situation was) that her ruses turned out to be only embarrassing. And after a little she gave them up.

Otherwise, things certainly went smoother with us than they had ever done when Father was alive. There was always dry wood in the shed, the water pails were always full, the clothes line was now spliced so strong it never let Mother's clean sheets down into the mud, and...well, that precarious bridge from one day to the next seemed to be completely shored up.

But how could a child love anyone for that kind of thing? How could that kind of thoughtfulness take the place of the knack Father had of immediately winning you over to his way of seeing that serious concern over *anything* belonged way down below fun?

It was queer about that, though. Once Mother lost the new scissors she'd spent the last cent in her purse for. "Now where could I have laid them?" she said, frowning with worry. "Did you have 'em openin' the flour bag?" Father asked. "No." "Didn't have 'em out clippin' flowers?" "No, I had the little scissors out there." He thought. "Sure you didn't have 'em cuttin' up citron for a pound cake?" She had laughed so we'd had to be stern with her to keep her from hysterics. But the minute her laughter had subsided her face looked as worried as before. Now, when she laughed with Syd about anything—though less often and not half as hysterically—an echo of the laughter would stay on in her eyes long after the laughter itself was done.

If only half-consciously, I resented that. I would think: if he'd ever once do something that wasn't so darned *sensible*, so darned predictable.

It was only when I would actually surprise myself in a moment of accepting Syd wholeheartedly that I was deliberately cruel to him.

I remember one day I was watching him make a birdhouse for me, completely engrossed in the expert way his large hands could manage the miniature splices. I was fingering absently a little gadget that hung from the buttonhole of my jacket. It was a tiny cube of wood, whittled so that only a sphere remained inside its open-faced cage.

He looked up. "Ronnie." he said, "one o' them edges there is way longer than the others. Let me square her up for you."

I bridled. "Naw." I said, "don't bother. That's all right."

"It won't take but a minute." he said. "Let's see it."

I moved off. "Naw, that's all right." I said. "My father made me that."

He didn't say a word.

Another day a cattle buyer was looking at the oxen. I felt just like a third man with him and Syd. Syd never said anything like, "Now keep friggin' with that sprayer till ya break it!" or "Look outa the man's way there." the way other men (even Father) did, to cut down kids in the barn.

"You oughta seen the rock that team hauled off last week!" I said.

The buyer grinned at me. "That's quite a boy you got there, Mr. Weston." he said, in a hearty salesman's voice. "I guess he's gonna be as good a judge o' cattle as his old man, eh?"

"He's not my old man." I said. "My father is dead."

I was glad Mother didn't see Syd's face then. Come to think of it, perhaps it used to give him away more often than I've made it sound.

❧

I think the fortnight before Christmas must have been the worst of all for Mother. She was very happy because we had more money for the mail order that year than ever before, and I knew she kept waiting for me to study the catalogue, so that she could glimpse which page I kept it open at longest. But I acted as if Christmas didn't matter to me in the least. Other years I used to nag and nag at her to get the order off early. But that year it was she herself who had to say: "My soul, this is the *fifteenth*. We better get that order off this very night or it'll be too late."

The night when we used to clear off the dining-room table and get out all the writing paraphernalia, pretending we were ordering each other's gifts from one page in the catalogue, while a finger was holding it open, secretly, to another; with her putting down the things for me and then folding the order sheet over her writing until I had put her gifts below; and making a solemn promise that when she added up the total she wouldn't even glance at anything but the figures—that night used to be almost as exciting as Christmas itself.

But that year I let her sit at the table alone. It gave me an almost sickening pang to see her there, taking as long as ever to elect those things for me which would be useful but still have something of the "present" quality about them, and sobered (but so unprotestingly) by my withholding of connivance in the spirit of the occasion thus made so desolate for her to support alone. But I couldn't help it. I didn't even pretend to glance at the numbers of the pages she was copying from.

Once she said, so extra-casually I knew it had come on her tongue and then faltered a good many times before she could speak it: "Would you like to put something down for your father?" Syd was outside.

I knew it would have delighted her beyond anything if I'd answered something like, "Yeah. What could I get him?—something that would really *surprise* him!" But what I said was, "No, I guess not. It'd be kinda foolish gettin' him something with his own money."

I didn't put anything down for him or, because it would be paid for with his money, for her either. Syd himself had never once enquired what I wanted. If he had, I was prepared to say, "Oh, anything. I don't care." with deliberate indifference. But just the same I almost hated him for not asking.

Syd took the letter to the post office the next morning. Any letter that needed a money order fixed up for enclosure Mother usually took. But he offered specially (almost insisted) to take this one. For a moment I wondered if he wanted to look at the sheet to see if there was anything on it for him (and for a moment I had another pang: to think of this little curiosity being rewarded by the sight of nothing more exciting than a work shirt). But then I knew that spying wasn't like Syd. This would be just like any other letter, to him, I thought.

δ

Times before, the day the Christmas order had finally gone off had been one of the wonderful ones. It had seemed as if we'd set in motion some benevolent mechanism which would be busy contriving something splendid for us all through the following days, even when we were not thinking about it. But that morning, this mood of indifference I had chosen spoiled everything.

About ten o'clock, Mother's hand froze suddenly on the pump handle. "Oh, dear!" she said. "I forgot to put down the tissue paper and seals. Now isn't that ...?"

She looked at me appealingly. I thought, if I'd only helped her (though the bitter regret which the "only" implied was disowned almost as soon as I recognized it). I wouldn't have forgotten. But I didn't say a word. And after that, Mother suddenly gave up trying to encourage my Christmas spirit.

It is curious how a child will prolong a sort of sulkiness that has started as whim until it hardens into obstinacy, resisting every effort to dislodge him from it; and how the most dismaying thing of all is when the others at last take his mood at its face value and leave him entirely alone.

I was, however, to know a dismay even worse before the next week was out.

Christmas was on Saturday of that week, and the order should come on the Tuesday or Wednesday before. But it didn't come on Tuesday. *Or* Wednesday. And when I went to the post office on Thursday, *certain* that it would be there (and thankful by this time that the excitement of the package arriving could save my face by seeming to sweep me out of my mood, rather than my having to abandon it of my own free will), the package was not there either. There was just a card, saying it had gone to the station. Whenever you have deliberately chosen to be perverse, it seems that everything else is quick to fall into line.

"Now what did they send it by express for?" Mother said. "I can't think of anything heavy in it."

"It's cheaper that way." Syd said.

"I know." Mother said. "But Christmas time … when everyone's in such a rush…."

"We can give the card to Cliff tomorrow." Syd said—Cliff was the mailman—"and he'll go to the station and get it for us."

"Why, yes." Mother said. "I never thought of that. Cliff'll get it. He's a good soul."

I was so relieved I nearly cried.

That night the snow came. When Syd came in from his late trip to the barn he stood in the porch almost solid white, with his arms angled out from his sides for someone to brush him off with the broom. "Why, Syd!" Mother cried, "Is it snowing? —like *that*?" And after I'd gone up to bed I kept my lamp lit for a little while to watch the great flakes float and eddy down past the window pane, like an infinite fragmentation of some beautiful white healing silence. Snow for Christmas.

But with it, while I slept, the wind came.

And when I looked out the window in the morning, the surroundings looked as strange as a landscape of the moon. The whole world seemed buried in a great sea of snow: huge, billowing, porpoise-backed waves of it, caught up around the corners of the buildings into long breaker tips that reached almost to the eaves. I saw Syd starting to shovel a tunnel to the barn. He didn't bend, but reached, at the drift before him. Here and there a spot of road would show bare as your hand in a trough of the waves, but on either side of the spot you couldn't even guess where the road went. I looked again at Syd's tunnel. He had scraped it right down to the grass, but I saw that already the wind had sifted enough snow back into it that a deep track could be made.

I knew that the men would not break out the roads until the wind had died down completely. Not till afternoon, anyway. I knew the mail would not go today. And this was the last day before Christmas. And so the order would never get here for Christmas at all.

I thought, for a second, how I had almost believed in my indifference to Christmas a couple of weeks ago. How could that have been possible? Was this storm, like the order going to the station, some sort of punishment? Perhaps even here, the mere focusing of memory on it tends to exaggerate a past despair. But it seems to me that those moments when I stood there at the window, realizing for the first time that the unthinkable *could* happen, may well have been the bleakest of my whole life.

Mother tried her best to console me. She said we had the tree, anyway (Syd had got that a couple of days ago, an absolutely perfect one), and we had lots of candy and nuts, and, well, the things would only be a little late. I could hardly keep from shouting when I answered, "What good are things *after* Christmas?" Especially with no tissue paper to wrap them in, and the time already past before which they must not be opened. It would be just like an order you'd sent in the summertime.

Syd didn't say a word. He didn't seem to be disturbed at all. And later in the morning, when I stood in the porch door, praying that by some last-minute miracle I'd see the ox teams come breaking the roads and the mailman's horse behind them (though the wind was blowing stronger now, rather than less), I heard Mother say to him almost frantically: "Syd, what could we fix up for Ronnie? We've just got to have something for him."

He said, "I don't know. What could we fix up for him?" But he didn't sound really concerned—in the next breath he asked her if she could get dinner early. I couldn't see what difference it made when we ate, or if we ate at all, with the whole long empty day ahead.

After an early dinner, we started to trim the tree. Mother and I. Syd got out his rifle and took it apart to clean it.

I helped Mother as conscientiously as I had ever done, because I was too desolate even to be sullen. And as we worked, as (with the glistening ornaments and ropes of tinsel) the tree changed more and more from a tree into an incarnation, it brought the texture of Christmas right into the room. But I worked with that awful docility with which you put on your best clothes as carefully as ever though the occasion is a farewell at the train, maybe for the last time. And then a shaft of how it *might* have been—trimming the tree on this cloistering day (the wind was shriller now), with the contents of the order hidden no more secretly than beneath the sofa and, because of that, my pledge not to look all the more torturingly sweet—would pierce me right to the bone.

About one o'clock, Syd came into the parlour. "I think I'll take a scout around with the gun." he said. So that's why he'd wanted an early dinner.

"Syd." Mother exclaimed, "you're not going hunting, a day like *this*?"

"It's a good day for huntin'." he said. "The wind'd be just about right in the spruce, and the snowshoein' ain't bad."

In one direction from our house was the road to town and in the other, across some narrow fields, was the dense woods. Twenty solid miles of it.

"Well…" Mother said resignedly. "But now you watch out a tree doesn't fall on you or something."

I was so shocked that Syd could leave us alone on this day that I didn't even resent it. I just watched him go across the field, lost in and then appearing out of the spasmodic gusts of wind-driven snow as if he were evaporating and then solidifying again.

We didn't pay much attention to the storm until we had finished working on the tree. In the morning the wind had blown hard, but unconcernedly. Now it was getting rough. Not vicious yet, but rough.

"I wonder if he took his compass." Mother said suddenly. She went to the pantry. The compass was still hanging on its nail. I knew you couldn't lose Syd if you tried—but just the same I was half-annoyed at her for checking up on the compass. It would have been more comfortable not to have known he didn't have it.

❧

About three o'clock the wind became really vicious, like an animal become ravening with the taste of its own violence. The air looked like one of those blizzards that sheep on an old calendar are seen huddling against. The trees bent and writhed constantly and the wind howled at the corners of the house as it sucked itself wildly across the fields.

And now, as if out of some place wrenched open by the wind, the cold came; depositing its sharp knives on the panes.

As the afternoon wore on, the uneasiness in both of us grew to active worry. But neither of us mentioned it. Partly as if by not naming it you could achieve protection, however flimsy, from the thing you feared, and partly because it had become so difficult for us to discuss Syd at all, let alone a mutual concern for him. We tried to fake an interest in small tasks. But the instant there'd be a slight lull in the storm, one or the other would immediately say, "I believe it's lettin' up." or "Of course, inside it always looks worse than it is." The next instant a redoubled clap of wind would make the chimney gasp as if the very breath of the house were being sucked outside, to be spun about, captured and lost forever, and our automatic glances at each other would seem to collide with almost physical effect—as glances do when smoke is discovered curling out from some place where no smoke should be.

And then we began one at a time to make excuses to peer out the frosted window toward the woods. The Christmas tree was like a mockery. It was like the guest from another way of life who happens to be staying with you when some private trouble strikes, so that you are denied even a natural as-with-neighbours reaction to it, because of appearance's sake.

It got so the only things of any reality in the whole house seemed to be Syd's unspoken name and the tick of the clock. And it was odd the situations my mind chose to recall him in: always one something like his maybe looking at the order sheet and seeing nothing for him there but the work shirt.

About four, Mother got supper. "Syd'll be hungry." she said." after the early dinner and tramping in the woods." But I knew that was only an excuse. I knew she had the foolish idea that supper ready would somehow beckon him home.

But supper was ready, and then growing cold on the back of the stove, and still he hadn't come. And then, supper *waiting* made the whole thing more clamorous than ever. It was early, but already there was a hint of darkness coming. As if the wind had broken into the hold of night too, and let dusk loose beforehand.

The clock struck the half-hour. Suddenly Mother leapt up. "He should be *home* now." she said. "I'm going down to Alf's and see if he thinks we ought to …."

I leapt up too. I felt an inexpressible relief, now that this intolerable pretence of casualness was over.

"I'm goin' with you." I said. I expected her to oppose that, but she didn't. "Well ... all right." she said. I got my heavy clothes on first, and went in to look out the parlour window once more—openly, avidly, now. There was nothing but that marching blur and the mourning trees. When she was ready she came in too.

"See any sign of him?" she said.

"No." I said. She looked as if the muscles of her face were starting to break up.

We were just turning from the window when all at once she put her hand on my arm. "Hark!" she said. "Wasn't that the back door?"

We both rushed to the kitchen. And there he was, standing by the door, the snow so driven into his clothes, and his eyebrows and mustache so encrusted with it, that he was hardly recognizable.

"Syd." Mother cried, "Oh Syd ...." She ran and put her arms about him and her face against his shoulder, snow and all.

"What's the trouble?" Syd said, startled. "What's wrong?" It had never occurred to him that we'd be worried on his account. He thought something dreadful must have happened to us.

"You." Mother cried. "You ... out in this. We've been almost crazy. Where have you *been*?" Her questions tumbled over each other before he could get out a single word. "Where did you come from? We didn't see you. We've been watching the woods all afternoon, haven't we, Ronnie? Where's your gun? Were you lost?"

"I didn't come by the woods." Syd said. "I come the road."

"The road? Here, let me shake that jumper off in the woodbox. You'll get your death." (I ran into the pantry for a knife to scrape the icicles off.) "Where's your gun?"

Syd sort of grinned. "In the barn." he said. The barn was way down from the house, in the opposite direction from the woods.

"The *barn*?"

Syd didn't answer. He opened the door and reached back into the porch. I thought he was reaching for the old broom.

When he straightened up, I couldn't believe my eyes. Everyone knows one miracle in his life, and this was mine. For in his hand he carried the Christmas order!

"Syd!" Mother cried. "You've been to town! You lugged that order all the way home!" Then, for a second, plain curiosity displaced her agitation. "Is that *our* order?" she said. "Look at the size of it, and the shape of it. I don't remember ...." It was a huge package, package-shaped at the top, but obviously containing some long almost unwrappable object at the bottom. No wonder it had gone to the station.

I couldn't say a word. I was inundated by the soft glow of danger past, the Christmas order was right here in the *house*, the tree had suddenly become an intimate again—and now the wind and the cold and the dark were not enemies anymore: just things that could be let go their way, their violence merely heightening the sense of our own containment.

ða

But it was not so much any of that as something else. It was as if I were seeing in Syd a different man. It wasn't that he had walked six miles to town and back on a day like this to get the order. It was that he had wanted to *surprise* us. It was that he had gone to all that manoeuvre of pretended indifference, of cleaning his gun, of actually going into the woods while we watched, and then cutting back across the field, leaving his gun in the barn, and skirting the pasture till he struck the road to town. It was that, for this effect of surprise (acutely embarrassed though he was, now that he had brought it off), he had done something that had so little common sense about it, that was so crazy, it was almost childish....

And when he fished way down inside the very last layer of heavy clothing and said, "Didn't you mention somethin' about forgettin' to order the tissue paper and seals." and I knew he had got even *them*, at some store in town... well, I had still another thing to bless them for: for not remarking on my speechlessness, for making their own voices loud enough to cover up the other sound I couldn't help—crying.

Syd brushed the snow from the package and took it into the dining room to unwrap, while Mother was taking up the supper. When she went down the cellar for the creamer he came to the dining-room door and beckoned to me. I went in and he closed the door.

He had put all the parcels under the couch except one. It was on the dining-room table. A bright enamelled case, with the top up and, inside, what I thought must surely be the most gorgeous comb, brush, and mirror set anyone had ever seen.

I gasped. He must have added that at the post office, I thought, the morning he took the order over. He (Syd!) must have asked the postmistress for her catalogue. I almost cried again: to think of what an effort that must have been for him, and of him trying to squeeze the article number and description in the tiny spaces provided, with that big handwriting of his that always looked as if it came so hard. I'd never

touched anything with such reverence as the heavy mirror I picked up
and then laid back again into its pleated satin socket.

"Think we could wrap it up kinda nice?" Syd said, almost sheep-
ishly.

"Now?" I said. "Right now?"

"Might as well." he said. "Case she goes snoopin'."

It did look nice when we were done. I wouldn't have believed Syd
could turn the corners of the flimsy tissue paper so deftly, and hold
them so perfectly in line while I put on the very biggest seals in the
whole package. We hid it in the sideboard drawer, beneath the tablecloth.

Mother looked at us when we came out into the kitchen again.

"Now what are you two up to?" she said.

"Ask him." I said, grinning. "Ask Dad."

Maybe I only *seem* to remember that a swift locking glance passed
between them before they dropped their eyes. But I do know that
Mother's face had the most indescribable look on it. As if something
had divided her between such happiness and such fear that the happiness might not last, that it was like a strickenness.

But the next morning, with the wind composed and penitent again,
and in the lamplight before dawn, when I saw the package beneath
the tree that *no* one could wrap—the bright, gleaming, new twenty-
two rifle that Syd must have added also at the post office—then, I think,
she knew it would last.

"D'ya like it?" Syd said shyly. He didn't touch the .22 himself, but he
kept standing right near it all the time.

"*Like* it?" I said.

"But, Syd." Mother said, "do you think he's old enough for a gun?"

"Oh, Mother..." I cried.

"Now, stop worryin'!" Syd chided her. "There ain't nothin' about a
gun, if anyone's careful."

She still didn't look too happy about it. But I think that, in a funny
way, this was the most rewarding thing for her of all: that Syd and I were
taking sides against *her*. With that peculiar sense of omniscience that
seems to come only with intense happiness, I thought (as a child thinks
such things, recognizing the essence *only* of words that would express
them): now, at last, with the man and the boy disputing with the woman
the wisdom of a gun for the boy, we are a family.

And I knew that, though I had no real gift for either of them, somehow I had managed to give them a present better than any to be found
in the catalogue.

And I knew too, if I could see it, wherever it was, my father's face would be right in on this with us; and that, if I could hear him, he would be saying: "Now, y'see? What did I tell you about your frettin'? Everything always turns out right."

Penny in the Dust

My sister and I were walking through the old sun-still fields the evening before my father's funeral, recalling this memory or that — trying, after the fashion of families who gather again in the place where they were born, to identify ourselves with the strange children we must have been.

"Do you remember the afternoon we thought you were lost?" my sister said. I did. That was as long ago as the day I was seven, but I'd had occasion to remember it only yesterday.

"We searched everywhere." she said. "Up in the meeting-house, back in the blueberry barrens — we even looked in the well. I think it's the only time I ever saw Father really upset. He didn't even stop to take the oxen off the wagon tongue when they told him. He raced right through the chopping where Tom Reeve was burning brush, looking for you — right through the flames almost; they couldn't do a thing with him. And you up in your bed, sound asleep!"

"It was all over losing a penny or something, wasn't it?" she went on, when I didn't answer. It was. She laughed indulgently. "You were a crazy kid, weren't you."

I was. But there was more to it than that. I had never seen a shining new penny before that day. I'd thought they were all black. This one was bright as gold. And my father had given it to me.

You would have to understand about my father, and that is the hard thing to tell. If I say that he worked all day long but never once had I seen him hurry, that would make him sound like a stupid man. If I say that he never held me on his knee when I was a child and that I never heard him laugh out loud in his life, it would make him sound humourless and severe. If I said that whenever I'd be reeling off some of my fanciful plans and he'd come into the kitchen and I'd stop short, you'd think that he was distant and that in some kind of way I was afraid of him. None of that would be true.

There's no way you can tell it to make it sound like anything more than an inarticulate man a little at sea with an imaginative child. You'll have to take my word for it that there was more to it than that. It was as if his sure-footed way in the fields forsook him the moment he came near the door of my child's world and that he could never intrude on it without feeling awkward and conscious of trespass; and that I, sensing that but not understanding it, felt at the sound of his solid step outside, the child-world's foolish fragility. He would fix the small spot where I planted beans and other quick-sprouting seeds before he prepared the big garden, even if the spring was late; but he wouldn't ask me how many rows I wanted and if he made three rows and I wanted four, I couldn't ask him to change them. If I walked behind the load of hay, longing to ride, and he walked ahead of the oxen, I couldn't ask him to put me up and he wouldn't make any move to do so until he saw me trying to grasp the binder.

He, my father, had just given me a new penny, bright as gold.

He'd taken it from his pocket several times, pretending to examine the date on it, waiting for me to notice it. He couldn't offer me anything until I had shown some sign that the gift would be welcome.

"You can have it if you want it, Pete." he said at last.

"Oh, thanks." I said. Nothing more. I couldn't expose any of my eagerness either.

I started with it, to the store. For a penny you could buy the magic cylinder of "Long Tom" popcorn with Heaven knows what glittering bauble inside. But the more I thought of my bright penny disappearing forever into the black drawstring pouch the storekeeper kept his money in, the slower my steps lagged as the store came nearer and nearer. I sat down in the road.

It was that time of magic suspension in an August afternoon. The lifting smells of leaves and cut clover hung still in the sun. The sun drowsed, like a kitten curled up on my shoulder. The deep flour-fine dust in the road puffed about my bare ankles, warm and soft as sleep. The sound of the cowbells came sharp and hollow from the cool swamp.

I began to play with the penny, putting off the decision. I would close my eyes and bury it deep in the sand; and then, with my eyes still closed, get up and walk around, and then come back to search for it. Tantalizing myself, each time, with the excitement of discovering afresh its bright shining edge. I did that again and again. Alas, once too often.

It was almost dark when their excited talking in the room awakened me. It was Mother who had found me. I suppose when it came dusk she thought of me in my bed other nights, and I suppose she looked there without any reasonable hope but only as you look in every place where the thing that is lost has ever lain before. And now suddenly she was crying because when she opened the door there, miraculously, I was.

"Peter!" she cried, ignoring the obvious in her sudden relief, "*where* have you been?"

"I lost my penny." I said.

"You lost your penny …? But what made you come up here and hide?"

If Father hadn't been there, I might have told her the whole story. But when I looked up at Father, standing there like the shape of everything sound and straight, it was like daylight shredding the memory of a silly dream. How could I bear the shame of repeating before him the childish visions I had built in my head in the magic August afternoon when almost anything could be made to seem real, as I buried the penny and dug it up again? How could I explain that pit-of-the-stomach sickness which struck through the whole day when I had to believe, at last, that it was really gone? How could I explain that I wasn't really hiding from them? How, with the words and the understanding I had then, that this was the only possible place to run from that awful feeling of loss?

"I lost my penny." I said again. I looked at Father and turned my face into the pillow. "I want to go to sleep."

"Peter." Mother said. "It's almost nine o'clock. You haven't had a bite of supper. Do you know you almost scared the *life* out of us?"

"You better get some supper." Father said. It was the only time he had spoken. I never dreamed that he would mention the thing again. But the next morning when we had the hay forks in our hands, ready to toss out the clover, he seemed to postpone the moment of actually leaving for the field. He stuck his fork in the ground and brought in another pail of water, though the kettle was chock full. He took out the shingle nail that held a broken yoke strap together and put it back in exactly the same hole. He went into the shed to see if the pigs had cleaned up all their breakfast.

And then he said abruptly, "Ain't you got no idea where you lost your penny?"

"Yes." I said, "I know just about."

"Let's see if we can't find it." he said.

We walked down the road together, stiff with awareness. He didn't hold my hand.

"It's right here somewhere." I said. "I was playin' with it, in the dust."

He looked at me, but he didn't ask me what game anyone could possibly play with a penny in the dust.

I might have known he would find it. He could tap the alder bark with his jackknife just exactly hard enough so it wouldn't split but so it would twist free from the notched wood, to make a whistle. His great fingers could trace loose the hopeless snarl of a fishing line that I could only succeed in tangling tighter and tighter. If I broke the handle of my wheelbarrow ragged beyond sight of any possible repair, he could take it and bring it back to me so you could hardly see the splice if you weren't looking for it.

He got down on his knees and drew his fingers carefully through the dust, like a harrow; not clawing it frantically into heaps as I had done, covering even as I uncovered. He found the penny almost at once.

He held it in his hand, as if the moment of passing it to me were a deadline for something he dreaded to say, but must. Something that could not be put off any longer, if it were to be spoken at all.

"Pete." he said, "you needn'ta hid. I wouldn'ta beat you."

Beat me? Oh, Father! You didn't think that was the reason...? I felt almost sick. I felt as if I had struck *him*.

I had to tell him the truth then. Because only the truth, no matter how ridiculous it was, would have the unmistakable sound truth has, to scatter that awful idea out of his head. "I wasn't hidin', Father." I said, "honest. I was .... I was buryin' my penny and makin' out I was diggin' up treasure. I was makin' out I was findin' gold. I didn't know what to do when I lost it, I just didn't know where to go ...." His head was bent forward, like mere listening. I had to make it truer still.

"I made out it was gold." I said desperately, "and I—I was makin' out I bought you a mowin' machine so's you could get your work done early every day so's you and I could go in to town in the big automobile I made out I bought you—and everyone'd turn around and look at us drivin' down the streets.... " His head was perfectly still, as if he were only waiting with patience for me to finish. "*Laughin'* and *talkin'*." I said. Louder, smiling intensely, compelling him, by the absolute conviction of some true particular, to believe me.

He looked up then. It was the only time I had ever seen tears in his eyes. It was the only time in my seven years that he had ever put his arm around me.

I wondered, though, why he hesitated, and then put the penny back in his own pocket.

Yesterday I knew. I never found any fortune and we never had a car to ride in together. But I think he knew what that would be like, just the same. I found the penny again yesterday, when we were getting out his good suit—in an upper vest pocket where no one ever carries change. It was still shining. He must have kept it polished.

I left it there.

The Finest Tree

"But Kate." I said, "aren't you going to *have* a tree? Don't think I feel it will not be different this year, but…"

"No," my wife replied. "Please. It's no use." Her face had that little paleness about the mouth which had been there ever since the day Nick went away, as if she were cold. "This business of forcing yourself to do the same things as if nothing had happened, I don't see it. Something *has* happened. It hasn't anything to do with being brave Dick, honestly. I could be brave enough if there was any *sense* in putting on that kind of show."

"I haven't cried." she added, almost defiantly. "Even when I was alone."

I knew that was true. That day when I came back into the house, the day our son had finished his last leave, she had not turned from the window. She had just said, "Was the train crowded?" The voice I shall not forget. But I knew she had not been crying.

I didn't quite know what to say, now. I had never seen Katherine like this, and it made me a little afraid. Apparently she mistook my hesitation.

"Oh, Dick." she cried suddenly, "please don't *make* me do it."

"Darling." I said, "whatever gave you the idea I wanted to *make* you do it? Anyway, perhaps you're right. Perhaps it *would* be better if we pretend it's just another Saturday." She seemed to relax.

This was the second day before Christmas, the day we always did get the Christmas tree when Nick was home. "Wouldn't you like to take a little drive?" I said, after a bit. I didn't want her to be in the house thinking about that, this particular day. And, driving, perhaps it would be different. In the house with her, just sitting there, there didn't seem to be anything I could say. Because I knew Katherine had the terrible conviction that Nick would not come back. I didn't feel that way about it, myself, and perhaps that is why I could say nothing to help her.

We took a strange road out into the country. It was a clean December day, with the morning crispness not quite relaxed, but the spruces cosy and personal and warm under their drooping shoulders of snow, and that strange expectancy in the air with the coming dusk so that it

212

seemed you would know it was Christmastime today no matter where you were and if you had no idea of the date at all. But perhaps it was just like any other day. It may only have seemed that way because of the things I remembered. I knew what Katherine was thinking … of all the times till this one when Nick had been with us, something eager and childlike coming back to him on this day … his good, really good, clear voice humming "Good King Wenceslaus." I knew Katherine was wishing the carols were over.

"I hope you will not think this is running away." she said, the only time she spoke. "If it did any good to …"

"Of course not." I said.

"I don't want to spoil anything for *you* …"

"Please don't think that." I said. "I don't feel a great deal of Christmas spirit this year myself."

"I know you don't." she said quickly. "I didn't mean that, either, but …"

I knew what she meant. I knew she meant, "but you don't feel that Nick is not coming back." I didn't, and that's why it was so hard to talk to Katherine that day. I knew it would be cruel to reason with her, for I knew that to force her to admit her fear, even to me, would make her feel guilty somehow, as if she were an ally in it.

I suppose it was selfishness that made me pick up the old man walking along the road with the axe, because obviously he was not going far. He was walking slowly, as if there was a weariness in him, but I am not always so thoughtful about such things. I guess I wanted a third person to talk to … desperately. He looked surprised when I stopped for him as if he had not noticed us coming, and for a minute he seemed reluctant to ride. He did not smile as he stepped into the car. I was somehow startled at his face, because from his back I had expected to see the face of a *very* old man.

"Nice this afternoon, isn't it?" Kate said pleasantly.

"Yes, it is." he said politely, but with a little surprise almost, as if the weather was a subject strange to him.

"Going far?" I inquired.

"No." he said. "Just up here a bit. I'll tell you. I was just going for the Christmas tree." Katherine sat around straight in the seat again, facing the road.

"Have you got *your* tree yet?" he said.

"No." I said, "we haven't." There was an awkward pause, and I switched on the radio. An announcer was speaking. "It has just been disclosed." he said, "that Canadian troops are spearheading the advance of the

Eighth Army in Italy." I felt the helplessness again, but I couldn't very well shut off the radio, immediately.

The old man seemed to be listening intently.

"Which way is Italy?" he said suddenly.

"Why, sort of south…yes, south-east." I said.

"That way, wouldn't it be?" he said, pointing.

"Yes." I said, "somewhere there, I suppose." I noticed that he did not seem to hear me. He looked in that direction a long time, without speaking.

"It's warm in Italy." he said, almost to himself.

"Yes, it's always warm there." I was wishing he would change the subject.

"About how far?" he said. "I know it's a long ways."

"Fifteen hundred…two thousand…miles. I'm afraid I really don't know."

"It *seems* like a long way." Kate broke in, and her voice was high and tense, as if she could be silent no longer, "when you have a son there. At least we think he's there. We haven't heard from him."

"You people have a son there?" the man said. He leaned forward almost eagerly. Then he hesitated. He did not seem to know whether he should go on or not. "I have a son there too." he added slowly.

"Then you understand." Kate said in a softer voice. "But you've heard from him." she added almost jealously. "At least you know where he *is.*"

"Yes." the old man said, "we … heard … from him yesterday morning."

"How…"

I'm sure it was "How nice!" that Kate started to say, but something caught her before it was quite out. Something in the man's voice seemed to strike us both at the same moment. We glanced at each other quickly.

"Oh." Kate said gently. "I'm sorry. I…I'm *so* sorry."

The man did not reply. I hope he understood why for the moment neither of us could find anything more than that to say. And I think he did. Because all of the awkwardness and something of the age left his face almost at once. There was no sound for a little but the soft sound of the car wheels on the snow.

"But you're going to have a tree just the same?" I said at last. It was a stupid remark, from all angles, but it slipped out before I could help it. He did not misunderstand me, thank heaven.

"Yes." he said. "We always *had* a Christmas tree. David always liked a tree. We thought we ought to have one, just the same. Do you think…?"

"I think…" Kate said softly, she seemed to be having a little trouble with her voice, "I think that it's … splendid … for you to have a tree just the same."

We drove on a little after we had let the old man out, and turned. There was not much talk between us. I knew we were both wishing there was something better we could have said to him.

But we were to have another chance. When we came back to the spot where we had left him, he was at the roadside again, holding a fir tree by the butt. He put up his hand for us to stop.

"Look." he said, "you folks haven't got a tree yet. I thought maybe if this was the kind of tree you liked…"

I glanced at Kate. But for the first time her face looked eager, and like itself again.

"Oh thank you!" she said. She looked at the tree. "Dick." she added slowly, "I think that's the *finest* tree we ever had."

"But your own…" I said. "We'll wait till you get your own tree, and you can go back with us. "

"No." he said, "thanks. It may take a little while."

"But we don't mind."

"No." he said, "thanks."

I put the car in gear. "Merry Christmas!" the old man said. He was smiling.

"Thank you." Kate said. She put her hand out to him, suddenly. "I wish there was something we could…"

"That's all right." he said slowly. "You have a son there. Maybe they *knew* each other. Maybe they… helped each other." I don't know why, but the remark I had made about "Christmas spirit this year" flashed through my mind.

"Maybe they did." Kate said eagerly. "Oh I *hope* they did." And I saw that there were tears in her eyes, the first tears since Nick had gone away. I knew it was all right with her now.

As we drove on, through the rear mirror I could watch the old man, and suddenly I knew why he had wanted to stay behind a little while. He was standing there, perfectly still, looking a long steady look towards the south-east.

It was a different kind of stillness between Katherine and me on the way back… not the loud kind at all. But I think we both felt a little guilty and ashamed. I think I felt guiltier than Kate, because I had felt all along that Nick was coming back.

The Dream and the Triumph

It was that March when, as people said, Chris and Mary Redmond had "just got where they could live." that Chris put the fork tine into his heel, bedding the horses. He thought nothing of it until he noticed the blood on his sock that night. Chris's face was lined with the big tracks of the big feelings only, no fretwork of the petty worries at all.

But even as Mary was bathing the tiny wound and he was laughing at her suggestion of a bread poultice, the tetanus germ was already entrenched. Mary was a small woman who took stature from her spirited expression, touched with something universal in its quiet moments.

"Let's see." Chris said, "when did we hear from Paul last?" He said this almost every night, just before he went to bed.

Paul was their grandson. They had brought him up from the time he was orphaned at ten.

He was away now at the city's engineering college. Even as a child he'd taken the mathematician's almost sensuous delight in surprising from a thing the equations that ran like hidden bones through it. The year he'd gone to high school in town and won the scholarship Mary hadn't been able to afford any new clothes. But she'd studied his grammar nights after her work was done so that she wouldn't say anything too wrong at graduation time to embarrass him.

"Ah, this is Wednesday." she said to Chris now. "No, it's Thursday, isn't it? I don't know why, but I seem to have lost a day this week. Well, then, we heard from him on Monday. Now, if that heel bothers you any...."

It's all right." Chris said. "The heat makes it feel good. Next time you write you better slip a few dollars into the envelope. I wouldn't want to think of him bein' strapped up there. And you know Paul... he wouldn't say, if ...."

"I know." Mary said.

"D'ya mind the time he lost the new purse you give him for Christmas." Chris said, "and he wouldn't let on and you got him another one just like it and pretended you'd found it where he was coasting, and you never let on either?"

"I remember." Mary said. "I don't believe he ever knew the difference." She smiled. "I must ask him about that when he comes home in May."

When Saturday's train passed over the river bridge, then blew for the station in town, Paul felt his nerves tauten. All along in the train he'd had only one thought, if I'd been home it wouldn't have happened. Bedding the horses, that was always my job. Your job ... your job ... your job ... the train wheels accused him.

The first familiar thing that caught his eye when he stepped onto the station platform was the old doctor's coonskin coat.

He put his suitcases in the back of the doctor's sleigh. But he didn't ask him any questions. Somehow he couldn't bear to, at the dingy station, in the town itself, where Chris has always seemed to be years rather than a few miles away from home.

When they came to the brook where Chris always stopped the horse for water and told him to "reach back in the big brown bag there" if he wanted some candy, Paul said, "How is he?"

"Well." the doctor said, "I thought it'd make your grandmother feel better if I came out again today, but ...." He shook his head.

The horse slowed to a stop. Paul's eyes fell on the skates tied to the outside of his suitcase of books. Somehow in the country men never seemed to skate after life stopped its circling just above their shoulders and settled on them. He knew he would never skate much again.

è

The next few days Paul could never get quite distinct. There are no equations for feeling.

Each time his thought tried to get things clear, a series of distracting images would block its path: His grandmother's Sunday dress and her awakened-in-the-night face that first afternoon when he and the doctor came into the house. His grandfather, raising himself on one elbow in bed, as if he couldn't talk unless his eyes were on the same level as the hearer's. His saying, with pain wavering his face like puffs of breeze on a lamp flame when the door blows open, "Ye'll find the axe where I started to clear the alders, Paul, and Fridays I always lay out to change the straw in the hens' nests." And, later, his grandmother's face, as her hand polished the nickel bar on the side of the stove, back and forth, back and forth, as she said, "No, it was Thursday. I don't know, I seem to have lost a day last week."

There was that final moment in the bedroom when three people there became two people there, unalterably, and nothing moved but the curtain, in and out a little, suddenly, like a sigh. And the moment when Mary first touched the pressing iron to Chris's good suit which, though he was a man to whom clothes mattered not at all, must have had *something* in its pattern that made him choose it rather than another.

"Paul." Mary said the second night after the funeral, "what made you bring home all your books and everything ... your skates and everything? You can't stay here. There's nothing here for anyone like you."

Nothing in Mary's tone had bid for pity or special consideration. It was merely the drained reasoning voice of one who has always been a foundation block in the household before, now feeling a helpless guilt for being there only as the hinge on which a cold practical decision, which none of them had ever dreamed of having to face, turned.

Paul couldn't answer. His tongue seemed out of connection with his mind.

As though to confront him with fact upon disrupting fact, his eyes staring out the window fell on Molly Gladwin walking down the road. If anyone had ever given Paul the word "girl" in one of those association tests, he'd have answered instantly, "Molly Gladwin."

There had always been a kind of unformed anchoring thought in the back of his mind that he and Molly might be married as soon as he'd finished his education. But now ....

"We could sell the stock." Mary said. "And I could manage all right."

And have it no less still all afternoon than when you blew out the lamp and went to bed? Never cooking anything to be divided. To have your thoughts creep back into your mind from the touch of table and chair which need two faces in the room to have a face of their own? And sometimes to sit, after your needle was put away, and stare mindlessly at your own hands and feet?

He was still silent.

"Or maybe I could go with Em." Mary said.

"You're not going with Aunt Em!" Paul exclaimed.

She had wanted to take *him* when both his parents died that same week of the black diphtheria. He would never forget his helpless dismay at the thought of going to live with Aunt Em and Uncle How. Nor would he ever forget his grandmother's gentle insistence, though without a word ever having passed between them, that this must not be.

And now she wasn't going there! It wasn't that Aunt Em and Uncle How weren't good as gold, but they only put one stick of wood in the stove at a time, and they never did the least thing that surprised themselves or anyone else, and even the air in their house seemed to be yellowing with disuse.

"You're not going with Aunt Em." he said. "I can tell you that!"

Mary took a long breath. "Maybe we should ... sell the place ... then. And I could...." She didn't finish the sentence.

"Sell the place." He knew what it had cost her even to pronounce the words. This place was the very rivers and mountains in the geography of her thoughts and feelings, and away from it they would crumble and decay.

"I'm not going back to the city." he said. "I can make a living here all right."

"Look at your hands." Mary said gently. "There's nothing but hard work here, Paul."

Well, his hands had toughened now. They stripped down the low branches of a standing tree with the axe or ribboned a perfect furrow with the plough, as if axe and plough were the only tools scaled to them. His dark face came to have the same countryman's grip in it as Chris's had had.

Yet the shadow of Paul's city life still lingered in him, disconcerting him. What kind, what better kind, of someone else might he have been if he had stayed there?

And Mary knew how he felt. Nothing either did for the other was in the least grudging. And to each the other was the projection of himself where injury or slight would sting sharpest. But he was restless, and she was beholden. That was always there. And so it came to be an area of constraint as tender and diffused as a blind boil.

They fell into the habit of examining beforehand whatever they said or did in each other's presence, to inhibit it if it threatened to touch on this sore spot. They couldn't seem to communicate a piece of news to each other with normal zest. One would have to lay it down as if he weren't looking, and the other pick it up slowly by the edge. A joke between them became impossible.

And though they didn't lie in wait to score off each other, they did fall into the habit of saying things like, "No wonder you have a cold. You never brush the snow off your clothes when you come into the house." Or, "You left the cellar door open last night." Or, "I thought you said you weren't going to wash today."

Most crippling of all, each knew (and knew that the other knew) that the prospect was a downhill one. Mary lived under the shadow of the day when she must ask his help inside the house, when she could no longer manage the care of her own person. And Paul fell into the awful stoicism that borrows no enlargement whatever for the things of today from the expectations of tomorrow.

ॐ

Finally, as it was bound to, there came the afternoon when the blighting accusation was spoken and the indelible response was put into words.

It had been for Paul one of those days of clenched, grinding mood which everyone knows occasionally. When there is a conspiracy among even trifles to frustrate you.

He had overslept. The single gust of wind that morning came at the very second the butt of the big spruce was severed, and took it into the thicket. He couldn't have found a rock in that part of the woods if he'd searched for one, but his axe found one all right. His watch stopped and tricked him into arriving home just too late to catch the dairyman he'd been waiting weeks to see.

And—Molly Gladwin. Her name stung suddenly in his mind like a spot these irritations had scraped the scab off so that the fresh blood came. Everyone else had a wife ....

When he stepped into the kitchen half an hour past dinnertime, Mary said to him, "I thought you were coming home early, Paul. The dairyman stopped in to see you, but he couldn't wait."

"What the hell difference does it make?" he flashed out at her. "Anyone buried in this damn ... all his life ... poor as a church mouse ... working your heart out for a few dollars ...."

He didn't know where the false words came from, how they slipped past his guard. They made no sense as an answer to her question.

Mary caught her breath. "Well, Paul." she said, "old people have to live till they die. Do you ever stop to think what it's like for me? You'll be old some day."

They turned away from each other's face, and each looked as if he wished he could turn away from his own. There is nothing so terrible as the silence after words like that in a country kitchen. There is nothing as terrible as sitting at the table and swallowing your food (it was spareribs; it was to have been special) after a silence like that.

It was the very next morning when Paul was fishing in the button box on the shelf for a piece of carpenter's chalk that the faded clipping tucked behind it fluttered on the couch.

He bent to retrieve it, and Mary said quickly, "Give it here and I'll put it in the stove. Trash collects so."

He passed it to her and she burned it. But he couldn't help noticing the big black headlines: DELICATE OPERATION RESTORES SIGHT TO 90-YEAR-OLD WOMAN.

Why did she read so little now and sew so little? The answer came to him like a blow. He narrowed his own lids and made the kitchen go like a snapshot taken when it is almost dark. To have it every minute of the day like that ....

He desperately wanted to say something, but how could he, with the punishing memory of what he'd said yesterday still so raw? The next day at dinner he forced himself to bring it up, obliquely.

"Why don't you go into town someday and have your eyes looked after?" he said. "Those old glasses must be...."

She hesitated. "I did." she said. "The day I took in the mats."

Yes, she must have. He remembered how that day when she'd come home she'd stood on the porch with her packages still in her arms and looked about the fields for several minutes, like someone committing them to memory before a long journey.

"What did he say?" he said.

"Oh," she said, "he didn't tell me much of anything different. You'll have to season that squash yourself," she added quickly, "I forgot the salt."

When she went outside to feed the hens, Paul phoned the doctor. Yes. Yes, both of them. Yes, progressive. Maybe six months ... a year ... it was hard to tell. Well, yes, sometimes they could ... there was this brilliant new eye surgeon in the city...."

Paul thanked him. The city... at her age it would seem like the ends of the earth to her. A hospital ... the word which all country people recoil from. The expense ... she'd never in the world consent to take his money. Never, after what he'd said.

And that evening he knew the answer to the question which two days ago his anger had flushed from behind her face. "Do you ever stop to think what it's like for me?"

What must it be like for the old?

Was being old anything they could help? Was it their fault that people were made half angry by whatever it is in people which makes them half angry at anything they might, if they let themselves consider it, pity?

He couldn't get to sleep that night. He turned one eye against the pillow and darkened the other with the palm of his hand, trying for sleep that way. But it was no use.

છે.

Mary had always liked to be in some small way somebody particular. It had nothing to do with pride, or ambition, or dissatisfaction with the country-woman's lot. But any little thing that won her recognition by outside standards (though she herself might know it was a silly thing to put any real stock in) gave her a curious glow.

She had never had but one ring with a stone in it, and it was not valuable. But she knew instinctively which things might be old and plain but still beautiful, as she knew which ones might be expensive but still just cheap. And whenever a stranger was coming she would slip it on her finger and hold that hand uppermost in her lap. She knew how to set her table just right for her kind of house, with no hint of imitation from a magazine page. She had, in her Bible, the letter the judge of a handwriting contest had written her once, awarding her first prize of five dollars and saying that she "showed an artist's touch." She still had the five-dollar bill, too.

She had kept in a twist of tissue paper in her top bureau drawer the little gold hoop which a tourist, stopping for a drink at the well, had impulsively taken off her own hair and put onto Mary's because she said—and Mary could tell that the spirit of the action was in no way rude or patronizing—it was just the thing to make Mary look like a character study for Renoir.

He got up and lit a cigarette.

He knew that just beneath her consciousness had always been the feeling that her life would reach some extraordinary little distinction, the thing she'd be remembered by. But instead of her life coming to any climax, it was like a room that gets silent and more silent as the fire stills and stills. It was as if a child's birthday were coming up when of course some plan must be underway, unknown to him, to put something splendid into his hand, and yet no one was planning anything at all.

He sat on the side of the bed, his last cigarette gone, alone in the deaf night-stillness that rings in your ears with every note of how you may have failed someone.

She was never to blame about Molly, he thought. It was the doubts my own imagination cast up. How would she and Molly get along? Would it be fair to either of them? And, deeper than that, it was my own crippling doubt. If you didn't know what kind of life was going to be yours later on, how could you tell which kind of girl you should ask to share it?

She didn't deny me wife and children. If there was ever any question of denial, I denied them to her—the family stir which should be there to shield anyone old from the bare still face of things as they are.

She rescued me from Aunt Em, but she never crowded me, like Aunt Em would have. She never put out a single tendril around my independence even then ....

His thoughts had seemed only to roil and writhe, but the glancing memory of Mary's handwriting prize must have struck root in Paul's brain. Otherwise a recurring notice in the farm periodical they sub-scribed to would have snagged his interest for the first time that very next night.

It was the announcement of a much bigger contest. Whoever the editors decided had sent in the best account of "My Favourite Memory" would receive five brand-new, hundred-dollar bills.

He had a sudden wild notion. If Mary had that much money which she'd won herself.... Why couldn't he fake it?

"Here's something." he said to her awkwardly. Speech between them still came like a startling sound. He read her the details. "Why don't you try it? You could think it up and I could write it down for you."

She gave the idea that particular smile you accord the preposterous. "Paul!" she said. "You know I could never put anything together that would ...."

But the next night when he said again, "Why don't you try that con-test?" she hesitated a minute, and then she said, "Well ... I suppose we wouldn't lose anything but the stamp, would we?"

She must have kept her mind on it all the next day. For that evening, diffidently, she brought out a whole sheaf of recollections to pick from.

He found it curiously hurting to see her so unsuspectingly serious over a choice. To know that, however she poked fun at her folly in pre-suming to chance this thing, she had a secret little hope in what she was doing nevertheless. But if his plan worked ....

"My husband was working away the day I lost my wedding ring." the memory she finally decided on went. "He didn't like to leave me with the chores, but that was the first year we were married and there was hardly any money. I hated to tell him when he came home. I was never afraid to tell him anything, but here I'd been supposed to be helping him out, and the ring had cost twenty dollars. I tried to make out I didn't mind as much as I did, but I felt heartbroken and naked with-out it.

"I was pretty sure I had lost it in the barn. We looked all through the barn. In the linter. In the feedbin. In the chaff on the barn floor. And he went over the whole haymow as cautious as a kitten poking the tines of the fork down through the loose hay and listening for a clink. We couldn't find it anywhere.

"He had a heifer he was raising for an extra cow. One day he said, 'I think I'll beef that heifer. She wouldn't make much of a cow.' I said, 'No, Chris, don't sell her, the money'll only go. Trade her in on another cow.' 'No,' he said, 'I think I'll sell her. One cow's enough for you to look after when I'm away so much.' I thought, he's going to beef her and sell her and buy me another ring. We couldn't afford it. But I didn't care to tell him not to spend the money that way because, if that wasn't what he had in mind, then he might think he had to.

"He killed the heifer and when they opened her, there was the ring, lodged in that part of her stomach they call the book because it looks a little like the leaves of a book. It must have got into her bran and middlings when I was swishing them up together in her feedbox and she'd swallowed it. It hadn't hurt her a bit.

"I remember the look on his face when he came in the door that day with his closed fist stuck out, and when he spread his fingers open and there was the ring in the palm of his hand.

"And I remember what he said when he slipped it on my finger again. 'This should be a lesson to us. We must never be afraid to part with something we need, to buy something we ....' He didn't finish, but I knew what he meant. And we never were."

The next day in town Paul went to the bank, and miraculously they did have five new hundred-dollar bills. It seemed like a blessing on his plan. The withdrawal almost emptied his account but he was reminded of Chris's words about the ring. The coincidence seemed like a good omen.

Then he bought an airmail envelope and stamp and a pad of typewriter paper. He used the typewriter at the library. He wrote, "Dear Mrs. Redmond: It is our great pleasure to inform you that your entry has been chosen as the best of all submitted in our recent contest. First-prize money is enclosed, with our heartiest congratulations."

He folded the sheet and put it into the envelope, with the bills, and sealed and stamped the envelope. It gave him a sudden pang to realize that all this forging of detail was probably needless. She could hardly tell one set of words, or one envelope, from another now.

She would need new clothes. He hesitated twice at the door of Chapman's Ladies' Wear and twice passed on.

The third trip by, he glanced through the window and saw Molly Gladwin standing beside the long counter.

With that heightened awareness you feel just after the ice of some daring project has first been broken, he seemed to be seeing her truly for the first time. He seemed to catch in this glimpse of her generous brown-eyed face, with that delicacy just below the skin which minimizes each feature and is more like the delicacy of hands, the essence of her. As if in a frame. For no good reason, it seemed to him to be a face that must be protected from ever going small with slight.

He went inside.

"I..." he said to her. "She needs a new dress and coat and hat and shoes. I thought maybe you.... How would that hat do, there in the window?"

Molly turned her back to the saleswoman and grimaced at him, just barely shaking her head and half laughing.

"No." she whispered, drawing him away from the counter, "Paul! That's kind of an old funeral hat. She wants something with ... there, more like that one ... with a little" — she made a motion with her hands — "in the front, and just a tiny little veil."

And when it came to the dress, she said, "No, Paul, she doesn't want a black dress. She wants a pattern, maybe great big flowers even, with some white around the neck...."

He had a picture of her and Mary deep in that special climate of settling on what kind of clothing looked best on each other and laughing at him for the mystery he found the whole thing. Or in that other special climate of planning the feminine touches inside a house which a man may find pleasant but must pretend not to notice except almost grudgingly, and which he'd envision wildly wrong if he were asked for suggestions.

He paid for the things and arranged to leave them at the store until the time came, he hoped, for Mary's trip to the city.

On an impulse he confided his plan to Molly. "Well, bless you ..." she said.

When he closed the door on the way out, he caught another glimpse of her, back at the counter again.

Her hand lay perfectly still on the bolt of cloth the saleswoman had rolled out for her. She was looking at him with that absorbed expression which gives such a wonderful feeling to anyone at whom no one else ever turns his head when the conversation is over and he has walked away.

Of all the people he knew, Molly alone could lighten his plaguing intentness instantly. And afterward he always felt like holding his head straighter and smiling at people and taking deeper breaths and longer steps.

The afternoon Paul slipped the airmail envelope inside the newspaper at the mailbox, Mary was trying to patch an apron.

"Paul." she said, "before you look at the paper, could you thread this needle for me? The eye seems to be so fine."

"In a minute." he said, opening the paper, smiling. "Look at this first."

She took the envelope in her hand and her hands began to tremble.

"Paul." she said, and her voice sounded frightened almost, "it isn't … is it? Open it."

"No." he said, "you open it. It's for you."

She opened the envelope and when she unfolded the sheet of paper, the bills fell into her lap.

He saw that she couldn't speak, and he picked up the sheet of paper to read out what was on it.

"Oh, Paul!" she cried. "I never *dreamed* … did you?" She put her apron to her eyes.

"Now, don't …" he said.

"I can't help it." she said, wresting the tremor of her voice into a shaky little laugh. "I'm such a fool when anything like this happens!" Her face shone. "Now you can get …. There's so many things. "

"I don't need anything." he said. "What that money's going for is to have your eyes seen to!"

She shook her head. "No." she said, "no. There's so many things we need."

Paul spoke with mock sternness. "Do you remember what Grandfather said, about what you need and what you …?"

She had to try hard, not to cry again. The way it is when mention is made of some affliction you have borne silently and without hope, which suddenly seems almost like a friend, now that a miraculous way is open to release from it.

"Of course, I suppose …" she spoke hesitantly, as if she were stating aloud to herself what she must have stated silently to herself time and time again, though knowing she could never give in to her own argument, " … if I let them go and was to get so I couldn't …."

She stopped again. Her voice could only support so many words at a time. "It almost seems like this was sent, doesn't it? I believe in those things!"

ᏋᎧ

Paul wouldn't have credited that anything could so alter the tempo of their living. Even the days seemed to have a new spring in their step.

Mary put up no real resistance to any of the things he had expected she would resist. Neither to her new clothes, now that she believed her own money had bought them, nor to the trip, nor to the hospital.

Molly came over and showed her at just what angle the hat should be worn, and he heard them consulting about what she should or should nor pack in her suitcase. (She'd have hated to take her own hairbrush if that should prove to be a homeliness which marked her as unused to the knowledge of outside ways.)

Of the trip he'd thought she'd say, "It seems like such an undertaking at my age." Instead, she said, "The plane from Greenwood would take us there in a couple of hours, but I suppose it'd cost a lot more that way, wouldn't it?" And he thought, how many small luxuries and excitements I've always taken for granted would have no claim on her, she must have had a secret little weakness for all along.

He was determined that nothing should spoil it for her. He gave her no hint of his one terrible misgiving. A taste of the city, and what fresh restlessness would he have to battle all over again when he came back home?

But there was no denying it. Each time she said jubilantly, "It will be a change for you too, Paul." it came to the surface like a treacherous fin.

It was only in aftersight that Paul recognized those times when the words "proud" and "exultant" had come closest to pronouncing their own name explicitly in his consciousness.

He was proud of Mary in the plane. Nothing about her pointed or exclaimed. You'd never have guessed that this flight might not be something quite usual for her. But he knew she was thinking, I am almost eighty years old and I am flying in an airplane and everyone is giving me a special smile.

He was proud of her in the surgeon's office.

The surgeon, who had that particular gentleness so often associated with great strength, came down from his doctor's eminence and balanced the grave risks and the tempting hopes for her as concernedly as if she were a member of his own family. She gave him her decision with a single nod of her head—no tears, not one—and a quick trusting grasp of his hand.

He was proud of her in the hospital room.

There the nurses kidded her ("The little one wanted to put lipstick on me today!"), asked her if they could try parting her hair on the other side just to see how it looked, made no secret to her of the fact that she was their favourite and bravest and most extraordinary patient, and confided to her little personal problems of their own. In an innocent and curiously affecting way, it was like a little court to her.

He was proud of her all that long punishing afternoon when all the fantastic contrivances of medical science up to this moment and all the magic of the surgeon's hands had learned up to now were focused on the face that flinched only by a moment's twitch of her smile when the needles stabbed. He was exultant for her that last day of all in the surgeon's office. As she read down the letters of the chart, while the gentle surgeon smiled deeper and deeper with each line.

She read them proudly and exultantly, as if she were passing her hand over a face believed lost. And then, yes, the two pardonable tears. And once more the impulsive touch, almost reverent now with more of thankfulness than there had been even of trusting before, on both her deliverer's miraculous hands.

"Isn't it odd, Dr. Key!" she said, smiling just right to discount the sentiment of her remark, "you told me things might be a little blurry at first, and your face does seem to have a sort of halo around it."

And right then the doctor made her the gift almost equal to his gift of sight.

He told her her case was so unique he was writing it up for an international medical journal. He would send her a copy.

"Mary Redmond." Her own name in learned print! Circulating all over the world! At last she'd been turned from a crowd-face into somebody particular!

Now her life wouldn't just thin away, absolutely unexceptional. Now she'd have this little fund of special notice, like a small treasure she could carry around in her pocket to touch reassuringly whenever she wished.

"You know I'm almost eighty." she said gently.

"I know." the doctor said, smiling at her that same special smile which the people in the plane had given her. "That's just it!"

The success of Mary's operation Paul had been prepared to rejoice in.

What he'd been totally unprepared for was the bloodless operation on his own vision. Face to face with this place where he'd expected to see everywhere he turned the torturing ghost of his other possible life, he was unbearably homesick. It was as simple as that.

Here where you left no track, where almost everyone was servant to something, where the memory of you stopped with your breath, he longed to be back where you could see the paths your feet had made on the yielding earth. Where your only masters were sun and storm. Where in your neighbours' registry of deeds any little individuality you'd ever achieved was perpetually recorded. And where your little kingdom would always be known as "the Paul Redmond place" as long as the windows of your house still looked out on the spot where you lay. It struck him that intensely.

A letter had come from Molly. He thought, with an unaccountable tenderness, I've never seen my name in her handwriting before.

He thought, she could never fit into the mould that seems to pattern most of these sure-faced wives here. I was right about that. But she has the one thing most of them haven't, the kind of understanding that's a passport anywhere that matters.

He had that wonderful feeling you have when it suddenly dawns on you that you really love someone, the feeling that, between you, an insight into everything is possible. He could hardly wait to tell her how ....

But that is Paul's story. This is Mary's.

There are two pictures of Mary that tell the rest of her story better than words.

One, a city reporter took of her for his newspaper the day before she left. She has the little gold hoop on her hair and the smile on her face honestly does give her the look of a Renoir. The smile was still on her face from having just said to Paul, though the contest itself she didn't mention, "Paul, do you remember the time you lost your purse and I pretended I came across it where you'd been coasting? Did *you* ever suspect the difference later?"

The other—and perhaps a better one still—was taken this last month. With Paul, Jr. A child with a quite ordinary face. But you can see by the way she looks at him that she's sure he'll be somebody. Really somebody, for all of them.

In the country, it doesn't matter in the least which member of the family that happens to be.

The Bars and the Bridge

Two scars have bracketed my left eye since I was ten. They have faded now to tiny commas visible only in cold or pallor. But they are really periods, not commas, in the syntax of my life. Not by reason of the accident that caused them, though. The reason has to do with my father.

I have never been able to put Father into words. Whenever I search for an adjective to describe him it's the comparative of it that comes to mind. Stronger. So1ider. Braver. (The time he crawled into a wounded bear's den to end her suffering became local legend, though he hated mention of it.) Or it's prefaced by the word "absolutely." Absolutely honest. Absolutely loyal.... Yet that doesn't suggest a true picture of him at all. Because the other adjectives which these summon up — severe, proud, uncompromising — don't apply in the least. (And I have made him sound like a "name." but he was a village farmer.)

The nearest I can come to illustrating this paradox is to say that he cast the biggest shadow, yet there was no darkness about him at all; that I never heard him make a sentimental remark in his life, but he took up the mousetrap the morning after the mouse had come out in the night and carried two peanuts into the toe of his rubber boot.

He was in no way forbidding (my sisters could swarm all over him without seeming to notice whether he responded with anything more than an indulgent gleam in his eye or not), yet there existed a curious awkwardness between us.

I suppose it was because we were so different. He never ran, he almost never laughed out loud, he was never flustered. I was tempery, mercurial, impulsive. I always made 100 in Arithmetic, but he could *judge* the exact acreage in a field while I was getting out my pencil.

We loved each other, but he never kissed me. He never took my hand even on the ruggedest log road. In a neighbour's house of a Sunday afternoon I might stand nearer him than anyone else, but I never got onto his lap as the other kids got onto their father's laps, mauling them and teasing them for candy money to go home. He never made me any of those small-scale replicas of farm gear that the other men made their sons—tiny ox-carts, tiny trail sleds. In any case, miniatures were not in his province. The plow was his instrument. On that scale, even without pacing or markers, the free-hand rows of his garden came out as beautifully straight as if they'd been done with a chalk-line.

One day he came across me poking seeds between the potato plants. "What's them?" he said.

I could be evasive with anyone else; I could never give him less than the whole truth.

"They're orange seeds." I said. I had saved them from the Christmas before. Oranges were such an exotic thing to us then that it was as if I were planting a mystery.

"They won't grow here." he said.

I dug them out and planted them, secretly, behind the barn. I knew it was farthest from his intention to deride anything I did, but whatever scheme of mine he watched seemed to turn suddenly ridiculous.

ॐ

The night of the accident was one of those cold drizzly nights in early Nova Scotian summer when animals in the pasture huddle like forlorn statues. The sort of night when the cows never come.

School had finished that very day. This was the third year I had graded twice and I was very excited. Next term I would have such occult subjects as Chemistry and Geometry! I felt cubits taller than the "kid" I had been yesterday.

I was prattling on to Mother about all the kings and queens of England I'd be studying and the new books I'd be exploring next term. Father took no part in the conversation at all, though he was not for that reason outside it—and everything I said was for his benefit too.

He was waiting to milk.

"Ain't it about time you got after the cows?" he said at last.

He never commanded me. I don't know why it would have been more embarrassing than punitive if he ever had.

Chemistry... cows. I winced. "They'll come, won't they?" I said. (I knew better.) "They come last night."

I never used good speech when Father was around. I'd have felt like a girl. Though he was a far wiser and better educated man in the true sense of the word than I've ever been.

"They won't come a night like this." he said. They're likely holed up in a spruce thicket somewhere, outa the rain."

"I'll see if I can hear the bell." I temporized. I went out on the porch steps and listened. There wasn't a sound.

"It's no use to wait for the bell." Father called. "They won't budge a hair tonight."

"Well, if they ain't got sense enough to come themselves a night like this." I said in as near as I'd ever come to sputtering at him, "why can't they just stay out?"

"I'd never get 'em back to their milk for a week." he said.

I went then, but, as he couldn't help seeing, grudgingly.

I sat on the bars and called, "Co-boss, Co-boss." but there wasn't the tinkle of a bell.

I loved to be out in a good honest rain, but this was different. I picked my steps down the pasture lane to avoid the clammy drops that showered from every bush or fern you touched.

I came to the first clearing where Father had planted the burntland potatoes last year. The cows were nowhere to be seen. But Pedro, the horse, was there, hunched up and gloomy-looking in the drizzle. I couldn't bear to see him so downcast without trying to cheer him up.

I went up and patted his rump. He moved just far enough ahead to escape my touch. It was the kind of night when the touch of anything sends a shivery feeling all through you.

I should have known that the horse wanted to be left alone. But I kept at it. I'd touch him, the horse would move ahead, I'd follow behind and touch him again. The horse laid back his ears.

I still retain the exact visual impression of the moment exploding. The big black haunch erupting, and the hoof, like a sudden devouring jaw somehow, right in front of my left eye. The horse wasn't shod or I'd have been killed.

I was stunned. But in a minute I got to my feet again. I put my hand to my face. It came away all blood. If there was any pain then, I don't remember it. I think it was the sight of the blood and that peculiar shock when some perfectly gentle object has suddenly disclosed a brutal face that made me start to scream.

Father heard me crying before I came in sight. He started off to meet me. When I came through the alders below the barn and he saw me holding my hand to my face he broke into a run. Before he got to the bars he could see the blood.

He didn't stop to let down a single bar. He leapt them. I'd never seen him move like that in my life before. He grabbed me up and raced back to the house.

Within minutes the house was a hubbub of neighbours. I gloried in the breathless attention that everyone bent on me. I asked Father to

hold me up to the mirror over the sink. "No, no, Joseph, don't…"
Mother pleaded, but he obeyed me. My face was a mass of cuts and
bruises. I felt like a Plantagenet borne off the field with royal wounds.
I remember all the headshakings:

"That biggest cut don't look too good to me. Pretty deep…"
and ministrations: "I got some o' that b'racit acit fer washin' out
wounds down home. I could git it in a minute…"
and injunctions: "No, *don't* let him lay down. Anyone's had a blow
on the head, always keep 'em movin' around…"

And I remember Mother beseeching me over and over, "Can you
see all right? Are you sure you can see all right?"

I don't remember anything obtrusive Father said or did. But he'd be
the one who called the doctor and told him *exactly* what the situation
was. When the doctor came at last, he'd be the one who rugged his
steaming horse and quietly put the extra leaves in the dining-room
table so they could lay me on it to have the stitches taken. The doctor
confessed to some anxiety about my standing anaesthetic, but it would
be Father's hand that held the "chlraform" cone for him, his hand as
steady as the doctor's own.

The doctor kept me in bed for three weeks. Father came in to see me
once each day and just before he went to bed. If I had the looking glass
in my hand, admiring my wounded eye which was now swollen shut
and the color of thunder sunsets, I would thrust it under the bedclothes
when I heard him coming. We exchanged almost exactly the same awkward words every time. He was the sort of man who looks helplessly
out of place in a bedroom. He never sat down.

Sometimes, with the pathetic transparency which children can see
through quickest of all, Mother would recount something he'd said or
done, trying to make it witness to some special bond between him and
me that I might not suspect. But I always squirmed, as children will
whenever a tender subject with them is put into words, however devi-
ous, and changed the conversation immediately.

All this is like a luminous patch on the general blur of childhood.
But the morning that is absolutely clear in every detail is the first morning I went outdoors again.

I'd planned to walk, but Father picked me up without a word and carried me. I didn't protest. But this time there was no tumult of excitement
as before to leave me mindless of his arms about me. The unaccustomed
feel of them made me aware of every ounce of my own weight. I suppose it was merely an ordinary fine summer's morning, but I remember it as the freshest, greenest, and sunniest of my life.

The moment we left the house behind it was plain that this wasn't just an aimless outing. He was *taking* me somewhere.

He carried me straight across the house field and down the slope beyond, where the soil was richest from the barn's drainage. Where I had stuck the orange seeds in the sod.

I saw where we were headed for before we got there. But I couldn't speak. I was struck almost atremble with a shaft of that distending joy that comes only a few times ever, out of all proportion to what provokes it. He had never made me any miniature wagons or sleds as the other men had for their sons. But he had made me a replica now of the one thing he had magic for.

He set me down beside a tiny garden.

Tiny, but the rows as immaculate as washboard ribs, and a miniature one for each of his own rows. This had been no job for the plow, though. It had been the patient work of fork and spade, and then the careful, even delicate, molding by his hands. He must have started it right after the accident, because the seeds were already through the ground. And he hadn't even told Mother about it.

"This can be yours." he said.

"Oh, Father." I began, "it's …" But how could I tell him what it was? I bent down quickly to examine the sprouts. "What's them?" I said, pointing to the strange plants in the outside rows.

"Melons." he said, pointing, "and red peppers … and citron."

He must have got them specially from the man who had the big glass hothouse in town. Things he'd never have dreamed of planting in his own garden. Things almost as fanciful as orange seeds.

"You never know, he said, "they might grow here."

I couldn't speak. But I think he could tell from the look on my face what silent delight was racing behind it. Or else what he said next would never have broken out.

"You don't think I'd a made you go for them cows if I'd a knowed you was gonna get…." he said almost savagely, "do you? I wouldn't a cared if they'd a never give another drop o' milk as long as they lived!"

I made him a crazy answer. But it didn't seem crazy to either of us then. Because of a sudden something that seemed to bridge all the gaps of speech.

"You jumped right over the bars when you saw I was hurt, didn't you!" I said. "You never even took the top one down. You just jumped right clear over 'em!"

He turned his face away, and it looked as if his shoulders were taking a long deep breath. He let me walk back to the house.

When we went into the kitchen someone said, "Where did you go?"

I don't know why there was a sudden understanding between us that this was some sort of secret.

"Just out." I said.

"Just out around." Father echoed.

I never again felt the old need to *adjust* myself at the sound of his footstep. Not ever.

Short Fictions

Long, Long After School

I ran into Wes Holman the very day I was collecting for Miss Tretheway's flowers. But it never came into my head to ask him for a contribution.

Miss Tretheway had taught Grade Three in our town for exactly fifty years. She had died the night before in her sleep. As chairman of the school board I had thought it would be fitting if all the Grade Three alumni who were still around made up enough money to get a really handsome "piece." She had no relatives. If I'd given it an instant's consideration I'd have known that Wes himself must have been in Grade Three some time or other; but I didn't.

Wes was just coming through the cemetery gate as I was going in. Wes "looks after" the cemetery, and I sometimes take a short cut through it on my way to work. I should say that Wes is our local "character." His tiny house up behind the ball park is furnished with almost nothing but books, and he can quote anyone from Seneca to Henry James. But that's his job: caretaker-about-town.

When I spoke to him about Miss Tretheway, a curious change came into his face. You couldn't say that he turned pale, but his stillness was quite different from the conventional one on such occasions. I had expected him to come out with some quote or other, but he didn't say a word.

He didn't go to her funeral. But he sent her flowers of his own. Or brought them, rather. The following day, when I took the short cut again, I surprised him on his knees placing them.

His little bunch of flowers was the most incongruous thing you could imagine. It was a corsage. A corsage of simple flowers, such as a young boy sends his girl for her first formal dance. And more incongruous than its presence in the circumstance of death was its connection with Miss Tretheway herself. I'm quite sure that Miss Tretheway never once had a beau send her flowers, that she'd never been to a dance in her whole life.

I suppose it would never have occurred to me to question anyone but Wes about his motive for doing a thing like that. But I asked Wes about it with no thought of rudeness whatever. Wes's privacy seemed to be everyone's property. There was probably a little self-conscious democracy in the gesture when we talked to him at all.

"She was so beautiful," he answered me, as if no other explanation was needed.

That was plainly ridiculous. That Miss Tretheway was a fine person for having spent a lifetime in small, unheralded services could not be disputed—but obviously she hadn't *ever* been beautiful. Her sturdy plainness was never transfigured, not even for an instant, by the echo of anything winsomer which had faded. Her eyes had never been very blue, her skin very pink, or her hair very brown. She wasn't very anything. Her heart might have been headlong (I think now that it was), but there was always that curious precision and economy in her face which lacks altogether the grain of helter-skelter necessary to any kind of charm. In short, even when she'd been a girl, she'd been the sort of girl whose slightest eagerness, more than if she were ugly or old, a young man automatically shies away from.

"But, Wes," I said, half-joking, "she wasn't beautiful. What made you say that?"

His story went something like this. He told it with a kind of dogged, confessional earnestness. I guess he'd come to figure that whenever we asked him a personal question he might as well satisfy our curiosity completely, first as last.

"Perhaps you remember how the kids used to tease me at school," he said. (I didn't. I guess those things stick in your mind according to which end of the teasing you happen to be on.) "If the boys would be telling some joke with words in it to giggle over, they'd look at me and say, 'Shhhh … Wes is blushing.' Or if we were all climbing up the ladder to the big beam in Hogan's stable, they'd say 'Look at Wes. He's so scared he's turning pale.' Do you remember the night you steered your sled into mine, going down Parker hill?"

"No," I said. "Did I do it on purpose?"

"I don't know," Wes said. "Maybe you didn't. I thought you did."

Maybe I did. I don't remember.

"I was taking Mrs. Banks's wash home on my sled, and you were coasting down the hill. The basket upset and all the things fell out on the snow. Don't you remember … Miss Tretheway came along and you all ran. She helped me pick up the stuff and shake the snow off it. She went with me right to Mrs. Banks's door and told her what had happened. I could never have made Mrs. Banks believe I didn't upset the stuff myself."

"I'm sorry," I said. I probably *had* done it on purpose.

"That's all right," he said. "I didn't mind the boys so much. It was the girls. You can't hit a girl. There just wasn't anything I could do about the girls. One day Miss Tretheway was showing us a new game in the school yard. I don't remember exactly how it went, but that one where we all made a big circle and someone stood in the centre. I put my hand out to close up the ring with the biggest Banks girl, but she wouldn't take it. She said, 'Your hands are dirty.' Miss Tretheway made us both hold out our hands. She said, 'Why, Marilyn, Wes's hands are much cleaner than yours. Maybe Wes doesn't like to get *his* hands dirty, did you ever think about that?' She took Marilyn's place herself. Her hand felt safe and warm, I remember... and I guess that's the first day I thought she was beautiful."

"I see," I said.

I did, and yet I didn't. The Wes I remembered would hate anything with the suggestion of teacher's pet about it. The only Wes I could seem to remember was the Wes of adolescence: the tough guy with the chip on his shoulder.

He was coming to that. But he stuck in an odd parenthesis first.

"Did you ever notice Miss Tretheway" he said, "when ... well, when the other teachers would be talking in the hall about the dances they'd been to over the weekend? Or when she'd be telling some kid a story after school and the kid would run off right in the middle of a sentence when she saw her mother coming to pick her up?"

"No," I said. "Why? What about it?"

"Oh, nothing, I guess." He drew a deep breath. "Anyway, I decided I'd be stronger and I'd study harder than anyone. And I was, wasn't I? I did. Do you remember the year they voted me the best all-round student in High School?" (I didn't. It must have been after I'd graduated.) "I guess I just can't remember how happy I was about that. I guess I was so happy I could believe anything. That must have been why I let the boys coax me into going to the closing dance." He smiled. "I thought since they'd voted for me ... but you can't legislate against a girl's glance."

Those were his exact words. Maybe he'd read them somewhere. Maybe they were his own. I don't know. But it was the kind of remark which had built up his quaint reputation as the town philosopher.

"I didn't want to go out on the dance floor," he said. "I'd never danced a foxtrot or anything. The girls all had on their evening dresses, and somehow they looked different altogether. They looked as if they wouldn't recognize *themselves* in their day clothes. Anyway, the boys grabbed hold of me and made me get into a Paul Jones. I was next to

Toby Wenford in the big ring. Jane Evans was right opposite me when the music stopped, but she danced with Toby instead—and the girl next to Jane just glanced at me and then went and sat down. I guess it was a pretty foolish thing to do, but I went down in the basement and drove my fist through a window."

"Is that the scar?" I said. I couldn't think of anything else to say.

"Oh, it was a lot worse than that," he said. He pulled up his sleeve and traced the faint sickle of the scar way up his arm. "You can hardly see it now. But I almost bled to death right there. I guess I might have, if it hadn't been for Miss Tretheway."

"Oh?" I said. "How's that?"

"You see, they didn't have any plasma around in bottles then," he said, "and in those days no one felt too comfortable about having his blood siphoned off. I guess no one felt like taking any chances for me, anyway. Mother said I could have hers, but hers wasn't right. Mine's that odd type—three, isn't it? Miss Tretheway's was three, too ... and that's funny, because only seven percent of people have it. She gave me a whole quart, just as soon as she found out that hers would match."

"I see," I said. So that was it. And yet I had a feeling that that *wasn't* it—not quite.

"She used to come see me every day," he said. "She used to bring me books. Did you know that books ... well, that for anyone like me that's the only way you can ...?" He hesitated, and I knew that that wasn't quite it either.

Not until he spoke again, when he spoke so differently, was I sure that only now was he coming to the real thing.

"Do you know what Miss Tretheway said when I thanked her for the transfusion?" he said. "She made a joke of it. She said 'I didn't know whether an old maid's blood would be any good to a fine young specimen like you, Wes, or not.' The thing I always remember, I knew that was the first time she'd ever called herself an old maid to anyone, and really felt like laughing. And I remember what *I* said. I said: 'Miss Tretheway, you're making me blush.' And do you know, that was the very first time I'd ever been able to say *that*, and laugh, myself."

There was quite a long silence.

"She was beautiful," he added softly. "She was a real lady."

The cemetery is right next to the river. I looked down the river where the cold December water lapped at the jagged ice thrown up on the banks, and I thought about a boy the colour of whose skin was such that he could never blush, and I thought about a girl who had never been asked to a dance. I thought about the corsage. My curiosity was quite satisfied. But somehow I myself had never felt less beautiful, or less of a gentleman.

Humble Pie

Sue-Ellen Price—she adopted the hyphen herself—was trim and flashy as a bird. She only came up to about here on Dave Marshall, but everyone said it was easy to see which one would call the tune in that match. Sue-Ellen just *had* to have the centre of the stage. "Look at that engagement ring," the talk went. "Wouldn't you know? A garnet wasn't good enough for her. Oh no, she had to have a diamond!" And the way she'd got Dave! Stealin' him away from Kate Weatherby. That's all you could call it, just plain stealin'.

Tongues buzzed faster than ever when Sue-Ellen got up the pie sale. The *idea* of a woman "goin' ahead" with that kind of a social! To buy a community bull! But Sue-Ellen said that if the men didn't have enough gumption to make the first move, why not have the social now, before the crew working on the power dam went away? If those strangers liked the looks of a pie, they didn't care how much they paid for it!

People are still talking about that pie sale.

It had always been a point of honor in Blighville that a girl didn't "tell her pie." Not even to her beau. He was considered a pretty lumpish fellow if he didn't find out, somehow, which was hers; but it was part of the game that she herself played Sphinx. The lengths to which he'd go to secure information elsewhere, including bribery of kid brothers or sisters, were a test and gauge of his devotion. Most of the girls brought their pies in a cocoon of wrapping paper (all poked up at the top so the trimmings wouldn't muss), and not a pin was removed until they reached that big table behind the screen.

But that wasn't Sue-Ellen's way.

"What kind of pie *you* takin'?" Dave kidded her the afternoon before the social.

"Cream chiffon," she said. Immediately. "It's got a lattice crust with showers on it, and it's in a basket like ... with paper roses around the bottom and a handle over top with roses all over *that*. You'll know it all right." She giggled. "I bet they'll run you up. You know how they always do, anyone's just engaged."

They always did. Oh, not so it wrecked the guy, but high enough to have some fun with it.

Dave smiled. "Maybe not." he said. "I got a scheme. I'm going to bid a little on every pie that goes up, to fool 'em. And if I have to go higher'n around two dollars on yours, so they don't get suspicious ... well, I give Pat Newlin the wink, see, and he bids it in *for* me."

Sue-Ellen's face went sort of slack. "Oh," she said. "Yeah."

As it happened, such a thunderstorm rolled up at dusk that only one of the engineering crew braved the long walk out from camp. He was a nice enough chap, I guess. But so much better looking dressed in his casual, stranger's, way, than any of us, dressed in our very best catalogue suits, that we resented him a little. His name was Steve Carter.

He was standing by the door when Sue-Ellen went in. She crooked a knee to take off her rubber and lost her balance. Some say she did it on purpose, some say she didn't. You never knew with Sue-Ellen. That's why anyone as straightforward as Dave couldn't see through her, they said. Anyway, the stranger put his arm around her, to steady her. The two of them had quite a giggle over it.

You couldn't say that Sue-Ellen made a bid for the stranger's attention, exactly. But when the dancing started it was the set Carter was in that she led Dave over to. Naturally, Carter asked *her* for the next polka quadrille. And when it came their turn to "polka out," they didn't just bob out in the centre and back, like everyone else. They made quite a thing of it. They took the whole circuit of the set, and turned the regular polka step into a kind of souped-up fox trot. As if they were poking fun at it. Dave, who was dancing that one with Kate Weatherby, just grinned.

Dimock Jodrey was the auctioneer. You know Dimock. A dead ringer for the Ancient Mariner, and just the thought of that suction trouble he has with his upper plate when the bidding goes wild is usually enough to spark things off right away.

But it didn't work tonight. He really extended himself. He shouted and cajoled. He threatened to sample the pies. He perched them on the tripod of his fingers and swooped them up and down at such perilous angles that all the women gasped. But it was still no good.

Dave started each pie off at one dollar. Then the youngsters took over, boosting one another by ten cent hikes until the limit of the one fifty or so each had in his pocket was reached. The men weren't much more venturesome. You could tell when anyone was particularly interested in a certain pie by the over-nonchalance of his bidding. But the others let the challenge slide. Shout and cajole as he might, Dimock had to knock the pies down at one eighty, two dollars, two ten...

Until Sue-Ellen's came under the gavel.

There are different versions of what happened then. Some say that when Dimock went to lift it up by the fragile handle affair, she made quite a fuss—so everyone would know it was hers. She didn't. She just shook her head at him. But what she did do (I was standing right beside her) she glanced at the stranger, and smirked her eyes up just the least little bit. He grinned back.

"One dollar." Dave started the bidding exactly as before.

"One dollar I have! Who'll say...?"

"One fifteen," came from one of the kids.

"One twenty," from another.

When it got to two dollars—and Sue-Ellen didn't look too happy with the way the bidding had dawdled—Dave stroked his chin. That was the signal for Pat Newlin to take over.

"Two and a quarter," Pat said.

"Five dollars." There was a sudden clap of thunder outside, but no one noticed it, for this clap inside. Five *dollars*? The stranger had spoken quietly, but he might as well have shouted.

I glanced at Sue-Ellen. She tried to appear as dumbfounded as everyone else, but that wasn't what her face showed most. It was sort of an "Ah *ha*?" look. There wasn't much doubt whose pie would bring the highest price now.

Pat tried frantically to catch Dave's eye. Should he go on a bit further, or fade right there and then?

'Five and a quarter." It was Dave himself.

You wouldn't believe so many people could be so quiet so suddenly.

They twigged what was going on, now. The duel was out in the open. Pat threw out his hands in a gesture of resignation.

"Six," Carter said.

"Seven."

"Eight."

That's when Dimock lost control of his upper plate altogether. He just stood there speechless, a man without a function. People shook their heads at Dave, frowning at him, shaping the words, "No. No ...," with their lips.

"Eight-fifty," he said.

"Nine," said the stranger.

"Drop it on him, *drop* it on him ...," Pat pleaded. But Dave just smiled.

"Nine-fifty," he said.

For the first time Carter hesitated.

"Nine-sixty," he countered. But his voice had lost its confidence.

"Ten dollars!' Dave said.

It was probably the good round sum that did it. With a good-natured wave of his arm, the stranger abdicated.

The hush lasted about a second. And then ... well, did you ever poke a stick into an ant-hill? Sue-Ellen herself fluttered around Dave as if he were a hero. She didn't give the stranger as much as another glance. Her pie was top banana, that's all she'd been worrying about. But Dave didn't seem to bear Carter any ill will. In fact, as soon as the buzz died down, he went right over and had quite a chat with him. They chuckled together as if the whole thing was a great joke.

You'd think any pie after that would have had a pretty tame spot in the billing. And I guess they all would have (the first few did, anyway) if it hadn't been for the accident. Whether it was the excitement or a swig too many, or whether he knew whose plain apple pie he was holding, Dimock prepared to give it an extra build-up. Halfway through a climatic wing dive the whole works scooted off his fingers and landed flat on the floor. The pie didn't smash, but the plate split right across.

You could have lit a match on Kate Weatherby's face when she pushed through the crowd. She went over and got one of the two extra plates she'd brought to eat from. She knelt down and slipped the pie off the split plate onto the new one. She looked as if she could go through the floor. So, for once in his life, did Dimock.

But Dave just smiled. He started the bidding on that pie too.

"Ten dollars," he said, very slowly, very deliberately, " ... and five cents."

No one moved a muscle. In *that* silence I could hear Sue-Ellen's whisper, ten feet away.

"Dave Marshall!" she said. "Are you raving crazy? Ten dollars and five cents!"

Dave just smiled. "Aw," he said, "it's for a good cause ..."

"And what do you want of *two* pies?"

"I ain't got two pies," he said. "Carter just took the other one off my hands ... give me a dollar for it. I figgered that's about what it was worth." The smile became almost a chuckle. "All the roses and showers take yer eye, I guess, but I figger maybe plain apple makes better chewin'."

I guess it must. Since Dave married Kate that smile seems to be built right into his face.

❦

Nettles into Orchids

The two women exchanged the smiles of women with their guards up. They hadn't met since Peter's death.

Margot Faith's fantastic hat seemed to be snickering at this small-town living room of Kate's, with its simple furnishings and its air of snugness. She had a handsome dark sure-footed face, and her speech had the actress's unmistakable resonance. Kate Elwood looked a little like Helen Hayes, but you could see that she had never been anything but someone's wife.

"Do you mind if I smoke?" Margot said. "Or is that still for hussies only, here in Greatbridge?" Her smile widened. "*Great*bridge. That name always amused me. How many people? Two thousand?"

"More or less." Kate said crisply. "And please smoke, if you feel like it. I do. Will you have one of these?"

"No, thanks." Margot said. "I think I prefer my own brand. They seem to be gentler on my throat. Which, naturally, is something I have to be very careful about."

She brought out a small lighter, filigreed with gold.

"But what a beauty." Kate exclaimed.

"Oh, that." Margot said airily. "One of my leading men gave me that. I can't remember which one. Maybe ... yes, it *was* the one in *Brief Candle*. Now what was his name? But I don't suppose you follow the Broadway plays, do you."

"No." Kate said. She returned to the lighter. "It's lovely." she said. You certainly don't see craftsmanship like that these days."

Margot's smile stiffened a little.

"I've been trying to think." Kate said, "how long it's been since you left Greatbridge. I don't believe you've ever been back since you won that drama scholarship way, *way* back when we were girls, have you?"

"No." Margot said. "The family moved away just afterwards, as you know ... and there was nothing to come back for. But this year I simply had to have a rest. I said to my agent, 'Play offers, television offers, movie offers ... for six solid months I just don't want to hear about them.' And the most restful and amusing place I could think of to start off my holiday was the old home town. It's so refreshing in these hectic days to find a place that hasn't changed one jot. I couldn't believe that the hotel still had that wonderful old umbrella stand in the lobby. And the people. Still so simple and unspoiled. So quaint..."

Kate crushed out her cigarette. "But what brought you here, Margot?" she said. "To this house? To see me."

Margot's eyebrows went up in mock dismay. "Why, Kate." she said. "What a question! We were always girlhood friends, weren't we? I simply thought you'd be glad to see *me*." She paused. Her face made the actress's lightning change. "And I wanted to tell you, of course, how very sorry I was to hear about Peter."

"*Oh* no." Kate said. "This isn't the stage, Margot. Let's have no more of this pretence. When you found out that Peter was dead you didn't come here to sympathize. You came here to crow, didn't you. To show me that when Peter died you won."

"Won?" Margot's expression made another lightning change. This time to utter perplexity. "Honestly, Kate, you *are* cryptic! You sound as if you and I had been in a contest for something."

"We were." Kate said. "For Peter."

Margot's brittle stage laugh was like glass breaking. "Oh Kate." she said, "you're too amusing. That little business about Peter. So long ago. Imagine your still fussing over that. I'd comp*letely* forgotten it."

"Oh no." Kate said again. "'Amusing' is a great word with you, Margot, but you're not amused at all. And you haven't forgotten a thing. You never stopped loving Peter. And you couldn't ever forget, not even after all these years, that it was me Peter loved best. A plain little nonentity like me! I can read you. You thought, I'll make her see that she's nothing but a widow now and I'm an actress. You thought what a sweet revenge it would be to be able to pity me."

Margot laughed again. "But you don't suppose for one minute that I ever really loved Peter?" she said. A whimsical girlhood crush maybe. I certainly wouldn't deny that. But... oh Kate, this is just too preposterous."

There was a silence and Margot's laugh seemed to hang in the air.

"I'm afraid you made a big blunder coming here, Margot." Kate said at last. She was perfectly calm now. "Because I'm still the winner."

"Now, Kate." Margot said indulgently, "you don't mean to pretend... seriously... that this life here ... without Peter..." Her bangled arm made a dramatic sweep to indicate the room's insignificance.

"How old are you, Margot?" Kate said abruptly.

"Really!" Margot's arm went rigid.

"You're forty-six." Kate said. "I know my own age and it's not hard to calculate yours. There always *was* a year between us. I suppose there still is."

Two small red spots burned on Margot's cheek bones.

"And what if I am?" she said. Her voice rose slightly. "A true actress is just reaching her prime at forty-six. The groping is all behind her. She's learned her art so thoroughly it's become a sort of instinct. She's on absolutely sure ground."

"That may be." Kate said. "But there is one part you can never play. Now."

"And what part is that, may I ask?"

"Come into the kitchen." Kate said, rising.

Margot shrugged with her hands, then followed. Kate crossed over to one of the windows and drew back the curtain.

Margot looked out. She saw two children in the back yard, a boy and a girl. They were throwing a battered tennis ball back and forth to each other, laughing almost constantly. The two women stood there side by side.

"You will never play the real life part of a mother." Kate said. She raised the window. The children's voices came abruptly louder into the room.

Margot didn't speak for a moment. "I understood you and Peter never had any children." she said finally. The tone was quite casual, but her voice sounded puckered.

"They came late." Kate said. "And, sentimentality or not, which would you rather have—a child of Peter's or that flossy cigarette lighter from a leading man whose name you can't even remember?"

Margot turned away from the window, but she didn't reply.

"You'd never have been willing to give Peter children." Kate went on unsparingly. "You told him so. You had a career to think about. Well, you have your career and I have ... Ann." she called. "Peter. Come here and meet the nice lady from New York. She was always so fond of children but she doesn't have any of her own."

"Kate." The word came suddenly from Margot like an arm held up crouchingly against a blow. "Please."

Kate looked at her face. And all at once the moment's relish turned to shame. She wouldn't have believed a face could change so subtly, really change, from one glance to the next. This was not acting. It was a face in total surrender. She remembered Margot's looks as a girl:

sparkling, high-spirited, and burning with an almost fierce pride and ambition—yet with a kind of great unconscious loneliness showing through. Now only the loneliness was left. And no longer unconscious.

"I'm sorry, Margot." she said gently. "I really am. I guess I was bitter." She hesitated. "And why shouldn't I be?" she continued haltingly. "Who had any better right? Because ... well ... I have the children, but ... I might as well admit it ... it *was* you Peter always loved."

"Did Peter ever tell you that?" Margot said.

"Not in words, no." Kate said. "But I knew. For instance, he used to make these mysterious trips to New York every time you had a play there. He told me they were business trips. But I knew. I remember finding a ticket stub for that very play you mentioned, *Brief Candle*, in the pocket of his good suit one time I was pressing it."

Margot looked as if she didn't know whether to laugh or cry. The two children's headlong entrance into the room gave her respite.

"Ann, Peter." Kate said, "this is Margot Faith, an old friend of mine and your father's. She's a great actress."

"Oh!" Ann exclaimed. "Are you going to stay with us?"

"Could you, Margot?" Kate said. It suddenly seemed like a splendid idea. "For a good long rest. For the whole six months, if you like. I mean it."

Margot didn't temporize at all.

"Yes." she said simply. "I could." The two women exchanged the smiles of old friends delivered from the prides that had separated them. "You see, Kate—but bless you for the try—there never was any play called *Brief Candle*. I had one Broadway success at the beginning and a few scattered shows after that. But there hasn't been another play—or anything else—for the last dozen years."

"Act some for *us*." young Peter broke in. "Right now. Will you? Please?"

Margot thought a moment. "Well, Peter." she said, "I'm afraid I'm not much good at it anymore ... and I never did get a chance at Shakespeare. But he has a splendid speech that begins like this. 'The quality of mercy is not strained ...'"

Peter understood nothing whatsoever of these words or the ones that followed, but as he listened to that suddenly luminous voice his eyes shone, because even without understanding he could tell that he was in the presence of some kind of magic.

The Doctor and the Patient

Doctor Austen's appearance was almost anonymous, as the appearance of the brilliant psychiatrist so often is. None of that transfixing eye business at all. His eyes just looked kind, and ready for humour, and a little tired.

"Smoke?" he said to the patient.

"Thank you." Walter Moore, the patient, had the incisive look of business about him. He happened to be a writer.

Dr. Austen noticed that Moore's hand didn't tremble as he lit the cigarette. But he was familiar with that look about his eyes: as if they were watching their own movements. He was familiar with that jerkiness about the smile.

"All right." he said gently. "Start anywhere. It's like the water, you know. Once you're in ..."

"It's driving me crazy." Moore said suddenly.

"A good many people feel that way about something." the doctor said. "More than you think. Some have reason. Some haven't. Let's see where your case fits in."

"It's hopeless." Moore said.

"Why?" the doctor said. He could tell the ones who'd come to the point without any shilly-shallying.

"Because I understand the whole thing, myself." Moore said. "I know exactly what's wrong with me. I wanted to be a doctor, and I turned out to be a writer. And it's too late to switch back. It's as simple as that."

He hesitated. "They say once you know what's wrong with you, you're okay. They're crazy. I know exactly what's wrong with me, but it's still driving me nuts."

"I see." the doctor said. His fatigue began to leave him.

"But *do* you?" That eager, spilling look the doctor knew so well came into Moore's face. "Lately it's as if ... I can't seem to think of anything else. It's as if the life I actually live weren't my real life at all."

Now, Dr. Austen thought. This is the first big hurdle. Unless you could make what you said next absolutely convincing, nothing else was any good at all. He drew a deep breath.

He said, "It's as if you'd been blind, isn't it, and then got your vision back … but just too late to catch the things you really wanted to see. It's as if the past were a sort of wall your eyes could see through but your hands couldn't smash down, to grasp the life that *should* have been yours all along. And it almost kills you to stand there helpless and stare at that life being lived by someone else doing the very things you were cut out for."

"Why, it is like that." Moore exclaimed, "exactly. I thought no one else in the world knew what it was like to feel that way."

"At some time or other." the doctor said, "I think almost everyone does. I think I hear more about that feeling than about all the rest put together."

He relaxed. The big hurdle was over. Once you got them to believe you really understood how they felt, made them really believe that they weren't alone in their particular dilemma … then they had confidence in everything you told them. They went right on arguing the case for their unhappiness—almost as if they didn't want to part with it. But now it was only a matter of patience, of watching for the right lead.

He asked Moore how old he was. Forty, Moore told him. You couldn't go back to medical school at that age, if that's what he was driving at. Well, you could … but seven more years' study. Forty-seven. Just beginning to practise. He'd be a freak, it wouldn't be the same at all.

Why did he want so much to be a doctor? He didn't know exactly. There were lots of things like that you couldn't explain.

What had stopped him from being a doctor? This damn writing, that's what had stopped him. If he hadn't had such unnatural luck with those first short stories, that very first year in medical school. That's what had blinded him!

Was there no other reason for quitting? No. Well, (jokingly), he hadn't been too fussy about messing with blood … but that was a trifle he'd have got used to.

Was that first year when he was actually studying to be a doctor the happiest year of his life? No. But the first year—study, routine, nothing for the imagination—you couldn't call that any test.

Would it do any good to tell him that there's always study and routine and the need for patience, above everything, in a doctor's life? Or that too much imagination can be a bad thing for a doctor? No, he was afraid it wouldn't …

Around the middle of the second visit they began to talk about writing.

"I've read some of your stuff." the doctor said. "You have a really first-rate talent, haven't you?"

"Well." Moore said. "All I know is that I'm successful. But yes, I suppose it's just possible that a successful writer might be a good one, too."

There it was. That touchy note of defending his work and his success. That was the lead.

"All right." the doctor said. "You're an excellent—believe me—and successful writer. And yet you'd be happier, and more satisfied, to be only a mediocre doctor?"

Moore looked at him as if he'd said something preposterous. "But I wouldn't have been just a mediocre doctor. I'd have been one of the best."

"How can you tell?"

"Well, that's another thing I can't explain, but ..." Egotism had nothing to do with it: the thought of his being only a mediocre doctor had simply never entered his head. "I mean, you couldn't possibly not be successful at something you wanted to do so much."

"Oh yes you could." the doctor said quietly. "That's quite possible. It's not always true that wanting to do a thing even desperately is any guarantee that you'll be good at it. In fact, it's often the thing, the very thing, that a man would do poorest that he wants to do most. I run across it all the time." He paused. "You know, in a way you're luckier than a good many people. You've found a thing you *can* do extremely well. So many people never discover what they're good at, at all. Maybe it's better to be doing what you can do, than what you want to. That you can do it so well, even when you think you should be doing something else, isn't that a pretty good sign that it's the proper thing for you?"

"You don't think I'd have made a good doctor then?" Moore said.

"No." the psychiatrist said frankly, "I don't."

"But why don't you think so? How can you know?"

The doctor hesitated a moment. Maybe this wasn't quite ethical, but ...

He got up and took several pages of typewritten manuscript from his files.

"Read that." he said.

Moore read the first paragraph of the first page carefully; then his eyes rabbit-hopped without interest through the rest. He looked up, puzzled.

"What would you say to the man who wrote that." the doctor said, "if he told you he was cut out to be a leading novelist?" He smiled. "That's his firm conviction."

Moore's bewilderment was almost comic. "Well, I don't know what I'd say to him." he said. "But I certainly know what I'd think. I'd think he was ridiculous."

"But how can you be so sure?"

"You're joking." Moore said. "I mean, it's grammatical enough and everything, but there's .... Good Lord, anyone could tell that."

"No, not just anyone, I think." the psychiatrist said. "In fact, I thought maybe all he lacked was practice. Isn't it that *you* can see this man would have no future as a writer because you're a writer yourself?" He paused. "Well, I can judge what kind of doctor you'd have made because I'm a doctor."

When Moore left the office, he walked as if his body had suddenly lost its nagging density. Doctor Austen felt the nice glow which always came when they went out smiling smoothly. His fatigue was gone. The method hadn't failed. Once you got them really to believe their situation wasn't unique, then some peace with it could always be made.

That manuscript business really hadn't been a trick, though, he told himself. This man wouldn't have made a good doctor. His impatience with anything short of absolute success. His imagination. With that much imagination, he'd probably always have been a little finicky about "messing with blood." Above all, the hastiness of his judgment—he'd barely glanced at the manuscript.

He smiled at the risk he'd taken. What possible tack could I have hit on, he thought, if he'd said the manuscript was actually good? But no, it hadn't been much of a risk, really. You could count pretty well on a writer's prejudice against any work that wasn't his own.

He re-read the manuscript, himself. Then he put it down on the desk and crossed out the opening sentence and substituted another. The fatigue began to return. And slowly that look came into his eyes as if they were watching their own movements.

If I'd only given my whole life to this, he thought ... It's driving me crazy.

You Could Go Anywhere Now

Mrs. Andrews held the parlour curtain back frankly when they passed the house without stopping, but she couldn't see either of their faces, David's or his wife's, for the little whirlwind of dust that spun behind the car down the hot summer road. A dull flash of hurt burned in her own face. David, who had been like her own son, would be like the others now.

୫

The others were never quite the same when they came back from the city. There was always that little defensiveness you couldn't help feeling with them. Even the special clothes they had for everything they helped with on the farm — the big coloured hats of the women and the white pants of the men, just soiled enough — seemed to make an awkwardness between them.

It was worse still with the ones that came with them, the real city ones. Their kind of friendliness made you feel foolish somehow. The funny eagerness of the women especially, as if the questions they kept asking about things in the country that were plain enough to anybody would please you right through. As if you wouldn't know it was just bad manners to act like that.

David's wife, she thought, is one of those.

She would have that sure look they all had in their faces, coming into the house to call on her. Picking up a shell or something off the mantle and saying, oh look, isn't that *darling*? As if it must flatter you all over to have your little keepsake amuse her. As if you didn't know she wouldn't think of acting that way in anyone's house in the city. Coming right around mealtime maybe and catching her before she'd changed her dress, but never thinking that would matter. Never thinking that a country woman would mind meeting another woman for the first time when she didn't look her best or have her good dishes on the table, or that she should give her own appearance a thought. Never thinking that a country woman was a woman in the same sort of way she was at all.

She would spoil David, too. The men became like their wives when they married the city ones. A sudden anger tightened in Mrs. Andrews's kind ready face.

Because David had never been like the others when he came back before. He worked in the same old clothes he had always worked in. And when he came into your house it was the same old way, quietly but at home, with no need to talk if there was nothing that needed talking about. He had come into her house now she was alone and lonely the same way he used to come in when he was a child and she had kept him those three wonderful years after his mother died, more tenderly than like a son because she had never had a son of her own.

David had seemed to belong to all of them here that way. There had never been any jealousy of David, even after he had gone so far beyond them that the city ones knew his name now too. It was as if one of your own family had *shown* the city ones.

That's why the thought kept circling in her mind, if there could only be some mistake — if there was only some way it could be Anna after all in the car with him today. Anna was a girl from home, and that would be the surest way of keeping him always among them. He had planned to marry Anna when they left this place together, and no one had ever dreamed that he would change his mind, because David would want a wife who had no strangeness with his own people.

Until the word came suddenly, not two weeks ago, that it was all over between David and Anna. That he was going to marry one of the city ones. It was as if the son you were surest and proudest of had gone over to the other side.

ঽৡ

"Well?" David said to his wife, silent beside him on the seat of the car.

"Do I have to say something?" she said, smiling.

"No." he said, "there was never any watching. That was the thing, right from the first."

He drove on slowly, letting the fullness of the minutes take that strange song in him, because he and she and this place could all talk to each other or be quiet together in the same way.

"Home —" she said softly, and she put one hand on his sleeve just tightly enough to feel the flesh beneath it. But she did not do it with any trickery, conscious that the light way was the right way. "Coming home with you, David —"

"It's home for you too, isn't it?" he said. "That's the nice part. After a while a man can't go home alone. You can't do anything alone, really. The unit is two people."

That was the thing about the other one. The one who had so nearly been with him in the car now. The one with only the bright city thoughts. This place today would mean nothing to that one — the way of it when the green mist of growing hung everywhere in the spring air, or later when the paler green of the long fields shimmered in the silence of the noon sun after the hay was cut and the little sadness of Fall was first quiet in the dark mountains, or later still when the Christmas kindliness was all through the living green of the white-shouldered spruces. Driving along with him today, it would have been as if she were leafing over an album of views, idly. None of the voice of this place would have come through to her, and he and she would have had to talk.

It had been so nearly too late when he found out that she despised him a little too. Because he could never leave this place. Because it would always be home to him. No matter what he did or where, the good slowness of earth and the little loneliness of it that was a man's best company, things like that, would always be in him as they were in the people who still lived here.

But with her he'd have had to keep that part of his heart secretly, and go to it alone. And you can't do it that way, if it's any good between you and your wife. You have to go all the important places in the heart together.

You could go home with this one beside him now, he thought. This one knew the light way, but because she had the quiet part too, because she could hear the same voice he heard in these places he had been young in, you could always go home now no matter where you were, just to speak of it to this one. You could go *anywhere* with this one now, or do anything, just to speak of it or think of it together, and there was no hunger in anything anymore.

"Dave." she said, "did you really understand about Mrs. Andrews?"

"Sure." he said quickly, because this was the first thing he hadn't quite understood with her. "This evening will be just as good anyway. It was just that I always *did* stop for a minute on the way by."

"I know." she said. She glanced at herself quickly in the car mirror. "But, Dave, can't you *see* what a sight I am? Look at my hair."

"You look fine." he said. "It wouldn't make any difference to Mrs. Andrews how you looked."

"Which is it, darling." she said, laughing, "do I look fine or doesn't it make any difference?"

"You look wonderful." he said.

"No, but really." she said, "I'd like to look nice. You *don't* understand … a little. You think it's some sort of vanity. But I'm your bride, Dave, and I'd just like to look nice for someone I think so much of and who thinks so much of you. I think I *ought* to fix myself up for Mrs. Andrews. Don't you see?"

"Okay." he said, seeing it her way now. "Come to think of it, tonight is better. I want to get her something. I always brought her something from the city, but I guess I had you too much on my mind this time."

"We *should* have brought her something, Dave." she said. "Something real nice." She thought a minute. "I wonder." she said, "would there be anything of mine …."

"Stationery?" he said.

"Dave!" she said, grimacing and striking his shoulder a little blow. "Not *stationery*!"

"Well then …?" he said.

"Dave." she said, "would you think it wasn't the nicest thing you ever gave me if I parted with that precious little bottle of Chanel?

He stared at her, half-incredulous. "Why, no." he said. "But for Mrs. Andrews? What in the world would a country woman do with a bottle of fussy *perfume*?"

"What do you think, silly?" she said. "Water the geraniums? You don't think a country woman likes things like that less than any other woman, do you? A little bit of really *nice* perfume for special occasions, she'd love it."

"She might, at that." he said slowly. "I guess I wouldn't know."

And the other one wouldn't either, David thought.

It was only last Christmas he'd spoken to her about something for Mrs. Andrews. "Don't ask *me* what to send her darling." she'd said. "A bungalow apron, I suppose. I can't think of anything else a woman could use back in *that* place."

Anna had been born in this place, he thought, but she had never really known it at all. But Katharine, the city one, who had never seen these people before, was coming home more even than he.

❦

The Snowman

The strange thing, there had never been any pain. Not even at the start. Just that painless blow somewhere inside his head, like a hammer blow of sound, and then his left side gone dead as a sound gone. He couldn't remember being carried from the barn, but when he came to in the bedroom his mind was as clear as it had ever been. He could see. He could hear. Bur he couldn't move his head, or walk alone — or speak.

They put a slate beside his good hand. On it he could write down any questions he had, or tell them of any needs. He hadn't written a word since he left school (at fourteen, because his own aging father had needed his stout muscle on the farm) and the slate pencil felt clumsy in his fingers, but he could make himself understood.

They were good to him: his son and his son's wife and the grandchildren. At first they'd come into his bedroom every evening and tell him all that had happened that day. What they'd done. The people they'd seen. What they'd heard and what they thought about it. Down to the last detail.

But gradually the tales got sparser, then dried up almost altogether. Gradually, not to bother them, he ceased to write any questions on the slate. Now all he wrote was "yes" or "no."

"Are you all right?"

"Yes."

"Do you want anything?"

"No."

Sometimes he wanted death. Anything to free him from the silence the walls ticked with and the pattern of purple ivy that stamped itself so tirelessly on the wallpaper. But he never wrote anything like that.

They never neglected him. They never left him alone in the house. And tied to his spool bed, on the rung nearest his good hand, was a bell he could ring if he had to get out onto "the chair." A tinkler off the string of sleighbells he had himself sewn to the leather thongs the day he drove Ellen in to town to marry her.

He minded the chair as nothing in his life before. Even when the son came. When the wife came (blushing the first couple of times, then with no more self-consciousness than if he was an infant she was tending) it was agony.

The bottle for urine he could manage without help. But one day he spilt it in the bed. The son, who had always bathed him, was nowhere around; so the wife had to change the sheets and wash him herself. At the pressure of the warm cloth in her hand he became alive down there — and when he saw the startled look on her face and then the suppressed grin, he had never felt such shame.

That night he heard her say to the son: "Maybe we should put diapers on him. Wouldn't that make it easier for everyone?"

"Diapers!" he thought. "I'd die first! I'd die!"

They put the diapers on him, though, and he didn't die. How could he?

They switched his bed around so that his head faced the window. So that he could see nearly all the fields and the movements in them, and the pasture that ran back to the steep spruce mountain.

He watched them sow the seeds in the land he'd been the first to break. He watched them hay where he had sown the first clover. The silence ceased to tick then. But he couldn't see the path behind the house that led to the meadow. He couldn't see the grove of silver birches where the son used to play under his eye while he cut the hoop poles. And sometimes when a movement would vanish beyond the edges of the rectangle of fields the window framed he would feel like tearing the walls apart.

All this last week he'd watched the grandchildren and their friends building snow forts in the field just outside the window. Mounding them to the height their arms could reach, scraping the edges smooth with a barrel stave, then playing Blindman's Buff amongst them the way he'd played it once amongst the cocks of August hay.

Today he watched them make a snowman. The air was soft as silk. The great globes of snow they rolled up to form the body left tracks right down to the aftergrass that was still green. They patted the small globe of the head into shape until it was perfectly round. There were two black coals for its eyes, one for its nose, and smaller ones for its teeth. They put a pipe he knew was his between its teeth. (How many times he'd tapped the stem of that pipe against his own teeth as he sat by the well curb in the Sunday sun and talked the week's work over with a neighbor.) And on its head they placed an old slouch hat that he saw was his too.

There was a game he had come to play with his memory. Off and on since he'd first heard Paul, the grandson who was named for him, counting 5, 10, 15, 20 ... while the others ran to hide.

A bitter thought had skimmed his mind. What blindfold God was forever counting 5, 10, 15, 20 ...? And where did you hide when the count was 55, 60? Years. But his mind had always "thrown" a bitter thought, the way a fish throws the hook. It did then.

And then it simply seemed to him that, yes, the years of his life had been grouped into just such sections. That if his mind could just piece these sections together again, like building blocks ...

è¿

In the kitchen, the son's wife said: "Did you tell him Jess was asking about him?"

"No." the son said, "I forgot. And ... I don't know. There's no way to be sure. But sometimes I doubt if he really takes things in."

è¿

5, 10 ...

He'd thought this block would be out of reach. So long ago. But when he closed his eyes it came back clearer to him than yesterday. It was as if he held it right there in his hand and could turn it from one windowed side to another ...

It was running ... and bread ... and mittens ... and sleep ... and moss ... and minnows ... and breezes ... and suppertime ... and dandelions ... and rock tops ... and tree forks ... and hills ... and hollows ... and sunburn ... and somersaults ... and hours and hours and hours and hours ...

è¿

And, yes, right at the centre was that one day, that one teeming June day when everything seemed to be so sparklingly in place. He'd been walking behind his father in the path of the plow. At the bottom of the third furrow his father said: "Would you like to ride on the horse's back for a few turns?" There was a moment's fear but he said yes. His father lifted him up and told him to hang tight to the hames. The hames, each with a gleaming brass knob on the end of it, curved upward from the harness like the twin arms of a lyre.

They started off again, and all at once it was as if his heart let loose a flight of birds. He felt so high above the earth that he could tell where the sky began. The roll of the horse's muscles under his legs seemed like a mightiness of his own, the roll of the turning sod like a song. He knew that the horse would keep straight to the furrow with no guidance at all, but he gripped the hames, veering them a little this way or that, as if through them he was steering the whole world. And always would ...

&

"Paul." the wife said downstairs, "go and see if your grandfather wants anything."

"Awww." Paul said, "can't Lennie go? I go *all* the time."

&

... 15, 20 ....

That block was easy too. Not as easy as the one before; here and there it was clouded by those feelings discovered for the first time. But he could remember it all if he tried.

It was striding. It was flesh. It was health in you like the flush of cider. It was never a thought of taking your time about anything, never a thought of caution, never looking back over your shoulder. It was the weight of things giving way to the strength (bottomless muscles of it) to lift them. It was straight ahead, but it wasn't scurry. It was news, always new, coming from everything you looked at. It was taking all the jumps, bare-hearted, in the solid stirrups of your blood ...

Sometimes it was the bright scarlet brawl of temper. Once he'd smashed the peavey stock to bits against a rock because a split in it had pinched his hands that were so quick to anger.

And once there was fear. One afternoon he and Karl and Leo, who were always together, decided to swim the lake at its widest, the naked three of them. Sun and water sang against their nakedness; it was naked glee. But when they were halfway across, the sun went in and the water looked like night water. He wished he could put his feet down, touching bottom, and walk ashore. He began to swim as if it was running after dark. He swam until the far shore looked so near he was sure that now he must be in the shallows next the bank. Forgetting how distance over water could fool you, he let his feet down and his head went under. In the moment before he flailed himself back to the surface he was seized with naked fear. For the first time in his life he had a glimpse of how the calmest second could suddenly open wide and show the terrible jaws lurking behind it.

But in less than five minutes more he *was* in the shallows, then climbing up the bank. The sun came out of the cloud and, as he rested on the bank beside Karl and Leo, with the three of them such sun-brothers that each was made three times himself, even the memory of his fear was swallowed up without a trace.

That's how it was then. It was knowing that, no matter what deep water you got into, the bank was always there.

It was striding. It was dreaming. And after the first so altogether different dream he'd had about a girl, it was the strut at the very centre of him. As if he carried in that sweet liquor of himself the power and thrust of all creation ...

જ

In the kitchen the wife said: "I don't mind anything else, but ... would *you* wash his teeth in the mornings?" More often than not, now, they spoke of him only as "he."

"All right." the son said.

"I'm not complaining. Now I don't complain much, do I. And no one can say I give him a cross word. But that's the one thing I ...."

"All right." the son said. "I'll do it. Someone has to."

She hesitated. "Karl Copeland was in again today, and he was saying again we should get him to fix up his business—while he can still sign."

"I know we should. But, well, it's a pretty touchy thing to ..."

"I know. I wouldn't have him think the property's all we're thinking about for the world. But as Karl says, it's only business—and if there's no will, you can't tell who'll try to come in, look what happened when Leo died."

જ

... 25, 30, 35 ...

A single pattern made these blocks as one. It was eating with Ellen, working with Ellen, sleeping with Ellen, having Ellen to turn to ... It was each being the other's listener and guarantee. It was having everything a safety away from striking him on any naked spot, because Ellen was with and in him like a hearth. Smoke rising, leaves falling, wheels turning, sun, rain, snow ... with Ellen there, it was having all the good things in the year's teeming calendar right next to his skin and all the stony ones a skin apart. It was day after day of wholeness. It was putting his own son on the horse's back when he plowed. It was the daily bread of hope—but more than hope, it was home.

Ellen … Ellen … Ellen … Her name flaked down through his mind as gently as the snowflakes eddied down outside the window, and he slept. He slept, and he dreamed.

≈⁊

He dreamed about the night Ellen died, the year he was 40. He saw the burning sunset paint the colors of pain he'd never felt the likes of on the blind church windows. He felt the beating his heart took from the skulls of everything he looked at that her hands would never touch again or her eyes ever see. Each leaf, each stone, each blade of grass had printed on it, each in its own alphabet, the one word "gone"—each of them itself as if gone out of reach. He saw the gaping socket of unrelatedness inside him, now that she was forever out of sight …

He awoke, nearly choked with the sound of crying his throat couldn't make.

≈⁊

Downstairs the wife was hearing Paul's spellings. "Trance … Tranquil … Transom … Transient …"

"What does 'transient' mean?" Paul asked.

She didn't know. She looked at her husband.

"I don't know, either." he said. "Go find it in that big dictionary of his." He looked at the sunset that was all bruise and flame. "You know." he said slowly, "he hardly went to school much but he was always reading. Anything he could get hold of. He was always thinking. He knew what all kinds of long words meant. If he'd been born somewhere else …"

"He slept a lot today." the wife said, her voice suddenly gentled with … was it twice tenderness because it was half-wish? "I think he's failing."

"Maybe … a little." the son said. "But he's always had that strong constitution."

"What does 'constitution' mean?" Paul asked.

≈⁊

The dream slipped away to wherever dreams go, taking its freight of feeling with it. His mind went back to its game. Or was it a task now? There was a new sense of urgency about it. A sudden drive to have it over with.

... 45, 50, 55 ...

Yes, yes, those blocks too were fairly clear. Clear enough, anyway, that in this new haste to reach the end he could skip them, come back to them later. Fill them in later, once the capstone block of 60 was, all conquered, fitted into place.

For they were endurance, simply; finding that if you put the sickened heart to work again, and soon, a different set of scopes and muscles grew; finding that whatever life might rob you of, you were always left with *some*thing worth its cost; learning that ... But surely all you had learned, any answers there might be, would be contained in that last block. He skipped to 60.

ૐ

"I left his window up a crack this afternoon." the wife said, "to air that funny smell out of the room. Would you go up and put it down? It looks like rain."

ૐ

60 ... 60 ... 60 ...

His mind wrestled with it—but to his growing dismay he found he couldn't force it into the shape of anything whatsoever. He was completely blocked. Why, why, he asked himself, could he call up those early years so easily and yet be helpless to picture the day he was 60? A day that was hardly a month ago, he was sure. His bafflement mounted almost to terror.

Again and again he tried; but each time, his mind caught itself, before he knew it, slewing senselessly off its target. 60, 60, sick-sty ... 60 seconds in a minute ... 60 minutes in an hour ... 60 pounds in a bushel of potatoes ... 60 degrees—and where was his carpenter's protractor now?—in each angle of a triangle that had all sides the same...

Again and again he reined his mind back to its object, trying to storm the image of his sixtieth birthday clear. But again and again he met a wall blanker than smoke, a nowhere louder than silence, a stare whiter than zeroes. Again ... and again ... and again ...

ૐ

The rain started softly, as if it was picking its steps, then poured in earnest all night long. The snow forts were dissolved, and the snowman melted gradually until there was nothing left of it but the coals and the pipe and the hat, drenched dark, but with the darker sweat stains on the band still showing.

In the morning, when the son went into the bedroom and found his father dead, there was one word scrawled on the slate. None of them could puzzle it out for certain. The wife thought it was "peace." The son, "praise." Lennie thought it was "price." Paul thought it was "please."

"How old was he?" the woman who wrote up deaths for the newspaper asked.

"I don't think he knew, these last months." the son said. "And we'd kind of lost track of it ourselves. But he'd have been sixty this coming Friday. It's right there in the Bible."

The Orchard

I was only eight at the time and no more impressionable, I think, than any other child. But I still remember that day of long ago, right down to its very texture.

I was watching what Mother was doing. The tissue paper, which lined the bureau drawer that held her keepsakes, had yellowed and she was changing it to fresh; then she dusted each object taken from the drawer before putting it back. She was humming a little tune as she worked, until she came to one particular box.

Her humming stopped then and she held this box in her hand with such a breathless sort of silence, it made me stare at her face. Mother always saved pretty boxes, and this one had once been pretty. But now it had faded with many years of age. Once, the cardboard cover had had a pattern of paper roses pasted on it, but as the glue had loosened, the flowers had browned and curled up at the edges.

I asked Mother to let me see inside the box. She still had that mute look on her face but she did as I asked.

When she opened the box, it was my turn to stare at what I saw. A tiny cardboard cross, the bare thread showing where wild flowers (now withered and fallen loose) had been sewn to the cross. A small, beaded change purse. A tiny braid of hair, so golden it must have been the envy of the sun.

I didn't have to ask the meaning of what I saw. I knew instinctively that these were the last of Ruby's things.

I never saw my sister Ruby. She had died at age six, years before I was born. But I had heard again and again what a rare and shining child she was.

"*Was* she so beautiful?" I asked Mother.

"Yes."

"Could she tame wild birds?"

"Yes."

"Could she really recite a dozen psalms without getting a word wrong?"

"Yes."

ॐ

I went outside to play. But things wouldn't seem to play *with* me. There was a quality in the air that I had never noticed before. Quieter than silence. Quieter than mysteries. Though it was June, there was none of that "whispering" together of things growing side by side in the fields. Things seemed oblivious to themselves. The leaves of the pear tree moved but without *deciding* to. Even the stones, which have their own way of speaking, were deaf and dumb.

It wasn't the hush of sadness. Sadness is active. It was simply the first time I had found out about *distance*, the cruelest word in the language.

The feeling didn't last. The shadow of a leaf moved, having decided to. A cloud drifted across the sun. The "nowness" came back to the stones. Everything in the day heard its own name and answered to it. It was as if something you'd taken to be an object had turned out, on nearing you, to be a face. And I lay on my back in the grass, squinting my eyes to make patterns of the shadows, luxuriously thoughtless.

Young or old, we nearly always discover the nature of things by a chance illumination, touched off by what need be no more than a seemingly irrelevant trifle.

Let your eye "happen" at the right moment on a moss-eaten shingle that has lost all but one of its nails to the winds of the years, and you will know all there is to know about melancholy.

Watch not a lark rising but a simple daisy, cleaner than diamonds, bowing to the sun-companioned fields and you may be struck in a flash with the victory of feeling over thought.

And so the chance discloser works in the case of hope. And so with sorrow. And so with pleasures and so with plans ...

My father was the quiet one of the family—outwardly at least. There were no fluctuating currents of feeling in his face as our activities bustled and eddied around his soberness. But I'm sure that he too knew moments when some small incident suffused him with total understanding.

I think of the morning we went to pick snow apples.

The ancient orchard was the site of what, years ago, had been my great-grandfather's homestead, but the forest had not quite reclaimed it and turned it into a wilderness. The apple trees still bore fruit and the narrow road that led there was still passable for horse and buckboard.

I don't know why the journey to pick the snow apples had a sort of magic for me but it did. And the magic never dimmed. I remember how it was when, in the dawning light, we neared our destination. When I knew that one more turn in the road and we'd be there, a shiver would run through me. And I'd close my eyes to the scattered trees at the edge of the orchard, so that when I opened them I'd all at once have the whole clearing in view.

It was like a place out of time. In another light the ancient trees, gnarled and twisted as they were, might have stood for torture. But here they spoke only of lasting, and the apples they still bore in plenty sang with a tart and tingling sweetness on the tongue.

A frost the night before had made them just right for picking, and when my father's burly arms shook the boughs, the fruit came down in showers. The whole day smelled and tasted of apple, and when we knelt in the clarion purity of the cidery October light to gather the apples in baskets, it was like the gentlest of peace made flesh.

As for my father, though his face showed no outward change, I know that, as he lifted the laden barrels onto the cart as easily as another man might lift a pailful and as he too felt the sanctity almost of this burnished day, he learned about strength and joy in their entirety.

When the containers were level full, Mother gathered apples in her apron to "top them off." and Father expertly packed them into such a tight crown that none would joggle free.

And then it was time to go home.

In a curious way it was Mother who then seemed to be the centre of everything. It was always like that when it was time to part with a splendid day. We were suddenly welded by the vow, silent but almost fierce, that we would always keep her safe from slight or harm.

My grandfather (I see him now) doesn't look old—although there is a far-off look in his eyes sometimes. A gaze that isn't there at all in the snapshot of him and grandmother taken (each young and smiling at the other's consciousness of the camera) the week before death overtook her so suddenly. The gaze is there now as he kindles the kitchen fire. He knows how good the warmth will feel against our flesh, now that the beginning night chill has subdued us. He tips up the back cover of the stove to see if the kindling has caught, and a tendril of smoke spirals for a moment in the air.

It is shapeless and yet an interlacing of *all* shapes as, ceaselessly changing, they twine and intertwine and melt, one into the other.

His eyes are no longer grave and inward-searching—they never are when I'm a chatterbox and he's my most indulgent listener. But as he watches the tendril of smoke, it is certain that he has discovered all there is to know about memory.

It would not be true to say that Ruby was constantly in the back of my mind. But ever since the day when Mother showed me the box of her things, the thought of her would sometimes cast a spell of silence on me. As if through silence (so like the silence of that first day) I could, *must*, somehow reach her.

One day in the quiet of the backfield, where I'd gone to search for four-leaf clovers, I had the strongest feeling that I could reach her if I called her name aloud. I looked around. There was no one or nothing to over-hear. I saw the golden hair again.

"Ruby." I called softly.

There was no answer.

"Ruby!" I called again in a stronger voice.

There was no answer.

"Ruby!" I called softly again. "Ruby!"

There was no answer.

I didn't find out about death.

Why Must It Sound Like a Cowboy Song?

You know how it is when they call across and tell you your friend is dead. You don't believe it. The sentence is alright but there is no meaning in it. It was only yesterday you saw him. But they tell it again and you know they do not lie. And you hate them. They do not know how good a friend of yours he was.

You believe it now, but you do not feel it. Then the morning is not so new and there is a stillness. And suddenly you see that the trees are dead and the sky is dead and the road is dead, and he is dead, too. So you turn and go inside the house. They do not know he was the best friend you ever had. And the thin spring sun that shines through the window seems stiller and deader than ever. You go in the room by yourself. And you feel alone. You never felt so alone in all your life. And the trees and the road and the sun and the tables and the chairs are all dead.

Now, through the day, when you move among them, they all speak of it and their faces are sad; but they talk about the weather again soon and you see that the other things, the bills they owe, their own hopes, are still important with them. You see they have forgotten and you feel alone. You talk the same in this strange husk of a day, but even when you forget, it keeps coming back suddenly, like a small coal touched against the heart. You did not have many friends. He was the best friend you had. He is dead. You move about, but you are lost in the long, dead day. And when the night comes, you are afraid. And your loneliness is tight and still because the heart has no tongue for it. We used to go out sailing when it was just coming light ...

It was raining the next day and I felt better. But that night the sun came out again and flamed lonesome in the church windows and he was still dead ... and I remembered when we were children together and now it was spring again but he was dead. You can't put it down, because there are only words, and when you read them over they are not true enough and you can never come any closer than that. They wouldn't know what you meant. They would have to feel the same way, and write it themselves, to know what you meant.

I went myself to see if it was true. They were not lying. His face was like a perfect drawing of his face and he never moved once. His fingers knew how to play the Hungarian Dances but they didn't move once. He was perfectly quiet. He would never speak again. He was dead, you see ... But the sun was still shining outside the blinds and the trees stood still in their tracks. Think hard, my mind, here in the sun and the dead tree-shadows and the lonesome day and the windows with their eyelids dropped around the silence ... what is it, *dead*? He was perfectly still. He did not move once. He was dead, you see. That's all you will ever know. And the sun still shines on the eyelids of the window in the bright-lonesome day and the trees stand still in their tracks. And the small coal burns steadily against the heart.

It was very easy when they buried him.

But when you walked home, bending against the drifting skirts of spring dusk-rain, you remembered going out in the boat with him when it was coming dawn and now you were alone ... and you never felt so alone in all your life. The bare, rain-black trees sighed, their arms dead in the bare wind, and there was the cast of ashes on the dead-lonesome day. The night falls quickly. There is a sick-heavy taste of defeat in your throat, and for a minute you beat your fists against a tree. You want to escape somewhere into the strange death-still night where this thing will not be true. But there is nowhere in the whole spring-sad night where it would not be true. He was the best friend you ever had. You will never have another as good. He is dead. And the bare trees weave their dead arms into the dark wind.

The Widow

The black of her borrowed dress made her look small, framing like a pale point of light the plaintive cameo of her face. Nothing moved in her slackened face, pale and wilted like a picked flower; nothing moved about her idle defeated mouth; no vagaries of pain twitched in her eyes. Nothing moved about her face but a loosened wisp of weary black hair and the dogged beat of a small blue vein that pulsed steadily over her left temple ... The sweet stagnant smell of chrysanthemums hung heavy about the dingy parlor. In the centre of the room, like a shrunken black kernel, the coffin lay.

Her large body, heavy with pregnancy, sat curiously erect, as if its weight were no longer felt. She gazed steadily at her dead husband. Steadily, like one who cannot recognize a vaguely familiar face. He seemed so still—as if smiling at some strange secret she could not share. The side of his face where the frantic steam had struck was powdered too white; and, before they brought him back, they had parted his hair on the wrong side to hide the perfect circle the iron splinter had made when it thrust itself through and took his life. Now and then, a blind unbelief in sudden death, she made little, saving movements toward his half-smiling face. Then, her quick rebellion spent, she would sink back, as from an obscure shaft of pain .... In their shabby setting, the chrysanthemums looked disdainful; but his mother, too old for grief, cackled over them with pride, showing them to the mourners as they came in and telling every one they cost sixty cents apiece and would last two weeks ....

Outside, the skeletal remains of late fall shivered patiently in a cold stubborn rain. The rain made ragged little furrows in the sawdust banking, soggy against the patched shingles of the house, and streaked the windowpanes with uneasy rivers meandering vaguely awry like an old man's tear. Monotonously, drops collected to bursting point on the upper sash, then trailed off into a thin stream. Outside, the steady drip drip drip and inside the strange taut quiet.

She nodded absently at the half-strangers who tiptoed silently into the parlor, walked to the coffin, looked a minute at the face there, and

274

sat down to make querulous grimaces of greeting to them who had come before. The women dropped easy tears while their slow gaze followed the subtly intruding pattern of the faded wallpaper. Some of them kissed her but she seemed to shrink away from their swelling sympathy. As if she found company in patient manipulations, she made, over and over, an odd unvarying pattern in the hem of her handkerchief—smoothing it out flat on her knee and puckering it carefully from corner to corner. With the other hand, she brushed, ceaselessly, a small flaw in the plush of the coffin. All things familiar seemed, to her, strange and far-off through the gossamer veil of grief. Once she turned and made a little gesture to his mother, asking her if she had borrowed the extra plates for supper. His mother nodded. A nervous cough broke the quiet self-consciousness in the room where time seemed to be a taut ribbon of suspense. Not before burial would these clustered, uneasily breathing fragments be released. Only the dull heaviness of her grief and the face in the coffin, serenely enigmatic with death, seemed at ease. Stubbornly the rain fell, repeating endlessly its treacherous lullaby.

When the first hymn began her eyes were suddenly wide and alive with pain. The balm of tears, for a swift moment, sprang up to dull the awareness. But one of the keys on the old organ stuck, and as the steady hum of its dissonant bass lent a mournful heaviness to the slow verses, her eyes were again lulled into immobility, dry and still. Nor, after the first eager bewilderment, did the long message of comfort rouse her. It was she, not they, who would wear the bruised remembering face at dusk. They would all sleep tonight. They would not feel, awakening, that strange kernel of stones in the heart. She looked at him harder. Outside the fall night thickened into a remote, cold, dusk, chiller, uncompromising. Bruised blue clouds banked themselves, shifting and restless, against the sun.

The one moment before the carriers, clumsy with reluctance, moved to the coffin, was stifling still, taut with that last intense loyalty to the flesh. A few of the women stifled sobs but she herself made no protest, no rebellious movement, no scream. When the six men, their faces strained to an unaccustomed solemnity, bore with awkward steps from the room their burden of flesh, she stood, uncertainly, like a balanced silhouette, but did not speak. As the door opened, suddenly the sun came out lighting up pitilessly, in form and shadow, the grotesque machinery of death. It would not be good for the coming child, the old women said, for her to go to the grave.

Alone, she sat at the window, kneading her handkerchief and watching the hearse rock perilously along the uneven rutted roads. Each time it lurched, she would make little movements of her arms as if to steady it. It passed over the hill and she stifled a small cry. Then she walked slowly across the kitchen floor, lit the oil lamp, trimmed its wick and set it carefully in the bracket. She picked up his old grey shoes and put them away. She filled the stove and sat down at the window again and began to knead slowly her handkerchief as it grew quickly darker.

The last time I saw her, she had grown quite broad and fat. They said she was having children too fast by her new husband.

It is not tragic that the bitter things are remembered, and live to lash with blunt edges and stop suddenly the forgetting, quick, laugh-long after they should be the dusty dead. The tragedy is their short sting, their dulled barbs, their replaced poignancy. It is tragic that they die unnoticed, like the old, and their pain is so mortal. For they are nearer than the laugh, more intimate than the greed and more of us than we can afford to lose, so unconsciously. It is strange that they are interred with such feverish haste, that such a vital present makes way so quickly for such a paralysis of future happiness, that mourners are so soon embarrassed to lift their veils for fear that they will be caught in a smile. The quick recovery is a mistaken salvation—only angle-worms should mend themselves so readily and so naturally. There is something fitting about a final scarred corpse. To have lived well is not to have laughed constantly—it is to have lost the laugh when it was merriest and to have felt the numb fingers of a varied death in a long handshake. It is to have staked everything and lost so that when they come out of the room and say "She is dead" there is no glib sob but a drowning man's full revelation. For the loneliness of contentment is emptier than the loneliness of loss, and to have stored one's long Gethsemane is to have furnished one's empty house. There is tragedy in the death of a stranger whom one cannot miss—there is rust in a long laugh and there is immortality only in an ache.

Muse in Overalls

The notion dies hard that the ideal spot for a writer to locate is at the helm of a small farm. In theory it sounds fine. Privacy and quiet. Plenty of exercise in the fresh air, amidst Nature's glories. Independence. Raising your own food. Setting your own mood. All this ensuring that inspiration be not hobbled.

Experience, alas, puts it another way. It speaks of boredom, exhaustion, seasonal slaveries, droughts, hurricanes, flue fires, fencing, hornets ... In truth, any writer who seeks to assuage the torment of his art with the balm of husbandry is merely exchanging one nightmare for two.

In the first place, cows hate a writer. They'll go to any length to thwart him. As surely as the rain shower knows the exact moment it can drench the hay en route from the field to the barn, a cow knows when you have a deadline to meet. That's the day your gentlest Jersey will suddenly change nature, taunt some cranky Herefords on the next marsh into pitched battle—and draw you away for a whole forenoon of arbitration (and restoration of the barbed wire) between them. That no sooner done than the *other* Jersey takes over. Ordinarily almost prim, she throws you a lewd glance over her shoulder, vaults the bars and, her mind suddenly on anything but her milk, races up the railway tracks in search of any old vagabond lover.

This kind of thing never ceases. One particularly vivid case of it still scorches my memory like a branding iron.

I'd just been assigned to do a rush piece on the function, if any, of poetry in the modern world: to be called "Verse and Universe." That morning, a rainy one, I had a Holstein whose "time was up." In all her previous accouchements she'd been a model patient, creating no difficulties for me of any kind. That morning, however, instinct told her her golden chance had come. The moment I turned her out to water and took my eye off her to fluff up her straw bedding, she vanished as utterly as if she'd been taken up into heaven.

So I roamed the pasture for three solid hours, soaked to the skin, until I located her (and son)—in a stand of hardhacks that would have daunted a machete. Did you ever trundle a calf, in a wheel-barrow, over half a mile of rocks and cradle hills? It was three o'clock in the afternoon before I got the two of them back into the barn. Another half hour to comb out my nerves and plait them together again and I thought the coast was finally clear for a run at the article.

Silly boy! Garbo (as we called her, she had such lovely bones) was not about to give up that easy.

For no discoverable reason except to spike my guns, she promptly came down with "milk fever." I called the vet. Naturally, he was having such a flare-up with his hemorrhoids that he couldn't come; but he did instruct me what to do. Blow up her udder with a bicycle pump, tie its four appendages off tight so the air couldn't escape, follow this with a hefty dose of Epsom salts and nux vomica, and by next day all should be well. When the operation was complete, I was too exhausted to notice how much like a Martian's Easter bonnet the four little bows of rickrack braid made her udder look, but Garbo glanced back at it and giggled.

The next day she was in no such mood. Cured of the fever, yes; but thorn scratches from the wild rosebushes she'd ploughed through were beginning to smart. Touch her udder and she'd let fly with both hind feet. I tried to hobble her with a patented device known as Anti-Cow-Kick, but it was no match for her at all. Nor would she let the calf near her, to nurse. So all morning was taken up teaching him to drink from a bucket. The method is simple, but tedious as hell. Let him lick your forefinger as you gradually lead his mouth down with it to the milk's surface. At first, he won't suck up any of the milk unless your finger is there. But after four or five hundred rounds of this, he may catch on and help himself.

Well, anyone who has ever spent hours on end pinch-hitting for a cow's teat knows that that (or a hoof in the groin) can knock the belles-lettres out of you quicker than a plugged gall duct. It need scarcely be added that the assignment went glimmering.

Nor are cows all. In league with them are scores of other things which know with equal precision just when the interruption of an idea will cause it to dissolve into thin air before you can get a word of it down.

Have it all blocked out how those brilliant passages of symbolism will put Bill Faulkner out of business—and the barn doors will swing off the hinges. Get all charged up with that death scene which will prove that you're tougher than Hemingway, yet tenderer than Fitzgerald—and the hens will fly over the coop for a ruining dust bath in the cucumber bed. Be all set to capture "sex" in such definitive fashion that

Mailer will hang up his tools—and the yearling bull will dash past your study window and mow the pea vines flat with the training crowbar he'd been tethered to. Have it right on the tip of your tongue to be Shakespeare himself—and the cellar drain will back up into the well.

As for bugs, let any writer "keep his ear to the ground." as he's supposed to, and what does he hear? He hears the cutworms (far more articulate than porpoises are said to be) hatching up plots of their own. In an accent more scraping than Bertie Russell's ever was.

Visitors from the city (all in spotless Bermuda shorts and burbling like wrens about the peace and quiet) toss out glib solutions to all these hassles. Just reverse the order, they say. Put your writing *first*—and if the farming has to be neglected, well, the hell with it!

They don't understand that, once you're hooked on farming, to neglect its claims is like trying to get through a day without brushing your teeth. That in any clash between a squash and a sonnet, the squash wins every time. That in any conflict between words and plowshares, words come out seeming like the furniture of a doll's house or wispy threads spun by a mixed-up spider out of his own gizzard.

Then *hire* the outside work done, they persist, and so outwit this Sword of Damocles. My reply is: With what? The average writer's income is roughly that of a Burmese coolie. And it would take nothing less than an army at action stations every moment of the day or night to give you constant protection. A cow-sitter, a calf-sitter; a hen-sitter, a hinge-sitter; a beet-sitter, a beetle-sitter ...

In any case, the only kind of help that doesn't bungle farm work so badly that you become perforce a *help*-sitter is another farmer. And you know how much ice your need for free time would cut with him! Break a leg and he'll come running, and look after everything until you're well again, without a grudging moment—but hire out to you so's you can make up them crazy stories? Like hell.

Even if he does come it's no good. First, you have to move your writing gear from the corner of the bedroom, where you normally operate, to the kitchen. If he came in for a drink of water and caught you, a *man* upstairs in the *day*time, you'd never live it down. (It would be like the time you passed a road gang laying asphalt on your way to the tennis courts and they all pointed to your white flannels and twittered "forty-love" at you.)

Second, how can you concentrate on your typewriter, anyway, when every time you glance out the window and see him wipe the sweat out of his eyes for another run at that matted grass with a hand-scythe you know what he's thinking? "Me leavin' m'own work to give him a lift, and him settin' in there pickin' away at that fool thing!"

All right then, the visitors keep at it, work along in the fields *with* him—that would at least halve your daily grind—and you could carry a notebook to jot your ideas down in as they occur. Ha. And ha again. Ask him to take the whole weight of a rafter you've both been hoisting, while you get out your little scratch pad? He'd notebook you!

In fact, I tried something like that once and, take my word for it, I got scorched with a look that peeled me like a sunburn! There may be some places where a writer's work is taken seriously. But in the country it soon gets cut down to size. About that of a split pea.

Don't get me wrong. Some of my best friends are neighbors. Mr. Billings, God love him (though he has pre-empted many an evening's work with his tales of "calling up" bull moose), who would lend you his last dollar. Mrs. Emery, bless her heart (though she is a mite prolix about her gallstones), who never bakes a tiptop pandowdy that she doesn't bring us half. And many more.

I would love the lot of them unreservedly, but for one thing: they saddle me with all their "papers." (A writer must be good for somethin'!) I've drafted more codicils to wills, composed more appeals from tax assessments, scripted more obituary and wedding notices to be lodged with the newspaper in town, concocted more entries for a woman who hopes to win a Purity Flour contest in twenty-five words or less, typed out more "parts" in a Christmas play, made more copies of a codfish recipe for a woman to distribute among her friends, filled out more applications for an Old Age Pension—ghosted more documents, in fact, than God made little green apples. It's got to the point that just the sight of a neighbor approaching with an envelope sticking out of his jumper pocket shrinks my heart like a prune.

So, all in all, if anyone is looking for a rural haven cheap, I have the very place for him. Interested parties will have no trouble to find me. Just drive down the Nova Scotian road from Bridgetown to Annapolis and I'll be in plain sight. If it's wintertime, you'll see me on the shed roof trying vainly to nail down the shingles a gale is stripping off like pinfeathers off a pullet. If it's summertime, I'll be chasing a sow out of the rhubarb. A mere thousand dollars, to help cover the cost of handling and postage, will take the whole place—rock, stock, and barrel churn.

Actually, I'm only kidding. I wouldn't part with it for all the ivory towers you could shake an elephant's graveyard at. Or for all the cities. If one is looking for laughs, it may not be the home where the boffo-

las roam, but—the elaborate cuteness which seems to be the occupa-
tional disease of writers-in-the-country notwithstanding—I'll "schtich"
with it.

Education at Mimi's

Mimi was born Mildred Pottie in Moose Jaw, Saskatchewan. But early on she changed her name to Mimi. Who could establish a salon of her kind with a name like Mildred?

Mimi has the same medieval face as the late Edith Sitwell and, to enhance this uncanny resemblance, she is never to be seen without a replica of the celebrated Sitwell turban on her head.

Everyone who is anyone in the Arts flocks to Mimi's Friday Evenings. An Eskimo sculptor who carves miniature ear trumpets out of walrus tusks. A musician who composes madrigals for the unaccompanied lute. The editor of an existential poetry magazine that carries only one single line per issue. An actor who twice bore a spear at Stratford. A truck driver turned Platonist. Devastatingly original types like that — as well as numerous gate-crashers who stray in for the free bourbon.

But it's writers that Mimi goes in for mostly. She finds their little cockfights so amusing. A tells B that he (B) is stuffed with desiccated words like dry bread dressing up a goose's ass. (Despite her regal air, Mimi makes it plain that she is also madcap enough to adore a touch of ribaldry.) B retorts that A's making a book of his own petty hassles is like the Aga Khan's selling his own bath water, including the ring around the tub. X tells Y that his characters have no more intricacy than a milk stool, and Y tells X that he's nothing but a ragpicker of psychological fall-out...

Yes, Mimi casts her net wide. Gore Vidal was once under her roof, for five minutes. And framed above her fireplace is a note from Norman Mailer *in his own handwriting.* "Regret must decline invitation to your gathering." it reads. "Expect to be laying a cornerstone, if nothing better presents herself, at the time you mention."

I gravitated into Mimi's orbit because of my literary credentials (I'd once had a stinging letter to the editor published in *The Beekeeper's Guide*) — and because of an ancient belief that books had instilled in me. This said that, against all reason, a spot like Mimi's was the very place to meet the real dream girls. Just watch for the quiet, withdrawn one. The one who takes no *part* in the buzz around her. The one who forsakes the dancing to wander out through the French doors to the terrace and lean her pensive elbows on the balustrade … In short, a puss in the corner.

Just spend a little *time* on one of these wallflowers, the idea goes, and what do you find? You find that she's as sensitive as an inchworm. That she sports (once enlivened) the most soulful eyes outside a beagle. Has an impish wit that (once disclosed) just matches yours. Can play Chopin that would make your toes curl. Will comprehend your subtlest sallies before they're out of your mouth … and where have each other been all your lives? That's, of course, if you're sensitive too.

Well, I'm as sensitive as only one who looks like the poor woman's Woody Allen can be, but my experience with these (apparently) pristine daisies amidst the hothouse orchidry, these (apparently) muffled Circes, has been something else.

The first specimen I encountered was at one of Mimi's intimate little *dansants*. She was all by herself, half-hidden in an alcove, while the rest of the company waltzed to Guy Lombardo recordings. (Another of Mimi's inspired ideas for making kitsch into a fun thing.) I asked Mimi who she was.

"I've no idea!" she exclaimed. "No one knows how she came to be here. She told me her name was Hester Sprockett—a plain fib if I ever heard one—but I couldn't get another word out of her." Mimi's cockatoo voice sank to a dramatic whisper. "Look at her brooding there! Those eyes! Those sensitive gams! That Garbo mystery! What'll you bet she's not an Icelandic poet or something? Shoo!" With that she slapped me smartly on both buttocks (Mimi adores a touch of vulgarity) and propelled me toward the lady in question.

By the time I had skirted the eddy of dancers, she had disappeared; but I found her as might be expected, leaning pensively over the balustrade. I thought of Juliet.

For a few minutes we said nothing as I stood beside her. And naturally my opening gambit was excruciatingly clipped, when it came. (I'd been practising on some old prose of Hemingway's with a pair of nail scissors.)

"A penny." I said.

"Whaa …?" she said. "Oh. Well, I was just wondering what day Christmas falls on this year."

Not quite the instant bridging of minds I'd been led to expect; but perhaps with my arm around her …

"Dance?" I said.

She shrugged laconically. "You're the boss!"

The aura of mystery that had surrounded her lasted just as long as it took us to get back into the light again and join the Terpsichore. Her name was indeed Hester Sprockett. Her eyes, at close range, were about as soulful as mine, which have been compared (unfavorably) to a titmouse's. And, sensitive gams notwithstanding, it became quite clear why she'd hitherto lacked a partner: she danced like Trigger. With not so much as a "Sorry." as she trampled my arches.

When these hoofmarks had healed sufficiently for me to be about again, I tried once more. Same balcony scene, but with another loner. I should mention that Mimi's terrace is an exact duplicate of the opening set in Noel Coward's *Private Lives*. So I walked up behind this one, brittle as you please, and spoke Ellyot's first line.

"Is that the Duke of Westminster's yacht?" I said—thinking, of course, that she'd quote Amanda's reply and we'd be off to the races.

Not at all. At first she let out a rude guffaw that brought the rest of the gang streaming out through the French doors to see what was up. Then her lips went thin as knife blades.

"I don't mind anyone taking a drink or two." she said. "But when you get so stoned you're seeing *yachts* yet—well, buzz off, Buster!"

Remember when Charles MacArthur offered Helen Hayes the peanuts at their first meeting, saying "I wish they were emeralds"? How suddenly I understood why that famous remark had come back to haunt him so bitterly all his days.

The third one I spotted at one of Mimi's wine-and-cheese parties. She was sitting on the floor all by herself, cross-legged. (This, I'd been given to believe, was another sure sign.) I squatted beside her.

"Lonely young man, bored by party." I said, "desires acquaintance of understanding young female seated like yogi." Not brittle this time: just cute, friendly, engaging.

Though she wasn't standing in the first place, she fell silent anyway. In fact, she hardly spoke a syllable during the whole encounter.

She just got up and went over to the big white Chickering piano. Those beagle eyes, that smile, that rapport! Here would be Chopin like I'd never heard before! She sat down and began to play.

She started with "The Road to Mandalay." She played by ear. She didn't use any of the black keys at all. She played the melody in chords around middle C, and then she encored it—with frilly little arpeggios which forsook all harmony whatsoever with the bass—two octaves higher up in the right hand. She kept the loud pedal down hard all the time. She played "The Road to Mandalay." and then she swung into the "Indian Love Call." and then "Good Night, Irene" and then "The Battle Hymn of the Republic."

I sneaked away while she was rolling up the heavy artillery.

Nevertheless, such an optimist am I that when the opportunity to test this thing again showed up within a fortnight, I couldn't resist giving it one last try.

It was Mimi's birthday, and we'd chipped together and got her a chamber mug that either Proust or Ronald Firbank, I forget which, was said once to have sat on. Those who weren't drinking punch from it were huddled in little coveys, in heated argument whether or not Capote's *The Grass Harp* had said anything *really* definitive about living in a tree house.

This gal was all alone on a divan, gazing into the flames of the open fire. She looked almost irremediably forlorn, this one—but what if she was only waiting for the right spark to irradiate her? I slipped down on the divan too.

"Hello." I said, smiling an ingenuous smile. I had abandoned all artificial approach by now.

"Huddo." she said. (*Ah-hah?* I couldn't identify the accent, but it spoke somehow of Persia and Omar Khayyam. I was about to launch into the "loaf of bread, jug of wine, and thou beside me singing in the wilderness" bit, when memory of my previous disaster in the field of quotes braked me.)

We didn't speak again for a long time. Just gazed, our heads almost touching, into the flames. Never had I felt such empathy. Finally, finally.

"Drink?" I said at last.

"Dough." she said simply. But, again, that haunting accent!

"Dance?" I said.

"Dough."

"Play some Chopin?"

"Dough." she said. "I dode wadda boove. I'b gudda code."

She had a cold all right. And don't think *I* didn't have a cold the next day. Whenever I catch a cold from someone else it never fails to settle in all six sinuses.

I go to Mimi's no more. I find that, as time passes, the company of ambivalent flautists and self-taught magi seems to weigh less and less with me. I find that the lacquered charm of kohl-lidded minxes wears thinner and thinner. But I owe Mimi's a perhaps greater deliverance from illusion. It has taught me one thing, if nothing else: the *sphinxes* are no bargain either. Unless, of course, they have money. Money at least talks.

Squares

Nowadays, most rural Nova Scotians have become as versed in the rites of slick courtship as their city cousins. They'd be quite contemptuous of the way of a man with a maid in my day. "Squares" they'd call us. I wonder, though.

It's true our amatory antics were almost as formalized and awkward as the mating dance of the penguin. But there were often some really memorable exceptions to the general pattern which I feel shouldn't go unsung. I still think of the lad whose particular technique was to visit his girl of an evening, lay wait for some errand to take her into the pantry, then post his chair at the pantry door and playfully keep her there hours on end with the threat of a kindling stick. I recall too the neighbouring swain who, on his wedding day, set off for the parsonage with his bride-to-be in the sleigh beside him. Halfway to town he suddenly remembered the ox shoes he'd planned to drop off at the blacksmith shop to be "corked." Nuptials or no, he swung around right there and came back for them. Everyone pelted the returning sleigh with cracked corn (in lieu of rice) and chopped-up catalogue covers (in lieu of confetti) — and they hadn't been within miles of the minister!

And I remember the time I myself bribed the kid brother of a local siren (we were both fourteen) to pin the following note on his sister's pillow. I had copied it verbatim from a book called "The Up-to-Date Practical Letter Writer" — an absolute classic published in 1902, which I had discovered one rainy day behind an old butter firkin in the attic. The book identified this specimen as: Letter from a Gentleman to a Lady Offering Her His Hand.

It read — and I quote accurately, because I still have the volume, right here beside me: "It is now nearly a year and a half since I first had the great pleasure of being received at your home as a friend. During the greater part of that time there has been but one attraction, one strong hope, and that is your personal charm and the desire of winning your favour. Have I been successful? Has the deep faithful love that I felt for you met any response in your heart? I feel that my future happiness hangs on your answer. It is not the fleeting fancy of an hour, but the true abiding love that is founded on respect and esteem, which has been for months my dearest life dream. Your maidenly dignity has kept your heart so securely hidden that I scarcely venture to hope I have a place there. I feel that I cannot endure suspense any longer, so write to win or lose all. Devotedly yours ..."

I snuck off home, feeling a mite sheepish, but tingling with the thought of all them fancy words a-workin' on her. Unfortunately her mother came across the note first.

For at least a month after that just to walk along the road was purgatory. Some wit would be sure to straighten up from his weeding and shout: "Hi, Ern. Goin' up to see her maidenly dignity?" Nowadays the persiflage that goes on between a boy and his girl is of no interest whatsoever to anyone else. In those days, a guy was just *watched* for some such ludicrous remark or action that could be pinned on him, like an identification badge, for the rest of his life.

Chronologically, our interest in girls began to sprout shortly after the polly-wog-nest phase had begun to pall. But the movies have it all wrong. We didn't carry their books home from school. The opening gambit was to shout some mildly defamatory remark at the object of your choice. Whereupon she brought said books down upon your head. Time and again I've felt the punitive weight of "Selected Canadian Prose and Verse."

The courage for such advances could only be found, of course, if you were in the presence of a group. If a single boy and a single girl discovered themselves to be alone together this bravado wilted into abject shyness. ("Your father set out his cabbage plants yit?" "I don't know. I imagine. Yours?" "I don't know. I imagine.")

At a later age the procedure was this. After the dancing at the wood-splitting "frolic" was over you sidled up to her while she was putting on her rubbers and mumbled, "Please may I see you home tonight?" Or if that many words were quite impossible to get out, "Comp'ny?" would do. She either "gave you a look" or tittered.

If she gave you a look, you had got what was known as "the mitten." And you never heard the last of it. ("Did you know Myrtle give Ed the mitten at the candy pull? And the simpleton went and bought her pie the very next night. I'd *see* myself!")

On the other hand, if she tittered you never heard the last of that either. You were "teased" about her from that day on. Though heaven knows little enough romantic guff shuttled back and forth during the journey to her door. A charming lady of my childhood acquaintance told me not long ago what happened the first night *she* was seen home. Not a syllable—not one—was uttered until they reached her gate. At which point her escort suffered one of those involuntary gastric rumblings which sound so thunderous in a conversational lull. He turned to her in the vibrant moonlight and spoke his one sentence of the night: "Did you hear my stomach a-rollin'!" And "stomach" is my own euphemism.

The next move was to drop into your girl's house of an evening. You put on your Sunday braces and your snub-nosed boots, but except for that no one would have guessed you were calling on *her*. You addressed your talk exclusively to her father ("Suppose pit prop's peel now?" or "That there Guernsey heifer o' yours looks like she's gonna make a good milker. I see she's springin' bag already.") Not till it was time to leave would you saunter over to pump yourself a drink and mutter, with your back to her, "You goin' to the tea meetin' in Parker's Cove?" She'd say, "I don't know. Is any of 'em goin' from here?" You'd say, "Some of 'em is, I guess. I am. You'd best make up your mind to go."

That was as definite a phrasing as the arrangement of dates ever took. Even when the affair had reached the stage of "setting up"—until two or three in the morning or until (as often happened) a particularly resonant tin receptacle in the parental bedroom upstairs was ominously sounded—we could be together for hours and say nothing whatever that would be of the slightest interest to either Dorothy Dix or the late Dr. Kinsey.

There were no movies to take our girls to, of course. Or cars to take them in. Our one medium of entertainment was the horse. Whereas nowadays the son says, "Can I have the car tonight, Dad?", we braided the driving mare's tail, hung scarlet tassels from her blinders, and asked Mother if we could borrow the sewing machine throw for a laprobe. A smart trotter gave you approximately the same prestige as a red convertible would now. If you happened to have a real showy *pacer*—well, you were the local Porfirio Rubirosa!

Sometimes we just drove. Sometimes we went to the next settlement and had supper there. That, incidentally, was publicly assessed as a mark of commitment almost as binding as a present.

The nature and order of these presents never varied. The first was always a box of chocolates. The next a pendant. And the next, substitute for the modern engagement ring, a muff. Engagement rings were thought to be a frivolous extravagance and the girl who angled for one a poor marital risk. ("She'll keep *that* poor boy's nose to the grindstone all right!") We didn't say, as they do now, "Did you know Helen has her ring?" We said, "Did you hear that Elsie got her muff?"

That is, if anyone knew about it. Secrecy was the keynote in all things. Extending, sometimes, even to the act of presentation.

I remember my first box of chocolates. I deposited it (in the dark of night) on a flat pasture rock where the girl of my choice would spot it on her way blueberrying the next morning. I know of another young blade who left the pendant in a barrel of scratch feed where *his* would come across it when she next fed the hens. And quite often the girl herself never exhibited a single one of her presents until after the wedding.

Which was typical of the girl's role. She mustn't make the slightest advertisement of her attachment to a boy. That would be "chasing him": an unthinkable disgrace.

This convention must have tried her sorely during the months of schoolteacher menace. Between September and June no girl sent to ask for whom the bell tolled. She knew darn well it might toll for her. But she could take no counter-measures. If her beau showed signs of transferring his affections, public sentiment was wholly on her side. ("There he's throwin' Clara over his shoulder and takin' up with that schoolteacher. And what does *she* want of *him*! She's just out for a good time while she's here and he ain't got sense enough to see it.") But she herself could only bide her time, and hope that come summer and a free field she could get him on the dotted line before the bell tolled again.

On the other hand, if she wished to "shake *him*," as the phrase had it, that took courage too. Especially after the muff stage. It could be done easily enough. She simply "told her pie" to someone else at the church social. But then it was she who fell afoul of the public's black looks.

The wedding date itself, of course, was the most closely guarded secret of all. The only dues we had were what information could be "pumped" from a child in the bride's household. Or if someone got wind of the groom's having been measured for a blue serge suit, or of his having buttonholed the minister some Sunday after church. Or, most positively, if someone surprised the dressmaker whisking a "shot silk" dress out of sight.

Nowadays in my old village the brides are decked out in more lace mittens and Tudor veils than you could shake Jacques Fath at. Then, the thing was shot silk. Trimmed with glass beads which, I remember, came in long vials, were strung onto thread, and sewn all over the dress's front "panel" in gleaming arabesques that would make the modern bridal get-up look like a dust cloth. If one of those appeared we knew this must be the very day.

And there the quiet ended. Salutings broke with a bang indeed. Old muzzle-loaders were dug out that hadn't known powder for years, clap-boards were belaboured with cudgels, every cow in the place was shorn of her bell.

When the happy couple finally "appeared" in the doorway, you filed past them into the house, muttering "Congratulations" to the groom and "Wish ya much joy" to the bride. Thereafter, protocol was entirely suspended. While the bride and groom were inescapably enthroned on the settee in the front room, even the most decorous of the company were already concocting designs on the nuptial bed.

A favourite trick was either to remove the slats or festoon them with cowbells, as a starter. (I remember once having volunteered our cow bells for this purpose. That's the last we ever saw of them. Next morning the groom simply got up and put them on his own herd!) And on or between the bed's covers was deposited anything from a layer of shredded horse mane to (as I witnessed once) a setting hen with all thirteen eggs.

Square it all was, I guess. But I've noticed this: that whereas in the more sophisticated romances of the present day, the gilt often wears off the gingerbread after a few years of marriage, ours, by gum, usually stuck.

Children

Call them Mark and Laura.

In a way they were odd ones too. Mark because he was smarter than anyone in school, and Laura because she was prettier. She was exactly as pretty as a flower, and as vulnerable. The reaches of Mark's imagination, which he traveled alone, left him vulnerable too. This drew them together.

Mark had a quick, flailing temper and sometimes he made her feel bad, but he never frightened her. The only time he'd ever seen *her* angry was one day an older boy snatched off his cap and sailed it up onto the shop roof. It was merely a routine joke, but Laura scrabbled up a rock from the frozen earth and would have thrown it at the boy's head if Mark hadn't held her arm.

Sometimes there seemed to be two of Mark. In the blacksmith's shop he'd guffaw as hard as the men themselves when Gus took a drill from the forge, held it in front of him and made a poking gesture with its red-hot tip in the direction of any woman going past—and when the New Testament reading in school was of miracles or mercy he'd close his eyes and make out he was Jesus.

Sometimes he was so serious Laura would feel him leave her—and the next minute he could make her laugh as she laughed with no one else. "Mark, you're crazy!" she'd say then: and more than ever then, she would see how the fondness in her voice lit up the corners of his glance.

Not everything they saw around them was a lilt of green. Men held the squealing pig on its back and dug the knife in and across its jugular. Rain lashed the sodden roses in the garden. Brook water drowned as indifferently as it sang. Fire and hurricane became great stunning fists when they slipped their leash. There was a bug for everything, a fly for everything, a germ for everything. There was rot for the wood, rust for the iron ... But wonder kept Mark and Laura warm.

Sometimes, when there was no school, they'd spend the whole day roaming around together. Aimlessly, but as if (Mark once thought, remembering the grammar lesson) each was the other's predicate.

Though both were older than their years, they still had fun with childish nonsense. Mark would trace the outline of Laura's hand on paper and then draw rings around all her fingers. Laura would blow the grey fluff off the bitter dandelion heads, split the hollow stems so they'd peel back into rosettes, and loop these into a necklace that she'd wear all morning.

That year, the morning of the King's birthday was perfect with holiday sun and breeze; and day of quicknesses and lulls that made it speakingly alive.

֍

Mark and Laura are sitting on the grass behind the barn, watching the darting swallows carry bits of mud in their beaks to the nests they are building under the eaves. They keep touching each other. Bouncing the crumbled hearts of daisies off the backs of their hands to see, by the number of yellow specks left clinging there, how many children they will have. Tickling each other's faces with little brooms of barley head (silky at the tip, with a sharp fish-hook at the bottom of each strand) to see who can keep from laughing the longest...

A sudden spatter of raindrops astonishes them, the sun is out so bright. They look at the sky, and far-off to the East the rain appears to be a solid sheet. They scamper into the barn.

The hay in the bay and on the head scaffold has been used down to the boards throughout the past winter. They have to walk a beam, high above the boards, to reach the main scaffold where the upland hay is still mounded almost to the eaves. Laura is scared, but Mark takes her hand and she dares it. They hollow out a small cavern in the hay and lie there. Mark feels his flesh stretch.

There is a swallow's nest, all finished, where a rafter joins the eave. He notices an egg that has fallen out of the nest onto the hay. He picks it up and holds it gently in his hand. And then for a moment, as if this strange new power widening in his flesh were putting words into his head, he has the thought: What if I should crush it? He makes as if to close his hand on the egg. Laura is startled, and begs him not to. He grins, and puts the egg back carefully back into the nest. He puts his arm around Laura, and again the thought returns. He squeezes her almost roughly. She is startled again; but again, when she looks at him he is grinning.

She thinks: he teases me, but he would never in the world harm me. He makes me laugh, but he would never poke fun at me. She doesn't know the word "betray." but she thinks: he would never betray me.

His eyes never hold anything back, so you don't know what it is, so you don't know whether or not it might be something they'd lift to strike you with. She thinks: I can have my back to him and I don't feel anything different coming out of his face, the thing you feel coming out of some people's faces when they know you can't see how they're looking at you. She thinks: his eyes never, never eat at me.

They go down to the barn floor. Mark tells Laura not to look. He searches out a brand new oxshoe nail. He bends it into a circle so that the square head of it can be taken for the jewel in the ring. Laura is standing in the doorway. The sky in the east has cleared completely, and nearby the sun has already dried off the scattering of drops; but there is a rainbow, its bands of color as clearly lined off as those in her hair ribbon. Mark takes the ring to her and puts it on her finger.

"Wait right here." he says, "and I'll get my kite."

He gets the kite and they fly it in the fields, Mark holding the string and Laura running along beside him. When it is as high as it will go, he passes the string to her. But she has none of his knack with it and almost at once the kite snags in the tall spruce at the edge of the graveyard.

Laura begs him to leave it there, but Mark is bound he'll climb the tree and get it back. He reaches the limb and tests it: will it hold him? He looks down at Laura. Her face pleads with him not to take the chance. He falters. But he can't give up now. He crawls out on the limb.

Just as he has the kite in his hand the limb breaks, and he falls. He keeps his grip on the kite and he's not hurt, but when the kite strikes the ground its frail wooden structure is splintered every which way. Laura picks it up and tries to fit the broken ends together. Mark snatches it from her and tramples it into a hundred pieces.

For a moment they don't speak. Then Mark says: "I wasn't mad at you."

"I know." she says. She shudders. "I was afraid you'd break your bones. You're sure you're not hurt?"

"No." he says—and all at once the whole thing strikes him funny—"I didn't break any bones. You saw me. I didn't even crack a smile."

"Mark." she says, "you're crazy!" laughing too.

"Do you want to play hopscotch?" he says.

"Yes." she says. "In our bare feet, will we?"

Mark takes a rib of the kite and draws a hopscotch court in the dust of the gateway while Laura searches for a flat round throwing-stone. The first game is almost finished when Mark looks up and sees a group of boys coming towards them. He feels childish and silly. He pretends he sprained his ankle. He sits down and puts on his sneakers. "I guess I'll go in the house for a while." he says. Laura senses that the spirit of the game is doused and goes off towards home.

When the boys have gone past, Mark comes out again. He sees the stone Laura had searched so long to find, lying there in the end square. One more chance and she might have finished with a perfect score. He picks the stone up and puts it into his pocket, to keep. Then he notices what the boys have scrawled in the dust: MARK LOVES LAURA.

His temper flares again. He starts to rub the scrawl out. But after the first scuff at it with his foot, he hesitates. He sees what Laura is doing down at her house. She is transplanting wild flowers from the field—clumps of violet, flowering daises—into a bare patch of earth beside the verandah. You can't transplant wild flowers, he thinks. They never live. She should know that.

He squats down and traces in again the letters of the word LOVES that his foot had smudged. He digs up some slips from the tall hollyhocks beside his own verandah and takes them down to Laura and helps her plant them beside the already wilting daisies.

"Where will I meet you after dinner?" he says.

"Wherever you say." she says.

"No. You say."

"All right. By the lumber pile."

è.

Sometimes, Mark has found, girls change after dinner. They put on an afternoon dress, and something that goes with it makes you feel clumsy and strange. Laura has put on a new dress, but she hasn't changed.

The boards of fresh-sawn lumber in the tall pile at the side of the road are stacked in triangles, to dry, with slats of air between each course. Mark and Laura climb up the outside and down the inside and lie on their backs on the ground, watching the patchwork of cloud that drifts slowly across the opening high above them.

They are playing another childish game: which cloud-shape looks like what? Mark names a map of Africa; in a moment Laura finds it too. She sees a whale; he finds that. A fountain, an alligator with its jaws open, a muffin (they laugh), a throne …

They hear voices and, getting to their feet, peer through the boards. Belle Herman and Annie Fred are walking by.

"You mark my words." Belle is saying, "that child is too pretty to live. Every time I look at her I think of my Ruby. You remember how pretty my Ruby was?"

"Who does she mean?" Laura whispers.

"I don't know." Mark whispers. "You know these 'forerunners' Belle's always talking about." But suddenly he feels that the boards are penning them in. "Let's go back the mountain road." he says.

They stroll back the mountain road. At first one walks in one wheel rut and one in the other; then they move closer together, their bodies almost touching, on the crown of the road. A bloom of well-being idles in them.

They dawdle along the road, entranced with everything. With leaves being all the different shapes they are, from the shell-ice patterns of the ferns to the coin shapes of the poplars ... and here. With all the different-colored birds, neater than arithmetic, having each feather perfectly shaded that the line on their breasts where the solid blue becomes the solid red or the black the grey is perfectly smooth, and birds being able to fly ... and *here*. With the deer-eyed deer roaming the woods like a thought and never stepping twice in the same track or sleeping twice in the same spot. With the water in the streams wrinkling its way to the sea ...

They lie on their backs on the pine needles beside the road and look up through the network of limbs at the sky. They are too lazed with the hum of the day to play the cloud game: it is too peaceful to set their minds that hard on anything.

"What will we think about?" Laura asks. Sometimes they do this, *pick* something to think about, just for fun, just to make sure that their thoughts are not on different tracks.

"Houses." Mark says.

They think about houses. Mark sees himself with Laura on his arm coming down the spiral staircase of the big mansion, to lead off the dancing in the big ballroom like the one his grandmother once told him about—the place where she'd once danced in England. Laura sees a house like any house in the village, with herself standing in the doorway at mealtime to call Mark from the fields.

"Stars." she says.

They think about stars. Mark tells her the stars are trillions of miles away—and that if you looked up out of a tunnel that was deep enough and dark enough you could see them in the daytime.

"But I'd just as soon look at these stars here." she says, pointing to the bunchberry blossoms.

They get up and go on. Until they come to a warm flat rock, where they sit down again. Mark makes excuses to touch her—half from fondness, and half from this new half-feeling that's nothing like anything he's ever felt before. She likes to have him touch her: his hands have nothing hidden behind their eyes either; their flesh is warm with all the warming messages there are.

With his hands together as in prayer Mark holds a blade of grass between his thumbs and blows a long note on it. Laura tries to do the same. No sound will come. Mark lines up another blade of grass between his palms and holds them up to Laura's lips, for her to blow against. He pulls a fern growing beside the rock and puts the sweet kernel of "meat" at the root of it into her mouth. He nests his hands together and tells her to put her finger in the crow's nest. ("Put your finger in the crow's nest, the crow's not home / He's gone to Ballyhackle, picking white stones.") When he pinches her finger quite hard with his thumbnail ("Oh, the crow came home!" the game goes) she is startled: but when she looks at him he is grinning and she sees it's just a joke. One taps out the rhythms of a tune with a finger on the other's cheek, to see if the other can tell what the tune is by the rhythm alone. Mark taps out "The Emperor's Waltz"—music he's heard on the cylinder records of the one "graffophone" in the whole place. Laura taps out "Pony Boy." the tune the mouth organs all play for the plain quadrilles.

Mark cuts a length off the tip of an alder beside the rock and loosens the bark with taps of his jackknife handle. He slips the bark off, grooves and notches the wood beneath, slips the bark back on, notches it where the wood was notched, and gives her what is now a whistle.

"Whenever you have anything to tell me." he says, "stand out by the gate and blow on that and I'll come down." She nods and puts the whistle into her dress pocket.

They move on. They see deer tracks in the road. Laura stoops down and traces their dainty outline with her fingers as if she were touching something of the deer's grace itself. The tracks follow the road and they follow the tracks, all excitement, nodding silence at each other, thinking they may turn a bend in the road and surprise the deer standing there—until the tracks go off into the woods and they notice the wildcat tracks alongside. They notice a tree stripped of its bark by a porcupine. It will die. On one of the rabbit paths along the road a strangled rabbit still lies, nothing left of it now but the skeleton with the wire drawn up tight around its neck. Laura wants to bury it. They scoop out a shallow grave with sharp-edged stones and bury it. Laura tries, clumsily, to make a cross with dry sticks. It keeps falling apart. Mark splits a sapling with his jackknife, peels its bark off, and fashions a cross that is shining white. But none of this really saddens them. They feel no omen in it whatsoever.

They come to the brook. Mark lies down flat, to drink. Laura starts to lie down beside him, then thinks of the rosettes of ribbon on her dress; she mustn't crush them. Mark never notices other girls' dresses, but now he thinks: What a pretty thing a girl is, in a pretty dress. Laura leans over the brook so she can see their faces shadowed in the water. She wonders where shadows go when they are gone. Mark strips some loose bark off a birch tree and makes a dipper. He scoops up some water in it and passes it to her. He holds his hand over the leak at the bottom until she has finished drinking.

The road turns, somehow turning old, and they both know at the same moment that it's time to turn back. They turn back.

On the way home they come to the church. They go inside. Their thoughts have an echo-mounting quality about them, like that of a church. Their faces are wary and subdued. They walk with the trespasser's tiptoe up to the chancel, but not quite to the altar. The sun coming through the small window of colored glass above the altar gives a coating of light to their upturned faces.

Mark cautiously opens the closet where the vestments hang. He touches the gold brocade on the stole. He sees himself wearing it. Laura feels him leave her.

Mark steps into the pulpit and reads a few sentences silently from the open Bible. He hears himself reading them aloud in a great, actor's voice. He swivels up the organ stool as far as it will go and sits down on it. He can only play by ear but he pretends to himself that he is playing by note from the open hymnal. Spreading wide the side flaps with his knees, for volume, he hears himself playing a great cathedral organ. He sees the great processional choir moving like kings up the aisle. Laura watches. She strengthens each long, held chord by pressing down a blending key two octaves higher.

When Mark surges backward in a flourish of calling up one last triumphant note the stool comes out of its socket. He falls with it to the floor. As if the crash were an oath, he rights the stool with shaking hands and they flee the church in a rush.

They wander through the churchyard. They linger at the grave of the child who died in 1851. Mark scrapes the moss from the lettering on the tombstone with his jackknife, and Laura straightens the line of sea shells that someone had once bordered the grave's edge with. Something hushing comes at Mark from the "Aged 14 years." from the long ago date.

He looks at Laura, and all at once there seems to be something fixed about her, like the sculptured lamb she is passing her hand over at the top of the tombstone. He tries to picture her face grown-up. He can't.

"Laura." he cries out, almost in panic. "Don't stand so still!"

"Mark." she says, "you're crazy!"

The sound of crows cawing in the wild-apple trees behind the church, where crows so often perch, suddenly distracts them. Mark and Laura, their faces totally revived, race across the graveyard to the open field to count the crows before they fly out of sight. There are only two.

"One crow sorrow." they jubilantly chant together, "two crows joy!"

While the whistle that had slipped from the pocket in Laura's dress somewhere among the million wheres along the mountain road, and the stone that had slipped through the hole in Mark's pocket, lay side by side with all the bits of wood and stone that hands had never touched and never would.

Appendix of Publishing History

Stories

Just Like Everyone Else

"The Balance" **V** "Another Man" *OB*, variant of "Snows of Christmas, Snows of Spring."

"A Present for Miss Merriam" **P** *Chatelaine*, December 1952, **C** *RYD*.

"The Clumsy One" **P** *Maclean's*, August 1950, **C** *RYD*.

"The Harness" **V** "The Rebellion of Young David" *Maclean's*, November 1951, **C** *MCS* under original title, *RYD*, anticipates *CM*.

"Just Like Everyone Else" (** original title "Snows of Christmas, Snows of Spring.")

"Cleft Rock, With Spring" **P** *Atlantic Advocate*, October 1957, **C** *RYD*.

"The Wild Goose" **P** *Atlantic Advocate*, October 1959, **C** *SAC, RYD*.

Desire

"The Quarrel" **P** *Maclean's*, January 1949, **C** *MC, RYD*.

"Goodbye, Prince" **V** earliest of three variants (original title "The Christmas That Faced Both Ways") *Canadian Home Journal*, December 1954.

"It Was Always Like That" **.

"The First Born Son" **P** *Esquire*, 1941, **C** *BCS, RYD*, anticipates chap. 24 *MV*.

"Return Trip to Christmas" **V** "Anything Can Happen at Christmas" *Chatelaine*, December 1957.

"The Locket" ** anticipates chap. 3 *MV*.

"The Choice" **.

A Million Things to Tell

"Thanks for Listening" ** anticipates the embedded story chap. 37 *MV*.

"Glance in the Mirror" **V** *Atlantic Advocate*, January 1957, **C** *RYD*.

"Another Christmas" **P** *Saturday Night*, December 1949, rpt. *Chatelaine* July 1959, **C** *RYD*.

"No Matter Who's There" ** (original title "No Matter Which People Are There") echoes of *MV*.

Sentiment/Sentimentality

"The Christmas Order" **V** of "Last Delivery Before Christmas" *Chatelaine*, December 1952, **C** *RYD*.

"Penny in the Dust" **P** *Maclean's*, December 1948, **C** *CA, CCL, VV, LC, RYD*.

"The Finest Tree" **P** *Saturday Night*, January 1944.

"The Dream and the Triumph" **P** *Chatelaine*, November 1956, **C** *RYD*.

"The Bars and the Bridge" **P** *Family Herald*, April 1958, **C** (shorter variant: "A Man") *OB*.

Short Fictions

"Long, Long After School" **P** A*tlantic Advocate*, 1959, **C** *RYD*.

"Humble Pie" **V** *Advertiser*, May 1960.

"Nettles into Orchids" **P** *Atlantic Advocate*, August 1961.

"The Doctor and the Patient" **P** *Atlantic Advocate*, July 1961.

"You Could Go Anywhere Now" **P** *Saturday Night*, November 1946, **C** *RYD*.

"The Snowman" **V** "Man and Snowman" *WS*.

"The Orchard" **P** *Review 3*, 1978, revised version of an earlier unpublished piece, "Snow Apples."

"Why Must It Sound Like a Cowboy Song?" **.

"The Widow" **.

"Muse in Overalls" **C** *W*.

"Education at Mimi's" **C** *W*.

"Squares" **P** (original title "We Never Heard of Dorothy Dix") *Atlantic Advocate*, January 1958.

"Children" ** one of three unpublished variants (along with "Hares and Hounds" and "The Day Before Never"), echoes of *MV*.

List of Abbreviations

** previously unpublished typescript
V fuller, earlier variant of a published piece
P previously published
C previously collected

MV *The Mountain and the Valley* by Ernest Buckler, McClelland and Stewart, 1952.
CM *The Cruelest Month* by Ernest Buckler, McClelland and Stewart, 1963.
OB *Ox Bells and Fireflies, a Memoir* by Ernest Buckler, McClelland and Stewart, 1968.
WS *Nova Scotia: Window on the Sea*. Text by Ernest Buckler, photographs by Hans Weber, McClelland and Stewart, 1973.
RYD *The Rebellion of Young David and Other Stories by Ernest Buckler*, selected and arranged by Robert Chambers, McClelland and Stewart, 1975.
W *Whirligig: Selected Prose and Verse* by Ernest Buckler, McClelland and Stewart, 1977.

Anthologies

BCS *A Book of Canadian Stories*. Ed. D. Pacey. Toronto: Ryerson, 1950.
MC *Maclean's Canada*. Ed. L.F. Hannon. McClelland and Stewart, 1960.
MCS *Modern Canadian Stories*. Ed. G. Rimanelli and R. Ruberto. Toronto: Ryerson, 1966.
CA *Canadian Anthology*. 2nd ed. Ed. C.F. Klinck and R.E. Watters. Toronto: Gage, 1966.
CCL *A Century of Canadian Literature*. Ed. G.H. Green and G. Sylvestre. Ryerson, 1967.
SAC *Stories from across Canada*. Ed. B.L. McEvoy. Philadelphia: Lippincott, 1967.

VV   *Voice and Vision.* Ed. J. Hodgins and W.H. New. McClelland and
       Stewart, 1972.
LC   *Literature in Canada* vol. 2. Ed. D. Daymond and L. Monkman.
       Gage, 1978.